STRANGERS IN THE AVALON DUNES

Also by Jane Kelly

Killing Time in Ocean City

Cape Mayhem

Wrong Beach Island

Missing You in Atlantic City

Greetings From Ventnor City

STRANGERS IN THE AVALON DUNES

Jane Kelly

Plexus Publishing, Inc.

Medford, New Jersey

First printing, 2023

Published by:
Plexus Publishing, Inc.
143 Old Marlton Pike
Medford, NJ 08055

This is a work of fiction. Names, characters, places, and incidents either are the product of the author's imagination or are used fictitiously. Any resemblance to actual persons, living or dead, is entirely coincidental.

Printed in the United States of America.

Library of Congress Cataloging-in-Publication Data

Names: Kelly, Jane, 1949- author.
Title: Strangers in the Avalon Dunes : a novel / by Jane Kelly.
Description: Medford, New Jersey : Plexus Publishing, Inc., [2023]
Identifiers: LCCN 2022040258 (print) | LCCN 2022040259 (ebook) | ISBN 9781940091129 (paperback) | ISBN 9781940091907 (ebook)
Subjects: LCGFT: Novels.
Classification: LCC PS3561.E39424 S77 2023 (print) | LCC PS3561.E39424 (ebook) | DDC 813/.54--dc23/eng/20220830
LC record available at https://lccn.loc.gov/2022040258
LC ebook record available at https://lccn.loc.gov/2022040259

President and CEO: Thomas H. Hogan, Sr.
Production Manager: Tiffany Chamenko
Book Designer: Jackie Crawford
Cover Designer: Erica Pannella
Marketing: Robert Colding

To my Pandemic 2020 buddies

To Carole Turk, bubble buddy, who shared her home as a place to hide out from Covid-19

To Matty Dalrymple and Lisa Regan, Zoom buddies, who shared inspiration to keep writing in isolation

Acknowledgments

Once again, I must thank my friends and readers for their insights: Marilynn Benz, Jim Clark, Matty Dalrymple, Linda Geiger, Denise Marconi Leitch, Mary McMahon, Lisa Regan, and Anne Tanner.

To my parents, Mary and Dick Kelly, who introduced me to Avalon during my elementary school years, to my niece, Kelly Henderson Sakowski, who provided me with updated information, and to Tish Mazza Ryan who could answer a wide range of questions about the town she loves over all those years. Thanks to Ellen Bocklet, Gerard Murphy, and Sandy Perron Davern for sharing their impressions.

Anne Tanner requires a second shout-out for connecting me through her daughter-in-law, Kathy Tanner, with Pat Beach who shared his memories of Avalon over the years.

Thanks to Carole Turk, Carolyn Anderson, Denise Marconi Leitch, and Carmen Pruna for checking out locations which were sometimes moving targets in these most unusual times. Thanks especially for donning masks as needed.

Once again, I must thank Bill Andersen who keeps an eye on my nautical references.

And last but not least, a big thank you to my colleagues at Plexus Publishing: Tom Hogan, Rob Colding, and Deb Kranz for their ongoing help and support.

Chapter 1

The fear kicked in after dark. Lying in bed, I saw nothing outside the window but the thicket that wrapped around the house. Trees. Bushes. Shrubs. I envisioned them all marching towards the house, crossing the driveway, scratching at the windows and, worst of all, carrying intruders with them. I can get a little overly dramatic.

"Andy, are you asleep?"

"Yes."

"You're lying."

"I don't believe sleeping men can lie."

I knew there was some play on words to be made there, but I didn't have the time or the interest. I felt too jumpy.

"Those woods are frightening. I think they are getting closer."

"Birnam Wood coming to Dunsinane?" asked Andy, back in college, and a Shakespeare class, after two decades.

"Exactly. And we all know how that worked out for Macbeth."

"Actually, I don't know," he mumbled. "We don't finish Macbeth until Friday."

"Trust me. It's not good."

"Maybe not," Andy hugged his pillow, "but I suspect his castle didn't have motion-sensing lighting."

No lights had come on. Not necessarily good news. "Anyone could be hiding in those trees waiting for their moment." I poked Andy in the side.

"I asked you to marry me because I thought you were a sound sleeper," Andy mumbled.

"Well, you'd better have another reason because I am wide awake."

He didn't open his eyes. "The first night in a new house can be disorienting."

Not for him apparently.

"I am here with you. There is no need to be afraid." He threw an arm around me.

"You're no help. You're asleep. Allegedly."

"Not quite, but hoping."

Small comfort. How much help would a semi-conscious man be? "There is someone in the dunes."

"There is no reason for anyone to be out there. Yes, there are some tall trees, but they are surrounded by low vegetation that makes those grounds virtually impassable." His voice grew weaker.

"Why did the Positanos need a house-sitter anyway? I mean really. Why would you pay someone five-hundred dollars a month to live in your multi-million-dollar house unless it was under threat?"

"There is no threat."

I turned my back to the window to face Andy. His arm fell away.

"Did Marc Positano tell you that?"

"No." He must have felt my stare. He opened his eyes.

"Did you ask?"

"It never occurred to me to ask."

"What kind of PI doesn't ask?"

"Ex-PI." He closed his eyes but opened them again when I continued to stare. "Housesitting came up in a casual conversation. He wasn't looking for someone. Just a lucky coincidence. Stop worrying. That's a dense thicket out there from street to beach. An intruder would not be able to get through. Besides, why would they when they could walk up the driveway?"

"You didn't close the gate?"

"The gate is meant to stop cars and trucks. Intruders don't even have to climb over it. They can walk around it."

"And come up here and hide in the thicket."

"Why would they? There are twines and vines and all sorts of vegetation. Even the occasional cactus. I would bet some of those plants would be pretty prickly." His voice faded. I was losing him to sleep.

"I saw some open spaces as we drove up." I turned back to watching for creepy creatures skulking around in the woods. "There is someone out there. I am not kidding you. They have a flashlight."

"Maybe it's moonlight reflecting off some wet leaves. It rained earlier." His voice sounded even weaker.

"It sprinkled earlier and there is no moon."

Barely awake, he mumbled. "That land is protected."

"I don't think we're dealing with law-abiding environmentalists. What if they kill us tonight?"

He groaned. "Why would anyone want to kill us?"

"They don't know it's us. They want to kill the Positanos."

"No one wants to kill the Positanos."

"You don't know that. What do we know about them?" I asked. "We only met them when they were guests at the Artistical."

He raised himself on one elbow. I suspect so I could see the desperation on his face. "He runs a chain of dry cleaners, and she operates a charity to feed the homeless. Just a hunch, but I do not believe they are involved in an international criminal cabal."

"I'm not so sure. Money laundering. Dry cleaning can be a cash business."

"He created a company with hundreds of franchises. It's a public corporation. Doesn't fit the profile of a criminal organization. Besides, I suspect in the age of the Internet, money laundering is a lot more sophisticated than funneling funds through your neighborhood dry cleaner. Now, if you'll excuse me, I need to be fresh in the morning." He let his head plop back on his pillow.

"Why did he want house-sitters all of a sudden?"

"He's always been a little concerned about the property sitting empty," Andy mumbled, but I was pretty certain that was what he said.

"You told me contractors come by to do maintenance."

"Occasionally. He likes the idea of the property being occupied. He seized an opportunity when I told him we were in South Jersey." Andy's last few words were barely audible.

I tried to keep quiet, but I wasn't convinced. "Why else would people be out there?"

"I would go ask but, personally, I think there's a better chance they would kill me if I went outside." He punched a dent into his pillow for his head and dropped it into it.

I slipped out of bed and crawled across the cold tile floor to the window. The eighteen-inch-high wall did not make me feel well-hidden. "The light went out," I called to Andy.

"Good." He rolled over in search of peace.

"Why is that good? I bet they know we are on to them. I bet people rob these houses in the winter."

"It's spring," he countered my claim.

"By a few days."

"I saw daffodils on the center island on Dune Drive." He wasn't ready to give up.

"I'm not quibbling over semantics. Let's agree on it's off-season."

He turned over so he could see out the window. "What do you see now?"

"The light. Now it's back and it's closer."

With great theatricality, he pulled himself out of bed and joined me on the floor. A white light flickered in the darkness. "See there it is again."

Andy came fully awake. "Something is moving out there."

"No kidding." I made an effort to minimize the sarcasm in my tone. Truth be told, I didn't try at all. At least, I didn't say *I told you so.*

Chapter 2

Andy added jeans and shoes to his attire. "I'm going out." He took the four steps necessary to get from our bedroom to the adjoining mudroom, grabbed a jacket and a high-powered flashlight. "Let's surprise them." He disabled the motion-sensing lights before pulling the door open.

If I weren't so frightened, I might have recoiled at the chill, but cold air was the least of our problems. Figuring my sleeping sweats constituted outdoor wear, I shoved my feet into old boat shoes and struggled into my raincoat.

He handed me his phone. "You be in charge of communications."

That meant calling 911 if needed. I hoped I'd never make the call.

Andy put a foot onto the gravel driveway and passed the weight of the door to me. The darkness provided cover, but the sound of his shoes on the loose stones seemed to drown out the crashing of the waves on the beach and the passage of the wind through the trees. No way his footsteps would fail to alert the intruders, human or other.

Someone was coming. I stayed hidden behind Andy, phone in hand, ready to call for help. Three feet from the edge of the thicket, we stopped. Despite the density of the underbrush, the intruder was making progress, backing towards the edge of the wooded area and us.

The Jersey Devil crossed my mind, but I didn't think the mythical creature left the Pine Barrens to visit the beach. I asked what I saw as a more realistic question. "What if it's a bear?" I whispered. "I read a lot of them are moving south."

"With their iPhones?" He pointed out the light.

Whatever the figure was, it fell into the driveway backward as if expelled by an angry forest. In my defense, the shape did resemble a bear.

However, it turned out to be a female human with a mass of long dark hair in tight curls that covered most of her brown jacket. Easy mistake.

The woman's arms were extended to guide another woman, older but far from elderly, wearing, and wearing only, a cotton nightgown far too thin to protect her from the late March air.

Without hesitation, Andy handed me the flashlight and slipped off his jacket. "Let me help."

The younger woman yelped. Her cell phone slipped from her hand. I flipped on the flashlight but pointed it at the ground to avoid blinding us all.

When the intruder who was not a bear turned and saw Andy holding out his coat, she accepted his offer and wrapped the jacket around the older woman. Before the coat covered her arms, the light revealed scratches, stripes of red running up her arms and across her chest. I suspected new wounds intersected with scabs and healing cuts, but her arms disappeared from view before I could be sure. Earlier injuries? From schlepping through our woods on other occasions? Based on the vacant expression on the woman's face, I doubted she knew.

"See, Mommy, the people who live here are nice," the young woman said as if speaking to a child. "They're not family, but they are nice."

"Daddy?" The woman gazed at Andy with wonderment.

"Your Daddy is not here tonight." Andy spoke in a soft tone, stepped past the daughter, and took one of her mother's arms to help her clear the final obstacles.

"He's not?" She sounded disappointed and not fully convinced.

"My name is Andy, and I know he would think it was okay if I helped you." With a gentle touch, he slipped her arm into his jacket sleeve. "We don't want that coat to fall off you. It's chilly out here."

The younger woman stopped hovering but comforted her mother with reassuring words as Andy bundled her into his jacket. "Mommy, see what good care they are taking of you. I bet they take good care of the house." She mouthed "thank you" to Andy as she bent to retrieve her phone.

I kept the flashlight pointed at the ground to help her.

Andy zipped the older woman into his jacket. "Let's make sure you are nice and warm."

She nodded although she seemed befuddled about what she was agreeing to.

"I see that you wore your beach shoes," he kindly misidentified slippers that were not meant to leave the house. "The gravel in this driveway can hurt your feet, so I am going to carry you." He spoke to her as if addressing a loved one.

With an expression full of wonder, she extended her arms and let Andy scoop her up. The younger woman reached out to stroke her mother's arm to calm her, but she did not need calming. She appeared happy in Andy's arms.

The young woman spoke to me. "I'm so sorry we disturbed you. My mother gets out of the house at night. She has dementia."

I didn't say it aloud, but a question formed in my mind. So young? Her mother looked worn and harried yet she did not appear elderly.

"Early-onset." The daughter, barely out of her teens, answered the question I didn't ask.

Instead, I asked, "How did she get here?"

"She walked. We live back on the bay but she moves fast. Her nighttime travels began about six months ago. At first, she could always find her way home, but that's changed. It's frightening. We are so afraid she will get out at night and won't come back. Locked doors don't stop her. It's as if she is a savant when it comes to finding hidden keys. And, she's not above going out a window."

Her mother stared with wide brown eyes, but I wasn't certain what she was hearing.

"Mommy and I should only go out together." She spoke to me but kept her eyes focused on her mother. "We tried putting bells on the doors, but she figured out how to keep them quiet. We agreed that if we couldn't stop her—*we* is my father and I—we would follow her, join her, retrieve her. Most nights my father falls asleep in front of the TV, so I've taken on the late shift. If she gets away, she always comes here. Tonight, I spotted her sneaking onto your property at the foot of your driveway. I swear she moves faster in those woods than she does on the street. Maybe she is reliving something that she did as a kid."

The young woman paused, fighting rising emotion.

"This is where she spent summers growing up. Well, for all her life, but it's the early years she talks about. Her mother only sold the house a few years ago. She knows she doesn't belong here anymore. Maybe that's why she stays in the thicket. It would be a lot easier on me if she used the driveway. And on her. She gets all scratched up."

Beside her, her mother, cradled in Andy's arms, smiled and nodded. Even the ravages of her disease could not hide that she was a beautiful woman. Her dark hair, pulled into a messy pile on the top of her head, was still thick and luxurious, And, those eyes.

"Again, I am so sorry we disturbed you. I hope we didn't frighten you," the younger woman said.

"Oh, no. Not at all." Andy and I lied in unison.

"Please, would you be willing to forget this? Clearly, I'm not here to rob you. Would I bring my ailing mother with me if I were?"

Good point.

"She just wanted to see her home, to visit her childhood." She paused and seemed reluctant to go on. "I can't promise she won't find her way here again."

"Hopefully not at 3 AM," Andy said with a smile.

"I will do my best to keep her at home."

"We'll keep an eye out. You two did startle us, but I'm more worried about her. Do you have a car nearby?" Andy asked.

"I parked at the bottom of the driveway. Right outside your gate."

"What's your mother's name?"

"Elisabeth."

"Elisabeth," Andy's tone was sweet, "I'm going to carry you to your car."

Tears glistened in Elisabeth's eyes. "That would be nice. My Daddy used to carry me sometimes when I got a burr in my foot. Did that ever happen to you?"

"It did," Andy assured her, "but I have shoes on tonight, so I'll be fine. Let's take care of your feet."

I handed the flashlight to the young woman, and she led the group down the driveway. I could hear the woman in Andy's arms chattering happily. "Daddy always told us to stay out of the dunes that we would get burrs in our feet."

"They hurt a lot. I remember," Andy cajoled her. "And they hurt when they come out. We don't want that to happen to you."

A few minutes later a bobbing circle of light rushed up the driveway. Andy shoved the flashlight into my hands as he flew by me into the mud room. His coat was nowhere to be seen.

I shut the door but still felt the chill coming off his body. He made a great show of breathing into his hands and rubbing them together to warm himself as he headed to the bedroom.

"We'll need to keep an eye out for Elisabeth." He stripped off his jeans and fell into bed in one graceful motion. "I have a feeling we might see her again."

Chapter 3

In the morning, I moved our clothing from the first-floor bedroom—which upon closer inspection proved to provide the least appealing sleeping quarters in the house—to a loft above the great room. The space offered panoramic views of the beach and ocean and the benefit of being two stories away from the reach of the encroaching woods. Mid-move, I heard a doorbell ring.

The Positano house had three doors that could be termed the front door. Where should I go? I turned and found the answer. Our overnight visitor, the younger one, stood five feet away from me waving through the glass door that opened from the deck. I checked the clock on the microwave. 9 AM. Early for someone who had been up in the middle of the night. Not only her, me too.

I'd had my morning Coke, but I still wasn't ready for company. Or dressed for it. But our would-be guest could see me. More importantly, she was holding Andy's jacket. That, I wanted. I stuck out a hand from under the clothes in my arms and pulled open the door.

"Remember me from last night? My name is Abby. Abby Douglas." Before I could even smile, which was my intention, she blurted out, "Why didn't you tell me?" She used an irritated tone.

How had the woman, girl, whatever, moved me to anger in under a minute? She had to have set a record.

"Tell you what?" I had no idea what she was talking about.

Without waiting for an invitation, she swept by me. "That you find missing people. That you could help us." A few steps into the house, she turned to face me. No, to confront me.

"How did you find out what I do? And who's missing?"

She dropped Andy's jacket on top of the pile of clothes in my arms. "My mother asked, and your friend told us your names. So, I Googled you. Just out of curiosity. I found stories about you, about how you find missing persons."

"That is not what I actually do."

"Then, what do you do?"

A good question. "I have done that sort of thing but only as a favor for a few people. Really."

"You can't do a favor for us?" If Abby took one of those *what dog do you look like* quizzes online, she would come up with a bulldog.

I felt no anger about her visit the night before. But her attitude that morning? A different story. I grew defensive. I held the door open with my foot indicating she should feel free to leave. "I am not in the habit of doing favors for people I find hiding outside my house."

"Don't be ridiculous. I explained that." She checked out the room and nodded at the dining area. "Can we work at that table?"

"Who said we are working on anything? I have no idea who you are or what you want." My assertive tone shocked me. I was usually more of a pushover.

"I anticipated that." She reached into her tote bag and pulled out a plastic sleeve. "I made a copy of my driver's license so you can check me out. There's also a copy of my resume, such as it is. I'm just finishing a gap year. I'd like to find a part-time job before I start college in the fall. There are personal references, too. I wouldn't mind working this summer. I'm available now. Feel free to pass it on."

Abandoning hope that she would leave unless I looked at her alleged credentials, I kicked the door closed and dropped the pile in my arms onto a chair. I extended a hand. "Let me see your original driver's license."

The document had not been altered. She was Abigail Kendra Douglas of Gladwyne, Pennsylvania. Nineteen years old. Height 5'3". Hair brown. The only thing that appeared dubious on the license was her weight which she listed as ninety-five pounds. Not that she was fat. She was fit, not skinny. Strong. She gave the impression she could win any physical altercation she got into and her expression in the picture suggested she might get into a few.

"My mother's father went missing over forty years ago. She wants to know what happened to him. I told her I would talk to you. Of course, I have no idea what she understands. She's slipping away." Words flew out of her mouth like bullets from a machine gun before she slowed her pace and softened her voice. "She's too young to do that. I'm too young to lose my mother."

Did Abby realize she'd hit a tender spot? She couldn't. No way she could know that I had not been much older than she was when I lost my mother. Could she?

"Listen, Miss Daniels."

"Call me Meg." My first mistake in encouraging her.

"All my mother wants before...well, before...is to know the truth about what happened to her father. He left just as she turned ten years old. And she never saw him again. Now, she is leaving us. Her mind will go before her body. The time for her to see him again is running out. Quickly."

Her tone was so full of pain, I couldn't control myself. I pointed to a chair. Mistake two.

"Tell me about it. You said she was ten when her father disappeared."

"My mother went to visit her grandmother thinking she had a happy home and came back three weeks later to find her father was gone."

"She never saw any trouble coming?" I asked.

"She was ten." Abby's tone accused me of stupidity.

"Kids know. Parents think they hide things from their children, but kids aren't dumb." I spoke as if I had training in child psychology. I didn't. I rarely encountered a child, but I'd been one.

"My mother said her father had changed maybe a year before he left. Mostly his appearance. She thought he was cool. Looking back, she saw he got caught up in the seventies. You know, the decade."

I knew. Disco. Free love. Clothes that suggested heavy drug use had been involved at the point of purchase.

She pulled an envelope out of her tote bag and emptied it onto the dining table. A few dozen photos slid out. "My mother grabbed pictures when my grandmother was moving. My grandmother was destroying all the ones with my grandfather in them." She passed me a few old snapshots. Two black and white photos of the same man. First with a baby, then with a toddler.

"My grandfather." She pointed to a man standing in front of a stone wall. "Holding my mother."

My guess? An Easter Sunday in the 1970s. Even if his face hadn't been distorted as he squinted into the sun, the photo quality made it difficult to tell what he looked like.

"His name was Kenneth Patterson. People called him Ken or Kenny. My grandmother always calls him Kenneth."

He, like everything else in the picture, appeared jaundiced. The photo quality of the pictures on the table improved as the years progressed, and the images grew more realistic as color photography improved to include colors other than yellow. Ken was a good-looking man. Long and lanky, thin without appearing weak. Not exceptionally handsome but with solid features. His dark eyes seemed a little dull, maybe a bit sad. A typical suburban dad. That is, until his daughter was about eight when his clothes became flashier, his sideburns longer, and his upper lip hairier. Much hairier. A bushy mustache made him stand out in photos with friends who, although dressed for the times, had not fully bought into the seventies disco look. Ken had.

"Brown eyes?" I asked.

"Like hers. Like mine. Or so my mother tells me. That's him with his brother." Abby pointed to two twenty-something guys in bathing suits standing ankle-deep in waves. "Gerald. He's the shorter light-haired guy. He lives in Sea Isle. I did a Google search."

I would not have taken the two for brothers. Slim, and well-built with coloring that would let him classify as tall, dark, and handsome, Ken was the more attractive of the two. Far more attractive. "Are there any shots of your grandmother in here?"

"Oh, wait." She rifled through the photos. "Here's one. Donna and Kenneth Patterson."

In the picture from the 1970s, Donna and Ken stood with their daughter between them. An unlikely couple. Donna was pretty, in a cute, all-American-girl-of-the-seventies way with long blonde hair parted in the middle with bangs feathered back. An aspiring Farrah Fawcett? Most American girls were. Donna's smile broadcast wholesomeness, the kind of girl I'd seen in films of old Miss America pageants. Ken on the other hand had taken on the look of a guy who stood outside strip clubs chanting "all nude, all the time."

"And the little girl in the picture is your mother?"

"Yes, Elisabeth Patterson Douglas." She leaned in close with a sentimental smile. "She tells me she was very proud of her Dorothy Hamill hairstyle. Her wedge."

"She was a cutie."

"She still is when she isn't in the grip of her disease. If you talk to her midday, you might think she's simply kind of shy." Any trace of sentimentality disappeared from her tone. "I made notes for you on the back of this photo." She handed a picture of a group of guys around thirty. The larger size and photo quality made it possible to see what each person looked like. I flipped the photo back and forth as I read the inscriptions on the back.

Ken Patterson (grandfather, mustache)
Dougie Hargreaves (long hair, sun-visor, dead)
Bobby DeMarco (black curls, nice smile, year-round at the shore)
Robin Carson (Alive – last known Stone Harbor and Philadelphia)
Francis Bloch (Freckles - dead)
Harris Meitner (Dead – Philadelphia)

The group seemed to suffer a fair number of premature deaths, but I didn't let my mind go down that path. I was only interested in the living and what happened to one of them: Ken Patterson.

I glanced at Abby and found she wasn't focused on the photos. She was looking around the house. "Are you living up here?" Her tone said she could hardly have disapproved more strongly.

By "up here," I assumed she meant the great room. A space Andy and I called the Juggernaut or more casually *the room* since it was the only one we planned on using. The multi-storied glass space that had once been most of the house now stuck out from an addition with five times the square footage.

"It's just the two of us. We hardly need eight bedrooms and eight baths. This suits us fine."

She nodded, but her face made no attempt to hide her disapproval. She took in the small kitchen area that was no more than an elaborate wet bar. "You know there is a gourmet kitchen in the back of the house."

Why on earth would I need a gourmet kitchen? Andy and I pretty much subsisted on take-out. "We have a small fridge, a coffee maker, and a microwave. We're pretty much set to go." I stuck to the basics and didn't mention the wine refrigerator or the cheese chiller. I tried to bring her attention back to the photos. "What is this sailboat?"

"Oh, that belonged to my grandfather. The *DonnaLisa.* My mother said her father always called her Lisa. Another thing my grandmother hated. Too trendy."

"She hated the name, not the boat?"

"No, I think she hated the boat, too. I guess that's why the painting is still here." She pointed over her shoulder at the watercolor of a sailboat. "Considering how she felt about the boat, I guess it isn't surprising that she left it behind. Given the new owner's taste, I am surprised it's still here."

I'd barely noticed the seascape hanging on the wall near the front door except the watercolor seemed like an odd intrusion in the otherwise modern space. I didn't get to ask about the boat's fate. Abby had changed the subject again. "Where do you sleep?"

I pointed to the space above our heads. "The first night we were here I saw a light in the thicket outside the window, and it made me aware of problems with sleeping on the ground floor right by the front door."

"Is that supposed to make me feel guilty?" Her tone suggested to me that nothing would ever make her feel guilty.

"Of course not. We only arrived last night and didn't realize we can awake to a gorgeous view upstairs."

"When I was a kid I used to hide in the loft," Abby said. "You know there is a little deck off it."

"Yes, we noticed." It was hard not to. A little deck in this house would be classified as a spacious deck in most.

"I loved coming here when my grandmother was in a good mood. When she wasn't I would take my toys and play in the loft until someone missed me and made me come down."

Imitating Abby, I made an abrupt topic change. "What did your grandfather do for a living?"

She leaned back. "He was a lawyer. I don't know what kind, but he made a lot of money. You know, this neighborhood is exceedingly prestigious."

A truth that was hard to miss.

"Back when my grandfather built this house, you couldn't call it a neighborhood. My grandfather built one of the first houses allowed." She waved an arm as if the neighbors' homes were visible. They weren't. The houses in the high dunes, and over forty years later there were still only around a dozen of them, sat nestled in thick vegetation that isolated them from their neighbors as well as the town of Avalon, New Jersey. Building this house let Ken show the world that he'd made it.

"How did your grandmother explain your grandfather's departure to your mother?"

"That he was *sick in the head* but when he got better he would come home. She said she shouldn't worry. My mother claimed my grandmother could never resist sliming him. Still can't."

"She hates him?"

"No way. She loves him. At least that is her story."

"But she threw away his pictures?"

"Yeah." Abby considered my question. "That was a little out of character."

Although believable after forty years.

"The way my grandmother…her name is Donna. Can we call her Donna? The way Donna told it, he left them enough money to live on *so he could avoid any legal problems*. He was selfish and took more for himself, but they would be fine until he recovered. They had a lawyer who would take care of all their affairs."

"Did she tell anyone the name of the lawyer?"

"Not that I know about. She may have." She flipped through the photos stopping to study each one before moving on.

"Did your grandmother ever talk about your grandfather to you?"

She kept her eyes on a photo. "In front of me. Not *to* me. Mostly whenever someone suggested she give up this house or the one outside Philadelphia. She said she wanted to be here when he came *crawling back* as she always put it."

"After thirty, forty years, she still expected him to reappear?"

She picked up another photo. "She remained convinced that he would realize she was right."

"About what?"

"About everything." She dropped the picture and focused on me. "At least that's how my mother sees Donna's attitude. *Saw* Donna's attitude. I have no idea what she thinks now."

I noted a catch in her voice, but she fought the sign of emotion. And won.

"I wish my grandmother had not sold this house." She got up and walked through the large living space to the windows overlooking the thicket and the beach beyond. "You didn't change anything but the furniture."

The room of mostly glass walls did not provide an opportunity for much change even if we owned the house, which we didn't. "This isn't our house. We're housesitting while my fiancé goes back to school. We're only here through May."

"Isn't he kind of old to do that?"

"Many people make changes in mid-life." I grew defensive. "You said you're starting college this year."

"So? I took a year off, but that doesn't make me middle-aged."

Middle-aged? That stung, but I ignored her comment. "So, I bet you discover that Andy is not unusual. I imagine you'll run into some dropouts from earlier generations or people who want to change tracks midlife."

"Like my grandfather."

"Not quite the same, but, yes, people sometimes don't want the same things they wanted in their twenties."

"Do you think staying until May will leave you enough time?"

"Enough time for what?" I watched her from the dining table.

"For you to find out what happened to my grandfather."

Mistake three. The biggest. I didn't say *are you nuts*. I did say, "Tell me what you've done so far."

Chapter 4

Abby stared over the treetops at the ocean. "Tide's going out. I can see the waves. I always loved coming here especially when I was little." She opened the slider and stepped onto the deck.

"It's kind of chilly, but, sure, go ahead." I granted permission that wasn't requested.

Out on the deck, Abby posed like Wonder Woman with her head tossed back so the breeze fanned her hair out into a cape. "I wanted to remember what it's like out here. The sun is warm."

Right. And the wind was cold, but I joined her.

"I did some work on my own, Abby said. "Internet searches. Couldn't find a thing."

"Did you check if your grandfather died?"

"No obituaries came up."

"What about gravesites?"

"I tried. Nothing. I checked to see if he was using another name. Like his middle name or his mother's maiden name. Or his middle name with his mother's maiden name. Still nothing."

"Did you post on any of the missing person sites?"

"Well, he's not actually a missing person, is he? He decided to leave."

"But..." I could counter that argument, but she didn't give me a chance.

"My grandmother would go ballistic if she thought I aired the family's dirty linen in public."

"Is your grandmother a heavy online user?" I doubted she was.

"She can barely send an email. But she has friends. Besides, what if someone does know him? I was afraid to give him warning. He hid once.

He could hide again. Don't forget, he left of his own accord. If posting for help is the approach you're going to take, forget it."

An opening to jump in and agree to forget it! I missed my chance and she kept going.

"We need to take him by surprise."

"You might not like what I find. Did it ever occur to you that he has another family?"

"It has occurred to my mother. Not my grandmother. Donna claims they are still married. He never contacted her for a divorce. She lived in the same two houses for years. Here and at home. He could have served her with papers." She paused. "I guess she could have ignored them and hidden them from the family. With her, you never know."

"Doesn't she ever consider that he might be deceased?" *Deceased* sounded so much softer than *dead.*

"She claims to sense that he is alive."

"But not where he is?"

"She's no psychic. She simply wants him to be alive."

"But never a single word or sighting?"

She shook her head.

"I should talk to your mother before I agree to do anything," I said.

She closed her eyes and took a deep breath. "I'm over eighteen. I don't need her permission. To do what? Ask a favor?"

Good point. It wasn't as if she'd be paying me.

Abby opened her eyes but didn't let hers meet mine. She studied the ocean. "My mother spent a lot of summers here with her mother, but her father was around for only a few of those years. Donna built the extension of the house after he left. It's bigger than the original building." She pointed towards a traditional cedar-shake-covered colonial structure that extended from behind the Juggernaut into the dunes for over a hundred feet. An obvious addition to the original home, built to suit different tastes. "Donna thought that all beach houses should be Cape Cod cottages."

Cape Cod, maybe. Cottage? No way. The addition was huge. "We only go back there to use the washing machine," I said. *Or we will when we run out of clean clothes.*

I came up beside Abby at the railing. The air felt chilly, but she was right about the sun. I was almost comfortable. "She never liked this house but never left it until a few years ago?"

"She wanted to be here when my grandfather came home." Abby made a great show of inhaling the ocean air.

"What did she think happened to him?"

She let out her breath slowly and turned to face me. "That he was suffering from temporary insanity."

"For forty years?"

I read the shake of her head to say *that's my grandmother*. "She had a theory that he might have amnesia. I know it sounds ridiculous. But you don't know my grandmother, Donna, and her will of iron. She doesn't listen to anyone. She knew how she wanted it to be, so that was how it was."

"I understand she had this sense that he was alive, but didn't she ever think about having him declared dead? There had to be financial benefits."

She turned back to the view. "I don't understand all that, but I do know that when he left, he had everything taken care of by an attorney."

"And you don't know the attorney's name?"

"What? Do you think I remembered it in the last five minutes?" Snappish. That's what Abby was. Snappish. This girl did not have a knack for getting people on her side.

"He was a friend of my grandfather's. My mother said whenever he was mentioned, Donna would say 'do not utter that man's name in my presence.'"

"Does Donna know you are trying to find your grandfather?"

She closed her eyes again and leaned her head back so the sun could bathe her face in light. "No way. She wants him back, but only if he comes crawling on his hands and knees."

"Yet she moved."

She opened her eyes and stared over the water. "I was surprised. About three years ago she sold this house and her house in Philadelphia. Outside Philadelphia actually. Villanova. Moved to Cape May full time."

"What about getting rid of the photos? Did she abandon hope that he would come back?"

"Not that I ever heard, and let's face it. She didn't go far. She talked about moving south to the Carolinas but ended up a couple of towns away still in New Jersey. I am sure so that if, excuse me, *when* he came back he would be able to find her." She studied the view for a moment. "She doesn't admit it, but she has some health issues. If you watch her, sometimes she stumbles over her words. Just for a few seconds. Maybe she figured she was getting older and didn't need two big houses to take care of."

"I find it hard to understand why she never made any effort to find your grandfather."

"In her mind, she does. She prays. We're Catholic. Donna goes to mass every morning. For years here in Avalon and now down in Cape May." She squinted into the sun as she looked up at me. It was rare for anyone to have to tilt their head back to look up at me. "My mother thinks she's gone to mass every day since my grandfather disappeared."

"You know he could be dead."

"He's not even eighty yet. I think he's alive." She turned away and took a deep breath of ocean air. "I love this house. Even more without Donna around."

I stuck to the issue at hand. "He could be anywhere in the world. I cannot afford to travel to find him."

"I can help. I had a part-time job over the winter."

I felt pretty certain her earnings wouldn't solve the problem. "I should talk to your grandmother, to Donna."

"Not a good idea. She won't even talk to me about him. Just about everything I learned came second-hand from my mother."

I didn't feel optimistic about the information Elisabeth could provide.

"Did your mother ever search for her father?"

"Yes, but I don't think she had the sense of urgency until she got her diagnosis. The Internet wasn't around to help when she was growing up. After she married, she wanted to hire a professional to look for him but my parents didn't have much money. When they had enough money, so much time had passed she figured the trail had gone cold."

"And the Internet?"

"I helped her, but we found nothing. We've tried more than once but never found a thing."

"I would really like to talk to your mother."

Abby hesitated, a surprising occurrence. "I'll see what my father says."

"I'd be happy to explain to him why it would be helpful."

"No. I'll talk to him." For once she let the conversation die.

"Exactly when did your grandfather disappear?" I asked.

"July Fourth. Want to know why I know?"

I nodded.

"Think about it. Given what I told you about Donna, what kind of celebrations do you think we had on the fourth of July? In this house, it wasn't like America was born that day. It was more like it died."

"And the year?"

"My mother always said he didn't wait until her tenth birthday on July 11th. She was born in 1967. I know that because her father used to tell her he could have been at the summer of love in San Francisco, but he was home changing her diaper. I think he said it a lot."

Or maybe her mother reminded her. What kind of father would say that to a child? What kind of mother would repeat that to a child? I'd put my money, in this case, on a quote from a bitter mother trying to recruit her daughter to her team. But what did I know? Nothing. Yet already, I didn't particularly like either of Elisabeth Douglas's parents.

Chapter 5

I stretched out on the sectional built to hold eighteen. Abby was gone. The loft was set up as our sleeping space. I was ready to execute my plan for the day—actually, for the sixty days we would be housesitting. *Do nothing.*

What would be so compelling that I would ever want to leave this glass palace overlooking the sea? What a gig! This was no ordinary house or setting. A prime piece of real estate in a town full of prime real estate.

I wasn't being a total slug. It wasn't as if I didn't have a fitness plan. If I wanted to see crashing waves at high tide from the main floor, I needed to stand up. So I'd be on my feet at least twice a day.

I turned on the TV and found a British mystery. I tried to enjoy it, but Abby Douglas kept popping into my mind. An argument ensued between my two views of the issue.

Why did you agree to help her?

It was a moment of weakness. She's only a kid.

An obnoxious kid.

An obnoxious kid who's trying to help her mother.

If you're going to help her, why are you sitting here streaming videos?

I can be contrarian.

You know you're going to help. Just get up and do it.

When this show is over.

You've seen this one a dozen times. The pharmacist did it.

I like watching it.

You like it because the detectives enjoy solving puzzles. Look at the pleasure they take knowing they help people. You could do that. You can help Elisabeth Douglas facing the end of her life, needing help, wanting only to know what happened to her father.

That side won the argument. I pulled out my laptop and searched for Kenneth Patterson. Abby was right. I found nothing. Finding his brother, Gerald, proved no problem. Why hadn't Abby pursued this herself? She was a kid but no shrinking violet. Was she afraid of finding the truth? Or had she found something that put her off? But then why hire me? Enlist me. A more accurate word since no money would change hands.

If a reason existed to fear Gerald Patterson, Google did not provide any warning. From what I could piece together, Kenneth Patterson's younger brother had retired from a large insurance company after thirty years of service and had been living in retirement in Sea Isle City, New Jersey, for twelve years. He had three daughters, all married, and seven grandchildren. Most of that information came from his wife's obituary. Veronica Lin Patterson had died three years earlier.

Gerald was…what? Ten miles, one bridge away. And no one had been in touch with him? I leaned back and stared out at the sun glimmering on the ocean.

What a nice day to lounge about. I told myself.

What a nice day for a ride. I argued.

Again, the side that favored helping Abby won. I grabbed my car fob and headed for the door.

According to every site I checked on the Internet, Gerald Patterson lived on 76th Street in Sea Isle City in what turned out to be a lovely Cape Cod-style cottage, a relic, dwarfed by houses from several generations of rebuilding in the town. No ocean view. No privacy. Not a hint of the opulence of his brother's house. Gerald's neighbors built as close to their property line as allowed, so when he looked out his windows Gerald saw walls, not waves. Still, he could smell the ocean air. I could, too, as I walked up his path.

I didn't abandon my project when no one answered my knock. I killed an hour entertaining myself with a cruise along the beachfront from Sea Isle to Strathmere. When I pulled up to the house on 76th Street for the second time, someone was sitting on the small porch. Someone who could be the Gerald Patterson I'd seen in the photo—plus forty years. I'd taken two steps up the short path when I heard a voice, a gruff and unwelcoming voice, call out.

"You have the wrong place."

"Gerald Patterson?"

"Who wants to know?" Now the tone turned hostile.

"My name is Meg Daniels." Lately, when searching for missing people, I'd been using the excuse that I was a historian, but that wouldn't work here. What was I researching? The fashions of the 1970s? That wouldn't fly. I had to be honest. "I am a friend of a family member of yours. I've come on their behalf."

If he was curious, which I would think a man with a missing brother might be, he didn't let on. "I don't have any family members that don't know how to get here themselves."

"This would be a great-niece. Your brother, Kenneth, had a daughter and she had a daughter. That's who asked me to come."

He looked off towards the ocean although he could not see it. "Well, if she's anything like her grandmother, she doesn't need to get in touch. I've been happy to grow old with that bitch out of my life."

"I don't know her grandmother, but I suspect she is nothing like her." That might have been a lie. I feared Abby inherited a few traits from the woman she described so negatively. "Your niece Elisabeth, Kenneth's daughter, is slipping into dementia and she'd like to see her father before… well, while she can still understand. Her daughter Abby thought you might be able to help."

I noted a flicker in his eyes, maybe a touch of emotion before he met my gaze and barked at me. "What in God's name makes you think I know where Kenny is?"

"So, you don't know where your brother is?"

"I guess if anyone would know, it would be me, but Kenny walked away before you were born without so much as a howdy-ho." He waved as if to say good riddance. "At first, I worried about him, but when I found out all the preparations he made without a word to me, I got mad. Real mad. He had no right to put me through that. I never heard from him. Never want to."

"I can see where you would be angry." I pointed to an aluminum lawn chair that matched his. "May I sit down?"

"Why? You staying?"

"I do have a few questions. If you could answer them for your niece's sake. Certainly, you can't blame her in any way for what her father did." I stared at him with wide eyes that begged him to agree. My eyes, the color of an Army jacket, were not my strong point, but he seemed to respond. Maybe he was a veteran.

For the second time, I detected a touch of emotion in his eyes, but not one he was going to acknowledge. He waved at the chair. "Help yourself." He waited until I settled into the seat before he continued. When he spoke again, the anger in his tone had disappeared. "I'm sorry to hear about Elisabeth. She was a nice kid. I don't feel right talking about Kenny, but if it's for little Lisa…that's what we used to call her. Kenny and I. Drove Donna nuts. Too common. No English queen had ever been called Lisa. We loved calling her Lisa."

I noted the hint of a smile at that memory. I did not want to interrupt.

"If I could ask Kenny what to do, I am sure he would want me to do anything I could to make Elisabeth's life better. He loved that little girl."

I tried to hide my skepticism.

"I loved her too. When she was little, I was crazy about her." He took a moment to remember. "I didn't have my own kids yet, so I used to hang out with Kenny and his family. Especially, when they got that big house on the beach in Avalon. You know it?"

I nodded. "That was how I met the family. Housesitting for the new owners."

"Then you know. Fancy schmancy. That was Ken. He had to have the best. Not that he didn't earn it all. He worked hard on cases I would never have touched."

Why? I wanted to ask but couldn't think of a discreet way to do that. "You're an attorney, too?"

"Not a big-bucks type like Kenny. Solid job. Solid salary. Solid life. That's me. Not like my brother."

His expression was more sad than angry.

"That wouldn't do for Kenny. No, my brother had to have the best of everything." He stopped. I waited while he decided if he was going to continue down this path. He decided yes. "I was never certain, but I suspected he cut a few corners in time, represented some people that I might call shady."

Aha. Now I understood why Gerald didn't want those cases.

"I was never certain. My brother was naïve in a way. I didn't think he would knowingly do anything illegal, but I worried he would make a mistake. You know. By accident."

I didn't interrupt to point out his brother was a lawyer.

"A few of his clients worried me. I didn't want to see him end up in jail. Or worse."

I didn't interrupt for an explanation.

"In a way, I was relieved when he went away, away from those types." He had more to say, but he didn't say it. "I shouldn't talk about him. He was always a great big brother to me."

"Until he disappeared off the face of the earth?"

He repeated what I said word for word as if reminding himself.

"Did it ever occur to you that he had met with foul play at the hands of any of those shady types?"

"Maybe." He thought for a moment and then corrected himself. "No. They were white-collar crooks. Not organized crime. They wouldn't have knocked him off." He mumbled. "I don't think. It wasn't a big concern of mine."

"Do you have any names?" I asked.

"Why would you need to know names?"

"I am gathering any information that might help me find him."

His eyes narrowed. "Most of them are probably dead by now. The only one I remember is Malcolm Maturi. You know him." He didn't ask a question. Apparently, I was supposed to recognize the name.

"Never heard of him."

"Really? Too young, I guess. Big celebrity chef. Even got his own TV show. Still around. Maturi, not the TV show. But Kenny was gone by then and, luckily, by the time Maturi went to jail. Some sort of financial hijinks in the 1980s. I forget the details. Kenny helped him get his business going, and I believe the two of them found some, shall we say, innovative means to raise funds. I never knew for sure. I'm just telling you so you can see the kind of people he worked with. Shady maybe, but dangerous no. No Tony Sopranos in the crowd."

His voice grew strong. I suspected he was fighting a smile. "Now, ask me about his wife. She was a different matter altogether."

"You suspected Donna killed him?"

"Look, I shouldn't talk about this. You're a total stranger. For all I know, you're out to hurt the family, not help them." Then, he chuckled. "Although I hate to pass up a chance to badmouth my sister-in-law. My former sister-in-law."

"Did you seriously believe she might have killed him?"

"Not really." He reconsidered. "Well, yes, at the beginning until I found out how Kenny had worked at arranging his escape. Closed his firm. Transferred his clients. Took care of every last detail."

"Did you see her after Ken disappeared?"

"I didn't go near the place. I realized I'd be persona non grata. Besides, Vonnie, that's my wife, and I were back in the city. "

"How did you find out he'd disappeared?"

"Lawyer called me, explained what happened, told me not to worry. Donna called me some night during that first week. Late in the week. Maybe Friday. She said it had occurred to her that I might know where Kenny had gone."

Four days later it occurred to her?

"It's a long time ago, but I remember that she was calm. Haughty and condescending as usual but eerily calm. She began every sentence with 'I guess you know…' I kept telling her I didn't know. Anything. I didn't. Kenny didn't give me any warning."

"And you accepted that he'd run off."

"After I heard from his lawyer."

"What about the rest of the family?"

"Our parents were dead. I was the rest of the family. Me and Vonnie. My wife. We didn't have any kids yet."

The conversation stopped while Gerald greeted a woman headed into the house next door.

"My neighbor." He mumbled. "That woman is a real pain in the neck. I am always super friendly to keep on her good side. She's likely to call the police and tell them we're talking too loudly out here."

Was that my cue to stop talking? If so, I ignored it but I did lower my voice which made my questions seem a bit sinister.

"Did all of his friends believe that story? Didn't anyone sound the alarm that he might have run into trouble?"

"Not that I ever heard. The lawyer who helped him was a friend. No one doubted him."

I said "hmh" in a way that questioned the lawyer's role.

"Look, his friends weren't my friends, so I didn't see all of them. The ones I did were annoyed he didn't touch base, but, for the most part, they wished him well. At least the ones who knew what Donna was really like."

"What was she like?"

His expression was an odd combination. Disgust and amusement. "With men or women?" Any sign of hesitation was gone. He was ready to bash Donna. "Most men didn't see through her. Almost all women did. When my wife, Vonnie—she died a few years ago—when Vonnie first met her, she caught on to her right away."

"On to her?"

"Donna was flirtatious. Very, very cute so she could pull it off. She wanted every man she met to find her adorable. Not sexy, mind you. Adorable. But you know how guys are. They take it as the same thing. So, she got a reputation as a tease."

"But she was Ken's girlfriend, his wife. She came onto his friends?"

"He loved having a girlfriend that everyone lusted after. He always had to have the best. He liked that she flirted. He knew she was going home with him. I always wondered exactly when he found out what a cold, controlling bitch she was." Gerald enjoyed sliming Donna. Even after all these years. I could tell.

"He married her," I countered.

"I guess he found out after the wedding. Certainly, after the kids were born."

Kids? "I thought Elisabeth was an only child."

"She had a younger brother. Two years younger. He died. Crib death. There was nothing anyone could do. Kenny was devastated. If Donna was, she didn't show it. I'd like to say the baby's death changed Donna, but it actually made her more herself. She seemed to have a toggle switch. Warm and flirty. Click. Cold as ice."

He paused as if digging for the right words to describe her. "She had this way of freezing up, of disapproving without saying a word, and she disapproved of everything. Everybody who wasn't her was wrong. Vonnie hated being around Donna. She knew Donna didn't approve of her. Didn't even like her name. Kenny told me she thought Vonnie sounded cheap. Donna did not like cheap. She insisted on calling her, Veronica. Not that she liked that name much better."

"I am hearing that she was two different people." I shivered. Not at the thought of Donna's split personality but at the touch of a breeze. The day was warm for March, but it was still March. At least for a day or two.

"I saw cute Donna at first. Took me a while to see judgmental Donna. I caught on before Kenny. He was crazy about her, at least about showing her off, taking her to parties. They were each a status symbol for the other."

I needed to meet this woman. I'd put pressure on Abby. "Abby, Ken's granddaughter, gave me this photo. Can you take a look?"

I passed him the picture, and his practiced disinterest vanished immediately. He pulled reading glasses out of his jacket pocket and held the photo close to his eyes for a better look. "I think I took this shot." He studied the photo. "They are all Kenny's buddies. I'm pretty sure that was the last time they all got together. This wasn't taken that long before Kenny disappeared. Possibly the same day. The Fourth of July. 1977." He stared at the photo some more. I didn't interrupt his thoughts. "You know thinking back on it, maybe Kenny did warn us all what he had in mind. This was taken at his house that morning, the day he left. Donna was having a champagne brunch. I know. Not traditional Fourth fare. They had another party to go to that night. Probably with more important people. So, the B-team got brunch. And champagne when what we really wanted was a beer."

Gerald Patterson
Ken Patterson's house
Avalon, New Jersey
July 4, 1977

Gerald didn't feel comfortable with Kenny's buddies. He was the kid brother and even as a married lawyer with a baby on the way, he would always feel like one. He hung around the drinks table trying to make small talk as each of them came up, but the conversation was strained.

His wife had the right idea. Vonnie was stretched out on a lounge at the edge of the deck. Away from the group, she could enjoy some peace and quiet along with a view of the ocean over the wooded thicket that provided the house with privacy atypical for the Jersey beaches. Gerald had to admit that Kenny had found a spectacular spot for his summer house although achieving his dream hadn't been easy. Raising the funds wasn't the only issue. Actually, that didn't seem to be an issue at all. Kenny had persevered through a lot of obstacles just to get the permits. And then, through the headaches of contractors and builders. Kenny never despaired and worked his way through problem after problem. Gerald guessed Kenny thought having a showplace was worth it.

Gerald wished he could give Vonnie a place like this so she could spend her summers sitting on a deck overlooking the ocean. She loved nature. She loved the sea. He envied the spot, not the home. Vonnie didn't need the flashy house Kenny built. He didn't either. His fantasy was a cottage nestled in these dunes with a screened-in porch facing the sea. He pictured sitting with Vonnie, not talking, simply enjoying the sound of the waves mixing with the joyful noise of beachgoers frolicking in the water or on the sand. His needs were simple. But the days of such simple structures in locales like this were long gone. He imagined when Kenny got new neighbors, they would be building houses as elaborate as his.

Gerald patted Vonnie's baby bump as he slipped onto the edge of the lounge beside her. "Do you feel like a walk to the beach?"

"No. I'm fine here as long as that bitch stays away from me."

"Donna?"

She stared at him as if asking who else she could mean.

"What did she do today?"

"Nothing, as usual. She complimented me on how I was giving the baby a good home and lots of nutrition."

"So?"

"She meant I looked fat."

Gerald trusted his wife's judgment.

"Then, she mentioned how lucky she was that she had a hairdresser she trusted at the shore so she could take care of her hair when she was pregnant."

"Well, I think your hair looks lovely." It shone with the sun reflecting off the straight black strands.

"I agree." Vonnie smiled. "And I don't even have to spend a hundred dollars getting it to look this way."

Vonnie laughed, but Gerald knew there was more.

"And she remarked on how lucky I saved old dresses from the sixties so I didn't have to buy new maternity clothes."

Gerald looked at his wife's flowered sundress. He thought she looked adorable. "Didn't you buy that especially for this party?"

She fought tears as she shook her head to answer.

"Why do you care what she thinks?"

"I don't but I want her to know I don't care, to realize I see through her."

"So tell her."

"She'd never believe me. She'd never believe that I had my own taste. She'd think I just didn't know any better. That's a big thing with her. 'They just don't know…'"

As if cued, Donna appeared beside the lounge. Had she overheard their conversation? He didn't care.

"Did you see your old friends, the Carsons, are here? They built a house down in Stone Harbor. It's big. I'll give it that."

"That's nice. I'll have to go say hello." Gerald smiled.

"It's not what I would have done." Donna looked as if she had just sucked on a lemon.

"What?" Gerald played dumb.

"Their house. They used brick as a base. People don't do that. Not in Stone Harbor."

Gerald had no idea if that was true or not, but he was prepared to defend the Carsons' choice. "I bet when those storms whip up the East Coast, they'll be happy they did."

Donna pretended to consider his point. "Perhaps. We don't have to worry about that. Even though we are right on the ocean, our house is set so high in the dunes the water can't get to us. Even during that horrid storm in 1962, these dunes weren't damaged. Not that we were here then. We were still in school in 1962, and now only fifteen years later, here we are. Whatever his shortcomings, Kenneth knew how to pick a location. Everyone can't get a spot like this."

Whatever his shortcomings? *Gerald glanced at Vonnie who was suppressing a smirk.*

"I think I'll go say hello to Robin Carson. Vonnie, do you want to come?"

His wife claimed she'd rather stay seated. "The clouds kind of come and go. I don't want to miss the sun while it's out."

"Yes," Donna said, "You should rest. Look at those ankles."

Gerald almost laughed aloud, but didn't say anything. He didn't need to strike back at Donna. Knowing he and Vonnie were in cahoots felt good enough.

"I'll be back after I see Robin." He gave his wife a light kiss, patted her belly and headed across the wide deck.

Kenny stopped him before he reached the Carsons. "Here you go, bro." He handed him a bottle of St Pauli Girl. "Don't let my lovely wife see that I am not adhering to her champagne standard. I see you've been chatting with her. Let me apologize for whatever offensive thing she said."

"Nothing overt."

"It never is. She thinks she's subtle." Kenny took a swig of his beer. "I almost said, 'she means well' but I don't think she does. She always wants the upper hand. I guess she was always like that." Kenny moved to the railing and leaned on it, watching the waves roll in and out in the distance. "Was I so besotted when I met her that I couldn't see clearly?"

"I don't know." What could Gerald say? He figured Kenny hadn't been thinking with his brain.

"She was so cute and all the boys liked her. I felt as if I'd won a prize."

"I guess she was sexy."

"Sexy? Hardly. It was 1965. I was a senior in college. I thought any sex was sexy. Even almost-sex was sexy." He took a long drink of beer. "You were what, the class of 1970?"

A rhetorical question. Kenny knew, but Gerald answered anyway. "Right, 1970."

"How many girls did you have sex with during college?"

"Well, you know I wasn't exactly a James Bond type."

"Give a guess."

"I don't know. A dozen. Maybe a few more."

"Five years. Five measly years. The world had changed so much. In 1965? I was a fool. Most of us were. If I knew then what I know now."

Gerald didn't want to think about what Kenny meant. He certainly wouldn't blame him for cheating, but he didn't want to hear about his brother's misadventures and run the risk of getting caught in the middle.

"At least she kept you out of Vietnam." Gerald, younger with a low lottery number, hadn't been so lucky.

"Vietnam is over. My marriage isn't. Legally."

"Look, I am sure Donna loves you," Gerald said although he was far from convinced.

"She loves her houses, she loves her cars, she loves her clothes. She used to love being seen with me, the big shot lawyer, but no more."

"You're looking pretty hip there, brother. Not exactly Donna's taste."

"She hates what she calls my new style. That's one of the things I love about this look. It annoys Donna. Plus, I feel free in these threads. Living with her is the opposite of being free. What is that Sammy Davis song, 'I've Got to be Me.'?" He sang the line that said he had to be free.

Gerald thought Kenny deserved the freedom of a new look if he wanted one. But in his opinion, his brother might have gone a bit too far.

"I'm just trying to move with the times. I'm not going to let her get me back into a Brooks Brothers suit." Kenny grew pensive. The serious look on his face frightened Gerald. What was he going to say?

"Yoah, Kenny-boy." Robin Carson called. "Come over here. Let's get a picture of Robin's Merry Men."

Whatever Kenny was about to say was lost. He lined up with the others, arms around each other. Robin Carson stood in front holding the camera.

"Here, I'll take it." Gerald took the Instamatic camera from Robin's hand. That was one thing a kid brother could be good for. "Turn around and put the ocean behind you. We want a nice view."

He snapped the picture. "That's a good one."

"Don't move," Kenny commanded. "Get one on my camera. Grab it from the table over there."

*****

"Of course, Kenny didn't have any old Instamatic camera. Always had to have the best. He'd bought himself a Leica."

"Funny, he didn't take it with him," I spoke to myself.

"What makes you say that?"

"Donna had this picture. Elisabeth saved it when Donna was cleaning out before her move. If no one heard from your brother, then he must have left it behind."

"That might be the one from Robin's camera."

I considered the quality of the photo vis-à-vis the other photos Abby had given me. I couldn't agree with Gerald but saw no point in arguing. "They look like a fun group," I observed.

"They were. At least, they had been. They'd been growing apart. The sixties, the Vietnam war, created rifts. The guy with the long hair like a hippie's. He lost a brother in Vietnam. He got angry, bitter. Had trouble with the politics of some of the other guys. Vietnam must have been over when this was taken, but he was still clinging to the counterculture. The others never even admitted the fifties ended. They were all living stereotypical suburban American lives."

"Do you know where any of them are today?"

"What so you can show up at their houses too?" He sounded annoyed on their behalf.

I guess that was what I had in mind. I admitted it.

"They won't have heard from Kenny either." He held the photo close. He didn't flip it over so he wasn't depending on Abby's notes. His take would either confirm or challenge her information. "Dougie is the guy with the long hair. I don't know if I ever knew his full name. He died years ago. Some sort of accident, I heard, but I wonder if he had issues with drugs."

Gerald pointed to a tall guy with a crewcut. "Francis, they called him Cissie, Francis Bloch. I heard he died."

"Who told you?"

He seemed shocked by the question. "I don't recall. It was a long time ago. I assume I saw the obituary."

"Now this guy is Harry. He's dead. And the other one is Robert something. Never read he died."

"Who's that guy in the back? The one holding the movie camera." It appeared to have a microphone on it.

"Robin Carson. They called him Robin the Hood, but he wasn't. A hood I mean. Nice guy. Always was. He had a brother my age, but Robin always treated me like a friend, not just some annoying kid."

"You still see him?"

"Ran into him the other day, which at my age means sometimes in the past ten years. I'm pretty sure he no longer has a house down here or in Philadelphia. He was in the middle of retiring, jabbering on about moving to Florida. He probably has done that by now." He stared at the photo. "Looking at this picture makes me feel bad that I got so mad at Kenny back then. Maybe he was telling me he needed to be free. I mean really, in actuality. I guess I missed that."

It seemed to me that Kenny was being pretty clear about needing to make a move. But, Gerald Patterson, good husband and expectant father, having never had those thoughts, didn't understand the words his brother spoke to him.

"You don't happen to know the name of the lawyer who arranged things for your brother when he disappeared, do you?"

He hesitated. "If I ever did, I've forgotten the name."

He was lying. I knew it. I just didn't know why.

"How did you get involved in this anyway?"

"By accident. Elisabeth got a little confused and came home to her old house by mistake."

"I am certainly sorry to hear about little Lisa, Elisabeth." He caught my expression and added, "I mean that. Truly."

I didn't think he was protecting himself. I got no indication that Gerald Patterson had ever thought about knocking his brother off. I saw nothing suspicious about Gerald Patterson except that he had a $100,000 Lexus in his driveway and a $50,000 Rolex on his wrist.

"Great watch." I probed.

"Oh, this. A gift. I don't know if it's real or not."

I hadn't been away from my job as a VIP concierge that long. I knew that watch was real. I bet he did too.

Chapter 6

The lightning drew my attention outside. Andy had gone up to bed around 10 PM. I was alone in the darkened great room on the huge sofa in front of the 85-inch TV screen watching *Midsomer Murders* on my phone when I noticed the flash. I hit pause and listened for thunder. Nothing. I walked to the window on the side of the house overlooking the driveway and the woods beyond. I told myself I was leaving it open to pull some fresh air inside, but I knew my real motivation. I wanted to listen for Elisabeth outside. I was worried about her even before I feared a storm might be moving in.

Only the usual sounds drifted through the night. Surf in the distance. A light breeze in the trees. And a rustling in the thicket. A loud rustling in the thicket. I couldn't imagine lithe Elisabeth creating such a large disturbance, but, if I abandoned my unrealistic fear of bears and monsters, the likelihood was I was listening to Elisabeth moving through the brush.

I stared hard. The moon, a sliver in the sky, offered no help. Was I imagining a shadow moving through the bushes? Maybe the shadow was leaves congregating in the wind. Then the shadow moved towards the road. I went downstairs and peered out the window beside the ground-level door. The shadow had moved farther away. My logical mind told me the image was not a wandering bear or the Jersey Devil. I slipped my feet into a pair of boat shoes and threw on a jacket and stepped onto the gravel driveway.

"Elisabeth," I called in a sing-song voice as if trying to lure a baby into nap time. I tried to find a level loud enough for Elisabeth to hear, but not the sleeping Andy.

No answer.

"Elisabeth," I called again, louder but still friendly.

I heard a bustling sound, but no answer. Could Elisabeth move that fast? And would she disrupt so many trees? She could if she was flailing around, and if she was flailing around, she was in trouble.

"It's Meg. Remember we met?" I could have kicked myself for my choice of words. I couldn't expect, or ask, Elisabeth to remember anything. "Elisabeth. Andy and I wanted you to come to visit. Tonight is good. Come inside."

No answer. No noise.

I kept talking as I headed toward the edge of the woods. I thought I saw a dark figure. "Elisabeth, I can see you in there." A lie because all I could see was a bulky item. Might have been Elisabeth. Or a tumbling bag of trash. Or a skinny bear. I told myself I was being ridiculous, but bears had been seen in every one of New Jersey's twenty-one counties. How a bear could make its way to a barrier island I couldn't explain, but I'd read that they were smart. Really smart. Smart enough to get to Seven Mile Island? I couldn't rule the possibility out or chase the idea from my mind that a skinny bear was a hungry bear.

I stopped to listen. The only sound I heard matched what I thought I saw. A person or a bear moving through the trees and shrubbery. The thought that it could be both terrified me. I pictured tiny Elisabeth being pursued by a bear. "Elisabeth?" I called again.

I heard something. A word? A growl? The wind was strong enough that I could not be sure.

"Elisabeth, you wait there. I am coming for you." I rushed towards the woods. Protected land or not, I needed to help Elisabeth.

"Elisabeth?" I stepped off the gravel onto a pile of leaves. The loose shoes weren't exactly appropriate for navigating the jungle that was our yard. I yelped as I slipped and grabbed onto a branch to steady myself.

"Elisabeth?"

No one answered, but I remained convinced Elisabeth was generating the noise. And, if she was, she could not be left alone in the brush. I turned on the flashlight on my phone but could see nothing but the vegetation I expected to find in the thicket.

"Elisabeth. It's Meg. You know me. We met here the other day. You and my friend, Andy."

No response except the swishing of leaves being disturbed. The noise was moving farther and farther away towards the road.

I stumbled back to the driveway and tried to keep up. "Elisabeth?"

It was late to make a call, but this was an emergency. I hit Abby's number.

"Abby. Your mother is in the woods beside our house. I can hear her, but I can't see her."

"Who is this?"

How many houses was her mother stalking? "Meg, up in the Dunes. You visited me today. I am outside our house. I called her, but she won't come out."

She sounded tired. "Are you sure it's my mother?"

"I want to err on the side of caution."

"You know it could be an animal. Maybe it isn't her. Let me check." Abby groaned as she moved. It wasn't as if I woke her up. I could hear the television in the background.

I followed the sound of the rustling in the woods as it continued to move away in the direction of Dune Drive.

"My mother is in bed."

"Are you sure?" People pulled covers up to fake it.

"Of course, I'm sure." Abby used a tone that made me wonder why I was doing anything to help her or her mother.

"Thanks," I said although the reason I should be thanking her eluded me. Her phone cut off before I got the full word out, a one-syllable word. At that point, my brain turned from whom did I hear to *what did I hear?*

I ran towards the house. I could not see three feet ahead which is why I ran headlong into something. Something big. Something hard. Something human. I fell to the ground.

"Why are you out here in the dark?" Andy picked me up.

"I thought I heard Elisabeth."

"You should have gotten me up. You shouldn't be out here alone."

"Aren't you the man who took me on an hour's walk today to prove that no one would trespass in these woods, to tell me not to worry? I figured it had to be Elisabeth."

"There could have been animals." He quickly added, "Probably not a bear. Maybe a fox or a coyote."

"I didn't really think about them. That makes me even more frightened for Elisabeth. She might not know what she is up against." I laid a hand on his chest. "Why have you been spending so much time at the gym?" I patted his developing six-pack.

"Going to a university is like joining a health club. I didn't say I was spending *all* my time in the library."

True. He hadn't.

"Don't expect any complaints from me. I like knowing you're in good shape in case I have to call on you to wrestle a bear."

Chapter 7

On our first day in the Positano's house, I had identified three doorbells. Each had a different tone. Beethoven's Fifth indicated someone was waiting at the ground-floor door from the driveway. Notre Dame's fight song meant someone wanted access from the garage. On Tuesday morning, I was already spread out on the sectional, remote control in hand, when I heard a traditional ding-dong, signaling me someone had come to the door on the deck.

Given the alternative, I hoped for a cable guy, a door-to-door salesman, or a religious zealot, but I knew that was unlikely. I sat up and saw over the back of the couch that the visitor was, as I suspected, Abby. She knew what door to use. If I didn't want to hide in the bathroom all day, there was no escaping Abby.

She was across the threshold as soon as I pulled the door open. "Hi, I know you are an early riser."

She knew nothing of the kind. I did not usually get up early although 10:30 was not exactly early. Even for me.

"I was on my way into town so I figured I would stop. Did you find out what was in the thicket last night? I hate to think of my mother in danger."

I didn't know how to explain the incident, so I didn't. "I have no idea."

"Maybe a fox." She planted her hands on her hips and stared at me. A confrontational pose. At least that is how I read it. "I thought I would check and see if you made any progress."

I hadn't even agreed to work for her. At least as far as she knew.

"I brought coffee." She held up two cups from Wawa. "Avalon Coffee is still closed for the season, but I like Wawa coffee."

"Come in, but you'll have to drink both cups yourself. I get all my caffeine from Coke."

"That's not good for you."

"It's caffeine and sugar. Just like coffee. It gets me going."

She slung her coat over one chair at what we called the kitchen island, definitely an island, although the concept of kitchen was dubious. She slid onto another. "So, what did you find out?" She sounded like a boss demanding answers.

I hesitated. I worried that revealing anything to Abby would make me lose control of the situation. Looking back, I was right.

"I talked to your grandfather's brother yesterday."

No *thank you*. No, *that was quick*. If she was surprised, she did not let on. "What did he say?"

"What I expected. That he hasn't seen your grandfather since 1977 and that no one he knows has seen your grandfather since 1977."

"And you believed him?"

"So far, yes. I need to talk to other people."

"Did you follow him after you talked to him?"

The thought hadn't even occurred to me.

Abby expressed horror at my lack of action. "Don't you think he would have gotten in touch with my grandfather as soon as you left?"

That actually was a possibility. "If he did, don't you think he would have used the phone?" I came across as defensive when, in fact, I was making a good point.

"I suppose." She thought long and hard. "We lost the opportunity if he was going to go see him last night. But he's old. He probably doesn't drive at night. He might go today. Luckily, we can get an early start."

"Abby, I have plans."

"What?" She stared into my eyes with a challenging look that made me want to disagree with her no matter what she said.

"Plans, errands, we just moved in."

"Those can wait. Come on," she whined. "We only have the advantage today if it isn't already too late to follow up."

I could have asked her why if she had Googled her great-uncle's address, she hadn't been in a rush years before, but I didn't. The situation had changed with her mother's illness. This search was no longer a matter of simple curiosity. This was a mission for Elisabeth's benefit.

I said, "Relax. Drink that coffee. I need a few minutes to get ready."

"That was quick," Abby said when I reappeared.

Was she being sarcastic? I didn't know. "I'll drive," I offered.

"No. I'll drive. My car is nicer. Plus, he might remember your car."

"No one remembers my car." I owned an innocuous silver hatchback, a couple of months old, that resembled at least 50% of the cars on the road.

"But he's never seen mine."

"That doesn't matter." I objected.

"He's seen yours." She made it clear she thought the decision was hers and it was final.

I wasn't in the mood for an argument. I considered myself easy-going but... *Think of Elisabeth. Think of Elisabeth.* Abby made it hard to remember that I liked helping people.

Abby slipped off her chair and piled one coffee cup into the other. She'd polished both cups off while I dressed. The thought of Abby fueled with that much caffeine was frightening.

"You can play navigator." She assumed the role of captain.

I took the empty cups and dropped them in the trash. "There's not much navigation required. Go up the Ocean Drive and turn left onto 76th Street in Sea Isle."

"Nice work. Your job is done." She led the way to her black BMW SUV. Her car also resembled 50% of the cars on the road. The upscale half.

The drive gave us time to talk about our approach, but we didn't. Abby wanted to talk about her mother. Abby needed to talk about her mother, and, if I was going to stick with this project, I needed to hear her talk about her mother. Describing Elisabeth Douglas's issues made Abby calmer, softer. Could I say even likable?

"I was in high school when her symptoms became problematic, but my father said there were signs even earlier. Can you imagine? She would forget things. Names. Nouns. My father said that was natural as people age. But then she forgot how to do things like starting the dishwasher. She'd go somewhere and forget how to get home. My father tried to deny what was happening, but memory loss is only one sign. She lost interest in everything. She began to slip away."

The control in Abby's voice shocked me. No emotion came to the surface. I guess she had been dealing with the situation for a large percentage of her young life. I didn't know how to respond. I had no experience with sick or ill parents. Both my parents had died quickly before they hit sixty.

Before I needed to contribute to the conversation, Abby continued. "I couldn't do much to help my father when I was in high school. He took the burden of her care. Luckily, he could work from home. He moved her down here to the shore for a quieter atmosphere. Even so, her condition has been a huge drain on him. So, I took a gap year thinking I could help. I believe I have. I don't know if my mother understands, but my father appreciates what I did. I can't imagine what he is going through."

This was the flip side of the Abby that I'd seen so far. A side, I suspected, she didn't often show. When she changed the subject without warning, I heard the more familiar tones in her voice. Clipped. Efficient. But at least, in this instance, not combative. "What is Andy studying?"

"He's taking courses to see what interests him."

"What did he do before?"

"He worked in hotel security at the Artistical resort in the Bahamas. I worked there too."

"Is that where you met him?"

"No. I met him in Ocean City."

"New Jersey?" She seemed shocked. Why? I had no idea. "How?"

"When my boss got murdered. Andy used to work as a private investigator."

"What did you do at the hotel?"

Really? She had no follow-up question about how, why, or by whom my boss got murdered? No, her mind had shifted gears. Again.

"I was a concierge."

"Oh."

I might have impressed her if I told her I was the hotel's VIP concierge, but I didn't want to go through the usual range of questions about my celebrity encounters. Who did you meet? How did they look in person? Were they as nice…snobby…funny as they seemed to be?

"What are you doing for money?" Abby asked.

"What?" A shockingly inappropriate question even for Abby.

"You aren't working. I wondered if you were rich."

"Sometimes."

"What do you mean by that?"

What did I mean? "Not that it is any of your business, but Andy and I saved a lot while we worked in the Bahamas. We got free housing."

"Did you get to use your own furniture?"

"Yes, but we lost almost everything in Hurricane Freida."

How did this girl's mind work? I could never anticipate her next question. So far, I'd told her my boss was murdered, my possessions were destroyed in a hurricane, and I was sometimes wealthy, but her follow-up question didn't stay on topic.

"When you met Andy did you know right away that he was the one?"

"Actually, no, but I did think he was cute." I didn't elaborate that I was reluctant to become too infatuated with a man who thought I might be a murderer.

"Don't you worry that he will want to hook up with some of the young girls in his class?"

"Now, I will." The thought had occurred to me, but I'd convinced myself Andy's classmates would see him as old. Not that I would tell Abby that.

"He's old but he's kind of hot." Abby's words killed my theory. "You should probably clean up your act a little."

"What?"

"I mean you have a look. I'll give you that, but it's not the latest. And it's kind of casual. I mean do you ever wear anything but those leggings and a tunic."

"I like having a uniform. It's easy. Plus, I didn't bring all my clothes with me." I didn't mention that the ones I left in our short-term rental were identical but in other neutral shades.

"The Lululemon store in town is open."

"Right. I'll keep that in mind." Did she think I was the type of woman who needed running gear?

I was relieved when she put on the SUV's blinker and made the turn onto 76th Street.

"Which house is his? We'll do a drive-by and then go back to the corner and wait."

"Fine." Internally, I grumbled. I resented going along with all of Abby's wishes but, the truth was, I had no basis for argument except my annoyance that she was right. It wouldn't hurt to keep an eye on her Great Uncle Gerald. At least until we cleared him. Cleared him? Of what? Hiding his brother? Communicating with his brother? Murdering his brother? I hadn't even considered that possibility.

"That's not much of a house," Abby sneered when I pointed out the modest Cape Cod.

"It looks better when it has a top-of-the-line Lexus in the driveway."

"You mean we missed him? He's probably gone to meet my grandfather." Her intonation stopped just short of outraged.

"Abby, maybe he went for donuts. Or to pick up a newspaper. Or to have coffee with friends. Or to the grocery store. Or to the liquor store."

She raised a hand to stop my recitation. "Well, we can take a ride. Maybe we'll find him. Lucky we have the license plate number."

"What makes you think we have the plate number?"

She turned slowly in her seat to face me. "You saw it yesterday and you didn't take down the number?"

Her judgmental tone made my blood pressure skyrocket. *Maybe you should have hired someone better. Maybe you should have hired someone actually you paid.* I didn't say that. I said, "Abby, I was doing you a favor dropping by for a chat with him. I wasn't pursuing a murder suspect." I sounded a bit apologetic as I added, "It was a Lexus."

She heaved a sigh, and I do mean heaved it, to guarantee I did not miss her exasperation. "What color was his car?"

Oh. Oh. "Dark." I hesitated. "Maybe maroon. You know, burgundy. Besides, I'll recognize it if it turns into the driveway."

"What? We're going to sit here and wait and do nothing?" The dial on her meter was headed to outrage again.

"That is a lot of what investigating involves."

"We should go look for him." She was calmer, but not calm.

Again, I hated to admit it, but she was right. We might get lucky. There were not that many commercial streets to cruise in town. It's what

I would have done if I'd been on my own, although I would have included a stop to check if the fudge shop had opened for the season. "Let's head for the Promenade," I suggested and waited for her to reject my idea, but she didn't.

"Okay. I'll go down Landis."

On the ride, I kept an eye out for any dark Lexus. I wasn't much of a car person. If I couldn't read a logo, I couldn't tell a $20,000 economy model from a $100,000 luxury car much to the frustration of my friends and acquaintances who went to the trouble of buying $100,000 models.

"Dock Mike's Pancake House says it's open. He could be in there," Abby said as we neared the center of town.

"I don't see a car that looks like his." I checked up and down the street.

"Maybe he didn't park on Landis."

"There a half-dozen spaces I can see." I was still counting when she interrupted.

"Maybe not when he got here. He has a nice car. Maybe he doesn't like to park on a busy street." She circled several nearby blocks searching for a Lexus. The only one we found was white.

"Not his," I assured Abby.

She repeated the search process for every business of any sort that was open. I was sorry to see that the fudge shop was not.

I felt we had done a thorough search of Sea Isle. "We can probably check back at the house," I said as if Abby would listen to anything I said.

She didn't. She continued north up the Ocean Drive. "Maybe he has friends up here."

He could have friends anywhere in the world, but I didn't protest. I loved riding up my favorite stretch of road that runs along the oceanfront from Sea Isle to Strathmere. Since I wasn't in the driver's seat, I could take in the scenery. Not that we could see the beach beyond the dunes. I cracked the window to hear the surf and breathe the ocean air. "I love this road. It's amazing how they fortified these dunes. I can't believe the amount of vegetation…"

"What are you doing looking at the dunes?" Abby made no attempt to hide her outrage. "I am driving. You are the one who should be checking for that Lexus."

"I'm watching," I said although I had not been. I redirected my attention to the row of houses that lined the west side of the road. I remembered a time when every lot was not taken. I always assumed that the Great Nor'easter of 1962 had cleared away a lot of the houses, but in the intervening decades the survivors of the storm, most small old-fashioned beach cottages that sat in the sand, had gotten new neighbors. The growth had happened over the years, but all the new builds appeared to have one thing in common. Every house stood on stilts. Yes, sitting high afforded them great views, but the new style promised a better chance of surviving the kind of destruction the area suffered in what was called the Good Friday storm of 1962. People still talked about that storm. Even people who weren't born until years after it had passed.

"I love the houses along this road. Look at the white one."

"Does it have a dark Lexus in the driveway?" Abby asked. Again, she made no effort to hide her annoyance. I didn't argue that I was capable of seeing a car and a house with a single glance. I sat in silence until we drove into Strathmere when I pointed out that the Deauville Inn opened at 11 AM. "We could drive through the parking lot."

"Good idea," Abby admitted but added, "I was going to suggest that."

Of course, you were.

Chapter 8

The car was barely into the parking lot when Abby jammed on her breaks and pulled into a space beside a dark color, late model Lexus. "Here it is." She turned off the engine. "I bet he's in there. Meeting with my grandfather."

I didn't disagree that he was probably in there. The restaurant had been around for years. It had a bar. It seemed like the kind of place a guy might go for a beer on a chilly spring day. I didn't agree that he would be meeting with her grandfather.

"Now what? Do we go in and confront him?" Abby was enthusiastic.

"No. We verify he is there and then we watch him."

I pulled a scrunchy out of my handbag and tried to capture my hair in it.

"What you doing?" Abby made it clear she was annoyed.

"Your great-uncle has seen me." I slipped on a pair of sunglasses. "If he recognizes me, he'll think I am following him."

"Right."

I waited for Abby to add a criticism. She didn't. She simply said, "You go first."

I stepped into the gift shop entrance first and got a clear shot of the bar from the entrance. I stopped dead. "Bingo."

"Where? Who? What do you see?"

"He's in there. He's at the bar. He's sitting with somebody else, a guy, a dark-haired guy."

"My grandfather?"

"I have no idea. That's what we are here to find out. He's facing us."

"Okay, let's go in." She sounded frighteningly excited.

"I think we have to wait for a hostess," I said.

"Yes, you do." A friendly young woman came into the room and picked up two menus to seat us.

"Before we sit down…" I bought a cap with a Deauville Inn patch on the front and tucked as much of my hair under it as I could.

"Ready?" The hostess asked.

I said "yes" but I grabbed Abby's arm and held her in place. "Promise me you'll be cool."

"Of course," she managed to infuse the phrase with disdain. "Although you look like a wanna-be Beyonce trying to sneak past your fans."

I wasn't going to complain about that comparison.

As the hostess led us past the bar to a table by the window, I kept my eye on Gerald. He was facing his friend and paying no attention to whomever came and went. I directed Abby to a chair with a view of the bar that left us with our backs to the water view. Gerald Patterson sat with his back to us. I didn't think he would notice us let alone find our position odd.

Gerald and his buddy were the only two customers on their side of the bar. One other group sat on the opposite side facing us. The place wasn't mobbed off-season. A curse. We could not blend into a crowd. A blessing. We could get a table with a view of Gerald Patterson and his companion.

I nodded at the bar. "The one with the Phillies jacket on the back of his chair."

"Is he my grandfather?"

"No. He is his brother." I expected a moment of thoughtful contemplation as Abby absorbed the impact of seeing her great-uncle. I was dreaming.

"I'm going to go talk to him." She tried to pull away, but I held tight to her arm and pulled her back to the table.

"We are here to observe."

She pasted a petulant expression on her face, but she fell back into her chair.

"Great. Lunch." Abby picked up the menu. "We could get a seafood tower."

I checked the menu. I actually checked the price, but I didn't use that as the basis for my disagreement. "Order something that comes out fast." I didn't add *and doesn't feed four.* "We might need to make a quick getaway."

The waitress appeared at our side.

"Why don't we start with an order of Brussel sprouts while we decide." I made a suggestion. It wasn't a question.

Abby made a face worthy of a five-year-old vegetable hater.

"You'll love them."

Her answer was to double down on her disgusted expression. She took another look at the menu. "Can I have the Bavarian Pretzel?"

"It's huge," the waitress said.

Abby's face answered that was fine by her.

"I'll help her."

We added two Cokes to our order and the waitress went off to retrieve our snacks.

"What are we going to do? I need to talk to him." Under the table, her legs bounced up and down at a frenetic pace.

"You wanted to see if he would lead you to your grandfather. Relax. Let him lead."

When her Coke came, she stuck the straw in her mouth, bent her head forward and stared at the conversation at the bar as she drained her glass. I heard the slurping at the end of her soda and then her assessment of the situation. "Appears to be a pretty serious conversation."

She wasn't wrong. The two men's body language suggested a topic heavier than last night's football game. Besides, football season was over.

"So that is my grandfather's brother?"

"Yep."

The waitress asked if Abby wanted another Coke and took the glass away to refill.

Abby never stopped staring at the man at the bar. "Shouldn't I feel something? You know, deep emotion."

In a similar situation, I might have, but I couldn't predict how Abby would react. "What do you feel?"

"Nothing."

I was surprised. "You said you missed your grandfather your entire life. That man is his brother. Your family."

"He was around. If he had wanted to be family, he could have been." She began using her two thighs as a drum. "Maybe that other guy is my grandfather."

"That is not your grandfather."

"How can you know? It's been over forty years since his last picture." She took a swig of the soda the waitress placed in front of her.

"He is too short." I waited until the waitress had pulled her hand clear of the dish before I stabbed a Brussel sprout with my fork.

Abby grimaced at my snack. "Old people get shorter." She had an answer for everything.

"Not from six-two to five-six."

"How can you tell how tall he is?" She pulled a piece off the oversized pretzel.

"That guy's legs are dangling off the ground." To me, he looked nothing like Ken Patterson, at least the pictures of Ken Patterson.

"How does that guy know my grandfather?"

"Abby you are assuming that as soon as I appeared at his house, Gerald Patterson's life became all about your grandfather. I am not saying you are wrong, but I am saying that we cannot know for sure. That man might never have heard of Ken Patterson."

"How are you going to find out?" Again, with the challenging tone that annoyed me.

"If you want to learn more, *you* go up to the bar and listen. Listen. Do not talk to him or his friend."

"I'll have to order something. Can I use your ID?"

"No, you cannot. Don't you have a fake ID?"

She shook her head.

"I never did either, but I thought I was just really out of it. You can order a soda."

"I have a soda."

I grabbed her glass and poured the remains of her drink into mine. "You're done. I'll pay." I gave her cash. I didn't know what she could do with my credit card, but I worried she'd figure something out and I'd end up serving time for procuring alcohol for a minor.

I watched Abby sidle up to the two men talking. At the mostly empty bar, she positioned herself a foot away from the twosome. The two men didn't even notice her. Their conversation was intense.

Her interaction with the bartender was almost as intense. She pointed to me and waved. I smiled and waved back. I didn't understand why she was pointing at the floor by my feet. I checked the spot out, but when I looked again she had turned her attention away and the bartender was off tending to her order.

Several minutes passed before she returned with a glass of soda and a towel wrapped around a large lump of something.

"Ice for your injured foot," Abby said.

"Which foot?"

"I didn't specify. Pick one. Fast."

A few seconds later the waitress placed a margarita in front of me. I smiled and thanked her.

Abby waited until the bartender left before she offered a full explanation. "I ordered a mixed drink. I figured what was the point of my ordering at the bar if he's going to scoop some ice into a glass and shoot some soda out of a gun into it. What could I learn in that time?"

"How did you get the drink?"

"I said it was for you. I told him you'd twisted your ankle and were in a lot of pain. You'd better keep that ice on your alleged injury or the bartender might think I was lying."

Imagine that. I was actually envious. Abby was better at my alleged job than I was. "I can't believe you pulled that off."

"I can be very charming."

Charming? I didn't think so. Threatening. Abusive. Bullying. Whatever. She'd bought herself some time to eavesdrop.

She went to take a sip of the margarita, but I pulled it away. "You're driving. Besides, we don't want the bartender to get suspicious." I took a sip. Alcohol would help kill the pain in my imaginary injury. I laid the ice pack on my ankle. I picked the left. "So what did you find out?"

"My Uncle Gerald seems like an okay guy. Not a deep thinker."

"It's a bar conversation, Abby."

"His friend calls him Gerald. He didn't call his friend anything."

"What were they talking about?"

"iPhones. Well, iPhones as cameras. The guy was telling Uncle Gerald that his iPhone took pictures as good as a camera, but Uncle Gerald wasn't buying it. He said Uncle Gerald still has a flip phone. I don't know if he was kidding or not. I hate to think I have a relative who's so out of it."

"Not really what we were looking for."

"They did talk about the old days, you know when flip phones were hot, but he was talking about the nineties. Not way back when my grandfather was around."

"All they talked about was phones?"

"The guy with no name said that 'he's been lucky. I thought he took a big chance coming here.'"

"Did he say why he came here?"

"Not that he, himself, came here. That someone other than *he* took a big chance coming here."

"Coming here or coming back here?" I asked.

Abby frowned. "I'm not sure."

"Here the bar or here Strathmere?"

"He didn't say. Do you think he was talking about my grandfather?"

Unlikely, but not impossible. "Assuming he didn't mean the bar, did he say anything specific about exactly where *here* was?"

"No. The guy didn't say where he came from either, but he did say this was a good place to meet. He didn't mind the drive. He said he didn't think Uncle Gerald should come to his place until things cooled down."

Until things cooled down. "What does that mean?" I was asking myself, but Abby answered.

"I have no idea. The bartender started talking to me again. He's cute, don't you think?"

I didn't simply sigh. Imitating Abby, I heaved a sigh. I wanted Abby to get my point that she was not staying on track. Abby didn't notice.

"Oh-oh. That other guy is leaving. That wasn't a long meeting. Maybe thirty, forty-five minutes." I should have timed it, not that I would confess that to Abby. "So, we didn't learn anything for sure, but this guy might know something." I was trying to placate myself as much as Abby.

The man, older than I thought when he turned, was going to have a clear view of our table as he left. I could only hope Gerald Patterson wouldn't feel the need to watch him go. I needn't have worried. He still had his beer to focus on. Or so I assumed. He turned to check for Mr. No Name. "Yoah, Facenda. You forgot your keys."

He tossed them across the room. Facenda had to lunge towards us to catch them. He missed.

"And that, Joey, is why you never made the varsity team in high school."

The men exchanged friendly waves without laying eyes on us, but just in case, I cupped my chin in my hands and covered as much of my face as I could.

I turned to Abby.

"Joey Facenda," she mouthed. Her eyes locked on mine.

"Virtual high five," I whispered. "Let's go."

She grabbed what remained of the Bavarian pretzel. "Don't forget to limp," she reminded me. "I'll pull the car up, you know, so you don't hurt your ankle."

I shoved a few Brussels sprouts in my mouth before I waved the waitress over. I tipped as if we'd had a three-course meal and limped out the door to where Abby was waiting.

Chapter 9

"Hurry, put this in your phone." She rattled off six characters, a mixture of letters and numbers.

"Joey Facenda's license number?" I asked.

"I notice those things," she said in one of her most condescending tones. She had a wide selection.

Think of Elisabeth. Think of Elisabeth. I said nothing aloud. I pulled out my notebook and recorded the number.

"What is that?"

"It's a notebook."

"No one uses paper anymore."

"At least one person does." I didn't bother telling her I'd made a special stop at Hoy's to get a new one for this investigation. She wouldn't appreciate the effort.

Joey Facenda had headed north across the Ocean Drive bridge into the south end of Ocean City. Lucky that Abby had gotten the license number on his Cadillac SUV. We couldn't see through the dark glass to confirm we had the right car.

"Is that shaded glass legal in Jersey?"

Abby shrugged. "I guess so. I see cars with it around."

To me, the windows suggested Joey Facenda had something to hide. Admittedly, not necessarily about Ken Patterson. But was I being rash to conclude that he was a secretive person? I didn't think so.

When Facenda turned onto West Avenue, we followed. "We'd better let him get a slight lead on us. Pull over for a couple of minutes."

"Why?" Abby protested.

"Just to change things up a bit. There's not much traffic this time of year. That cuts both ways. It's easier for him to notice us and it's easier for us to catch up with him."

"If he's going straight."

"Okay, go ahead." I let her think she'd convinced me but, in truth, during our argument, we had put three cars between us and Facenda's SUV.

We followed the car up the Ocean Drive over another bridge through Longport, Margate, Ventnor and into Atlantic City where Facenda drove his car into an indoor garage that belonged to a high rise right on the Boardwalk.

"Should I follow?" Abby's asking for my opinion startled me.

"No," I said instinctively. "We don't know what he is doing here. Do we know if he was going home?" I asked.

"He didn't say," Abby said. "Well, that place sucks."

"Why? It looks lovely."

"Yes, but we can't see in the windows." She threw her arms in the air in frustration. "Even if we could figure out what windows we wanted to peek into."

I keyed his name into the phone. "Do we know the address here?"

"Try social media. He's old. He may be on Facebook."

I hated it when Abby was right. Joey Facenda had a Facebook page. His cover photo was a shot of him, standing in front of this apartment building which I assumed was his home but could be his workplace.

"So, what do we do now?'

I knew she wouldn't like my answer. She probably envisioned us scaling the outside of the apartment building and eavesdropping on the balcony. My plan was much simpler. "We go home and we do our research. At least, I do. We find out who Joey is, where he's been, we check out all his photos. On a computer screen where we won't miss anything. Then we figure out if he could have any possible ties to your grandfather."

"He's younger."

I agreed. "Not that much. Don't even think about him. I will take on all of that responsibility for checking out Joey Facenda. You do nothing. Swear to me. You will do nothing. Leave Joey Facenda alone. For all we know, he's an unsavory character."

"You think my uncle associates with unsavory characters?"

"I don't know your uncle. I wouldn't think so, but we can't be too careful. We only have one shot at this guy before he knows what we are up to. Let me take the lead. Let me take charge."

She said yes, but I didn't trust her. I was becoming more and more convinced that some of Abby's traits were hereditary and had skipped a generation. I hoped for her sake, and mine, she had not inherited Donna Patterson's personality.

Chapter 10

Abby pulled up our driveway to drop me off at home and waited for an invitation to come in. She didn't get one.

"I need to operate independently." I didn't explain why. If I did find Ken Patterson, I needed to verify that he was willing to be found before I told Abby. I'd heard too many horror stories about investigators who put people in harm's way by divulging their whereabouts. Okay, only a few, but one was too many. It put the fear of God in me.

Within five minutes of arriving home, I was on the sectional in position to do nothing. The problem? My body was on the couch, but my mind wasn't. I kept thinking about how I was going to find Ken Patterson. In truth, I kept thinking about how I was going to get Abby out of my life. The sooner the better. I had a few hours left in the day, but I didn't know what to do with them.

Normal steps, like talking to the neighbors, didn't make sense. Most of the nearby houses—and nearby was a very generous definition—weren't even built when Ken Patterson lived here. After he was gone? Donna remained in the house, but she was a resident of an exclusive enclave. We couldn't even see any houses from our location. I wouldn't have been shocked to find that Ken had been living next door for forty years. An exaggeration? Barely.

No, I would have to depend on the list of contacts Abby gave me.

I pulled out my laptop. It didn't take long to confirm that Francis Bloch and Harris Meitner had died. Both in the past few years. Dougie Hargreaves had never appeared on the Internet even as an obituary. That left me with Robin Carson and Bob DeMarco. I had no idea of the best place to begin. I picked what I thought would be easiest, the guy with the broadest smile.

If Bob DeMarco had a presence on social media, I couldn't find him, but I found his Avalon address easily. I found him just as easily. At least, I assumed the man in the garage rummaging through the trunk of a high-end model Mercedes was Bob DeMarco. Although he must have been in his late seventies, he bore a striking resemblance to the photo from four decades before. Some lines surrounded his eyes and mouth, and his curls were now almost solidly gray with occasional traces of black. What remained unchanged was the smile that he flashed at my approach. Unlike Gerald Patterson, Bob DeMarco seemed delighted to find a stranger in his driveway.

"Excuse me, are you Bob DeMarco?"

"I am indeed." His tone was downright jolly. His expression matched. "And to whom might I be speaking?"

"My name is Meg Daniels. There is no way you should know me. I have recently become acquainted with the daughter of Kenneth Patterson."

He barely paused. "Little Lisa? I remember little Lisa. Her name was Elisabeth but Ken always called her Lisa." He extended some beach towels towards me. "Would you mind holding these?"

"Of course," I grabbed the pile of toweling. "You've been to the beach recently?" I asked, surprised by the amount of sand falling from the towels.

"Last summer. I'm not conscientious about cleaning out the car, but I swear I left a pair of sunglasses in here somewhere." He raised other summer items, Frisbees, flip-flops, and boogie boards to run his free hand underneath. "I knew it." His hand emerged with a glass case. "I lost a pair somewhere around the house and I recalled having backups."

He took the towels from my arms and threw them back in the car. "Got a few months before I have to worry about them." He slammed the trunk lid closed. "Is little Lisa okay?" He pulled the expensive sunglasses from their case and polished them on his shirt. "I guess I shouldn't call her little Lisa anymore." He kept his eyes on his newly discovered sunglasses. "I used to see Elisabeth around town sometime. She didn't have any idea who I was, of course."

Of course?

He plopped the sunglasses onto his nose and made a great show of checking them out. "Okay," he sounded pleased." So, little Lisa. I'd see her with Donna once in a while, so I'd recognize her even when she wasn't with her mother. She had features like Donna but with Ken's coloring. I never said anything. Elisabeth wouldn't know me from Adam. How do these look?" He put his hands on his hips and threw his head back striking a pose worthy of the Lands End catalog.

"Camera-ready," I assured him.

He pulled the glasses off and again cleaned the lenses on his Polo shirt as he spoke. "Anyway, once Ken disappeared, I was persona non-grata at their place. Not that I wanted to go there. At first, my wife would want us to stop by to see how Donna was. I could feel the hostility. As if it was my fault Ken flew the coop. Crazy, right? I even offered to help Donna with some tasks around the house, but things were…" He searched for a word and came up with "awkward."

I nodded, although for all I knew he was the mastermind behind an elaborate plot to help Ken disappear. Or even worse, *make* Ken disappear.

"I see Donna on the street. Rarely. Only down here at the shore. She pretends she doesn't see me. This has been going on for, what? Thirty, forty years. It's ridiculous. Although I must say it's remarkable how she kept her looks. You know, for her age." He appeared wistful but only for a few seconds. "Anyway, I did see Elisabeth grow up from afar. Very far. Donna wouldn't come near me. The weird thing about Donna's anger was that I didn't even approve of Ken's behavior. What he did to his daughter! She didn't deserve that. Anyway, why are you here?" He hung the glasses on the neckline of his shirt and smiled at me.

"Elisabeth is not good. Early-onset dementia. All she wants is to learn more about her father."

"So she can forget it right away?" His question seemed to spring from confusion, not cruelty.

"So she can be happy in these bad times," I suggested.

He appeared embarrassed. "I'm sorry. Of course. Of course. That came out wrong. Brrr. It's chilly out here. Come in. I'll be happy to help Elisabeth."

He directed me across the garage. I told myself there was no reason to feel uncomfortable that the garage door was sliding closed behind us. He led me into the house, through a mudroom and a laundry room to the elaborate hallway that visitors entering through the front door saw first. Instead of leading me to the circular staircase, he opened a wooden door and indicated that I should step inside.

"It's an elevator," he said. "From the expression on your face, I can guess that you are afraid I am going to lock you in a closet."

He wasn't far from right. Actually, he was right. I had thought he was going to push me into a closet. I couldn't think of a come-back, so I lied. "I wasn't worried."

"Darn. That is one of the problems with getting older. No one worries anymore."

I chuckled and stepped inside, leaving room for at least three more people. Three large people.

"This would have made Ken jealous." He pulled the door shut behind us and then slid a gate across to cage us in. "He was like that. He liked to be top dog, to be the first to have anything. I must admit I was a little competitive too. Not that I could keep up with him back then."

When we stepped off the elevator, I could see that Bob DeMarco had done well for himself, although I guess the elevator made that pretty obvious. Maybe not as well as Ken—there were about a dozen houses in the exclusive area where Ken had built—but DeMarco and his neighbors appeared to be living quite nicely. Two lots back from the beach, his house was dwarfed only by the huge deck overlooking the street and expansive beach and ocean views beyond.

His wife wasn't home, but I assumed he had one. The same person who took care of the car in the garage did not take care of the house that suggested a decorating magazine would be doing a photo shoot that afternoon. DeMarco caught me checking his ring finger so I flashed my engagement ring so he wouldn't worry that I was checking him out.

"Are you here all year?" I asked.

"I retired ten years ago and have spent pretty much all of my time down here since then. We sold the big house in the suburbs a few years ago. My wife keeps a small apartment in the city. Philadelphia. I want her to retire, but she's not ready, although she has cut back. She's coming down tonight." He adjusted the coffee maker on the countertop by an inch. "I broke my back getting the place ready. She's kind of a stickler. I live in fear she'll surprise me someday and find out what this place looks like when she's not here."

The single item currently out of place was a glass of orange juice on the kitchen island. DeMarco held it aloft. "Mimosa?"

I explained it was a little early for me.

"Screwdriver?"

His offer was tempting, but I had to keep a clear head. I was, after all, working. Unpaid but working.

We settled into adjoining armchairs pointed down the street at the beach and ocean.

"So what do you want me to tell you about Ken?"

"I am searching for clues about where he might have gone. Did he tell you?" I could hope.

"He didn't tell anyone. None of us had a clue."

"Do you know why he left?"

"Where to begin?" He sipped his mimosa and seemed to savor the taste as he considered his approach. I must admit I was startled when he finally spoke. "What year did you graduate from college?"

I told him and he whistled. "You're a young one."

"Not that young."

"I graduated in 1965."

My turn to whistle. I told him I would "but, the truth is, I try but no noise comes out."

"What do you know about 1965?"

"I know that the sixties were just getting started. The swinging sixties."

"Maybe in New York, San Francisco, London. But in Philadelphia where we went to college, it was still the fifties. Do you know what boys did when they graduated from college in 1965?"

"I'd like to hear."

"They became adults. They graduated, got married and found jobs they would grow to hate if they didn't hate them from day one. Husband and wife went to work to save money for a starter house which, if they were lucky, they moved into before baby number one arrived in 1967. Then, the wife would stop working and stay home to take care of the first child and the second one that arrived in 1969."

My mind turned to Andy's "Women's History" course. Tonight, I would have something to discuss with him.

"Some of us threw in the pressure of night school, graduate or law, like Ken did."

The life he described sounded exhausting. No one frittering away their lives in prolonged adolescence.

"That was what was expected and that is what Ken and I did when we graduated in 1965. I don't think either of us had a second thought. It was what was done."

He stared at me for my reaction, which was a sad sigh that I tried to suppress.

"There was a silver lining. Vietnam heated up, and married men were exempt. At least until August of 1965. Those of us who got married in June were lucky. Those who had a wedding planned for the fall had to elope to avoid the draft. A couple of guys I knew made the deadline, which wasn't easy because they got short notice—hours not days. So, I guess we married guys figured we didn't have it so bad. We got to live with a woman, not a platoon full of sweaty guys in Southeast Asia."

I knew this had to have something to do with Ken Patterson. I waited for DeMarco to get to the point.

"You know what happened next?" he asked.

I shook my head. I had no idea where this was headed.

He drank, wiped the bottom of his glass and set it on a coaster before he continued. "May I speak bluntly with you? I understand the current times require some decorum."

Good grief, what was he about to tell me? "Of course."

"What happened next was the sexual revolution." He took a drink and waited for my reaction. I had none, so he went on. "Do you know how different life was for the kids who entered as freshmen when I was a senior? They got to live the summer of love. You know the summer of love? 1967."

"And your class missed it?"

"By that much." He made a gesture leaving a tiny place between two fingers to indicate the tiny margin by which sexual freedom had eluded them.

"We were making mortgage payments and changing diapers. I loved my wife and my daughter, but I was still a kid myself. I couldn't help looking at those hippies and thinking that could have been me. Of course, without my married-status exemption, I probably would have gotten drafted and ended up in Vietnam. But I didn't think about that. I thought about what I'd missed."

I could understand his reaction. I didn't have to say so. DeMarco wasn't finished.

"I don't mean we didn't have sex before marriage, we did, but pretty much after we were engaged or at least committed. I bet a student's life was different when you went to school." He held up a hand. "Don't answer. It's none of my business. So, anyway, you asked about Ken."

I said "yes" so DeMarco knew I was still alive.

"Look, guys back then, we didn't have heart-to-heart talks, so I only suspected what was going on with Ken. Football. Baseball. Later on, hockey when the Flyers came to Philadelphia. Those things, I knew how Ken felt about. The Eagles. The Phillies. We talked about them. But his marriage? I knew only what I could see."

I felt optimistic that his long drink was a ploy to pull together more thoughts.

"Ken and Donna—that's his wife—always appeared happy, you know, when we were newlyweds. Before then too. But I always wondered. I mean Donna was quite the looker." The way his eyes lit up told me he could still see the young Donna. "Ken once told me how proud he was walking into a party with her. He knew everyone looked. Donna knew she was cute. She flirted with all the guys. Ken loved that they all were attracted to her. And they were, but on a playful level. Most guys, the smart ones, recognized she was a tease. No action, if you get my drift."

I nodded. I got his drift.

"Ken and Donna were very different. Maybe not at first, but he changed. You heard of key parties?"

"Every man puts his keys in the bowl," I said, "and then a wife picks out a set and no one goes home with the same person they came with. I always thought they were an urban legend."

"They were real. I would never have asked my wife to go to one of those. But Ken did."

"I'm thinking Donna didn't go for parties like those." I'd already learned that much about her.

"Hah. I said he *asked.* She never would have gone to one."

I couldn't tell if DeMarco saw that as good or bad.

"But Ken? He wanted to try everything."

"But he couldn't go without Donna," I suggested.

"And he couldn't go *with* her." He stopped as if he'd suddenly heard himself. "You might wonder why I am telling you all this."

I got the impression he had wondered why he was telling me all this.

"I hoped this information might help you understand Ken. You can edit what you tell his daughter." He sipped his mimosa. "Anyway, Ken worked with this woman. Actually, she worked for him. That arrangement wouldn't fly these days but back then...." He shrugged as if to say what can I say? Things were different. "Anyway, she was a single woman. He conned her into going with him. Eventually, they dispensed with the parties. He got hot and heavy, as we liked to say, with her."

"When was that?" I asked.

"I'd say 1973, 1974. For some reason, I connect her with Watergate. I guess Ken talked about Watergate and her at the same time."

"Did Donna realize this was going on?"

"Hardly. She couldn't handle the seventies. She couldn't handle the sixties. In Donna's world, it was always 1955. Look...." He took a sip of his drink.

In my opinion, a delaying tactic. I hoped he wasn't reconsidering spilling his guts to a surprisingly inappropriate extent.

He wasn't. "I could kind of see where Ken was coming from. It occurred to me that I had missed some...stuff. That's life. If he were married to anyone but Donna, I might have pointed out that married life wasn't a bundle of laughs for the woman either. Staying home all day taking care of kids was no picnic. I bet plenty of wives would have liked to be in San Francisco for the summer of love, but that wasn't true of Donna. She had exactly what she wanted." He took another sip. "She never imagined that her husband would cheat on her."

"What happened to the other woman?"

"I'm not sure. She left the firm. As far as I know, he never heard from her again. Not that he missed her. He preferred the more casual attitude towards relationships that developed during that time. Family guys who envied the free love of the sixties wanted a taste. A lot of divorces."

"But not Ken and Donna?"

"She would never have agreed to a divorce. She probably would have killed him first."

I went for it. "Do you think she did?"

He didn't look as shocked as he probably should have. He hesitated. His tone was defensive when he answered. "No. Nobody said anything like that to me." He gulped most of the remainder of his drink and leaned back in his chair. "Did you know I saw him the day he disappeared?"

And I would know this because? You tell me the life story of your generation and now you mention this? I repeated the sentiment but only to myself.

"Yes, at a party at our friends, the Blochs. They had a beautiful house back on the bay. It's still there. They both died young. In their fifties. She went first, and I think he died of a broken heart. They never got to retire to their place down here." He launched into a detailed description of the property. He was on a roll. I didn't want to interrupt the flow of information. I let Bob De Marco talk.

****Bob DeMarco****
Avalon
July 4, 1977

Bob couldn't believe Ken's outfit. The rest of the group wore clothes considered up-to-date. His own jeans flared, and his shirts had the long, pointed collars that made his old clothes look outdated. But Ken? He certainly stood out in the crowd in his blue and white striped pants and loud red shirt open way too close to his wide, white leather belt to show way too much chest hair. And the white shoes! No guy they knew wore white shoes unless they were in tennis sneakers. A person had to step way out of line for Bob to notice their outfit. Bob noticed Ken's outfit.

He had to laugh. How had Donna let Ken leave the house in that getup? The distance she kept from her husband and the tightness around her mouth suggested she hadn't wanted to. Of course, there were so many things about Ken that Donna disapproved of, her demeanor might have nothing to do with the clothes at all. Although that outfit must have been the icing on the cake.

He watched Ken and Donna as they made their way into the party. The stern woman who walked in the door became cheerful, almost giggly as she made her rounds. As usual, she looked perfectly put together. The other women followed the trends, but Donna was a classic. She wore neat white pants and a blazer, a little oversized—her concession to the current style even though the evening was too hot for a blazer. Eventually, she would lay it across a chair so the label would show. He'd watched her position clothing that way at other parties. He didn't recognize the label, but his wife would. She would sneer at Donna's pretentiousness, but a similar item would show up in the next month's bills. No way around it. Donna was a trendsetter.

"Bob." Ken peeled off from his wife as soon as he could. He approached Bob with a bottle of beer in his hand. "Looking good, my man."

Looking good, my man? Did Ken dress to match his new lingo, or adjust his speech to his new style?

"You, too. Very patriotic."

"Now you have the right perspective. Donna hates my new threads. Probably because Brooks Brothers doesn't sell them. You know she can't abide clothing without a label that she approves."

"At least you're not wearing a gold chain."

Bob heard it said clouds passed over people's faces. A cloud passed over Ken's. "Only after dark." As if the two things were related, he went on. "Donna isn't thrilled, but I've been learning to disco dance."

Bob hated his reaction. Judgmental. He would never want to treat Ken the way Donna did, but he could empathize with her reaction to that news. Not just dancing, but disco and all that it implied. He understood rebellion. Bob wasn't blind to her physical attributes—she was still a looker—but he'd rebel too if he was married to Donna. But maybe 'go away with the boys for a golf weekend' or 'a weeklong fishing trip' rebellion. But learn to dance? To disco dance? "Just promise me I won't see you roller-skating around town."

Another cloud passed over Ken's face. "I wouldn't pooh-pooh what you haven't tried. You can't imagine how freeing it is. It's a gas."

A gas? Who had Ken been talking with? Bob moved to safer topics. "Is that why we haven't seen you around the club lately. Too busy for golf?"

"Partially." A sly smile crept across his face. "I've got better things to do."

"Care to share?" Bob asked, although part of him hoped Ken didn't want to.

Ken did. "Bob, we missed so much in life. We can't get the sixties back, but I'm not letting the seventies slip away. The world is changing. There's a lot going on out there. I asked Donna if she wanted to come to disco class. She told me that was ridiculous. That people like us don't disco dance. So, I went on my own."

Bob let out an imperceptible sigh of relief. Too soon. Ken wasn't finished.

"I'm glad I did. There are women all over the place at those clubs. Not all too young for me. I never went for those sixties types. You know the hippies with the long silky hair and bare feet. Good thing because they wouldn't have given me the time of day, but these girls are different. They don't see me as 'the man.' And if they do, they don't think I'm the enemy. They get me. They appreciate nice things, like wearing sleek silky clothes that show off everything they've got."

Bob was growing uneasy. Anyone could walk by at any minute and hear this conversation.

"It isn't the way it used to be, Bobby Boy. No big build-up. If you get a kiss, you're in. If you know what I mean. No commitment. No promises. Most times? Not even a second date. Date? What am I saying? There was never even a first date." He chuckled. A smug, self-satisfied sound.

Bob knew what Ken meant, but it didn't sound appealing. He was relieved he was married, that he didn't have to be out there dating. No, he might be a little bored and boring, but his life was fine. He liked the routine. The sameness of every day. He had more money than he ever thought possible. He wasn't rich, but life was good. Sure, sometimes he would look at a pretty girl. The young ones were showing a lot more skin and shape these days, but he never wanted to connect with one. Not really. Looking was enough for him. He liked going home to Sally. She wasn't glamorous, but she was devoted. A good wife. A good mother. Open and honest.

He didn't know how to respond to Ken. Donna was Ken's wife. She deserved better.

"I haven't told anyone else about this. Well, except my lawyer who is working on the financial details, but it isn't going to work out with Donna."

Isn't going to work out? Wasn't that something you said when you decided you weren't going to propose to a woman? Not what you said twelve years into a marriage.

"Does she know?"

"No, I'm not giving her any warning. God knows what she would pull. Nope, one day, she'll wake up and I'll be gone, and she will never understand. You know why?"

Because the two of you were a classic mismatch. He didn't say that. He raised an eyebrow to ask why.

"Because it isn't done. Because people like us don't leave their marriages. She'll never figure out that I am not and do not want to be 'people like us.' One day she'll find out."

***

"He just didn't tell me that 'one day' had arrived." DeMarco took a final gulp of mimosa.

"And that was the last time you saw him?"

"He left after the party. That night. I was shocked. I figured he was full of hot air. He often was, but after I heard he'd gone, I thought back and figured out he executed his plan. Sure you don't want a drink? I'm having another."

"I'm positive."

I didn't consider the discussion complete. I directed my question to his back as he headed for the kitchen. "No one worried about him or investigated?"

"Not to my knowledge. Why would they? He had it all set up."

"But you didn't hear that in advance."

DeMarco focused on preparing another mimosa. He never even glanced my way. "Harry Meitner, a friend who was working as his attorney, called me within a day or two to let me know. Don't expect to hear from Ken. Don't try to find him."

"Is that Harris Meitner?"

"Yeah. Harry. Harris. We generally called him Meitner. I heard he died a few years back. Nice guy. Nice guy to handle that for Ken."

"And you simply accepted his explanation?"

"I did. My wife saw Donna a few times, and she had some cockamamie story about how Ken had to flee, how he did it to protect the family. Just a tiny little part of me accepted maybe Ken had to go on the run. He did make an incredible amount of money, really fast. I suspected that not all his clients were on the up and up, but they weren't mobsters."

The memory amused him or maybe he was just pleased he had another drink. He was smiling as he returned to his chair. "They might have hidden some dollars off-shore and shaved some money off their taxes, but the real crime, as far as I could see, was their wardrobes."

"So, he appeared in public with them."

"A few. I wouldn't know about the rest, would I?"

I twisted my face into a position that I hoped said *I guess not.*

"The most famous one was Malcolm Maturi. You heard of him?"

I nodded but didn't say why.

"He got involved in some tax fraud or something. Not exactly the type to rub people out." He chuckled. "Except with sea salt." He eyed me waiting for me to match his amusement.

I laughed as best I could. "Did anyone else seem suspicious?"

"No one who shared it with me, but I imagine people talked. Ken made a lot of money. A lot. He got a couple of huge settlements. That's how he got the house on the beach. I thought he spent it all, but seeing how he left enough to keep Donna and Elisabeth going all those years, his spending was only the tip of the iceberg."

"If you thought that his clients were dodgy, didn't it occur to you that they might have killed him?"

"Not really. Like I said, they were people like Maturi. He did eventually serve time for some sort of financial skullduggery, but they were never able to pin any sort of violent act on him. Not because they didn't try. He ended up being a sympathetic figure and went back to being a celebrity. A bigger celebrity." De Marco frowned. "I can't believe you haven't heard of him. He has a show that went national."

I didn't tell him that not only didn't I like to cook, I didn't like to watch it happen.

"Anyway, I trusted Harris and he said Ken had closed down his business, relocated and was doing fine. So, I believed him. I knew he hadn't killed him."

"How?"

"We were friends since elementary school. Hey." He climbed out of his chair and knocked on the window. "Don't sit there," he explained to a sea gull who didn't understand or pretended not to grasp that he was not welcome on the porch railing. "Come on," he hit the window harder. The gull stared at him but didn't budge. "If he poops out there my wife will go nuts." He waved at the bird with disgust.

"Did you ever hear of a Joey Facenda?" I directed my question to his back.

DeMarco made a final obscene gesture at the bird and turned towards me. He gulped his drink and thought long and hard. "Not that I can recall. Was he from Philadelphia?"

"I'm not sure. He might have been a friend of Ken's little brother, Gerald."

"Not Little Joey! Gerald had a buddy he went everywhere with. I never knew his last name. It might have been Facenda. He moved down the shore when the gambling jobs opened up. I imagine he went to Atlantic City or one of the towns up that way. Back in the day, I used to see Little Joey once in a blue moon if Ken and I saw Gerald."

"You went to the champagne brunch that Donna gave the morning Ken left. I saw the pictures."

"Wow. You are asking me to dig deep into the old memory. Although, I've got to say some of those old memories are easier to call up than yesterday's." He came close to emptying his glass in a single gulp. "As I recall, Sally and I dropped by."

"I know Gerald was there. Was Joey?"

"You gotta be kidding. Not that I can exactly remember, but Joey was not a champagne brunch kind of guy. Donna never would have invited him. She probably didn't want to invite Gerald. Or his wife. Donna could be a snob. She didn't like that Gerald was in the war. No one else she knew had relatives who served."

"So she was opposed to the war in Vietnam?" I asked.

"Donna? That woman never had a political thought in her life. She would have been okay with Gerald if he was an officer and had a nicer uniform. She went crazy at the way he looked when he came home. She thought he was a hippie, and his friends were degenerates."

"Was he a hippie?"

"Far from it. Not a true hippie. Smoked a little weed. Dressed a little bit like one. Long hair. Bell bottoms. Sandals even in winter. Even before he left for Nam, a lot of his friends were hippie types. I never really knew any of them. I think they drifted away when Gerald came home, got married, had a kid. But Little Joey that you asked about? Little Joey stuck. I ran into Gerald a few times over the years after Kenny disappeared. Usually, he was with Little Joey. Kind of an odd couple. They were both successful, but Gerald looked like a middle-aged lawyer. Joey looked like an emcee from a strip club. Maybe that was what he did. Whatever he did paid for some expensive, if appalling, clothes and fancy cars. He looked good, barely aged a day."

"Have you seen him lately?"

"Twenty years, I bet." He dropped back into his chair. "Why do you ask?"

"I wondered if he might know something about Ken's disappearance."

"I doubt it. He wasn't Ken's friend. I guess Gerald talked to him about Ken, but he wouldn't have known anything Gerald didn't know."

"Was Ken's disappearing act a big topic of conversation?"

"Of course, in our small group, but everyone I knew believed Meitner."

"Didn't other people ask about him?"

"I am sure people did." He plucked a speck of dust that I could barely see from the table. "I am sure they asked me if I knew. Without being too specific, I would have indicated that I was not surprised. He wasn't happy. He left Donna enough money that she didn't complain. At least about money."

He paused, but he had more to say. I could tell. I stayed silent.

"After a short period of time, people didn't rally around Donna. She didn't know what to do without a mate. The women didn't want her near their husbands. For being such a prude, she was still a flirt. I felt sorry for her for about a nano-second." Despite the decades that had passed, he sounded disapproving. Maybe a little angry.

"Ken filed for divorce?"

"Like I said, he had worked out the details. I am certain he took care of the divorce. He probably thought he was divorced but Donna would never accept that. She was a rule-abiding Catholic. When she said until death do we part, she meant it."

"So she never looked for anyone else?"

"From what my wife told me, she didn't want anyone else. It didn't always appear that way. I guess she couldn't stop flirting." He paused to take a drink of his mimosa. "Donna believed she was still married to Ken. She swore he'd come back. I heard she kept their houses—one here, one in the city—for years. Years? Decades. The story was that no one could ever convince her he wasn't coming back. I heard she sold both houses eventually. Not that long ago. You ever see the one down here?"

"That's how I met the family. My fiancé and I are staying in it right now."

He seemed surprised but didn't ask any questions. "You can see how extravagant the house was. Donna never liked that style, but she did like that it was expensive. I am certain she liked living in such a prestigious area. I wonder what changed her mind about selling after all those years. Maybe she finally accepted that he wasn't coming back."

"Could I check with your wife?"

"My first wife? I guess I could give you her address. Sally DeMarco."

"Oh."

He read a lot into that one syllable. "Yeah, I was pretty horrified by Ken and those seventies girls, but the eighties girls in their neat navy-blue suits and their little ties, spouting stock prices and marketing theories? I found those irresistible."

Chapter 11

I heard the downstairs door open and Andy's voice call out. "Sorry. I should have texted when I got sidetracked by a student in my Women's History course. She wanted to interview me for her paper." He called from the mud room. "She wanted my opinion of *The Feminine Mystique.*"

"Your opinion?"

I heard him start up the stairs. "You know, a man's opinion. She's quite the chatterbox. She caught me in the parking lot."

"No problem. I went ahead and ate."

Even though the couch accommodated eighteen, he plopped beside me. "What is that?" He crinkled his nose as he looked at my plate.

"An old family recipe." I held it up for his review. "Chips de pommes de terre au gratin."

Andy waved my culinary masterpiece away. "I am not much of a linguist, but even I understand that means potato chips with cheese."

"Yeah, we didn't have much in our little dorm fridge, so I took some potato chips, put a few squares of sharp cheese on top and microwaved it for twenty seconds. Voila! Would you like me to whip you up a serving?"

He plucked a chip from my plate. "I'll have a taste." His face screwed into a horrified expression. "Sometimes I don't understand how you stay alive."

I ignored him.

"I see you have a new notebook in your hand. Does that mean you have committed to helping Abby?"

"I stopped at Hoy's yesterday. I'm in for a full $5.98."

"No backing out now."

"Yep. I caught up on all my notes from the past two days. I've been checking out Joey Facenda."

"Who is?"

"A guy Abby and I saw with Gerald Patterson."

"You and Abby? Isn't that kind of risky taking Abby along? What if you found Ken Patterson? What if he didn't want to be found?"

"I already told her to back off. I didn't worry about today because she knew where her uncle lived. She gave me the information. We didn't do anything today that she couldn't have done on her own. He may not want to be found, but I don't believe he is in any physical danger from his family. Except maybe from Donna, and she has no idea what I am doing."

"So, what did you do today? You talk. I'll forage around in our *kitchen*." He used air quotes to emphasize the concept.

"Yeah. We should go to the grocery store sometime. I'll find one."

"If I'm not mistaken there is one right on Dune Drive."

"I think it's closed for the season."

"Do you think there might be another food source within driving distance," Andy was teasing. At least I hoped he was.

"Luckily, lots of restaurants. We don't want to dirty that kitchen. We're only going to be here a couple of months, and we'd have to clean it when we leave."

"I can't argue with that." Andy gave a little shrug. "So were you out getting to know Avalon today?"

"In a way. After Abby dropped me off." While Andy foraged, I brought him up-to-date on my morning with Abby and my afternoon visit with Bob DeMarco. "He really likes to talk. He's down here by himself for most of the week while his wife stays in Philadelphia. I think he gets lonely. Solitude might be hard on him, but it worked for me. He was more than willing to chat. And then I came home and did some follow-up research on Joey Facenda."

Andy came back to the sofa with a pack of peanut butter crackers and a carton of milk he'd gotten at Wawa.

"Between Facebook, Instagram, and Twitter, Facenda revealed a lot. Plenty of pictures—none of Ken Patterson or a likely candidate to be an older Ken Patterson. At least, none that I could identify. A lot of group shots. Joey Facenda likes parties. So does his wife Joy and their three children, although they are all married and living on their own now."

"But no sign of Ken Patterson?"

"I poured over Facenda's photos, and there were a lot of them, searching for anyone who might be Ken. I found Gerald at quite a few events. Gerald is a pretty ordinary-looking guy but he was always with the same beautiful woman with distinctive long dark silky hair. His Vonnie, I assumed. Some faces were blurred or facing away from the camera. If one of them was Ken, I'd never know."

"So you have no further interest in Joey Facenda?"

"I see no point in focusing on him. Abby is convinced that he met Gerald today because of my visit. If we followed her lead, we'd be surveilling Joey Facenda 24/7. I am not discounting him, but I feel okay moving him to the back burner."

"And who is on the front burner?" Andy asked.

"No one. Bob DeMarco was a good friend of Ken's but, in my opinion, he doesn't even warrant a burner. I didn't get much from him. Nothing new. Ken planned to leave. Donna was a nightmare. One of Donna's stories was that Ken left to protect Elisabeth and her from Ken's unsavory clients. Even if we had names, a lot of those folks might be dead so I can't question them. The only name is a guy who is a celebrity chef."

"What? Do they think maybe he skewered Ken and..."

I held up a hand to cut Andy off. "Don't put the image of serving Ken in one of his restaurants in my mind. Oh, God. Too late. I did it myself. His signature dish. Ken ala Maturi."

"Maturi?"

"Yeah, Malcolm Maturi."

"The guy who's opening the new restaurant in the Harbor House Hotel."

I shrugged. "I have no idea, but I can't imagine too many celebrity chefs are called Malcolm Maturi. You know him?"

"When I was still with the Artistical, we talked about his new restaurant a lot in staff meetings. Big competition for the Atlantic City property. You've met him."

"I met him? That's unlikely."

"He ran some cooking school at the Bahama property. Just for a week. You would have been the concierge who took care of him."

"Me?"

"I'm sure. I have a vague recollection that he offered you a seat in one of his classes and you wouldn't take it."

"There's a shocker." I had zero interest in cooking.

"You told him you had to work. The people who came were paying $10,000 for the course, and he offered it to you for free. I bet he'd remember you. He wasn't pleased."

"How old is he? What did he look like?"

Andy fiddled with his phone and then passed it to me. "Recognize him?"

I didn't. "I can't remember everyone. Many of the celebrities I took care of were only famous for a short time. And sometimes only in the minds of their publicists."

"Maturi's been around for ages. Big deal in the culinary world probably before we were born. Survived some scandals. I think."

"Nice looking man. Distinguished." I didn't know how tall he was, but he fit the other two components of tall, dark and handsome.

"I probably remember him better than you do because, as head of Security, I had a hard time keeping the ladies away."

I swiped through the other photos Andy retrieved. Many of them were of Maturi and groups of happy ladies.

I did a quick search to check his date of birth. "He would have been a kid when he worked with Ken. Maybe I should talk to him."

"What would he know?" Andy seemed skeptical.

"I have no idea. That's why I should talk to him."

"What are you going to say?" He took a long drink of milk.

"That's a good question." I hadn't thought that far.

"Try not to accuse him of murder. Suppose you are right, and someone did kill Ken Patterson. It might be he planned to slip away but the people he was avoiding, personal or business, caught up with him and killed him. It might have been a professional hit. There is no statute of limitation on murder."

He popped the last cracker in his mouth and crinkled the cellophane wrapper. "Now that we've finished dinner," he said without an ounce of sarcasm in his tone, "why don't we take advantage of this romantic setting. I'll build a fire. I'd say we could admire the moon but with those clouds, that's not a possibility. Maybe we could talk." He paused. "About something other than Ken Patterson. If we discuss *The Feminine Mystique*, technically, I won't even be goofing off."

"Let me crack a window so I can listen for Elisabeth."

"Let me go. I'll check outside too." He stepped onto the deck and listened for a full minute before he called Elisabeth's name.

"Better you, than me. I always feel like someone is out there, watching me." I came up behind him and wrapped my arms around his waist. "Did you hear something?"

"No. Only wind. I'll check again later."

"I was hoping you'd be too busy later." I squeezed him tight.

He turned for a long kiss. When he pulled away, he stared deep into my eyes. "The thing that floored me most about *The Feminine Mystique* was the story about the college seniors who blew off their finals for their wedding showers."

"Interesting. Why don't we go settle onto the couch and you can tell me all about it?" I took his hand and led him inside.

We had a relaxing evening chatting by the fire interrupted only by two Elisabeth false alarms and my reminder to Andy to buy bear repellent and whatever might deter any fox or coyote visitors.

Chapter 12

Andy was up and out to school early. I poured my morning Coke and took it, a pack of chocolate chip cookies and a heavy quilt to the deck off the loft. I stared at the ocean, watched for the sunrise and awaited inspiration on how to track down Ken Patterson. The rising sun silhouetted a lone jogger passing at the water's edge. I envied him. Not that he was running, but that he wanted to run. His energy made me feel like a slug. Sitting in the cool morning air didn't help. The chill might have energized the runner but it made me sleepy.

I went back to bed but not to sleep. I took my laptop with me. Since meeting Donna Patterson seemed unlikely, maybe I could observe her. Our Lady Star of the Sea in Cape May had weekday masses, and I could make it if I hurried. I hurried—at least what I call hurrying before noon.

I arrived before the Mass began. The twenty or so people scattered throughout the pews were visibly devout as I would expect from worshipers who gotten up on a weekday morning to attend mass. Donna was not among them. Not yet. I wasn't worried.

I imagined that, like Donna, these churchgoers made the trip every day. They were tastefully, but extremely casually, attired. I, with a blazer over my uniform of leggings and tunic, appeared overdressed making me feel even more like an intruder.

I settled into the last pew and waited. Sitting in church surrounded by religious icons made me feel guilty and a little afraid that I would be punished for sacrilege. I rationalized. Yes, the purpose of my visit was deceitful, but the ultimate objective of my project was charitable. I was trying to help Elisabeth. And wasn't I giving Donna a chance to give me a more positive impression than I'd gotten from those who knew her? Not that I would talk to her. I had come to observe. Maybe I would sense that she had mellowed, that she was a deeply spiritual person. I bought my explanation but wasn't sure anyone else would.

My feelings of guilt escalated when I spotted Donna Patterson. At least the woman I assumed was Donna Patterson. I heard the door open and then the click of high heels. All the other late arrivals had entered with reverence, but not Donna. She swept past me down the center aisle as if she owned the place. I only got a good look at her when she turned to enter a pew a behind the other attendees. She caught sight of me and stared for a few seconds. That gave me enough time to judge that she was about the right age, meticulously groomed, stylishly dressed and, unbelievably, a dead-ringer for her forty-year-old picture. In a tailored pantsuit and designer accessories, she snatched the title of *best-dressed worshipper* away from me.

I am here now God. As if he'd been waiting for her arrival, the priest came onto the altar and began the Mass.

I moved into the far-right corner of my pew so I could get a side view of Donna standing, sitting, kneeling on cue always keeping her back ramrod straight and head held high. I tried to find a single word to describe her. Brisk. Brittle. I sought another *br* word but only came up with unbreakable. Her will of iron was visible. She was here to remind God that she wanted, needed, deserved her husband back.

Despite her appearance, I found myself drawn to another theory. Was she doing penance? Maybe no one I'd talked to was promoting the idea that Donna could have murdered Ken, but neither had anyone dismissed it.

I pictured her forty years earlier slipping into the confessional to ask for absolution for killing her husband. The priest's vows would have prevented him from turning her in, but not from giving her a killer penance. A killer penance for a killer. She may have gotten to walk out of the church a free woman that day but she had to return every day for the rest of her life. Which, if that day's behavior was any indication, she did as if making a banking transaction with the efficiency of a businesswoman. I detected no sign of a regret-filled murderess.

As the only attendee who did not go up for communion, I could watch each person return showing respect for the sacrament they'd received. Each one but Donna. She hustled down the aisle as if she had seen some unsavory character making a move on her handbag. At least, she did fold her hands as expected. I suspected to display the cluster of diamonds on the third finger of her left hand. Her jewelry broadcast that she was a woman of means, and perhaps more importantly to her, she was married.

Donna waited until the precise second when it became permissible to leave and then did so just as officiously as she had entered. I stepped out of the pew and walked to the door at an appropriate pace. I should have moved at an inappropriate pace. When I descended the outside steps, I checked the mall and the street but saw no sign of Donna. She certainly knew how to make a quick getaway.

Chapter 13

I cruised down Beach Avenue to check out any changes to the town and saw no reason to bypass Uncle Bill's Pancake House which had not changed. Despite all the choices, I ordered basic buttermilk pancakes. My booth had a view through the dunes to a slice of ocean, but I spent my time on my phone researching celebrity chef, Malcolm Maturi. I was surprised to find his name in the news. While he was in the process of opening what he said would be the last restaurant added to his empire, rumors were circulating that he had been negotiating to sell his brand. I had no idea how big a deal that would be. I never watched food shows. I had no interest in food before it was cooked to perfection and neatly arranged on a plate by someone who *was* interested in meal preparation.

Word was Chef Maturi was currently living in the Harbor House Hotel and running Taste of Maturi, a small cafe that, from noon to three each afternoon, offered a sample of what was to come in the restaurant due to open that Memorial Day. The article said he liked to mingle with and check the reactions of his customers. And, there had been a lot of customers.

This guy was a big celebrity. Why would he talk to me? How could I approach him? *Say, I heard you were one of the shifty clients Ken Patterson dealt with back in the day. Did you happen to kill him? Or maybe you know who did?*

As I drove to Atlantic City, I struggled to keep my objective clear. I was not looking for a killer. I was looking for a missing father. Who wouldn't want to assist me with that mission? I was simply offering Malcolm Maturi an opportunity to help.

When I saw him in person, charming a group of women in his café, I recognized that I'd met him before. I never would have known where.

He was tall, slender with his hair, graying but still thick, pulled into a low ponytail. He was a type and I had seen a bunch of them, older gentlemen who frequented the Artistical in the Bahamas with women of a certain age much younger than theirs. He was well-tanned, well-groomed, well-dressed, although in his case I could only judge by his shoes. He was wearing a white chef's jacket.

I didn't mind waiting for a table. It gave me time to work up an appetite and to observe the chef. Maturi charmed. He flirted. He basked in the adoration of his fans, excuse me, customers. Most women, but not all. Male. Female. Young. Old. He posed for pictures and helped them all take selfies. If anyone had any complaints about A Taste of Maturi, I didn't see them register them.

I finally got a table and my turn to bask in his charm. If he remembered me, he didn't let on. He smiled politely, expectantly. Most likely accustomed to bigger reactions, he gave me a few seconds to have one before he asked my name.

I saw no reason to lie.

"Do you live locally?"

"Yes," I told the truth, the short version without elaboration, explanation or any hint that I had ever worked in the Bahamas.

"Perhaps you would like to taste our escargot. It is a special we are offering."

I hadn't seen him offer it to other people but for the sake of ingratiating myself with him, I smiled and accepted. Four snails don't look big but following close on a stack of pancakes, even an unfinished stack, they made for a large meal.

The chef hovered to make sure I ate them all.

"I am not a huge escargot fan, but these are delicious." Actually, they had too much garlic. Okay by me, but I was a huge fan of garlic.

"I thought you would think so. Let me bring you a sampler of our shrimp scampi."

He did and then followed quickly with small plates of Fettucine Alfredo, Chicken Marsala and a dish called Lamb Maturi. The chef showed no concern about cleansing my palate. The dishes came fast and furious. He kept an eye on my table and arrived with a new dish as soon as I took the final bite of the one before. Some might call his smile flirtatious, but I would have called it devilish. He enjoyed overfeeding his guests. At least me. My table seemed to be getting more attention than most.

"And" he produced the dessert with a flourish, "my Berry Mélange Crème Brulé to finish." To finish me off was more like it. He was trying to kill me. I accepted his behavior as killing with kindness until he slipped onto a chair across from me.

His smile turned cold. His teeth still showed but he wasn't smiling. "I know why you're here."

How could he possibly know? Was he a friend of Gerald Patterson? I guess if Gerald Patterson had lied about knowing the shady types, it made sense. In a situation like this, I cautioned myself not to speculate. I took a bite of Crème Brulé. Nice but not special. Although, to me, any Crème Brulé is a nice Crème Brulé.

"Aren't you even going to try to deny it?" His tone was not customer friendly.

"Deny what?" I wasn't feigning ignorance. I had no clue what he was talking about.

"You think that you can come in here and I won't recognize you? You? The woman who rejected my offer to share my most precious gift, my magic, my ability to turn the most mundane of nature's offerings into heaven on earth."

"I had to work." Thank God Andy had reminded me of Maturi's trip to the Bahamas or I would have had no idea what to say.

"So you said, but I knew your job. You took care of the celebrities, and I was the biggest celebrity in residence that week."

At least in his own mind.

"My job was to minister to your needs not to take advantage of your generosity." I thought that sounded pretty good.

"I need to be generous, to share my gift." He laid a hand across his chest.

"I am sorry if you didn't understand..."

"But I did, and I do now." He spoke with chilling civility. "You did not like my food and yet here you are tasting all my best dishes."

He kind of coerced me into eating them.

"Spying on me. You have the audacity to come to my restaurant thinking that I would not realize that Howard Bing sent you."

"Howard Bing?" My shocked tone was genuine. Maturi believed my old boss at the Artistical sent me to report back on his competition which, now that he mentioned it, wasn't a bad idea. I would send Bingo an e-mail when I got home.

"Bingo has no idea I am here. I don't work for him anymore."

"Then, why are you here?"

"Look around you. The place is mobbed. Everyone wants a Taste of Maturi."

I saw in his eyes that my flattery made a dent in his anger. A dent.

"But you are right. I do have an ulterior motive."

"I knew it." He pointed at me and his fingertip stopped precariously close to the tip of my nose.

"But it has nothing to do with your restaurant. It has to do with a man who went missing long ago. Over forty years ago."

He shook his head with exaggerated motions and waved his hands in the air with gestures I read as saying *what are you talking about, you are crazy, spit it out.* He stared at me, waiting for me to go on.

"I am helping a family that has not seen their husband, father and grandfather in four decades."

"And I would know this man?"

"He was your lawyer for a time. Kenneth Patterson."

He froze for just a few seconds while the blood seemed to drain from his face. "Wow."

I waited while he flipped through his memory.

"As the kids say, that is a blast from the past."

The kids who said that were now in their golden years, but I didn't challenge him.

He stared across his café but didn't seem to see the crowd. "I haven't heard of him in years. I guess I thought he was dead." He shrugged. His action appeared casual but the expression on his face did not.

"He may be. His family wants to find out what happened, to find him if he is alive. His daughter is ill." No need to elaborate.

"Ken Patterson. That takes me back a lot of years. A lot of years. Why on earth would you think that I could help you?" He smoothed the front of his white jacket.

"I heard you were his client. I wondered if he had ever said anything to you that might help me."

"How?" His tone was defensive.

"I don't really know. I guess the most obvious information would be if he told you where he was headed."

"I don't understand."

"He vanished in July 1977. I hoped he might have told his clients more than he told his friends. I am grasping at straws."

"Why on earth would he have confided in me? In any client? I was just a client. Not a friend. We might have had drinks a few times in my restaurants, but that was business." An unctuous grin spread across his face. "Although any time spent in one of my restaurants is a pleasure."

I laughed before I realized he wasn't trying to be funny.

"All I knew was that he closed his business. I think that was quite a while before I heard he had left town. I'm not sure if he had provided a forwarding address or not. It wasn't as if we were going to stay in touch. He'd transferred all my files."

"I am trying to verify that he did make his getaway as he planned."

"He planned to disappear? I don't recall that. All I knew was he left me in the lurch and I had to adjust to another lawyer."

"Was that a big problem for you?"

His eyes narrowed and he stared into mine. "Do you mean did I get angry and kill him? Hardly. I barely knew the guy"

"Of course, I didn't mean that." Of course, I did.

"I've had many lawyers in my life, some of whom I would have been happy to kill, but I can assure you, Kenneth Patterson was not one of them."

Maturi forced a laugh. "Luckily, I am not the type to hold a grudge," said the man who remembered a hotel employee who had rejected his offer of cooking classes five years before.

Chapter 14

When I got back to the Positano's house, a man in white overalls holding a rake was standing by his van in the driveway. A gardener? Kind of a shock. I didn't know we had a gardener. I didn't even know we had a garden.

The tall man loaded the rake along with some other tools into the back of his vehicle, but I felt his eyes on me as I pulled by him into a parking space by the front door. He didn't move any closer, but he did wave as I climbed out of my car. "Hello, there. Sorry to disturb. I told the Positanos I would come by and check the garden if that is what you can call this little patch back here."

"Oh." I didn't want to sound upset. After all, he could easily convert his tools to weapons. "I didn't realize you were coming."

"I thought Marc Positano would have told you. Maybe not that I'd be here today, but that we would be stopping by to check on things. You know. Clean up the driveway. Check around the perimeter of the pool. We can call in advance from now on if needed."

I glanced at the side of his van, but there was no logo. I had no idea who "we" was.

"No, that's fine. I do recall my fiancé saying that there were workmen who came buy on occasion. I didn't realize…"

"Are you folks going to be here for a while?"

"The Positanos will be back for the summer."

"Nice of them to lend you the house. Marc a relative of yours?"

"No. No. Just friends. They, he and Phyllis, like having someone in the house."

"Nice couple. Not like that woman who was here before. You know her?"

I blushed. "No, not really. We've never met."

"She was a piece of work."

Pumping the gardener for information seemed indiscrete, but this source had just fallen into my lap. "You knew her?"

He shook his head. "Not really, but you hear stuff."

I was figuring out how to wheedle that *stuff* out of him when he continued.

"Guys talk about how she drove her husband away. They found that easy to believe. Poor guy moved to California, or somewhere on the West Coast, to get away from her and was never heard from again."

"Did you know him?"

"Me? No. That was way before my time."

He was flattering himself. Maybe before his time as a gardener but not his time on earth.

"Just gossip. Folk lore. You think we gardeners are just working, but we're watching and listening. I could tell you tales about most houses we serve."

"Well, I'll be sure to hide my life story from you." I laughed.

"You live here alone?"

I stopped laughing. The question, or the way he asked it, scared me but I did not let on. I maintained a grin. "No, like I said. With my fiancé. Spread the word. I live here with a big brute." Okay, that was an exaggeration and probably a transparent one. "A private investigator. No one to mess with."

"A PI, eh?" He seemed displeased by that information. "Well, I'm finished here. We'll be back to put some planters on the deck. Would you like me to show you what we had in mind?" He took a step towards the house.

"No, that's fine. As I said, we're just housesitting, helping out the Positanos. We'll be gone soon."

"You from around here?"

Now that was a good question. At this point in our nomadic life, where were we from? "Yes" seemed like the easiest answer.

"Well, if you have a lawn keep us in mind."

"Do you have a card? We don't currently have a lawn, but we can tell the Positanos you were here."

The man made a great show of checking every pocket but came up empty. "Hold on." He reached into the front seat of his small van.

I was aware that this was the point at which the killer would pull a gun out of the glove compartment, but this guy turned around armed only with an apologetic smile. "I am embarrassed."

It appeared that he actually was a gardener.

"Foley's Gardening," he said. "Marc will know us."

I thanked him. "I'll let you finish here."

I was being neurotic, but I made a great show of pulling out my phone so he knew I could summon help in a flash. I climbed the outdoor stairs to the deck, but I didn't open the door. Part of me envisioned the stranger charging up the steps behind me and forcing me into the house. I knew that was ridiculous. At least part of me did. The other part of me suggested hanging out on the deck. After lingering on the deck for a few minutes, I heard wheels on gravel as he headed down the driveway.

I peeked around the corner of the house half-expecting the man to charge me with a butcher knife. But his truck was gone. I let out a sigh of relief and went back to enjoying the sun. I stretched out on a chaise and closed my eyes. I wasn't paranoid to worry about finding a strange man in the driveway. I needed to get a list from Andy of the workmen who might be showing up. Some of them might need to get into the house, and I wasn't about to let just anyone inside.

I enjoyed a half-hour on the deck marred only by the persistent smell of tuna fish. I guess that wasn't that odd. I was sitting facing a sea full of fish. But when I stood up and saw the spot of mayonnaise on my pants, I was pretty sure the fish I was smelling came from a can. My foot knocked a brown paper bag with something hard inside. I opened the top and found a crumpled potato chip bag, a dirty napkin, and an empty bottle of St Pauli Girl Lager.

That guy had eaten lunch on our deck. The nerve. I bet he did it regularly. He probably didn't realize there were house sitters. Had he done any work at all, or did he simply drop by for lunch? Maybe he dropped a few tools outside of his truck in case anyone came back and discovered him.

If they were his tools. Oh my God. What an idiot I was. Those tools probably belonged to the Positanos and I had watched him steal them. I dropped the bag back onto the deck and ran down the steps and back to the garage doors. I couldn't even describe the guy. Young? Old? Not young. Forties? Sixties? I didn't know. Hair color? He had on a Phillies hat. Eye color? He had on sunglasses. Weight? Average. Height? Okay, that I knew. He was tall. Not ridiculously tall, but tall. I could probably identify where he came up to on the van. What kind of van? White. Plates. Jersey. At least I'd noticed that.

The keypad beside the garage door was easy to locate. Now all I needed was the code. Andy had used the garage on the one occasion the air had been warm enough to leave the top down, but I knew the code. Now I just had to remember what it was. I was too flustered to get my mind under control. It took me a few moments to remember that the code was someone's birthday. Not mine. Not Andy's. But whose? I tried to remember our conversation with the Positanos when they left the Bahamas. "The code is easy to remember. It's…" And then I remembered the word birthday, but what word came between "it's" and "birthday?" Why would any of the Positano's birthdays be familiar to me?

I closed my eyes and tried to recall the conversation. And, then I remembered. The Positano's had relayed the code as part of an elaborate explanation. They hadn't had to change it when they bought the house. Turns out the code matched a birthday. It might have been his birthday. It might have been her birthday. It took a few seconds before I recalled that whoever's birthday it was had been born on the fourth of July. Were there only four digits? I had no idea what year either of the Positanos had been born. Not even a guess. And I didn't want to guess. How many tries did I get before the cops showed up?

Could four digits be enough? I hoped so. My hands were shaking as I raised them to the keypad. 0704. I didn't even have to press the Enter key. Both garage doors slid up.

Technically, the Positanos had a two-car garage but with a wide expanse of space on either side. The only car in residence was a yellow Jeep Wrangler. One space remained open for whichever car Andy and I chose to put away. The right wall resembled a sporting goods shop, with kayaks, ocean kayaks, boogie boards, surfboards. The selection equaled any display I had seen at the Avalon Surf Shop. On the left side was the equipment I assumed was used for pool and yard maintenance. Everything had a place, and everything appeared to be in its spot. The equipment looked pristine, so I found it easy to believe that the gardener brought his own. I let out another big sigh of relief. This one because nothing appeared to have been stolen.

I was relaxing when I glanced to the back of the garage and saw it. I walked up beside it to make sure I was seeing what I thought I was, hoping I'd be wrong.

I wasn't.

Chapter 15

"Why do I have to go with you?" Andy had barely gotten his coat off.

"I don't want to do this alone. I don't believe I should do this alone."

"Do what?"

"You'll see."

I led Andy through the back of the house, the part we would never venture into except to do laundry. I pulled a key off a hook and opened the door to the garage. The light came on automatically as I stepped inside.

Andy wrapped his arms around his torso. "Brrr. It's cold in here. Why were you in the garage?"

"Checking that the gardener didn't steal anything."

"We have a gardener?" Andy sounded as surprised as I had been.

"Apparently, and he brings his own tools. And lunch."

"And doesn't steal anything when he's here. That's good news." Andy rubbed his hands together thinking his sign to move along was subtle.

"That is good. This is not. What do think this is?" I patted the top of the large container.

"I know what that is. It says it right here in the logo. It's a freezer."

"What kind?"

That question seemed to throw him, but he answered. "An old-fashioned chest-style freezer. What's inside?"

"I don't know. I wasn't going to open it on my own."

"Why not?" He appeared puzzled.

"What do you think I would find?"

"Oh, I don't know. Frozen things. Frozen meat. Frozen fish. Frozen vegetables. Maybe if we get lucky some ice cream."

I challenged him. "Do you really believe that?"

"I do. Unless it's empty. It looks pretty old." Andy patted the top gently as if afraid to damage the weathered appliance.

"Exactly. Old enough to have been here when the Pattersons were here. When Ken Patterson was here."

He turned to me with eyes that danced with amusement. "I see where this is going. This old freezer would be perfect for storing bodies, or body parts. I am thinking you didn't want to open this because you're afraid we'll find Ken Patterson inside."

"You aren't?" I asked.

"This is the Positano's freezer." His tone added he didn't think we'd discover any bodies.

"It's plugged in. I checked. Why would they use this ancient relic? They have two, count them two, beautiful upright freezers in their kitchen."

"What were you doing in the kitchen?" Andy sounded truly shocked.

"I needed ice."

He nodded, accepting my excuse. "Maybe they simply like freezing things. Maybe he hunts and has tons of venison to store."

"Andy, I've met Mr. Positano. His only hunting takes place on the sale rack at Nordstrom's."

"So you think Donna killed her husband and left his body behind when she moved?"

"See, you thought that too."

"No, I thought, why would anyone risk leaving a body in a freezer when the house changes owners?"

"Who knows how Donna thinks? Maybe she made some deal with the Positanos to come back for it." I waved my arms in a move that made me appear a little frenzied.

"Or" Andy paused for dramatic effect, "maybe Ken's body isn't in there. You want me to open it?"

"I do."

"Okay." He put his hand on the latch but didn't pull on it.

"Why the reluctance? Did Positano give you instructions not to open the chest-model freezer in the garage?"

"Nope. I have no fear of opening it. Ready?" He had to fiddle with the catch for a few seconds, but then he lifted the lid and pushed it up. "Oh my God."

"Oh my God." I echoed his reaction. "What is that?" I felt sick. "Is that hair I see?"

Together we gazed into the deep freezer and were hit with an unpleasant, but not overwhelming, odor. Andy pulled a piece of cardboard out of the freezer.

"What is it?" I asked.

"A list." Andy read aloud. "Marianne. Labradoodle. Died 2020. Age 12. Sylvie. Poodle. Died 2018. Age 15. Kenneth. Human. Died 1977. Age 34." He paused briefly. "I made that last one up."

I punched his arm in a playful enough manner that he couldn't file charges against me. "He could be under there."

"Really? Can you imagine how that phone call went? 'Hello, Mrs. Patterson. Marc Positano here. You know that old freezer in the garage. Well, I just went to put my deceased and beloved poodle Sylvie in there and I noticed you forgot to take your husband when you moved, but don't worry if it's inconvenient for you to drop by and pick him up. We will lay our beloved poodle to rest on top."

"Well, just because Ken's body was gone when the Positanos arrived, doesn't mean he wasn't in there previously. Maybe Donna warned Marc Positano not to use the freezer for storing food but didn't tell him why."

"And in the forty years Donna lived here after Ken left, no one once thought to open the freezer?"

"Do you open freezers in other people's homes? He could easily have remained in there undetected."

Andy shrugged. "I won't tell you that is impossible, but I don't think it's likely. I wouldn't build my investigation around this possibility." He hesitated. "Do you think you are being objective? Maybe you like the idea that Ken never got away and Donna killed him."

"I'd prefer to think that Ken is happy somewhere, although if someone did kill him it would mean that he never abandoned his daughter. That would give Elisabeth some peace. And if he is dead, Donna is the likely suspect. I haven't met anyone who likes her."

"That doesn't mean she's a killer. She'd be a more likely victim of one of the people who hate her."

I ignored his comment although I agreed with it. "If she didn't know he was dead, why did she never try to strong-arm information out of his attorney?" I held out my hands, palms up, in a gesture that added *Eh? Tell me.*

"Are you sure she didn't?"

"Well, no, but I think he was dead and she probably knew it. I think someone killed him, most likely Donna."

"Admit it, Meg. You're rooting for Donna. What about the questionable clients people mention?"

"So, you agree he was murdered?" I heard what I wanted to hear.

"No, I don't think that is what happened. The fact that he had a lawyer take care of everything would cover his tracks for a while. He expected to take over control of his affairs eventually, right? If he were dead, things would have fallen through the cracks. The IRS would have come looking for him. My opinion? He got away as planned. Anything else is too big a coincidence."

"Unless his attorney set him up and killed him. No one ever even questioned him."

"A lot of women your age just wile the day away on Facebook," Andy said.

I stared at him until he let his eyes meet mine. "You say women my age because all the kids from school are into Tik Tok?"

He responded with a wry grin. "Well, they are. Or they were earlier today. Who knows what they have discovered by now?"

"I'll consider devoting my days to Tik Tok dances after I find Ken Patterson or discover his fate."

Andy didn't try to dissuade me. He pulled me into his arms and hugged me hard. "Just promise me, you won't run around making accusations. Swear that you'll be careful. Don't go all lone wolf on me." He released me from his grip and took my hand. "In the meantime, let's try to forget about Ken Patterson, get out of the garage and enjoy the ocean breezes."

Chapter 16

If Andy hoped to enjoy the ocean breezes without talk of Ken Patterson's disappearance, his hopes were short-lived. We had hardly settled onto two loungers and covered ourselves in quilts and blankets before I returned to the topic.

"I did get some new information before I found the freezer. I went to see Malcolm Maturi."

"Did you tell him why you were there?" Andy passed me a glass of wine.

"I did."

"Did it bother him?"

"Not as much as when he thought I was there to spy on him. On Bingo's behalf. He did recognize me from the Bahamas."

"And thought you were a corporate spy! At least that pays." He raised his wine glass to salute me.

"You can put your glass down. I am not actually a corporate spy though it might be something to consider. Do you want to hear what happened when I mentioned Ken's name?"

"Of course. But first, would you like me to get some hors d'oeuvres?"

The mention of an edible item made my stomach churn. "I'm fine. I had a bite at Maturi's. Actually, about five-thousand bites. I think he was trying to kill me."

"Spying is a tough game," Andy said. "Do you think you could handle it if I nibbled in front of you?"

"Sure," I lied.

When Andy returned with cheese, crackers, and other items from the mini-fridge, I glanced at the plate and turned away.

"You were going to tell me what happened when you mentioned

Ken's name." Andy plopped a piece of cheese in his mouth quickly as if I wouldn't notice.

"He blanched. I doubt I've ever used that verb before, but he blanched, he did. Just for a second, he turned as white as his chef's jacket. And his face froze." I attempted an imitation. "He made a big deal of remembering Ken. Fake."

Andy said nothing.

"Well?" I prompted.

"I'm trying to come up with a blanching joke. You know because he's a chef." Andy smiled.

"Why would he be so rattled by my mentioning Ken's name"

"Was he nervous the entire time?" Andy asked.

"Not really, but I can't forget his initial response." I shivered not because of Maturi's response but because the temperature was dropping.

"Everyone told you he was one of Ken's shady clients. I can see him recalling an uncomfortable situation. That doesn't mean he killed him."

"Do you think he was involved with Donna?" I asked Andy to speculate.

"I doubt it. He was a dozen years younger. Plus, the way you describe Donna, she doesn't seem like the type to cheat." He broke a cracker in four and slid a tiny piece in his mouth.

"You can eat in front of me. It's not as if I'll get sick all over you."

"Based on the expression on your face, I'm not so sure."

"It's not the food. Well, not only the food." I sighed. "I'm just feeling a little discouraged."

"You're finding some helpful information. Don't get discouraged unless you want to stop."

"I don't want to quit for selfish reasons. I feel I might accomplish something good."

"It would be important to Elisabeth." He held up a hand to call for silence. "Did you hear that?"

We sat in silence. I didn't.

"Wait," he said.

This time I did hear it. "The bear?"

"That might be the least of our problems."

"Maybe you shouldn't have gotten rid of your gun when you closed your PI business," I said, although I was the one who urged him to do that. I was afraid of bullets when they weren't even in a gun.

"Whatever is out there, I don't believe we should take care of it with gunfire. Let me check things out. It might be Elisabeth."

"That was a lot of noise though." I was still thinking bear.

"I'll look. You call Abby."

Abby answered and said, "I'm walking to her room now. Oh, my God. It must be her. She isn't here. I am on my way."

I ran down the steps to catch up with Andy who was walking along the edge of the wooded area calling Elisabeth's name. I joined in.

"Andy, I see her." I saw a patch of pink amidst the vegetation.

I pointed and he plunged into the thicket. When he emerged, he was carrying Elisabeth, this time dressed in a pink flannel nightgown heavier but not heavy enough to protect her from the chill night air. I tucked my jacket around her.

"Look, Elisabeth. Here is Meg. Meg and I live here now. You came to visit before."

Elisabeth appeared concerned but not frightened. "I didn't want Mother to see me. She doesn't like it when I play in the woods. I'm sorry."

"Nothing to be sorry about, Elisabeth," Andy assured her. "I wonder if we should take her inside. Will it upset her more?"

I had no idea. "Abby should be here in a few minutes. Let's walk her to the foot of the driveway and wait there."

I ran back to the deck for a quilt and wrapped it around Elisabeth. She chatted happily about her years in the house as we walked down the driveway. Her eyes glistened at the memory.

Abby pulled up, not in her SUV, but in a car that made it easy for Andy to settle Elisabeth into the front seat. She smiled and waved out the window as they pulled away.

"I'm not going to walk away from this search, am I?"

Andy wrapped an arm around me to fight off the chill. "Not a chance."

Chapter 17

Abby was at our door before 9 AM. "Sorry about my mother last night. I must have dozed off. I cannot figure how she got out. But, all's well that ends well. Tell Andy I said thank you." She brushed by me moving as fast as her mouth. "I brought donuts. I would have brought them from Kohler's, but they are closed for the season. Theirs are the best. Trust me." She dropped a Wawa bag on the counter. "But these aren't awful. I hope you haven't eaten."

"As a matter of fact…."

"These cream donuts are good. Not Kohler's but how bad can a cream donut be?" She pulled one from the bag and bit into it.

"Oh." I ditched explaining that I had already eaten in favor of a cream donut. In my world, there's always room for a cream donut.

"I came by to find out what you discovered."

It took me a minute to chew before I answered. I reached for a napkin and handed one to Abby. If I needed one half as much as she did, I needed one badly.

"From what I can gather your grandfather did plan and execute an escape as you've heard."

The anger in her voice was aimed at me, as was the cream donut she waved in the air. "I know that."

"I wanted to make sure that he did, in fact, get away as planned and to find out if he left any clues as to where he was going." I didn't mention my growing suspicion that her grandmother killed him.

"I finished my coffee on the way over." She headed for the coffee maker and touched the pot. It must have felt warm. She opened a cabinet door and issued a theatrical harrumph.

"My grandmother kept mugs here."

"Oh."

She moved on to the next cabinet and pulled out an oversized mug with an anchor on the side. She blew into the cup before pouring the coffee and taking a sip. She grimaced and spat it into the sink. "This is horrible."

"Andy made that before he left for school over two hours ago."

She dropped the mug into the sink and left the mess for me to take care of.

"Don't you feel stupid saying your boyfriend, I mean your fiancé, goes to school?"

"No."

I waited for her to squirm at the inappropriateness of her question, but she didn't.

"I would."

My phone lit up from an incoming message that I ignored.

Abby leaned over to check out my cover photo. "Andy looks a lot different in that picture. Kind of like a surfer boy." She turned the phone to study my screen.

"And you think he looks different now?"

"Yeah. More like a professor. He's changing. He wears sweaters and his hair is neater. A sign of change."

"That picture was taken on a windy beach in the Bahamas. Not too many people wear sweaters in July when the average temperature is in the eighties."

She shrugged. "You know what happened to my grandmother's marriage? She didn't recognize change coming."

I ignored her. "So far I've learned nothing about your grandfather after he left. Are you sure your grandmother never heard another word from him?"

"I've heard her say it many times. 'Not a single word.' Do you have any bottled water?"

"In the refrigerator. Under the counter."

When she reappeared with a bottle of water, she had more advice for me. "You should stay through the summer. Do you know they say Avalon is 'Cooler by a mile?'"

"I do."

"Do you know why?"

"Because it sits a mile farther out to sea than other towns down here on the southern end of the Jersey Shore. I would really like to speak to your grandmother."

She twisted the cap off the bottle and held it aloft. "Glass?"

"Behind you."

"Well, that—meeting Donna—isn't going to happen. She does not want anyone searching for my grandfather."

"But wouldn't she be happy if he came back?" I bit into the donut again. It was disappearing alarmingly quickly.

"If he crawled back. She would hate for him to believe she cared enough to look for him."

"Can I at least *see* your grandmother?" I didn't admit I already had. "I promise I will not talk to her." I sucked the extra cream that was escaping from the remainder of the donut into my mouth necessitating a slight delay before I continued. "I promise I'll be subtle. I just want to see her." *And maybe interact with her under false pretenses.*

"You mean spy on her?"

"Yeah. I guess I do." I popped the end of the donut in my mouth.

"She goes to mass every morning at Our Lady Star of the Sea. She lives in Cape May now."

"I wouldn't get to see her in action there." I blushed as I said the words. I couldn't admit I'd already tried that approach. "I want to get an idea of what she is like."

"Why?" Abby snapped.

I wasn't quite sure, but I had a story ready. "To help me understand your grandfather."

Abby accepted that answer although I found it rather generic and weak. "I'll call you if I hear she is going anywhere. It may be a while. She tends to spend her days in her condo reading romance novels and waiting for happy hour."

"Before you go, do you know if Donna still has a relationship with a woman named Sally DeMarco?"

"If you call ignoring each other if they happen to run into each other accidentally which happens every five years or so having a relationship, yes. Otherwise, no."

"I thought I might try to talk to her. Her husband was friends with your grandfather, so she knew him too. I don't want her running to your grandmother and tipping her off to what I am doing."

"My first reaction is *go for it*. She isn't going to call Donna. They hate each other. I don't know why but they do. One time I had to hide my grandmother so Sally wouldn't see her."

"They hate each other that much?"

"I think the dislike is mutual. No. Not dislike. Hate is the right word. More than you can imagine."

That was great news. A woman who hated Donna Patterson might be willing to talk. Not just willing. Eager.

Abby rose and wandered over to the lone painting on the walls of *the room*. "Did I mention that Donna always kept her wedding portrait, their wedding portrait, here? So you would see it as you came in the door. She said she left it there as a signal so no matter which door he used when he returned, my grandfather would understand he still belonged. She had another shot by the door in the mud room downstairs. And, get this…" Abby paused for dramatic effect. "She kept another one hanging in the garage, I guess in case he drove back."

Why was I not surprised?

Chapter 18

I located Robin Carson through his social media. He and his wife lived on their boat. Florida in the winter. Cape May in the summer.

I was hoping that the retiree could add information that did more than confirm Donna was a horror and Ken was lucky to get away from her. He agreed to see me because, he claimed, "he was doing it for Little Lisa" the child he remembered. He messaged me that he and his wife had a small condo in Cape May where he'd be happy to meet with me. He insisted on providing detailed directions in case my GPS wasn't up to the job. It was and I found the spot easily.

Robin seemed happy to see me. His smile was warm, genuine, soft. He projected an aura of peace and contentment. Not quite as extreme as that of a cult leader. But a member? Possibly.

"Odd you caught us at the shore at this time of year." He waved me through the door of his apartment. "Generally, we'd be on our boat, but we came north for a wedding. We'll go back down to Florida and bring the boat up for the summer."

As conservative as his appearance was in the group photo, Robin now looked like the kind of guy who might have run off with Ken. A twenty-first-century version of a free spirit. He pulled his hair, a gorgeous shade of steel gray, into a loose man bun. Aside from a nod to winter in his hiking boots, his wide khaki shorts and Hawaiian shirt suggested he was still in Florida where he hung out with Jimmy Buffett. Metaphorically. Not actually.

"Stacy," he called. "We have company."

He introduced me to a woman dressed in the distaff version of his outfit, although in deference to the northern latitude, she had replaced the shorts with a pair of jeans.

"Nice to meet you, Meg," she greeted me warmly, although I figured out she had no idea who I was or what I wanted.

"Do you have any lemonade out there?" Robin pointed at a closet-sized kitchen that made the wet bar area at the Positano's look like a gourmet setup.

"I'll bring some. You make yourself comfortable." She directed me to a couch that ran along one wall. Robin took a seat directly across from me. We sat six feet apart facing each other. The Carsons certainly had the knack of living in small spaces. I suspected there might be more space in the cabin of their boat. Even the view out their sliding glass door was small. A similar apartment twenty feet away and a tiny sliver of the bay beyond.

"Sorry, it's a little snug in here. That's how we like it. We downsized over ten years ago now. We live on our boat. This is just a port in a storm." He laughed. "I imagine you figured out we don't do much entertaining."

I had guessed as much but didn't admit it. I matched my chuckle to his.

"We view this place as more of a storage unit. There is a bedroom." He pointed over his shoulder to tell me what was on the other side of the wall. "And, of course, a bathroom. That's all we need. Funny, we spent our entire life accumulating things only to find out we're happier living like this."

"Although I do still have my grandmother's china boxed up under the bed. Some items I just couldn't part with." Stacy said as she stepped back into the room with lemonade in Baccarat water goblets.

Looking at the couple, I figured out Ken might have been the first in his crowd to step away from his wife, but he had not been the last. Robin's wife was not young, but she was younger. "I never met Ken Patterson. He was gone before I arrived on the scene."

"But you heard about him?" I asked.

Stacy shook her head. "Not much. He was just a guy from the group who left. Everyone once in a while someone would say 'I wonder where Ken is today'."

"And then we would all say, 'In a better place.'" Robin leaned forward, glass raised to click against mine.

I forced a puzzled expression onto my face as if I had not heard a bad word about Donna. I didn't want to lead the witness.

"Did anyone mention that his wife wasn't popular?"

I didn't lie. I provided basic information. "I talked to Bob DeMarco. He indicated Donna and Ken were not well matched."

"Ah, Bob. I imagine he'd give you the most positive opinion of anyone in our crowd."

"Really?" What DeMarco had to say was the most positive opinion?

Robin read something on my face that surprised him. "Maybe he finally saw through her. I used to feel sorry for his girlfriend, later his wife. She was a great girl, but not a looker like Donna."

The surprised expression on my face was genuine. I'd trusted Bob DeMarco.

"I guess that is not something Bob would want to admit. He tried to go along with the gang on the topic of Donna, but it was hard to miss that he was infatuated. Donna knew and would toy with him. He would have done anything for her. I have no idea if anything ever happened. I tend to think not. Donna was a tease."

"Now her, I've heard about." Stacy laughed. "To know her was to hate her."

"So why are you asking about Ken now, after all these years?" Robin asked.

I explained Elisabeth's illness and how Andy and I came to meet her and her daughter.

"I remember thinking that Ken's daughter was sweet. Nothing like Donna. At least at the point that I knew her. She was still little, but I was always watching for tell-tale signs that she would end up being a little Donna, a pretentious snob."

I didn't think she had, but what did I know. I left his comment hang in the air and moved on. "So, I am doing this, asking questions, for Elisabeth. I guess I need to ask three. One, do you believe Ken disappeared willingly as was said? Two, have you been in touch with him since? And three, were there activities he liked to do that he might have continued throughout his life?" To signal I was ready to listen, I took a long sip of the lemonade. Not a hardship. It was delicious.

"Okay, number one first. I definitely believe that he left of his own accord. I could see his...what should I call it...discontent growing for years. Years. I remember we were all together for a Christmas party in Philadelphia. 1969. I never forgot. They kept playing *Abbey Road*. You know, the Beatles."

I nodded. I knew.

"It hadn't been out that long. I think that album made a lot of us think about the parties we were not attending that night." Even then, five decades later, he appeared wistful. It took him a few seconds before he spoke again. "Anyway, Ken, he starts bending my ear about what we were missing. You know the lottery?"

"Yeah?" I dragged out the word to make it a question.

"Not the money lottery. The draft lottery."

"I know it happened, but not the details."

"People would get drafted according to their birthday. Every day of the year got a number."

****Robin Carson****
Philadelphia PA
December 1969

"Nice of our government to run that lottery right before Christmas, eh?" Ken was on his way to a monumental drunk. Robin glanced over his shoulder at Donna. Looking perfect although she'd given birth only three months before. She was across the room from her husband but, like always, keeping tabs on him.

"Doesn't matter for us, Kenny boy. We're too old. Besides, we're married. We were married in time."

"Yeah. You made it under the wire."

"I would have married Myra no matter what. We were lucky that when the exemption was pulled we were near Maryland and could get married that afternoon."

"What's your number?"

"My lottery number? I have no idea. I didn't look because the lottery doesn't apply to me. I was born two months too early. No more worrying about the draft even if I were single."

"You know what my number is, Robin?"

Robin shook his head. "It's not your number I'm worried about, Ken. What about Gerald?"

"Oh, he's the big loser. He's gonna go. But me? 361. I would never have to go. I don't have to be married." He stared at Robin waiting for a big reaction.

Robin did not provide one. "It doesn't matter. That lottery isn't for guys our age. I told you. We are too old. By a hair's breadth, by months, but too old. 1944 was the first unlucky year. Besides you've always been exempt. First, college. Then, marriage." Robin couldn't believe that Ken couldn't get that, wouldn't get that.

"You know, we did not have to get married, Robin."

"Ken, you didn't get married to avoid the draft. I mean being a married man came in handy, but you were set to tie the knot anyway." What was wrong with him? Married four years, with an adorable daughter and infant son and Ken's telling him he doesn't need to be married.

"Look at that hippie girl over there."

Robin knew who Ken meant. Only one girl wore bell-bottoms, clogs and a gauzy top covered with embroidery that looked as if it had come from India. Her long straight hair almost reached her waist. He had no trouble picking her out in the crowd of suburban moms and dads.

"I bet she gets it on with whomever she wants, whenever she wants."

Robin was embarrassed. He didn't want to talk about the girl like that. He said nothing.

"You can tell by looking at her." Ken was almost salivating.

"Never judge a book by its cover." Robin tried to lighten up the conversation.

"Why? Look at us. I can judge you by your cover. Nice house. Nice car. Nice job. Nice wife. Nice kids."

Robin noted the order he listed his assets even as he wondered if Ken considered them liabilities.

"But no damn excitement."

"I like my life," Robin stated without anger.

"You do? You really do?" Ken patted him on the shoulder. The action of a drunk. "Good for you." He shook Robin's shoulder vigorously. "Although for God's sake I can't figure out why."

"Listen, Ken, you're not going to do anything stupid, are you?"

"Me? Honor student Kenneth G. Patterson?" He made a sputtering noise that Robin took to mean that was impossible. Not undesirable. Impossible. "Are you asking if I am going to try my luck with the little hippie lady?"

"I…I…" That was exactly what Robin was asking but didn't want to say so. Ken might consider it a dare.

"No. I am not going to try my luck with the little hippie chick. And do you know why?" He dropped his hand back on Robin's shoulder and leaned in as if he were about to tell him a secret. "Because she wouldn't give me the time of day. She will look around this room and she won't even see me. I am invisible to her. If someone did force her to meet me, you know what she would think?"

Robin pulled his head away from Ken's and shook it slightly.

"What a jerk! To her, I am the man, *the enemy."*

Someone moved the needle back on the record player and the sounds of "Something" flooded the room. Ken sprung back as if someone had pushed him. His eyes filled with tears. "Can you imagine feeling that way about someone?"

"Yeah, Ken, I can."

Ken shook his head. He was now looking very drunk. "I can't, Robin. I didn't know it was possible, so I didn't look for it. You know, that feeling." He stared into Robin's eyes with such intensity that Robin had to look away. He's just drunk, *Robin told himself.* Maybe something put Ken in a bad mood. He'll get over it. *But even as he reassured himself, Robin was not convinced. He knew he should have felt sorry for Ken, but he'd gotten himself into the situation. The main emotion Robin felt was joy, joy that he did not feel the same way as Ken.*

*****

"So, you think as far back as 1969 he wanted to leave his wife?"

"Years before he left. I think, at first, he wanted to have his cake and eat it too."

"Is that what he did?"

"Not that night. But after that?" He fell silent and stared at the little slice of bay visible behind the building across the way.

I was about to prompt him when he continued.

"I can't say when his marriage went off the track. He and Donna were living the good life. At least, it looked good on the surface. He made a lot of money. A *lot* of money. I never asked how. He was a big-time lawyer, right out of the gate. So I guess all that money made sense. And he bought a big place in Villanova. Then, he built himself a fancy house in those high dunes in Avalon. One of the first to go in there. That meant a lot to him. He grew up poor. He wanted more. He wanted it all. That Avalon house? No place fancier on the Jersey Shore. But that was Ken. He liked to show off. That's how he ended up with Donna. He had to have the hottest girlfriend. No. Not hot. Maybe cutest."

He stopped. He had more to say but seemed reluctant.

"Was that what it was all about with Donna? The physical attraction?"

He waited and took a long drink before he answered. "I'm not sure if passion was ever involved. Not like in that song, "Something." He loved showing Donna off. He did from the first minute he saw her. We were probably at a frat party. One of those stories where he looked across the room and said I'm going to get her. He was a nice-looking guy, and she was a great-looking girl. Perfectly groomed. Knew all the latest styles. Always dressed right for every occasion. Ken told me I couldn't imagine what it felt like to walk into a room with her. I got his point. They made a good-looking couple."

I sat through an awkward silence hoping he would continue. I was hoping for more dirt about Donna.

"She knew all the rules, and she believed there were rules. All the rules Donna believed in, if they were real in the first place, went away in the sixties. But not in Donna's mind. But Ken liked the way she looked. The way she kept the house. Elisabeth always looked like a little model. But then came the seventies. What's your impression of the seventies?"

"Disco music. Really bad clothes," I said

"You're right. But things got pretty wild, even for some married folks, if you get my drift."

I nodded. I would have gotten his drift even if Bob DeMarco hadn't already filled me in.

"But I never joined in on all that. Myra, my first wife, and I were happy. I liked being married. I liked having a family."

I wanted to discover what went wrong, but I have a hard time asking questions when I fear the answer. I didn't have to.

"Myra died. Cancer. Forty-two. Left me with three kids. I was lucky. I was thrilled to meet Stacy." He reached over and laid a hand on her knee.

She covered it with hers and intertwined her fingers with his. "And I was just as lucky," she said.

"I never had that urge to get out there like Ken did. He felt he was missing something and he blamed Donna."

"So, you feel he was unfair to Donna?"

"Oh God no. She was a horror show."

I changed the subject. "I have a question that I realize is kind of crazy."

"Go ahead. Shoot. I am probably saying too much, but if anything I can tell you helps Little Lisa, I'm in."

I pulled out the picture that Abby had given me. He took it from my hands and smiled. "Wow. The old gang. Bittersweet, you know. Several of them are gone." He pulled reading glasses from his shirt pocket and leaned in to study the photo.

"I noticed that in the photo you're holding a movie camera."

"Ah. Super 8. For a while there, I didn't leave home without it."

"This sounds crazy, but you wouldn't happen to have that film would you?"

"From what year?"

I expected his tone to add "are you nuts?" but it didn't.

"I believe that photo was taken the day Ken disappeared. July 4, 1977."

"1977," he mumbled as he got to his feet and disappeared into the next room.

"Ah, he'll be proud to show off his system," Stacy laughed. "Set your watch. He'll be back with the right DVD in under a minute."

She was almost right. He was back in under two. "I had all those films converted to DVD." He opened bookcase doors to reveal a TV with a cable box and DVD player. "If this old player goes out on me, I don't know where I'll move them next."

When the disc loaded, the screen said 1977 in psychedelic colors. "I made a lot of movies that year. I loaded them separately so we can skip to July."

He hit the remote to skip through the clips with some brief stops to look at his kids and to point out his first wife, Myra. As we skipped past someone's graduation, I figured July 4 was coming soon. "Here we go."

I recognized the view from what was now the Positano's deck. The vegetation on the dunes was much thinner, but a couple of trees that stood close to the house had survived from the seventies. The camera panned the party crowd. In the corner, I spotted Gerald Patterson sitting at the bottom of a deck chair where his wife Vonnie lounged. Just as he had said. Seeing the past that

I had heard described gave me a chill. I wasn't sure why. I saw another woman approaching and wondered if I was going to see Donna, but the camera panned by her quickly and focused one by one on what Robin called his gang. He turned up the volume.

The voice behind the camera said, "Hello, Dougie Hargreaves. Do you have a message you'd like to leave for future Americans on this momentous day?"

Dougie responded with a colorful expletive. "Bicentennial's over, Bud. I used up all my inspirational thoughts last year. Catch me in 2076."

The cameraman moved onto a redhead with freckles. "And now I am interviewing the great Francis Bloch. What's up Cissie?"

"You call me that again, you'll get my Irish up."

"You're not Irish." The voice behind the camera challenged him.

"A technicality. I still have red hair and a temper," the man said with a broad smile.

The film cut off and I worried that I would not get to see the Pattersons, but a new clip began.

"Here is our gracious hostess, the lovely Donna Patterson," said the voice behind the camera although Donna looked anything but gracious. She made no attempt to hide her annoyance at the sight of the camera, but when she spoke the flirtatious Donna emerged. "Robin, you are a regular Cecil B. DeMille these days. When you go to Hollywood, take me with you."

Robin thanked Donna for taking time to talk to his camera, and she giggled as he moved the camera to Bob DeMarco standing beside Donna.

"Are you enjoying the Fourth?"

"Our beautiful hostess is doing a superb job." DeMarco flashed his signature grin.

The conversation continued but I wasn't listening. In the background, I saw the man I assumed to be Ken Patterson. His ridiculous 1970s outfit would have been a good clue even if I had never seen his picture. He was standing alone, taking in the action around him. He studied a young girl who walked by him in a two-piece bathing suit that was probably considered revealing at the time. He never took his eyes off her, but he didn't look lecherous. He looked sad.

Chapter 19

I figured I could think in the Princeton Inn as well as at home. Plus, they had food there. While I waited for my cheeseburger, visions of the young Pattersons and their friends played in my head. Smiling people. So young. So unsuspecting. Except for Ken who knew change was coming. But were they the changes Ken anticipated? I still wondered if he got to execute his plan. I had no reason to believe he hadn't gotten away, but the feeling nagged at me. Not one single contact in forty years? Not one accidental sighting? Not even one suspected sighting? It just did not seem possible that Ken had made his escape as planned. And if he hadn't? I had my prime suspect, but I had my prime suspect before I had any facts. Despite all her protests of loyalty and fidelity, possibly because of those protests, I did not understand, or trust, Donna Patterson.

I had just started perusing the menu when Abby slipped into the booth across the table from me.

"So what have you found out?" No *hello.* No *nice to see you.*

"How did you find me?"

"I saw your car outside."

How? Even I walked by it in parking lots. As far as I knew it had no distinguishing features. It had Jersey plates, but there were millions of cars just like it within a ten-mile radius. Okay, maybe not millions, but hundreds. I bet. At least dozens.

"How did you know it was mine?" I stupidly asked the girl who was shocked I had not memorized Gerald Patterson's license plate number.

"A hunch."

I let it go.

"I thought I could get a report."

She hadn't done anything specifically offensive, but somehow Abby managed to rub me the wrong way. A skill she inherited from her grandmother?

I would probably end up doing everything she wanted, but her attitude made me reluctant to admit that. "Abby, I really want to help you with this, but I am not your employee. I am doing what I can as fast as I can. These things take time." *Although I am putting a rush on this project simply to get you out of my hair.* I kept that last part to myself.

"But did you do anything today?"

"Today isn't over but yes, I have made some progress today." Not that I was going to share the details with her. Maybe someday, I would show her the DVD that Robin Carson insisted on burning for me, but I wasn't in a mood to open that can of worms. Not yet. "Nothing definitive. Nothing I'm ready to share."

At that moment help came in the form of a young woman dressed all in black. "Hi, my name is Madison. I'll be your server today."

Pretty much just to annoy Abby, I let the waitress chat for a bit before I gave her my order. Abby wanted a mineral water.

With the waitress gone, talking with Abby was inevitable. But what was there to say? I went on the offensive.

"Did you talk to your father about my visiting your mother yet?"

"I will. He works at home. I don't like to interrupt him. He loses enough time helping out with my mother."

"I've got to have more to go on. I want you to tell me everything you ever remember anyone saying about your grandfather."

She leaned back in her seat, sulking. "I told you we didn't talk about him. By the time he left, it seemed everyone hated him."

Everyone? I suspected that meant Donna and anyone she could influence. "They must have said why."

"He wouldn't go to church anymore."

"See you remember something."

"He liked to golf too much. But Donna thought that might have been a cover. You know, so he could get out of the house."

So maybe when he was out of the house for good, he went back to golf.

"He liked to disco dance. I heard he even roller-skated."

"Great," I said although I'd already heard that from Bob DeMarco.

"He loved the ocean. Remember you have a painting of his sailboat near the front door. Donna would sometimes say he would never surface in the middle of the country because he would not leave the ocean."

"That's great information. Anything else?"

"My grandmother was talking about how she detested cigars, and she mentioned that my grandfather had 'tried to take up that filthy habit' but she had stopped him."

Of course.

"Did he smoke cigarettes?"

"I never heard that he did or didn't. My grandmother would never have approved."

"Anything else?"

"I told you he was never a big topic of conversation. I heard Donna refer to how he embarrassed her because he liked to be the center of attention and would tell dumb jokes that weren't funny."

From what I heard, I wasn't sure I would use Donna as an arbiter of anyone's sense of humor.

"We didn't talk about him. Asking about him made my grandmother mad and my mother sad."

"Keep thinking, and if you come up with anything else let me know. I imagine that your grandfather might have tried anything your grandmother disapproved of."

My tone was joking, but Abby's face was consumed by sadness. "I wonder if my mother would have had a happier life if he'd taken her along. She only got to do things her mother approved of."

Chapter 20

I checked my rear-view mirror on my way to Sally DeMarco's. If Abby was tailing me, she was doing a good job. I didn't notice a suspicious SUV.

Sally DeMarco wasn't living in the same style as her former husband, but I would have been happy in the condominium complex on the water in Stone Harbor.

In this day and age, stopping by isn't a common practice and the former Mrs. Robert DeMarco should not have opened her door to a stranger who knocked. But she did, and I explained my mission in general terms. She didn't ask for specifics, and I didn't offer them.

Mrs. DeMarco asked me to come in and turned her back so I could follow her up the steep staircase to her second-floor apartment. Or, had I wanted, locked the door behind me before attacking and robbing her. I didn't point that out. A safety lecture didn't seem a wise way to launch the conversation.

Sally DeMarco's condo had the look of a 1984 suburban colonial home with the furniture, knick-knacks and mementos of a three-thousand-square-foot house crammed into one area that served as living room, dining room and den. Sally dressed to match the décor which, while extremely tasteful, was completely at odds with the casual view of boat docks along the inlet.

"What a lovely view even on a cloudy day," I commented.

"Thank you. Yes, it's lovely. Please have a seat, Ms…"I'm sorry. I know you said your name, but I didn't catch it."

"Daniels. My name is Meg Daniels."

"Of course, Meg. It's strange. As you get older names are a problem, but I'll remember Meg. Let me get us something to drink so we can have a relaxing conversation. Tea?"

I didn't like tea, but I said yes to keep the meeting moving.

She left me alone in her living area as she went to prepare drinks. Bringing the water to a boil left me plenty of time to steal any number of expensive knick-knacks—the condo was overflowing with them—and make a run for it. I might not have been a cover girl for fitness, but she was in her late seventies. I didn't think she could catch me. Again, I chose not to lecture. I had not come to do a security audit.

"Here we are, Pam." She poured the tea into china teacups and presented cookies on a plate to match on the coffee table in front of me.

"Thank you." If I proved to be a criminal, she wouldn't even recall the right name to give the cops. I no longer had a mother but if I did, I hoped she'd be more cautious with strangers.

"Oh no. I forgot." Mrs. DeMarco scurried to the kitchen and back. I was pleased to see that, this time, she remembered to bring the sugar, but forgot the napkins. She made another trip. My mission was dependent on Sally DeMarco's memory. I wasn't feeling optimistic.

We made small talk for five minutes or so. Sally—she told me I must call her Sally—chose the topics. How wonderful Stone Harbor was. It was. How beautiful her view was. It was. How lovely the weather was. At that moment, it really wasn't, but overall the last week had been sunny and dry. I didn't nitpick.

Sally was entertaining and upbeat. Then, I mentioned that Donna Patterson's granddaughter had asked me to learn as much as I could about her grandfather and his disappearance.

"Does her granddaughter know how I feel about that woman, her grandmother?" The emotion in Sally's voice was unmistakable.

"She knows you are no longer friends."

"She doesn't know why?"

"I think if she did, she would have told me."

"It isn't the kind of tale a grandmother would confide in a granddaughter." She made sipping tea look like an act of aggression. "Donna was always the kind of woman other women could see through." Her cup hit the saucer with a frightening amount of force but stayed intact.

"And the men?"

"They thought Donna was adorable."

Should I mention that I talked to her ex-husband? Better not. "I've heard that she was kind of cold."

Sally passed the plate of butter cookies. I never refuse any cookie. She took one for herself and chewed a tiny bite slowly. "I find this difficult to explain. Donna was completely rigid about everything she believed. Always had to be in control. She never simply said, yes. Me: Would you like to go to Restaurant A for lunch? Her: Yes, that would be fine, but wouldn't you rather go to Restaurant B. Me: I'm going to wear my green dress. Her: I like that dress, but for the event wouldn't you prefer the blue one. Got the picture?"

I did.

"I tried to avoid giving in to her." Sally chuckled but I heard real anger in her words. "If we went shopping, she'd badger and badger until you bought what she wanted. A woman at a darling little boutique in Stone Harbor told me that she knew 90% of what people bought when shopping with Donna would come back."

"A control freak?"

"Totally. But the issue was bigger than that. She was implying not only whatever you selected was not what she wanted, it was somehow wrong." She straightened her posture and looked down her nose in what I assumed was an imitation of Donna. "She always knew better." She let her shoulders sag. "If our husbands hadn't been college buddies, I never would have befriended her."

"Her personality caused the rift between the two of you?"

"Oh, not that side of her personality. The other side. Have you seen her?"

"Pictures." I wasn't about to share the story of my trip to Our Lady Star of the Sea with Sally. I had a feeling that was one thing she wouldn't forget.

"Then you can tell she was pretty, but what you can't see is how cute she was. She liked to think she was zany. She would flirt to get what she wanted. And man, could she flirt. I told Bob after Ken disappeared that she was going to have a shock when she wasn't invited anywhere. No wife was going to invite her around her husband."

"Was she included in things after Ken disappeared?"

"Rarely. Once she wasn't half of a couple she was pretty much on her own. It wasn't that she would have stolen someone's husband. She would have wanted them to ask so she could reject them." She bit into the cookie and stared into space for a few seconds before she let her eyes meet mine.

"Got the type? Everyone steered clear of her except for Bob and me. We invited her to go with us to a few events after Ken left. I got the hint from the other women that we should not invite her again. She was all over the men."

I had a feeling I knew where this was going. "Including Bob?"

"Including Bob." She took a long drink. "So, I can tell what you're thinking. She seduced Bob and slept with him."

That was the obvious conclusion.

"Oh no. What she did was worse. She seduced him, but she turned him down."

"Wait, how do you know she tried to seduce him?"

"She told me."

I felt the punch in my stomach, and it hadn't happened to me.

"I saw what she was up to and told Bob to watch out. He laughed. 'That bitch. You forget. Ken told me what she was really like. He would always say *I might as well have married a missionary.*' If you get what I mean."

I got what he meant.

"You must have encountered women that men are drawn to like flies to honey. Donna wasn't one of them. She worked at it. She giggled and acted silly. Her zany routine. They all bought the act. Eventually, even Bob."

I knew it was thirty years too late to save this marriage, but I heard myself try. "But he didn't go through with it."

"As I said, that only made it worse." She shook her head as she sipped her tea. Her voice was surprisingly calm as she continued. "She set the entire thing up. She called and asked Bob to help her move an armoire." She slipped into a flirtatious voice. "'Being alone and all. I can't budge it.'" Sally dropped the coquettish tone. "I shouldn't have let him go alone but Felicity, my daughter, was taking a summer course and she needed help on a book report on *The Red and the Black*."

Now that was a specific memory from a woman who couldn't retain my name.

"I never knew exactly what went on that night, but Bob was at Donna's for three hours. To move an armoire? Not that I suspected at the time, but two days later, Bob called her and arranged to meet her. She agreed. You know why she went? To turn him down. She called me the next day because she had 'given it careful thought' and felt I needed to know. She was 'so sorry.' She 'never meant for it to happen.' She had never 'done anything to encourage him.'"

"But she had?"

"She wanted me to think that she was apologizing, but her real message was *I am irresistible. I may not have a man, but I could have anyone I wanted and that includes your husband.*"

I hoped she would go on. Not that it had anything to do with Ken Patterson's disappearance, but I wanted to hear what happened when her husband came home.

"Obviously, we never got in touch with her again. None of the others in our circle were dumb enough to do that in the first place."

I had no reason to ask but I did. "Is that when your marriage ended?"

"Not immediately. I confronted Bob and he confessed all, said he had been a fool, but I couldn't forgive him. He knew her game, yet he couldn't resist. Something inside me shattered. Nothing was the same after that. Eventually, he met someone at work who didn't hate him like I did. Adriana. You may have heard they had a whole other family." She took a sip of tea. "I guess I have always blamed Donna. If Bob and I had been on better terms, I doubt he would have fallen for that Adriana girl when she came along. But who knows? I've moved on."

I couldn't control my eyes. They traveled to the third finger of her left hand. A traditional engagement ring with a small diamond and a gold wedding band. Donna Patterson might have been able to make the excuse that she still wore her wedding jewels because she had a knuckle-full of precious stones. Sally could make no such claim. Her rings were plain. The lone diamond tiny. A sweet ring. A sentimental gift of a young man struggling to give a ring to the woman he loved.

I glanced around her living room and saw no signs of her having moved on. I'd bet anything that the furniture was from the years of her marriage. The family pictures on display still included Bob. He'd walked two daughters down the aisle. He held what I assumed was their grandchildren. He came to family birthday parties. Her family with Bob had been her life. She had to hate Donna Patterson.

"I never spoke to Donna again. Never saw her at least on purpose. We're talking thirty years. What am I saying? More."

"But you've run into her?"

"Rarely. From what I hear, we're both down the shore full-time, but I don't encounter her once a year. I bet I haven't seen her in two or three years. Have you?" Her tone was cheerful. "I hope she looks awful."

I shrugged. No need to rub salt in the wound.

Sally took a long drink and stared across the water. She wasn't going to say more.

After such emotional revelations, I hesitated to move on to the matter of Ken Patterson's disappearance, but the topic was better than Bob's second family. Then I realized I was the one who felt emotional. Mrs. DeMarco seemed ready to discuss other topics. "So, what did you want to know about Ken's disappearance?"

"How did Donna react?"

"I think she wanted to keep the story hush-hush at first. Nobody heard from her for a few days after the lawyer broke the news to her. Nobody knew what had happened, so it wasn't like anyone found it that odd. I believe she kept the news to herself until she could figure out how to present the situation and her position in it. When she surfaced she was going full-tilt for the wronged-wife role."

****Sally DeMarco****
Patterson House
Avalon, New Jersey
July 18, 1977

Sally didn't want to visit Donna, but the girls had agreed that they would drop by, one each day, to cheer her up. "Can you imagine how horrible she must feel? Being abandoned by her husband? Left with a child to raise? We would support you if that happened to you." *Sure, they would, but would Donna if the situation were reversed? She doubted it.*

Sally had expressed sympathy she actually didn't feel and agreed to drop by on Monday, the two-week anniversary of Ken's disappearance. She didn't share with anyone that she was happy for Ken. He saw an opportunity to get away from Donna and took it. She pictured him somewhere far away golfing, sailing, or even disco dancing.

Sally found his recent behavior and change in appearance ridiculous, but she understood its roots. She always felt the urge to rebel when Donna was around. If Donna said go, she said stop. If Donna said red, she said blue. Not that it mattered. In the end, Donna always got her way. She imagined poor Ken had to deal with the same behavior. Well, luckily poor Ken was anything but poor. He had the money to disappear and used it.

As she approached the big house in the dunes, Sally could hear the happy screams coming from the pool. Elisabeth with her friends. Unsuspecting. Unaware of the pain that lay ahead. What Ken had done wasn't fair to Elisabeth, but she couldn't imagine he wouldn't make arrangements to see his daughter in the future. He had always seemed like a decent father. She judged him by the depth of emotion that surfaced when his baby son died. Of course, no one ever really knows what goes on in someone else's house or head. God knows she never knew what was going on in Donna's.

When Sally walked onto the deck, Donna was stretched out on a lounge chair with a cocktail in her hand. At 1 PM. Afternoon drinking wasn't Donna's style, but if there was ever a time to pick it up, Sally figured this was it.

"So, is it your turn to babysit me?" Donna's smile was insincere, verging on hostile.

"No one wants you to go through this alone. You would do the same for us." Sally was not convinced the last part was true but the way Donna's expression softened made her feel she'd said the right thing, told the right lie.

Despite her drinking, Donna was perfectly groomed. Clothes pressed. Makeup on. Her hair was barely mussed by the gentle breeze blowing across the deck. Her sole concession to the situation she found herself in seemed to be a couple of broken nails, but even those she had filed into a neat curve. "Can I get you a drink?" Donna said but made no move to get up.

"I'll grab a soda from the fridge."

She held up her cocktail. "While you're there can you grab me another. It's getting hot out here," she said as if the sun and heat were the only reason she needed a drink. "The glasses are out. There's a pitcher in the refrigerator."

When she returned, Donna's glass was empty. She offered the replacement, and Donna reached for it with a badly bruised hand. A yellowing bruise so not recent. "What happened?"

Donna took a long drink before she held out her hand and studied it.

"I'm not quite sure. I hate to admit this, even though I had a perfect right to react as I did, I ripped through what was left of Ken's possessions throwing them into bins. I guess I was slamming doors and banging drawers, and after I finished I noticed this had happened. I guess I'm not good at losing control."

"So you got rid of all his stuff? That's good."

"Actually, I didn't. I let them sit for a few days and then I put them all back just as they were. He'll need them when he returns."

Sally didn't argue that she found it unlikely Ken would be back. Let Donna's fantasy get her through these times.

"Did you hear that bastard, Harris Meitner, helped him? He had the nerve to make nice with me at all those parties and the entire time he's helping Kenneth plot his disappearance. How irresponsible! He shouldn't have helped him. He should have taken Kenneth to a doctor, put him under medical care. He should have seen the man was having a breakdown." Donna took a huge gulp of her drink. "Does he think that a family's concerns are only financial? Do I care that Kenneth left me with enough money to live comfortably for the rest of my life? That is not what is important."

Sally listened and nodded although she had heard all this before. Donna had told her story to anyone who would listen, and her friends had compared notes at the yacht club over the weekend.

"You know when this breakdown is over, when he realizes what he has done, he'll be back." She turned to Sally and her eyes demanded that she agree. "You know that this is a temporary condition. He's been under stress at work lately. Taking on too many clients. Clients that are not our type of people. Remember, I told you." She gulped her drink. "That is not what I signed up for. I never would have married a criminal lawyer."

Sally recoiled when Donna sat straight and turned to face her.

"Do you think that was why he had to go? Do you think he was in danger? Do you think he didn't say a word to protect me and Elisabeth? The less we knew the better."

Sally knew she had asked all the girls these same questions. Like all of them, Sally didn't believe that explanation but saw no point in disagreeing. "I guess anything is possible."

"He'll be back. I am going to sit here and wait for him. If he isn't back by the time school starts, I'll go to our house in Villanova to wait. I mean what

if he has amnesia? When he recovers, he'll need to know where to find me. And Elisabeth."

Sally didn't have any response, but Donna did not appear to care.

"I'm prepared to wait for him. As long as it takes for him to get over this craziness. He will return. He will figure out how wrong what he did was. He will crawl home. And I will welcome him. I will help him recover. Because this is what a good wife does. I made a vow that I would remain faithful to him until death do we part and I will. I honor my vows."

*****

"Did you give any thought to foul play?"

"You mean that nonsense she said about unsavory clients? No way." Sally looked at me and read in my expression that was not what I meant. "Oh, you're talking about the bruise. Do you mean do I think Donna killed him? No." She drew the word out into five syllables. "Okay, it occurred to me at the time, but how would Donna kill him? How would she dispose of a body? Besides, his lawyer would have raised an alarm. Wouldn't he?"

I suspected she was reconsidering the possibility. I raised my shoulders along with my eyebrows to indicate I was open to the thought.

Sally said, "No way. Donna would never kill Ken," but she didn't mean it.

At least, she wasn't convincing me.

"I don't even think she wanted to. She wanted him to shape up, do things her way. She believed he would come around no matter how many times he told her no. She wouldn't kill him."

I repeated my shoulder/eyebrow-lift maneuver. Most people find it hard to believe anyone they know could kill, until someone they know kills. I let the thought hang in the air and pursued a different line of questioning. One more in line with my stated mission. I reminded myself that I was supposed to be searching for Ken Patterson not proving his wife killed him. "Did you like Ken?"

Sally thought long and hard before she spoke. "I didn't dislike him. He was a friend of Bob's. Part of the package. I never minded if he didn't come to some event, but I never complained if he did. He was kind of a blowhard, a name-dropper." She sipped her tea. "But one night, years before he left, when we were all on a ski trip, Ken and I were the last two awake. We were sitting outside by the firepit, drinking wine, and we got into this surprisingly intimate conversation. Nothing romantic, not even any suppressed desire. Just an honest conversation about life and what we wanted from it and what we were afraid we wouldn't get. Ken did most of the talking, not because he was overbearing, which he often was, but because he had the most to say."

She paused and I waited, hoping she would go on.

When she did, her voice was almost a whisper. "He seemed so sad," she shook her head as if still amazed. "I never would have guessed given his outward personality. As I said, he was a bit of a blow-hard, a big talker. He liked being the center of attention. On the one hand, he appeared sophisticated, but on the other, he was kind of corny." Her smile was affectionate. "If you do find him, don't ever ask him to tell a joke."

"And he changed?"

"On the surface. I never had another deep discussion with him. We never referred to the one we had that night, but I saw his outward changes as reflective of his inner battle. Doing what he thought he should vs. doing what would make him happy."

"What about Ken's new persona, his new self. Did he add any new friends?"

"I wouldn't know. Except for this girlfriend that Bob told me about. Beverly Glenn."

"You remember her?"

"Not her. Her name. Bob and I had a running joke. I'd go with him when he had to go to LA on business and whenever we drove by Beverly Glen Boulevard, Bob would make some stupid joke about how Ken would never pick someone up off just any street, it had to be in a nice neighborhood. I'm not saying we were funny, but it made her name stick in my head."

"That's amazing. After all these years."

"Not really. One of my daughters lives in LA off Beverly Glen. So, the name crosses my mind fairly often."

"Do you know what happened to her?"

"Not a clue. Sorry." Sally's expression supported her alleged regret.

"Have you ever seen her around Avalon?"

"I never saw her in the first place. You could be Beverly Glenn for all I know. I wish I knew more. I'm sorry."

Sally had nothing to be sorry for. "You've given me some useful leads."

She walked me down the steps to her front door. I sensed she didn't want me to go. She put her hand on the doorknob but didn't pull the door open.

"Can I confess something horrible to you?"

"Of course." I tried not to appear too eager.

"I wasn't quite straight with you." She lowered her voice to a whisper although I saw no sign of a neighbor. "For a while, I did believe that Donna killed Ken. I figured Ken told Donna he was leaving, and she wasn't having it. This was before…you know…the episode between Donna and Bob. At first, Bob didn't think I was serious. He saw our discussions as a joke. Our long discussions."

"About?" I prompted her.

"About how she did it. We figured poison. She'd never get her hair or clothes messed up." She glanced around nervously. "We even figured out it happened that night everyone talks about. We just couldn't figure out what she did with the body. Ken disappeared while Elisabeth was on a visit with Donna's parents on the Cape. That gave Donna plenty of time to take care of that problem."

"I would have wondered the same thing. Did you tell anyone? Did you go to the police?" I lowered my voice to match hers.

"We had no evidence. And then as time went by, people would tell us she made such a big deal for years of waiting for him, that he would come back. I don't think she even thought about having him declared dead, and I bet he had plenty of insurance."

"Unless she was afraid to invite an investigation."

"I suppose. She claimed she never moved so he could find her when he came back. Villanova in the winter. Avalon in the summer. She always professed to hate the shore house, to find it flashy, but she never left. Why else would she stay except to be there when he resurfaced?"

If she'd hidden the body somewhere on the property?

"Bob and I could think of one other reason. We thought she might have hidden the body on the property." Sally echoed my thought.

Why hadn't DeMarco mentioned that? Of course, he hadn't mentioned his attempt at a fling with Donna either.

"Do you remember the last time you saw him?"

"Bob?"

"Ken."

"Oh. At a Fourth of July party. We saw them twice that day. At their house in the morning and at the Bloch's in the evening. Aside from his ridiculous clothing, I don't remember noticing him." She described his red, white, and blue outfit slightly differently than her ex-husband had but the general impression was the same. "I remember he left early because Bob dropped him home."

A detail DeMarco had failed to mention.

"So, you didn't notice anything odd about Donna's behavior?"

"Again, Bob and I talked about it later. She never noticed Ken had left until Bob gave her the car keys."

"Was she surprised?"

"Yes. And it wasn't as if it hadn't happened before. Ken seemed to have a lot of legal emergencies. I can remember more than one time we had to give Donna a lift home, but this time he left her the car. It was kind of odd. It was kind of an odd night."

Yes, it was.

"Did she stay, or did she follow him home?"

"It's hard to recall from a party like that. Bob and I must have talked about it. I just can't recall."

The one thing I really needed to know, and Sally couldn't remember. At least, she claimed she couldn't remember.

"And you never heard anything about him in the years after he disappeared."

She shook her head and stared into the distance. "I never heard a peep."

"And your ex-husband never heard from him?"

"Not that I was aware of, but I only see Bob at weddings and funerals. Ken Patterson isn't on our minds. Even if Bob had contact, the topic would be unlikely to come up."

I thanked Sally DeMarco for her help.

"My pleasure, Kim. Very nice meeting you."

Chapter 21

"Is ABBA here?" Andy called as he climbed the stairs to the side deck where he found me stretched out on a lounge gazing across the thicket.

"They've been here all afternoon. Along with Donna Summer, Gloria Gaynor and the BeeGees." I hit the remote to shut the music off.

"You know there is an ocean out there to your left. Hear it? If you shift in your chair, you could see it. Why are you facing Dunsinane?"

"I think she murdered him."

"Who?" Andy leaned against the railing ready to listen. "Who got killed and who killed?" He held up a hand to indicate no answer was required. "Why did I ask? I can figure out that you are thinking Ken was murdered. You believe Donna did the dirty deed. Why this conclusion and why did it lead you to sit here?"

I waved towards the thicket. Nothing but a web of tangled trees and shrubs as far as the eye could see which, given the thickness of the foliage, was not that far. "I believe he is out there. I think she buried him in Dunsinane."

Andy didn't argue but neither did he agree with me.

"Want to hear my scenario? I found out today that Bob DeMarco dropped Ken off right out here at the bottom of our driveway and returned to the party where he gave the car keys to Donna."

"Do you know how long he was back at the party before he gave her the keys?"

"No. I don't, but I imagine he would have given them to her as soon as possible. So he wouldn't forget."

"An assumption but a reasonable one. Do you know how long the drive back to the party was?"

"Aha. You think because this happened forty years ago that I don't.

However, I asked Bob DeMarco about the party's locale. He remembered the hosts and knew where they had a house for years. So, I timed it. And don't ask me if I checked the speed limit from forty-some years ago. There are variables, but the ride took roughly six minutes."

Andy crossed his arms across his chest. "So, if you assume Bob went directly to Donna when he returned to the party you have to add five minutes for him to park and walk to the house. So even if Donna snatches the keys and runs out the door to the car parked right there she doesn't get home for another six minutes. That gives Ken a seventeen-minute lead. If I were going to disappear, I would be ready and packed to go. I'd be in and out of that house in under five."

"Not if there were a few items you wanted to take with you, items Donna would have noticed were missing. You'd take two minutes to walk up the driveway, one to open the garage, two to back the car out. That's five right there. You'd go in the house to grab what you'd left. That could take five." My eyes asked him to agree.

If he did, he gave no indication.

"Look, I accept that it's a close margin. Nonetheless, she catches him," I said.

"Okay," Andy said without conviction.

"She confronts him. Some sort of altercation occurs. She kills him, maybe by accident. Sally DeMarco said she had a bruise on her hand and a couple of broken nails. She is alone in the house but she doesn't have to rush. She has plenty of time to drag him to the freezer. Then, she takes her time disposing of the body. She had all winter. Does sandy soil freeze?" I didn't pause for an answer. "Even if it does, she had months of privacy before a freeze set in. I texted Abby to ask her to find out when the gate went in. I know the pool was installed before her grandfather left. I can only assume it's the same pool, but I asked. She's going to find out."

"With all this land why would she bury a body down near the road?" Andy made a good point.

"Why is the gate set so far back?" Not exactly an answer, but something to consider.

"My guess? To leave some spaces for parking so people don't drive up the driveway." Andy seemed to have an answer for everything. "That reminds me. I asked Marc Positano about the gardener. He requested that we ask them to park down by the gate." Andy leaned against the railing. "Ken was a big guy which raises two issues. Where did she hide him until the season ended, and I'm pretty sure you're going to say the freezer? So, let's go to number two. How did she get him to his burial spot?"

"Yes to number one. So let me take number two. She could have had an accomplice."

"Who?" Andy sounded skeptical.

"No idea. I am still fine-tuning my theory."

"And getting Ken into the freezer. How did she pull that off?" He shifted his weight and relaxed back onto the railing.

"She was alone. Elisabeth was away. She had plenty of time." I waved a hand to emphasize how easy that would be.

"Any idea who this accomplice was?" Andy asks good questions.

My imagination had been running wild on that topic. "I came up with two main characteristics of any accomplice. It's a basic assumption. He was strong enough to move the body. Possibly both in and out of the freezer. Aside from that, one, he had a boat or, two, he was a butcher or a surgeon."

"Given what you say about Donna's being a snob, I would have to vote for a surgeon, or even better a surgeon with a boat." Andy humored me.

"Good thought. If only I could find her with the Leica. I didn't understand why he wouldn't take his camera. That photo that Abby gave me did not come out of a Kodak Instamatic. I swear it is the picture Gerald said he took with Ken's Leica on the day Ken left."

"Which means someone got the film developed and it wasn't Ken." Andy got my point. "He could have removed the film, left it behind and taken the camera."

"I don't buy that. He specifically asked Gerald to take the picture. He wanted it. And, he was embarking on the trip of a lifetime. Why would he leave a camera like that?"

"Even if he did, I don't think that proves he was murdered." Andy said.

I didn't have an answer.

Andy crouched in front of me and stared into my eyes. "If you seriously think you are investigating a murder, don't you think you should have other suspects?"

"The obvious one is Meitner, his attorney, who could have set the entire plan up and then absconded with all the money. He had access. Because of what he said, no one searched for Ken. All the arrangements had been made."

"Anyone else?" Andy asked.

"I'm not buying the whole shady character bit."

"He did make a lot of money, fast, right?" Andy stood and rubbed his hands together as if we were lingering in sub-zero weather.

"He did, so of course, people would speculate about how he got so rich."

"Doesn't mean the rumors are true." He blew into his hands as if we were in the middle of a snowstorm.

"I'm taking a hard look at his friends. Bob DeMarco was the last one to see Ken alive. Robin Carson thinks he had the hots for Donna, but if that provided a motive, why kill Ken when he was going away?"

"What about girlfriends? Donna might not be the only woman scorned."

"I did get one name, but finding her might not be easy."

He clapped his hands together. "I hate to disturb you but do you think we could move this conversation inside. The sunlight is fading. I am getting cold and I'm starving."

Andy returned the chair to the front deck and met me in our kitchen area where I was pulling out all sorts of cocktail snacks. I handed him a bottle of wine to open. "Sorry to go on and on about Ken and Donna Patterson. How was your day?"

"Fine. Nothing new unless you want to discuss dialectical materialism."

"I am not quite sure what that is, but I am pretty sure I don't want to talk about it."

"So, what do want to talk about?"

"I want to whine on a different topic."

"Be my guest? Topic?"

"Abby."

"Go on."

"Today she dropped in on me while I was having lunch at the Princeton. She said it was a coincidence, but I suspect she's stalking me. I hear horrible things about her grandmother. I think Abby inherited some of her grandmother's worst traits."

"Examples?"

I went back to the beginning of my acquaintance with Abby and recited every insult or inappropriate remark I could remember. It took a while. Andy carried the wine, and I followed with what we were willing to call our dinner to the main seating area. He nibbled while I continued my list. I took a deep breath when I finished. "And now that I unloaded all that on you, I feel guilty. She is young and dealing with issues that a girl that age should never have to face."

"You are under no obligation to help her, but I think you are hooked. I mean, you did invest in that notebook."

"Everyone talks about how extreme Donna's reaction to her husband's desertion was but was it? Really? She did not make one attempt to find him. It appears she accepted every term he offered through his attorney. I don't believe we can learn that much more. I do not believe a man could vanish so successfully. No sightings. No contacts. No nothing. I didn't even uncover one rumor where someone thought they spotted him. Not one. Of course, I'm just getting started, but rumors spread. No one heard anything."

"Do you like Ken?" Andy reached for the photos on the coffee table.

"He's not likable. Actually, from what I've heard so far, he sounds kind of reptilian. He threw himself into the sexual revolution like one of those slimy characters you see in movies. Most of them working in gentlemen's clubs. Yet, there seemed to be a deep need underlying the whole personality transplant. He knew what he wanted." I turned my laptop to face him.

"What am I looking at?"

"Video of the day Ken Patterson died. I mean left."

Andy sat on the couch next to me and studied the video.

"I suspect I spotted him in the background before he talked. He was hard to miss."

"I guess women liked men in those get-ups back in those days." He shook his head. To indicate he didn't understand? Or, to shake the image out of his head? "Any particular love in his life?"

"I don't expect he always got names. Think seventies. Sexual freedom. The entire country seemed to act like teenagers on prom night."

"Got it. So Ken was really into the seventies."

"Watch his greeting."

On the screen, Ken spoke in a deep voice distorted by the old technology. "Robin, my man. So great to see you. Far out that all of us are here today. My brothers. By birth and by spirit." He flashed an exaggerated grin at the camera.

"And his wife?" Andy asked.

"I found her in here too." I waited until Donna appeared and then froze the screen. "His wife thought it was still 1955."

"They look badly mismatched." Andy kicked off his shoes, stretched out and propped his feet on the couch. "From what you say, I find it likely that he would want to disappear."

"But also, that she would want him to disappear if he wouldn't change. He embarrassed her."

"Did the police ever investigate Donna?" Andy asked.

"Not her. Not anyone. Technically, legally, he was never missing. He was simply hiding from his family, and he took more than adequate financial care of them, so no one went looking for him."

Andy lay his head back on the couch. "I'm listening. Just resting my eyes."

"Bob told me that men his age felt they had missed something. They were settled down and married when the sexual revolution hit. He said Ken believed if he had been a couple of years younger, his whole life would have been different. His friend Robin confirmed that idea. His brother said Ken was jealous that he was younger."

"So?"

"Ken wanted a different life. One that certainly didn't include Donna, one that didn't have room for a daughter. That was a horrible thing to do to Elisabeth. Especially from what Elisabeth told Abby. He gave her the impression he loved her, all the while he was plotting to abandon his family."

"You don't know what he was thinking. Or what he did after he left." Andy wasn't defending Ken. Just being objective.

"No, but I know what he didn't do. He didn't keep in touch with Elisabeth. He deprived her of a loving father."

"So what's your next step?" Andy asked.

"I found out the lawyer's name was Meitner and that his wife is alive. I'm going to see her. She lives outside of Philadelphia. I have an appointment."

"Don't you prefer surprise visits?"

Andy was right. I did, but I didn't want to drive to Philadelphia for no reason. I might risk a fruitless ride for a paid investigative job, not that I ever had one.

"I didn't want to make a visit at all. I called today and tried to talk to her on the phone, but she said she didn't know who I was. She wanted to see me. She also stated that she did not have her husband's files."

"Did you ask?"

"No. Maybe she was hoping that would put me off. She also made it clear that she will not be alone in the house with me."

"I can understand her concern. I worry myself." Andy plopped a cracker in his mouth.

I ignored him. "I need to move beyond his old friends. They all tell the same story. I need to find someone who knew the *new* Ken Patterson. From what Abby told me, before he left, aside from his lifelong love of the ocean, her grandfather liked disco and roller skating. I'd be fine if I could find a disco roller rink on a pier."

"Hmmm" was all Andy said. His eyes shut. Within moments, he was asleep.

I cracked the window on the side of the house so I could listen for Elisabeth. Andy was out cold for over an hour before I heard the low rustling of the wind in the trees disrupted by what I feared might be Elisabeth on one of her nocturnal walks. I stepped onto the deck and called her name. No response.

"Elisabeth? You need to come inside." I listened but the movement seemed to have stopped. Just to be safe I dialed Abby. I didn't have to explain what I wanted.

"She's in bed, but I'll check." Less than a minute later she added, "Safe and sound in her bed, but thanks for checking."

I was shocked at Abby's warm tone. I swore I detected a glimmer of appreciation in her voice.

I closed and locked the window. I covered Andy with a blanket and left him where he had fallen on the large sofa. I left a note on the coffee maker. PLEASE PICK UP SOME BEAR REPELLENT. WILL THAT WORK ON COYOTES AND FOXES TOO?

I wasn't thinking about myself. I knew enough to avoid predators. I wasn't so sure about Elisabeth.

Chapter 22

If Harris Meitner stole all of Ken's money, he didn't put it into his house. The Meitner home was lovely, in a neighborhood of split-level houses that, even at current prices, could probably be bought for far less than Ken Patterson left behind when he fled.

I assumed the woman standing in the doorway at number 402 was Leslie Meitner—either that or a model who had escaped from a Land's End catalog wearing sporty-grandmother clothes. She scrutinized me as I walked up the path. "Your name is?"

I told her.

"I've made a note on my calendar that you are coming and the number you called from. I noted your license plate number when you pulled up." She made it pretty clear that I'd be apprehended easily if I made a bad move. Apparently, it had occurred to her that I had come to kill her.

She didn't ask for identification, so I offered it.

"No need. I have enough. It's a beautiful day. I thought we could walk."

Smart woman. Unlike Sally DeMarco, she was not inviting a stranger inside her home. She closed the door leaving the two of us outside.

In sneakers, she was dressed for walking. In ballet flats, I was dressed for sitting. To me, she seemed to have an unnaturally fast gait as she led the way. I struggled to keep up.

"I guess you wonder why I agreed to see you."

"I did."

"I've been waiting for years for someone to come for information about Ken Patterson."

"So you have some?" I felt optimism sneaking into my attitude.

"Very little."

Pessimism started knocking any optimistic thoughts out of my head.

Mrs. Meitner continued. "I didn't want to talk to just anyone. Now that I can see you, you seem like a decent person. People say not to judge a book by its cover, but, in this case, that is my only option. Well, that and a Google search. I feel I can tell you what my concern was." She stopped abruptly and turned to face me. "Why didn't anyone ever try to find him until now?"

"I don't know. I've only met the family recently."

"And they asked *you* to locate him?" Her emphasis on *you* added a level of complexity to what appeared to be a simple question.

"His granddaughter did. Her mother, Ken's daughter Elisabeth, is slipping into dementia and she wants to see her father."

"But Elizabeth never tried to find him."

"I think his wife, Donna, controlled the situation."

"Ah, Donna. Harris, my husband, had steeled himself for an attack. He was dreading having to deal with Donna Patterson, but he never got a complaint from her. He heard through the grapevine that she trashed him horribly, but she never said a bad word to his face. Ken left during the summer, so Harris took the trouble to drive down the shore to meet with her. He said she followed every instruction. Very serious about the entire process. No emotion except haughtiness. She was always pretentious, and that didn't change when Ken left. She never tried to wheedle any clues about Ken as to where he had gone."

"And your husband knew?" I sounded as hopeful as I felt.

"Only the initial destination, which I did not know and still do not know. Harris would never break confidentiality, but I do know he changed his plans at the last minute."

"Do you have any idea why?"

"No. Harris kept a home office. One night he asked if we could delay dinner a few minutes because of a hiccup in the plans he made for Ken. He made a call, but I didn't listen. When he came to dinner he said it was just a hiccup."

A hiccup? "Did he say what it was?"

"He would never."

"Do you think Donna understood that when Ken left, he left town?"

"I assume my husband told her."

"Your husband had no idea where he went aside from that interim destination?"

"I never asked."

Not a direct answer.

Mrs. Meitner continued. "At that point, I still had somewhat of a superficial friendship with Donna. I wouldn't have wanted to know. I didn't want her trying to pump me for information. I rarely saw her after Ken left, but when I did she didn't even try to wheedle anything out of me."

She stopped walking. I read her facial expression as non-verbal hemming and hawing.

"Before Ken left, my husband asked our son to help him out with a case. My son was eighteen at the time."

I couldn't imagine what type of assistance he could have provided.

"Ken had a Porsche. A 911. A pricier model. He loved that car. So much that he never brought it to the shore. He didn't want it near the saltwater. I understand that when Donna returned to the house in Philadelphia, the car was gone. She called Harris. She wondered if Ken took it or if she should report it stolen. I didn't hear this from Harris. I heard it from the girls. You know, the wives. Our crowd."

What did this have to do with her son?

"The job Harris hired Sethie for, my son, was to drive a car to a boatyard in Maine."

"And you think he drove that Porsche."

"Sethie never flat-out told me, but he let some details slip. That he couldn't believe his father let him drive a Porsche. That he was really careful not to get stopped. That the hotel they put him up in was on the water right by the boatyard. Wasn't Maine a beautiful state? What would you think?"

I would have thought that Ken's lawyer hired his son to drive his client's beloved Porsche to a boatyard where he could sail to meet it. "The same as you, I'm sure."

At last, I had a clue as to where Ken had gone, but Maine was a big state. Big but beautiful. I wouldn't mind taking a ride up there, but only after our time in Avalon was done. But where would I begin? Would

Harris Meitner's son possibly remember where in Maine he had taken the car? What would it matter? Ken's plans had changed.

"So he planned to sail away to Maine."

"That was my assumption."

"But he changed his plans?"

"I have no idea what part of his proposed strategy he changed." She pulled her jacket tight around her. "It's getting chilly. I thought Spring had really arrived, but I guess it fooled us. As usual."

I accepted her claim that she knew nothing about Ken's destination and moved on. "From what I can gather, Ken never filed for divorce. Do you know why?"

"Again, confidentiality. Harris never told me what reasons he gave, but I can guess. Donna would not have agreed to a divorce. He would have spent years in court. We had mutual friends. Years after he was gone, Donna would tell them he was still her husband, marriage was for life. I didn't see her often but when I did she was never without her wedding rings. I heard that she would always give her marital status as married. I guessed that Ken had taken good care of her and somehow would retain more control of his finances if he didn't get the court involved. He simply wanted out."

"I am surprised she didn't talk to your husband about getting more money with or without a divorce."

"She got plenty. She probably could have gotten more. She certainly had grounds to file for divorce, but as I told you, she didn't want to. Her position was that he would be back."

"And she never tried to pressure you or your husband to tell her where he had gone?"

"Never. She just went along."

"Was that typical of her behavior?"

"Oh lord, no. She wouldn't even let someone pick a restaurant. I suspect she was in shock. She felt certain she had Ken under her thumb. I would have seen the writing on the wall. Most people would have. He changed. Anyone could look into the marriage and see that Ken was rebelling."

"But Donna couldn't see it?"

"My take? Donna thought she could control him, that he would do what she wanted. Even after he left, her only position was that he would realize he was wrong and come back."

"But she did nothing to make that happen." My tone asked for confirmation.

"Maybe she prayed. Rumor was she became extremely religious after Ken left."

"She'd never been that way before?"

"No. She went through the motions, but she was not devout. I guess she had everything she wanted. Nothing to pray for. But after Ken left? She was in that church almost every day. At least that is what I heard."

"How long had your husband been Ken's lawyer?"

"Ordinarily, he wasn't. Not until Ken wanted to arrange his separation."

Nice word separation. I would have said disappearance. Desertion. Abandonment of his wife and child, but I didn't interrupt.

"Harris was never his business lawyer. He never would have been."

"This might be a touchy subject but you said 'he never would have been.' Was he concerned about Ken's business dealings?"

"Let me put it this way. Some, not all, of his clients were not the type of people that Harris would have dealt with. He never would have partnered with them. Harris told me he was glad he knew Ken was alive or he might have thought that one of those guys had knocked him off."

Was my refusal to consider rough characters wrong? Why would it be when it seemed so obvious—at least to me—that Donna was the offender? "Do you have names for any of those people?"

"No. I only remember one because I found it horribly annoying that Harris would refuse to eat at certain restaurants owned by a celebrity chef, Malcolm Maturi."

Why interrupt the flow by saying I'd met him? I let her tell me.

"He was just getting his start. Everyone raved about his restaurants. He had about five of them across the Philadelphia area. I felt like an idiot. All my friends would recommend them, and I'd have to say that Harris refused to go."

"But he told you he was Ken's client?"

"It came out somehow when Ken wanted to take us to dinner at one of those restaurants and Harris refused. Ken was the one who said, 'But he's my client. He'll treat us like kings.' We never went. Harris claimed to know things. Turned out he was right, but Ken was long gone before Maturi's problems became public knowledge."

"Maturi's problems?" I was interested in hearing her version of what had happened.

"Financial chicanery of some sort. I heard he went to prison, but that was nothing compared to the mess with his wife. If you want to know about that incident, Google it. It's an old story, but I am sure you'll find the basics if you dig."

I wasn't concerned about gathering information about an event that happened years after Ken disappeared. "When Ken's plans changed after he left, you knew nothing of that?"

I studied her face. She was struggling. She had something she wanted to say. "Not officially. It is important to me that you understand I am not betraying a confidence. Not even after all these years."

"Of course."

"Let me give you the overview. Ken and Harris set up a plan. The day or two after Ken was supposed to execute the plan, Harris received a telex in his home office from Ken saying that plans have changed."

"A telegram?"

"Not really, but close enough. A telex was an electronic transmission. No signature. It's typed in somewhere else and prints out at your office. In this case, Harris's.

"Ken didn't call him?"

"No. A few days later a letter showed up at our home. Regular mail. No return receipt. Sent from Ohio. Harris explained that it outlined some changes that Ken wanted to make. Harris said it was no big deal that he decided to sell the boat and the Porsche."

"Which was then in Maine?"

"The car was. I have no idea where the boat was."

"And you think the telex wasn't really from Ken."

"I wondered."

"What did your husband think?"

"I'm happy to see the forsythia are blooming. I hope we aren't going to get a frost. I love what Harris and I used to call the yellow spring. Forsythia. Daffodils. Tulips." Her face relaxed into a smile. Remembering her beloved?

I hadn't meant to ask what her husband thought about spring flowers, and I feared that was going to be her only response.

After a few seconds, she returned to my preferred topic. "He found the requests within reason. He said the signature on the letter was clearly Ken's. Ken had a distinctive way of making a K and a P."

Which to my mind made it all the easier to forge his signature.

"He confided all this to you?"

"Not the substance of the correspondence. Just the news that he would be selling the car and the boat. He wanted to know if I wanted either one. I knew our son would want the Porsche, but he was too young. The last thing I wanted was a sailboat."

I couldn't formulate my thoughts quickly, but could this mean Ken was dead and Meitner was planning on taking the car and boat for himself? Leslie Meitner was staring at me.

"Did he sell them?" I asked.

"I am sure he did. He would do whatever Ken asked. It's hard for me to remember the details. This happened so long ago."

"Was your husband concerned about Ken?"

"He had to be worried, but he didn't admit it. Ken told him not to try contacting him, but that had always been the arrangement."

In that case, the situation did not seem so alarming.

"But he had to be somewhat worried if he even mentioned it to you."

"I don't know if he was, but I was." She stopped again and checked around her as if someone was within hearing range. No one was even within sight. "I understood Donna pretty well. I worried that she found out what he was planning and killed him."

Chapter 23

As much as I enjoyed painting Donna Patterson as a killer, I was supposed to be hoping that Ken Patterson was still alive. On the way back from Philadelphia, I took the exit off the Parkway for Sea Isle City. What harm could a detour by Gerald Patterson's do? I might get lucky and run into Ken.

Okay, I'll admit it. I drove through Sea Isle partially so I could report my action to Abby. Usually, I don't want to let family members down, but my motivation was different with Abby. I didn't want her to tell me I had let her down. I was letting her bully me, just as her grandmother had bullied her husband. I had to admit to a certain level of understanding for the guy.

Even as I came over the bridge into Sea Isle I had no idea what I was expecting. To find Gerald Patterson sitting on the porch with his long-lost brother, Ken? That would have been unlikely in seventy-degree weather, let alone on a forty-five-degree day.

I flipped on a baseball cap and slipped on sunglasses as I headed past 70th Street. "Well, I'll cut back this street to Central," I said aloud as I turned onto 76th Street as if I were making a loudspeaker announcement to the neighbors.

Gerald Patterson's car was in the driveway. A Porsche was pulled in behind not quite clearing the pavement. Two SUVs were in front of the house. One a BMW. One a Mercedes. All the other spots on the street were open, so I could only assume the cars' owners were visiting Gerald Patterson's house. I continued to Central and made a right. It was too soon to circle back so I headed into town. I did a drive-by to make sure the fudge shop had not decided to open unexpectantly. It had not, so I parked and walked up onto the Promenade to breathe some salt air and listen to the ocean on the far side of the dunes. Yes, I could do that at my own house, but old habits die hard. I love taking sentimental journeys—in this case back to my college years.

I took the sandy path through the dunes until I found a spot where I could stare at the ocean until enough time had passed for me to take another spin by 76th Street. My timing was perfect, or perfectly imperfect. Two young men, well young in comparison to Gerald, were walking down the path and waving to him. He was holding the storm door open and watching the two climb into their cars. One headed for the BMW. One headed for the Mercedes. I headed for Central Avenue. My stomach turned but I had nothing to fear. Neither of those men had seen me before. Gerald wouldn't recognize me or my car. Still, I felt panic. For no good reason. What had I discovered? That Gerald gets visits from young men with expensive cars. Neither of them was Ken Patterson.

I could circle again to see who got in the Porsche. On my second trip, I saw the Targa emblem but no one approaching it. Why would I waste more time?

Chapter 24

I was half-asleep when I heard footsteps on the stairs to the deck. Probably Andy. Lying on my back on a chaise that equaled the comfort of the furniture inside the house, I was too relaxed to worry about the Jersey Devil or even a bear emerging from hibernation. The air was a little more than chilly, and the wind was a lot more than a breeze. Definitely not yet deck weather, but I counted on some red wine to convince Andy to join me. I didn't even open my eyes when I called out, "Andy, I'm out here." I pulled the comforter up under my chin.

"How did you know it was me?" he asked.

"Who else would it be?" I opened my eyes and smiled.

"A bear?" He gave me a light peck on the cheek and perched on the edge of the lounger.

"Only if the bear drove up the driveway. I heard your tires on the gravel. Join me. You made it in time for the moonrise. Not a full moon but headed in the right direction. I put a quilt on that chair for you. There's a bottle of wine and a glass on the table."

He grabbed the wine and offered to top off my glass. "I'm actually drinking Coke, but it tastes better in a wine glass."

He filled his glass and settled onto the lounge. "Aside from the fact that the Coke will make you burp, this is very romantic."

"I know and wait until you hear what I found out about Malcolm Maturi."

"That is not very romantic." He adjusted the comforter and settled in.

"What I found is the opposite of romantic. Didn't you guys do a security check on him when he came to the Artistical Bahama site?"

"Based on your tone, apparently not an adequate one. Did you check out his background?" He sipped his wine.

"I was simply checking to make sure I knew what his career was about."

"And you found something else? Something juicy? What did you find? Am I about to find out that he did have shady dealings with Ken Patterson?"

"This has nothing to do with Ken Patterson. At least, I can't see how it could. Ken was long gone, or at least for a few years, when all this happened."

"All what happened?"

"Malcolm Maturi was suspected of killing his wife."

"Charged?" Andy sipped the wine and displayed no reaction to my news.

"Never. They couldn't find enough evidence. It's an old story, 1980, so there was limited info available, but luckily a few years ago some website did a podcast on the entire situation."

"I'm going to get a synopsis, aren't I? Let me prepare." He lay back. "Ready."

"So, Malcolm Maturi married his high school sweetheart right after graduation. A girl named Brenda. Sweet thing according to her friends and neighbors. Always supportive of Malcolm as he made it big around Philadelphia. He wasn't a national celebrity yet."

"Which is why we didn't hear about this even when we encountered him?"

"You mean investigated him? Good excuse, Andy, for hosting a wife-killer at the hotel."

"You said his guilt was never proven." he defended Malcolm Maturi. "I rest my case. Besides it isn't as if this story popped up at the start of your research."

"True. But listen this is an interesting tale. You see, his wife, Brenda, was sweet, nice, and pretty, but she didn't match Malcolm's new image. He was really hot stuff around town. Sophisticated. Brenda wasn't one for the nightlife. They had a baby girl, and she liked staying home with her. Which was probably good because whenever they went out, Malcolm would demean Brenda for her appearance. I saw pictures. She was still pretty, but a bit pudgy. Her clothes were slightly trashy. The two did not look like a matched set."

"Malcolm and Brenda?"

"Right. Rumor had it she was worried he was cheating on her or even worse that he was going to divorce her."

"Do we have any cheese?" Andy asked.

"In the refrigerator. And crackers. I got them at the Bread and Cheese Cupboard. I didn't have time to get to the grocery store." I didn't mention I hadn't located it yet.

Andy made no complaint. He was back in a few minutes with a nicely arranged plate of cheese and a bowl of crackers. "When I left Malcolm and Brenda were headed for divorce." He put a slice of brie on a water cracker and handed it to me."

I took a quick bite and got back to my story.

"They never had to get divorced because, conveniently, she died."

"I'm thinking conveniently is your word selection and that perhaps the cause was not natural."

"A robbery, and it was convenient. Friends and family said she would never let him have that kid."

"And, I bet, he would never let her have half of his empire," Andy added.

"They said that even more," I admitted.

"So assuming motive is not a problem, how did he pull this murder off?"

"Wait until you hear. Malcolm's business was flourishing. He got big on the charity circuit. So, he sponsors this big event out in Doylestown where they live. It's for some education fund, and they are giving tons of cash prizes. He has it all arranged with the bank to get the money ready, but low and behold, he gets delayed in downtown Philadelphia. So he asks his wife to do a simple favor for him. Pick up $10,000 in cash.

"In 1980? That was a lot of money."

"Exactly. So poor dumb Brenda…"

"Again, I assume dumb is your word." Andy popped some cheddar into his mouth.

"Okay, poor trusting Brenda, pulls into the bank, gets the money and starts her drive home. Little does she know that a *completely random* bank robber has noticed her taking out gobs of money and crawled into the backseat of her car—which she never locks because of their safe location. As the story goes, he held a gun to her head and forced her to drive into the country where he shoots her dead and takes the money."

Andy raised his index finger. "I have a question. The sarcasm in your voice when you say 'completely random' is yours?"

"I think the police felt the same way for a while, too, but it took them years to identify the shooter. Then, they could never find any connection between Malcolm and the killer, or I should say alleged killer. They only got him because he crossed his girlfriend who picked him up at the murder scene. She turned him in."

"That's why I never cross you. Never will."

"Very reassuring, Andy."

"Did they convict the shooter?" he asked.

"He was killed in a shoot-out with police when they tried to arrest him, not for murdering Brenda Maturi, but for murdering his girlfriend, which is what happened after she talked. She didn't have time to incriminate Malcolm."

"So Brenda Maturi's murder was never solved." Andy seemed interested.

"The cops had the girlfriend's testimony that the shooter had done it, but nothing tying it to Maturi."

"Why did the girlfriend nail her boyfriend but not Maturi?"

"Maybe she didn't know about him." That was the only answer I could come up with.

"Did she know her boyfriend had done the hit for hire?"

"It sounded that way." I thought back to the research I had done.

"But he didn't provide any details?" Andy shook his head. "I don't buy that. She picked him up after a job she knew was a hit.'

"So she said."

"Let's role play." He sat up and dropped his legs onto the deck so he sat facing me. "Let's say tomorrow morning over breakfast I say to you, 'I've got to go out tonight. I have a job.' What would you as the loving girlfriend of a contract killer say?"

"That's nice, honey. Will you be home for dinner?"

"You? I don't think so and not just because it would be unlikely you'd make dinner. You'd ask, 'what's the job?' We're having breakfast. You'd want to make some conversation."

"This scenario doesn't work for us because we never sit down for breakfast." I took a sip of Coke.

"Well, let's assume for once that we made an exception." He was determined to win his point.

I put myself in the mindset of a criminal's moll. I tried to think like a moll. "This job pay well?"

"I'd say so. Rich dude. Willing to pay. Wants his wife offed." Andy continued the act.

I shook my head. "I think you gave up the information awfully quickly. But I see what you mean. He wouldn't say an individual offed. A person offed. He would say his wife. So maybe she did know about Maturi, and he paid her off." I sat and faced Andy. "Assuming she knew the shooter did the hit for Maturi, she probably thought there was something to be gotten from the rich guy and she got it. He was making more and more money. When she went public and accused her boyfriend, she gave an interview saying she was so sorry she didn't come through sooner to spare that poor Mr. Maturi the pain of being falsely accused."

"And you bought that story?" Andy stared at me over the bottom of his wine glass.

"I didn't, but I bet you Maturi did. Literally. He paid for it. Apparently, the world at large believed her. Maturi became an innocent victim. The whole episode ended up helping his career. That's a pretty juicy story don't you think?" I lay back on the lounger.

"Yes, but does it have anything to do with Kenneth Patterson?"

"No, but it's a lot juicier than anything I can find about Kenneth Patterson. Although he did associate with a guy who killed his wife."

"Three years after he disappeared and after he was no longer Maturi's lawyer. He probably never knew. Here comes the moon." Andy was enthusiastic. "You can forget about Ken Patterson, and I can forget about school and totally relax."

"Absolutely." I wasn't ready to forget about Ken Patterson's association with the kind of person who would kill his wife, but I'd have to explore those possibilities later. I sat back and enjoyed the scene. For a moment. At least until the moon cleared the horizon. "Andy, you're a professional. If we rule out the freezer, where would you hide a body in this house?"

"This again." He sighed but played along. "Why would I hide it in the house when I had a huge body of water outside my front door?" He waved an arm at the Atlantic Ocean.

"Maybe you're not strong enough to get it into the water. And, putting it in from the beach, it could wash right back ashore."

"How big is the body?"

"Six feet or so. Muscular build."

He turned his head to stare at me. "Since we decided we were no longer discussing Ken Patterson this evening, I can only conclude that you're planning to kill me. Is that correct?"

"At the moment it seems unlikely, but I don't want to be unprepared."

"Smart. Preparation is key. Look." He rolled onto his side to face me. "I'm offering you an honest opinion. I'm not saying this because I am a potential corpse, but I can't think of a spot in this house unless a body was buried in the cement foundation when that extension went on."

"When was that?"

"No idea. The Positanos have only owned the house for three years. Before that."

"Forty years ago?" I asked.

"I guess it's possible, but I suggest that we not dig it up to check. I don't want to lose the security deposit."

"We didn't pay a security deposit."

"Still not a good idea." He leaned back and gazed at the moon rising out of the water.

"How about in the thicket?"

"That is dry sand, but it is sand. It's hard to dig a hole that doesn't fill up again."

"That might be helpful."

"But you also have lots of vegetation to deal with. I guess it could be done, but it wouldn't be ideal. You know what would be ideal?" He sat to face me. "Not killing your fiancé."

"But if I did and dumped his body in the thicket and no one noticed, there might be traces of him."

"We wouldn't be talking about a body dumped in the middle of a summer forty years ago, would we?"

"We haven't ruled out that someone could keep a body in a freezer for a short time and then in the off-season drag it into the thicket."

"I'm beginning to see a search in my future. What? To look for bone fragments? I hate to be a naysayer, but we cannot disturb those dunes." He relaxed onto his back. "Have you given any more thought to planning a wedding?" Andy asked.

"We haven't even been engaged a year."

"But don't most couples use that year to plan their wedding?"

"I want to enjoy being engaged." I held my hand up and admired my ring. "I thought we should wait until you graduate. That's what all the kids do. I think."

"And I certainly want to fit in with all the kids." He rolled onto his side so he could stare at me. "To tell you the truth, I'm more worried that I'll be mistaken for the father of the bride."

My friends find it odd that I find Andy Beck as cute years into the relationship as I did on the day I met him. His cool green eyes never changed, even if I could detect some fine lines around them. I hadn't spotted any gray hairs yet, but if I had, they wouldn't matter to me. "Even if you looked like the grandfather of the bride, I'd still be thrilled to marry you."

He smiled.

"This is where you say that even if I looked like the grandmother of the bride, you'd still be thrilled to marry me."

He smiled.

"Andy?"

"I'd be happy to marry you then, but do you think we could plan something a little sooner." The moment was sweet and romantic and interrupted by footsteps coming up to the deck. My eyes met Andy's. We both had the feeling we knew who the feet we heard belonged to. Andy held a finger to his lips to silence me.

I heard the ding dong of the upstairs doorbell. Then knocking. Then more footsteps.

"Here you are! I guess you didn't hear me." Abby pulled a chair from the table, plopped it down and sat on it replacing the view. "I was in the neighborhood, so I thought I'd stop by and see if you had an update for me."

"I am still talking to your grandfather's old friends. No one has heard from him since he left."

She opened her mouth to complain. She got out three words "I don't understand" before Andy jumped in. "Meg has been working her butt off for you this week. She had a nice leisurely vacation week planned, but she has been at it non-stop to find your grandfather."

"She hasn't found much though, has she?"

I jumped in. "But tomorrow is Saturday, and I've got a big day planned. Andy is going to help me."

That was news to Andy, but he played along. "Happy to get away from my school work."

"So, you won't need my help?" Abby didn't sound so much disappointed as doubtful.

"No. We have our day planned and two investigators are enough. We don't want to overwhelm people."

"Right. Because I can make myself available whenever you need me. My dad can watch over my mom."

"It's Friday night. You should go out. Have some fun.." I encouraged her.

"I would but all my friends are in the city or away at college." The first-rate manipulator looked to each of us in turn. "You guys are my best friends now."

"Can I get you something to drink?" Andy and I spoke in unison.

Chapter 25

I hoped something Bob DeMarco recalled from the night he drove Ken home would crack the case. I needed to press him harder. I should have hoped he would incriminate himself, but I was really hoping for dirt on Donna.

A good detective visiting Bob DeMarco might have gotten a phone number. As Abby would have been quick to point out, I wasn't a good detective. I might have countered that I was not, in fact, a detective. No matter. I didn't feel guilty. She got what she paid for. She got a lot more than she had any right to expect.

I called the number I found online. The DeMarcos still had a land-line. His wife answered and said he was at the yacht club. She didn't seem to care who wanted to know, but I explained who I was anyway. She still did not appear to care.

"The Avalon Yacht Club?"

"He used to keep a boat there. We're still members, but his sailboat is a bit big for their slips." She didn't seem ready to continue.

"So, is he at the Stone Harbor Yacht Club?"

"No, they have pretty much the same profile. He needed someplace with bigger boats."

Although she wasn't reticent about giving out information, she didn't seem ready to say where that space was.

"Ah. Where did he find a place?"

"Down near Cape May. The boat was in the slip when he bought it. He just kept it there."

"Do you have a name?"

"ME SAID LORDY."

"Could you spell that?" I thought I heard her say "ME SAID LORDY'." Turned out when she spelled it out, she had. "The boatyard is called 'ME SAID LORDY'?"

"Don't be ridiculous. The boatyard is Smitty's Marina. His boat is called *ME SAID LORDY.*"

"Do you have a cell number for him? I want to tell him that I'd like to drop by."

She gave me the number. I was wondering if I should ask for his PIN number next when she added, "Of course, he won't answer it."

"Any particular reason?"

"His boat is his castle. He always leaves his cell phone in the car."

I said, "Thank you" but I heard the click on her end before I finished the second word.

When I told Andy where I was off to, he dropped his copy of Hamlet and insisted on coming along. "We told Abby we'd be working together today. I'd hate to think we lied. Besides, there might be some clue about boats that I can help with." I suspected he had another motive. He always said he was feeling free without the burden of owning a sailboat. His had not survived Hurricane Freida. The truth? He felt lost without the *Maggie May*. And as the weather grew warmer, he would probably miss her more.

Having Andy along did come in handy. He was familiar with the boatyard which was not easy to find. At least by land.

Andy took a long time moving down the dock stopping to chat with owners spending the beautiful day getting ready for the season.

"We can chat on the way back," I said when he'd finished admiring a catamaran with the owner.

"I wouldn't worry about rushing. It isn't likely DeMarco is going out. What a treat to have a day like today to work on the boat this early in the year."

I heard the yearning in Andy's voice.

"I see him." I pointed out Bob DeMarco.

"Nice boat," Andy said, again with yearning.

"Bob DeMarco," I called from the dock.

He turned and raised a hand to shield his eyes from the sun and blocked my view of his reaction.

"Elisabeth Patterson's friend."

"I'm sorry. I don't recall…"

"Little Lisa's friend. Meg. Meg Daniels. I stopped by your house. Sorry to bother you again, but I had a question."

"Of course, Ms. Daniels. Come aboard. Nice to see you again." He seemed genuinely pleased. No fear. No anxiety. Not even a modicum of discomfort.

"This is my fiancé, Andy Beck."

"Nice to meet you." Andy followed me onboard.

Bob greeted him with a warm handshake.

"How long have you had this boat?" Andy asked.

"Forty some years now."

"This is a classic. You're not the first owner, right?"

"No. No. I'm not. The previous owner had it for about ten years."

He seemed uncomfortable admitting it.

"It's a beaut. Your name? An unusual name."

"I know. People ask me about it a lot. The previous owner named it. His story was he got a good deal and when he thought about buying it, he said, *lordy why not*? or *Me Said Lordy*."

"Well, you're a lucky man." Andy took it all in. "Thirty-five?"

"You got it," DeMarco answered. "Thirty-five feet of pure joy. Have a seat."

He cleared some tools off the bench to make room for us and placed them neatly in a toolbox that bore no resemblance to his car trunk. There was a place for everything and when he closed it everything was in its place.

"You've got some nice tools there." Andy nodded at the toolbox.

"I got lucky. The previous owner left everything. Everything was top of the line. For the most part, I still use the same tools. Added items as new technology came available, but the basics still work just fine."

Then the two of them chatted about DeMarco's boat for about fifteen minutes without a break. Without a break? Without a breath! I was interested for about five of those minutes.

I sat on the bench and watched the proud boat-owner give Andy a tour of the deck. He caressed the boom and the sails as if they were loved ones. Andy would follow suit with a gentle touch. DeMarco asked if I wanted to see the cabin, but I said the two of them should go ahead. At least on the deck, I had a nice view.

Hard to believe the man who owned the Mercedes with the messy trunk owned this truly ship-shape boat. At least it looked ship-shape to me, but I didn't have DeMarco's eye. As he came up the ladder from the cabin, he reached over and rubbed a spot at my feet.

"I should probably replace the decking. There were a few stains on it when I got her. I tried everything to remove them but figured I was making things worse." He leaned forward to trace a few spots at my feet with his finger. "All these years and they haven't completely faded. I've almost grown to admire them. If I didn't point this out, would you even notice?"

"Never," I feigned enthusiasm.

Although I tried to convey that sitting on a sailboat on a sunny day is not an unpleasant activity, Andy sensed I was growing bored. "But I should stop monopolizing your time. We came here because Meg had a question." He turned towards me to direct DeMarco's attention my way.

"Sorry. I get carried away." He flashed his signature wide grin.

"No need to apologize, Bob. I am still trying to help Elisabeth Douglas, you know, Elisabeth Patterson. I was wondering why you didn't mention that you drove Ken home from the party on the day he left."

He screwed his features to display confusion. "I told you he left, right?"

"So what happened?"

"Nothing happened. I drove him home in his car. I dropped him at the foot of his driveway. Never saw him again."

"Did he give any indication he was going away?"

"You mean like a long, sentimental goodbye? No. He said thanks mate, told me to give Donna the keys and said 'see you on the flip side.'" DeMarco used air quotes to emphasize the way Ken said goodbye. "He did not tell me there would be no flip side."

"And what happened when you gave Donna the keys?"

"She wasn't too happy with me. Not about the keys. She was furious that Ken left without telling her."

"What did she do? Did she stay until the end of the party?"

"I don't remember. I am sure I avoided her all night."

"But you don't recall seeing her?"

"I can't say I remember running into her again, but that was a very long time ago. My memory is not what it once was."

With that information, I was ready to go, but we had a long goodbye because DeMarco and Andy had to have a detailed discussion about spinnakers. I tried to appear interested but I was dying to get back to the car. Once I was safely inside, I dug in my handbag for my notebook and recorded my thoughts.

"It's an anagram."

"What is?" Andy asked.

"*ME SAID LORDY.* While you two were chatting, I had plenty of time to figure it out. There had to be more to that weird name for a boat." I held up the paper. "Me Lisa Roddy. The names of the two Patterson kids. Lisa was a nickname used only by her father and his friends."

"I didn't know there was a boy."

"He died before his first birthday. The fact that Ken remembered him and included his name changes my image and my opinion of him. I had viewed him as heartless, but he remembered."

"Or so you think." He stared for a minute to make sure the anagram was correct. "It could be a coincidence."

"Really?" My tone told him I did not agree. "The weirdest name ever for a boat."

"So you think this is, was, Ken's boat."

"I feel certain. Abby told me he had a boat named the DonnaLisa. If he was going to disappear on it, he had to change the name."

"Whoa, that's bad luck," Andy said.

"Maybe something bad made him change his plans."

"I think you're onto something. Any idea what it is?" He asked.

"Bob DeMarco knows a lot more than he's saying about Ken's disappearance. He bought his boat. Did he say anything to you about the previous owner other than he selected the name?"

"Only that it was a friend. Do you want to go back and ask him?"

"No. I don't want to alert him that I think it is an issue. I need to figure out a way to run into him. Casually. Subtly. Subtlety is my specialty you know."

Oddly, Andy didn't answer.

Chapter 26

On the way north, I convinced Andy to ride by the address I'd gotten for Beverly Glenn, now Hines according to her social media. Well, *some* Beverly Glenn's social media. I was convinced I'd identified the right Beverly Glenn.

When we arrived at the house in a development off Route 9, I saw that we had gotten lucky. Beverly, at least this Beverly, was hosting a garage sale. Actually, a house sale. Buyers were free to roam anywhere they wanted through the house and property.

"I see a pretty nice collection of vinyl over there. I'm going to have a look." Andy went to check out the records leaving me beside a lifetime supply of porcelain figurines.

"I'll see if I can locate Beverly," I called after him.

"You looking for Beverly?" a woman manning the payment desk asked. "She's inside."

I thanked her and headed through wide double doors to a linoleum-floored entrance hall that might have once been lit by a since-sold chandelier. All that remained were some dangling wires.

Stepping from the bright sunlight to the dark interior left me stunned and unable to see beyond a swath of light on the bright blue carpet ahead. As my eyes adjusted, I saw that time seemed to have stopped over thirty years ago inside the Hines home. The furniture, what was left of it, was dark and heavy with the formal style of an English manor house. Quite the style in the 1980s. I wandered through a mostly empty living room. In the dining room, a couple argued if they needed a complete set. The wife was arguing that the furniture would not look so dated if they painted it. I didn't see anyone browsing in the kitchen, but the arrangement of the utensils, dishes, and cookware suggested that early shoppers had made a considerable number of purchases.

I walked down a hallway and peeked into the bedrooms still decorated in 1980's Laura Ashley. Each room had a different border. Pink. Lavender. Blue. Green. Some of the bedroom furniture had been sold, but there were a few pieces as well as bags of linens left.

I heard Beverly Glenn before I saw her. At least, I assumed I was listening to Beverly Glenn's voice carrying from the room ahead of me which I expected to be the master bedroom.

"I hate to give up this house. Marty and I had a wonderful life here. We used to give quite the party. In the seventies, we were a bit on the wild side, but in the eighties? Oh those parties were elegant. I'd offer you Marty's tuxedos—they were classics—but I didn't keep them after he died. It was too painful to see them every day. Plus, I could never put a price on his possessions."

I stepped into the room and found a couple in their forties backing towards the door. The woman looked at me as if I were a flotation device that had been thrown to her before she went under for the third time. The petite woman doing the talking, the woman I assumed was Beverly Glenn, didn't notice the woman's expression or my arrival.

"In his last years, Marty and I stayed here all year. He died right in this room. Right in that bed." She stared at it and tears rose in her eyes.

Scratch that sale.

"You two should value every moment you have together. Make memories. One day that is all one of you will have."

The woman's face suggested she made enough memories with Beverly Glenn, but the husband remained locked in the conversation. Well, the monolog.

"He was a great husband. I was so lucky to find him. Actually, he found me."

The story went on, but I tuned out and checked out the master bedroom and the items for sale in it. The room appeared to be the only one that had been updated in the last few decades. The remaining furniture, two bedside tables, one bureau and, of course, the bed where Marty had died, huddled together along one wall. Sliding glass doors with access to a pool and patio covered most of another wall. The doors on the long closet lining the opposite wall were pushed back to provide a view of gorgeous party clothes indicating an exciting social life, at least until the nineties. Slinky seventies outfits. Puffy-sleeved eighties ensembles. Then nothing.

I wondered why.

A woman walked up behind me. "I was a tiny little thing."

I turned and found the chatty woman who was, to my mind, still a tiny little thing. No more than five-three without an ounce of fat to be seen.

"I hoped I could salvage some of those outfits from the seventies, but I seem to have thickened somehow. Same weight just not in the same places. It's a shame. I'm moving to a cruise ship. I figure there will be some social life there. If not and the situation gets too bad, I'll throw myself overboard."

"Are you Beverly Glenn?"

"Yes. This is my house." She leaned in to stage-whisper in a conspiratorial tone. "I am not seriously contemplating jumping overboard. To the contrary, I am hoping to have some wonderful times. A merry widow." A look of horror crossed her face. "I don't mean to say I wasn't happy being married. I was. But now that I am single, I need a little more excitement."

"I hope you find it. *I* was hoping to find you."

Oddly, she did not appear surprised.

"I've been asking around to see if anyone has run into Ken Patterson lately."

Bemusement. That was what spread across her face. No shock. No fear. Just bemusement. "If by lately you mean the 1970s, then yes. If you mean this century, then no. Why on earth would anyone be looking for him? How did you ever find me? Who told you to talk to me?" She hurled questions at me in rapid-fire succession.

"His granddaughter is feeling sentimental. She wants to learn about her family."

"So why are you helping her?"

Because I'm a sap. "In the past few years, I've had some luck researching old stories. She came and asked for my help."

"I can't see why she'd want to learn more about him. I only knew him for a short time, but he was kind of a jerk."

"Oh. I thought you were involved with him."

"I was. I was involved with more than a few jerks in those years." She shook her head as if disgusted, but I caught the hint of a smile on her lips. "But then I met Marty and everything changed. I had him for a lot of years. I miss him. I think I always will." I saw tears welling. Maybe she was not the merry widow she hoped to be.

"Anything you can tell me about Ken might help."

"This is not the kind of stuff a granddaughter would want to hear, but I'll tell you if you want. You're not his kid or anything?"

"Total stranger." I raised my hand as if swearing an oath.

"I guess it's okay then. Back in the seventies, I'd seen him around for a few summers. He looked like just one of the husbands, one of the straights. Straight meant something different then. Not hip. Not with it. I was a party girl. I could tell he had money and probably a wife. I wasn't interested. I only wanted to have fun. But then I met him when I was out dancing one night."

****Beverly Glenn****
Wildwood, New Jersey
July, 1975

Closing time was getting closer. She'd had a few dances but not with anyone she wanted to end the night with. Then, she felt his gaze. She let her eyes meet his but turned away quickly. Even in the dim lighting, she recognized him. She knew he was the same guy who had approached her before. Not in this club. Not this year. Last year. Maybe the year before. In Fred's in Stone Harbor. Looking like the straight he was.

Now it appeared he had caught up with the times and finally figured out what the seventies were about. At least his style had.

She knew before she glanced back that he was still eyeing her. She felt his stare. He was coming on to her. Again, she turned away, but her smile suggested she'd be looking his way again.

He'd let his hair grow both on his head and on his upper lip. He'd updated his clothes. Tight pants flared at the bottom. Tight shirt in loud colors. Gold chain. He looked kind of ridiculous but maybe because she had seen him before. The preppie had turned into this hip-looking guy.

He was younger than she'd thought. Nowhere near forty. He still had at least ten years on her, but he was a nice-looking guy and, she suspected from previous years, had money. A lot of money.

She lowered her head and gazed up at him with eyes that invited him to move down the bar. She flashed her most seductive smile. She thought the look was kind of ridiculous, but men went for it these days.

He moved next to her, just a little too close. Their arms weren't touching but that was a technicality. They were drawn together, generating heat.

"I've seen you around here before." He wasn't making a simple observation. She understood what he was really saying. I wish I had spoken to you before. I am happy to see that you are here tonight. I am going to invest all my effort in bedding you. *That's how it was in those days. Flirting felt like a commitment. If she was going to reject him, she should do it now.*

Instead, she smiled up at him. "I've seen you before. At Fred's in Stone Harbor. A couple of years ago. You've changed."

"I've wised up." He leaned closer. "Can I buy you a drink?"

"I've got one thanks, but I'll be happy to drink it with you."

He took out a five-dollar bill and waved down the bartender. He ordered a Coke. A Coke?

"No rum? Just Coke?" She asked.

"Well, the DJ plays until 2 AM, and I want to make sure I have the stamina to keep dancing. Do you think you can keep up?" He bounced on his feet and moved his head in time to music.

She turned to face him so her breasts brushed his arm. "I can keep up."

He downed his Coke and took her hand. "Let's see what you can do."

She followed him onto the dance floor and stayed with him through five disco beat dances. He hadn't lied. He was not only a great dancer, but he also got lost in the music.

When The Hustle came over the speakers, they parted for a line dance. She followed his lead. The song and the craze were brand new, but he had mastered all the moves. He looked so spirited she sometimes wondered if he remembered she was there, but as the song drew to an end, he pulled her out of the line and held her close. Frankie Valli came over the sound system singing "My Eyes Adored You," He stared into her eyes. "My name is Ken and I believe I could adore you."

*****

"Corny, I know, but effective. Made an impression, I tell you. I still remember the entire night. He took me home. I figured we'd had a great one-night stand, but he kept coming back. I thought it was a summer fling. Then, vacation season was over, but we kept seeing each other in the city. He spent plenty of money on me. Wined and dined me. I knew he was married, but I wasn't looking for a relationship."

She pulled a slinky gold jumpsuit with sequined trim from the closet and held it in front of her to check herself out in the mirror. "I mock his outfits, but back then I made some daring wardrobe choices myself. We looked great together. Mutt and Jeff. You know them?"

I shook my head.

"Cartoon characters. One was tall. One was short. Just like Ken and me." She put the outfit back in the closet. "Ken's wife hated everything about his new style. He told me that he kept his clothes in his office in Philadelphia and in his car when they were at the shore. When he grew his hair, he couldn't hide his change from his wife anymore."

She held up what appeared to be an orange tent with turquoise and lime accents. "This kaftan would fit you."

If she let down the hem, it would have fit Babar.

I had no idea what she saw on my face, but she reacted. "No offense. You simply have a bigger frame than I do."

"It's great. I wish I had somewhere to wear it."

She shrugged and hung the dress back in the closet. "Ah right. Ken Patterson's clothes. "His wife…."

"Donna," I interrupted.

"If you say so, Donna wouldn't be seen with him in them and probably would have thrown them out if she found them. She was preppy. I saw her a couple of times. Nice jeans. Sweater with those rings around them, you know?"

I didn't know.

"Some Scottish style. Anyway, trust me. Sweaters with turtlenecks underneath. She loved turtlenecks even in the summer. She couldn't handle Ken's transformation. Or match it. She presented not one ounce of sex appeal."

We moved aside to provide two teen-aged girls with access to the slinky seventies outfits in the closet. The girls giggled with glee as they made their way down the rack. I wasn't sure if their admiration was sincere or not. By the expression on Beverly's face, she was wondering the same thing. "I had some great times in that purple outfit." She pointed the girls to one of the more garish selections. "This would be fabulous with your black hair."

The girls giggled as she took it down from the rack. I waited for the worst but then Beverly held the jumpsuit in front of the girl with a body that matched hers. "Look in the mirror." She pointed to a standing mirror with a price tag of five dollars. When the girl asked the price of the outfit, Beverly showed them the tag. "Fifteen dollars. You can pay at the door."

"Groovy," the raven-haired girl said. "Did you say groovy back in the day?"

"Not so much," Beverly smiled. "Although that outfit is, in fact, quite groovy." She looked at the taller blond girl. "I'm sorry, you have four inches on me. My shoes will be a little small for you, but maybe you can find a handbag." She pointed across the room.

"Oh my God!" the dark-haired girl cried out, "shoes," and followed Beverly's directions.

Beverly and I stepped out on the patio to give the girls room to browse racks of footwear from platforms to spike heels.

"Have a seat." Beverly pointed to two chairs that I assumed had at one point been pulled up to a table beside the pool. "Although I might have to ask you to stand. I'll sell that chair right out from under you."

I settled onto the dining chair and Beverly continued her story.

"This is awful but to tell you the truth, I didn't like Ken that much. But," she dragged the word out, "he had a lot to offer. Dinner in New York. Weekends in Vegas. Weeks in Hawaii. We had an arrangement for a few years. I was sorry to see it end."

"Did you end it or did he?"

"I guess he did. He just disappeared. The kids call it ghosting. Had a fun night and then I never heard another word."

"What did you think?"

"I figured his wife murdered him. The way he talked about her. She was one cold bitch."

"Did he seriously think she might kill him?"

She laughed. "That was a joke, but she was capable."

"You thought it was possible?"

"He would tell me stories. She wanted a lifestyle. Not a husband. She got a lot more than she bargained for when he made it so big. She was perfectly happy as long as he behaved. Poor guy didn't wanna behave."

"Did the police investigate?"

She shrugged. "No one talked to me. I heard he left town. We didn't travel in the same circles, but some acquaintances caught rumors." She paused. She was holding back. "He liked to fancy himself as kind of an operator. A wise guy. Not on a big mob level, but I think he enjoyed being around tough guys. Not rough. Hotshots. High rollers. I sometimes wonder if he had to leave town."

"Did he ever mention any of those guys by name?"

"No. Only that chef guy. He was a real hotshot at the time. Ken took me to a couple of his restaurants. Thought he'd impress me that he knew the guy. You know, the one who was accused of killing his wife."

Suddenly everyone mentions the wife. "Malcolm Maturi?"

"Yeah. That's the guy. He's still around. Career shot up like a rocket. Big deal. Ken loved showing off that he could get a table at any of the kid's restaurants. They were all local at that point. Around Philadelphia. Eventually, he went national. Great looking guy. Charming, too. I can't believe that they thought he killed his first wife. It was a big story. You're too young. To my knowledge, he was never charged but there were rumors. More than rumors. The press was all over the story, but it never held the kid back. Probably helped his career. Poor single dad falsely accused."

"What did Ken think about it?"

"Ken was long gone. And well rid of Maturi. The guy did time later for some sort of financial crime, but he wormed his way back into the public's good graces. Not sure how exactly. Shifted blame. Played the victim."

"Do you think Ken was murdered?"

"By Maturi?"

"By anyone."

"That would be too big a coincidence. Not that he ever told me, but the rumor was that he had cashed out quite a lot before he disappeared. Made some elaborate plan. Left his wife and kid well provided for. I didn't hear all that much. We didn't know many people in common. But what he did wasn't cool. He had a daughter. I'm not sure if the cops got involved." She chuckled. "Once they met the wife, they probably would have figured that's what they would have done. Although I would have thought he would have said goodbye to me."

"And you never saw him again?"

"Nope. He got up one morning, and by morning I mean 3 AM, and left as if everything was normal. Fourth of July. I never expected to see him on a holiday. He had to be with his wife. Then, he vanished." She smiled at shoppers roaming around the pool. "Bedroom stuff is through that door." I worried she would not continue, but she did. "I thought I saw him once." She seemed reluctant to explain. "Not that long ago."

I kept quiet waiting for her to speak.

"I was probably wrong."

"Where?" I was going to have to push for this.

"My husband flew. A small plane. When he died, I wanted to sell the plane. A guy called about it, even before I placed it with a broker, and he came out to see it. He kept asking if I would be the one meeting him."

"And you thought it might be Ken."

"No. That never occurred to me, but something was not right about the transaction. Not just because the guy didn't buy the plane, but that he came to look. I know nothing about planes, but enough that I realized there were some basic questions a buyer should have asked. How many hours on the engine? Has it been hangered? This guy didn't have a clue about planes. He was not who he said he was. He wasn't Ken. I was sure of that, but he got a ride with a friend who never got out of the car. He pulled up to the gate where he could see the plane and just sat there. Sunglasses. Baseball cap. Not odd-looking at all, but I felt as if he was watching me. And for some reason, I thought of Ken."

"Did he look like Ken?"

"Not particularly. I mean, we're old now aren't we?"

"The guy looked your age?"

"Yeah. Maybe a little older. Definitely not younger."

"I don't understand why you thought he was Ken."

"I'm a little psychic sometimes."

As much as I didn't want to believe her, I had to admit that sometimes I felt a little psychic myself.

Chapter 27

"What's in the bag?" Andy asked.

"I bought some kitchen utensils."

"Why on earth would you buy kitchen utensils?"

"I felt I had to buy something." I eyed a new collection of vinyl records he was loading into the back of his car. "But I can see you took care of that." My cell rang. "Abby," I mouthed as I picked up.

"My grandmother is going to lunch. She left our house a few minutes ago." Abby's tone was conspiratorial.

I felt the same urgency I heard in Abby's voice. "Where is she going?"

"The Princeton."

"What is she wearing?" I asked just in case I had observed the wrong woman at mass.

"She just stopped by. Pantsuit. Navy. Blouse. White silk. You'll recognize her by her Bottega bag. You know Bottega?"

"I do." Long ago from personal experience and recently from my work with celebs. I ended the call and turned to Andy. "So, do you want to have a bite to eat before we head home?"

Andy checked his watch. "I'd like to do some schoolwork this afternoon." He stopped as if shocked by his own words. "Who would have dreamt I'd be talking about doing schoolwork again. If I had said those words twenty years ago, I wouldn't have to be saying them now. I was hoping to take you out tonight."

I explained that there was more than food at stake. "We don't have to linger. I may never have another chance to get a look at Donna. I won't talk to her. I want to see her in action."

Andy didn't question why I believed that was important. He drove to Avalon and found a space across from the Princeton Inn facing the 9/11 memorial.

I ran into the dining room to check. I took a glance around and saw a variety of diners. Donna wasn't one of them.

"I gather Donna Patterson is not in there," Andy said as I climbed back into the car. "Was Abby sure about this?"

"She seemed to be. Maybe Donna made a stop."

"What kind of car does she drive?"

"You think I would have asked, wouldn't you?"

A few minutes later, Donna Patterson parked her car across the street from us and climbed out of a silver/blue BMW. At least, I assumed I was looking at Donna Patterson. If not, I wasted my time recording her license plate number in my notebook.

"Let's go." Andy was ready to join in the game. He grabbed my hand and led me across the street and up the stairs to the hostess stand. "Table for two."

"Could we have that table?" I added and nodded at a table close to the booth occupied by two attractive women in their seventies. One was the woman from early morning mass, the same woman who drove the blue BMW. She wore a blue pantsuit and tucked a navy Bottega bag on the seat beside her. Undoubtedly Donna Patterson. Besides, even though the face had thinned and life had etched fine lines around her eyes and mouth, the face was easy to identify from the 1970s photos.

I didn't know what my stereotype of a 77-year-old woman was, but Donna Patterson did not fit the mold. Seeing her up close, she appeared at least ten years younger than her age. Her clothes and hairstyle were a lot more stylish than mine. She had forty years on me, yet she wore heels on a Saturday that I wouldn't have endured at the social event of the decade. If I were ever invited to the social event of the decade. As I had been warned, she looked perfect.

I tried to be subtle as I observed the woman and her friend. Donna was seated so that I could check out her left hand. The cluster of diamonds I had noticed at church proved impressive. It took a few stolen glances to conclude I was looking at a tiny solitaire diamond, a huge solitaire diamond with two smaller side diamonds, and a band of moderately sized diamonds plus a few spacers. I concocted a story that the tiny solitaire was the original engagement ring that a young Kenneth had presented to her. I was surprised she still wore it since it appeared the successful Kenneth had replaced it with something far more impressive. Maybe she did love him. I reminded myself, people kill those they love.

"I am trying to do the table assignments. Can you help?" Her friend unfolded an oversized sheet of white paper on the table.

"Of course," Donna laughed. "You know I have the best understanding of what's going on in that crowd."

"So, here's table two. I put you at table one with us."

"Why Marjorie that is so kind of you." Donna sounded almost nice until she added, "Thank you for sparing me." She gazed at the diagram and jabbed her finger onto what I was assumed table two. "They don't like each other, and I can see why."

"Should I move them to another table?"

"No. Let's put them together. We don't like either of them."

The two women laughed. It was easy to see what they had in common. I glanced across the table at Andy, but he was engrossed in the menu.

"The rest of the table meet with your approval?" Marjorie asked.

"Kathy will drive Alice nuts. I call that a win for us."

Again, the two women laughed. I kicked Andy under the table. He looked up assuming the blow was accidental but when I nodded my head to the left, he caught on. He was discreet, but listening.

Table 3. Bores and braggarts.

Table 4: Wannabees and climbers.

And so it went on. Each table populated by guests that Donna and her friend disdained.

"Psst." Andy caught my eye. "Your eyes are shooting daggers at her."

I nodded. I was trying to be subtle but finding it hard.

Unless we missed something said while we were ordering, Donna and Marjorie had nothing positive to say about any of the guests. Andy's eyes met mine occasionally to confirm we were hearing the same thing until the waitress returned with their order. Marjorie appeared satisfied with her food, but Donna found no more to like on her plate than she did on the guest list.

"Look at this. They call this a sandwich? This is a disgrace." She lifted the top of the roll and dropped it onto what appeared to be a pile of crab cake. "Can you imagine?"

I could. It looked fine to me. Tasty actually. But Donna waved at the waitress as she brought us our drinks.

"Waitress, over here. This is horrible." She went through a list of the sandwich's shortcomings, jabbing her crooked finger into every item on the plate with the same energy she had attacked the seating chart. Finally, she leaned back in her chair and pantomimed a gesture to sweep away the plate. "Just bring me the soup and a roll with butter."

Donna and Marjorie devoted the few minutes until her soup arrived to discussing the shortcomings of the meal. Then, they returned to gossip. This time at table twelve. "I never thought Tad and Jackie should have married in the first place." Donna was the ringleader. Marjorie didn't seem as pleased about the end of that marriage or any of Donna's nasty observations.

"Donna, you are an attractive woman. You look so great for your age. Much better than Jackie." Of course, she had to make a comparison not to make Donna feel good as much as to denigrate their *friend*. "I am sure you could find someone for yourself if you made the effort."

"I have someone. You know how I feel."

"But someone real. Someone here to help you."

"I'm still married."

"But when you gave up those houses, I thought you gave up waiting for Ken to come back."

Donna took a big bite of her roll giving her time to think as she chewed it. "I figure this is the time he might try to come back. He's old. Probably decrepit given his lifestyle. This is when he'll figure out he needs me."

"What would you do if he showed up on your doorstep?"

"He's my husband, Marjorie. What can I do? I will take him back. Of course, I will. That's really why I sold the houses. Neither of those places would have worked, you know taking care of an old person."

Andy's eyes met mine across the table. I'd known him long enough to recognize that the slight raising and dropping of his shoulders meant he believed her. The twist of his mouth indicated her explanation seemed reasonable to him.

I wasn't prepared to view anything Donna Patterson said as reasonable.

Chapter 28

I protested that we had a big lunch, but Andy was determined to take me out to a special dinner. He gave no hint what special meant.

When I heard gravel under our tires, I suspected we had arrived at our destination for dinner. "This must be some special restaurant." I held my hands over my eyes as Andy instructed.

"I found this surprise for you, and I didn't want to let it wait." Andy pulled the car to a stop. "Okay. You can uncover your eyes now. Here we are." He sounded proud and happy.

"Oh my God, Andy. How did you find this place?" I stared at the lights forming an arch above a double door.

"They invented this thing called the Internet. I opened up Google and typed in Roller Disco New Jersey. And, voila."

The long, low building reverberated with a disco beat. Through the opaque windows, I could see the flashing of red and blue lights. I couldn't believe such a place still existed. I couldn't believe I was going to be inside *Dolly's Roller Disco*.

Clearly excited, Andy jumped out of the driver's seat and ran around the front of the car to help me onto the rough surface.

"Andy, this is perfect."

He briefed me as we walked across the parking lot. "I was looking for a roller disco as a goof, to get you in the 1970s mood. I couldn't believe I found one although they only do pure disco on Saturday night."

"Pure disco?"

"Other nights their music collection is more eclectic, but he told me if you come here on Saturday night you travel back to the 1970s."

"He?"

"Part of your surprise."

"Ken Patterson?" My stomach did a black flip.

"Not that big of a surprise. Now that you say that I realize mine is sort of a paltry surprise." He feigned a frown and I kissed it off his cheek.

Walking under the neon lights at the entrance got me into the seventies mood. Andy held the door and we stepped into a red, white, and blue cinderblock entryway. A disco beat filled the room. I had no idea what music was playing.

Andy stepped forward to a ticket booth and spoke through the small round opening in the window. "Two adults, please."

The young guy behind the glass didn't appear particularly happy to be serving us or to be wearing the orange and brown polyester shirt featuring a long collar with points so sharp they might have qualified as weapons. His space included a wall full of skating accessories, but he didn't seem interested in selling any to us. He pulled two red tickets off a roll and pushed them through a slot cut out at the bottom of the window. "Need skates?"

"Yes," said Andy.

"Pick 'em up inside." Without making eye contact, he slid two blue tickets under the glass and pointed towards a door painted with red and white stripes with IN painted in navy blue.

"Did we ever discuss that I can't roller skate?" I told Andy.

Andy appeared crestfallen. "But you ice skate."

"It's not the same. I'll try but don't set your expectations too high."

"Don't underestimate yourself." Andy pulled the door open and the 1970s engulfed us. Donna Summer was singing "On the Radio." Not my favorite, but I was fairly sure management saved my favorite, "Last Dance," for the final skate of the night.

We headed for a booth filled with hundreds of skates and more skating accessories. The same cashier took the two red tickets he had just handed us. Andy then surrendered two blue tickets.

"Size?" the attendant asked.

We told him and he pushed one pair of skates at me and the other Andy's way. Identical. Tan with orange wheels. The effort appeared to wear him out. He pushed a wall panel and disappeared, I assumed into the back room to recover. Andy and I turned right to the area with benches designated for lacing up our skates.

I checked out the rectangle the size of an Olympic ice rink and found it difficult to see myself fitting in with the skaters circling the floor. But Ken Patterson? It wasn't a stretch to picture him skating under the mirror ball reflecting the flashing red and blue lights at either end of the rink. Donna? A different story altogether. If this was the life Ken Patterson wanted, he was most likely right that Donna would never deign to share it.

Although I'd never known him to roller skate, Andy tied his skates with the speed of someone who skated at least three times a week "I'll put our stuff in a locker."

He skated off with my shoes and bag and reappeared seconds later to find me still fiddling with my laces. "Let me help you with them."

I leaned back, let Andy kneel in front of me and do the hard work with my laces. "This would remind me of when you got on one knee to propose to me if you'd gotten on one knee to propose to me."

"You would have hated that."

"True. I would have told you to get up and stop making a fool of yourself."

"I should have thought of using the old skate-tying gambit. Undercover proposal. I might propose again."

"I'll still hate it, but I could always use a second ring." I made a show of polishing the one I did have. "I have to admit that if I don't break a leg, this will turn out to be a great surprise."

"This isn't the whole surprise." Andy beamed.

I glanced across the rink to the skate-up food stands. I had a horrible feeling I'd spotted our dinner restaurant. The rink's mood was definitely 1970s but, upon closer inspection, the menu items appeared to be updated, although I couldn't see myself ordering sushi in this place.

"Dinner?"

"Still not the whole surprise." He pulled two pictures of Ken Patterson out of his shirt pocket. The original snapshot and a close-up cropped from it.

"He's not here?" I couldn't believe Andy could have held that news back.

"I doubt it, but I don't doubt that the guy who runs this place has encountered him. He has been running this rink for fifty years. For twenty-five of those years, he had other rinks around New Jersey. One in Atlantic County. If Ken was big into roller disco, this guy will know him."

"Okay. Let's go find him."

"We don't have to search," Andy said proudly. "Unless he called in sick, he's the DJ." He pointed to the far end of the rink where I could see a man standing behind a large console.

"I bet I can reach the DJ's booth." I held out a hand to ask Andy for help getting to my feet. He did but when he let go I rolled away in the wrong direction. "This doesn't happen on ice skates."

He grabbed ahold of me, rolled me to a ramp and helped me descend to the rink level. Only three feet at a twenty-degree angle but it struck me as a major design flaw in the rink's architecture. No one else seemed to mind. I let them all go first and then I moved down clinging to Andy with my left hand and the railing with my right.

He suggested we circle the rink a few times and get the lay of the land before we approached DJ, Diggs Decker. Andy took the lead as we merged into an eclectic group of skaters. Some were dressed to kill. A few wore costumes. I spotted a lot of affection for the seventies in outfits minimally altered to reflect current-day styles.

Donna Summer had given way to the BeeGees and "Stayin' Alive." "Music seems appropriate."

Andy laughed, but I wasn't sure he understood completely. At least until he saw my attempt to skate.

Roller skating did not come back like riding a bicycle. On ice, I would have found fitting in easy. Bounce a little. Wave my arms. At least on ice, I could have turned from forward to backward. On wood, I edged forward. In truth, I wasn't skating. Andy was dragging me. I wasn't the worst person on the rink. I was, however, in the running for the title. My main competition came from the under-eight crowd.

Andy appeared completely at home. I did not. I was a little jealous of the ease with which he moved. He was having fun.

Based on the little I'd heard, I assumed Ken Patterson got good at this. How free Ken must have felt. Even I felt free, and I was pretty much terrified. His experience must have matched mine on ice skates when I was flying as if my body had superpowers. Ken probably didn't mind the people leaning on the railings around the roller rink watching. They terrified me and fed my fear of humiliating myself. I clung to Andy's hand.

"Why did I not know that you could roller skate?" I asked.

"You never asked."

"It doesn't seem like something you would do."

"Notice the scoreboard?" He pointed at a far wall.

"If I look, it's likely I'll wipe out. I'm going to have to trust you."

"You knew I played hockey."

"Ice hockey."

"You knew I spent time in locations unlikely to have an ice rink."

"I get it. You play hockey on roller skates."

"Not anymore, but I can still stand up."

"Luckily, one of us can."

"Do you want me to let you go?" Andy lightened his grip on my hand.

It had to happen someday. "Go ahead I'll follow you to the DJ booth."

Andy turned and skated backward about three feet ahead of me. More likely to catch me when the inevitable fall came. But it turned out I made it to the DJ booth in an upright position. At least I got close. I rolled a few feet past the booth and slammed into the railing to stop. I inched my way back to where Andy was standing, waiting for Diggs Decker, according to the neon sign over his head, to finish adjusting his console. Cheers around the rink greeted the Village People singing "YMCA." Diggs slipped off his headphones.

Andy yelled to introduce himself and explained that they had spoken earlier. "This is my fiancé, Meg Daniels, she is a friend of a family searching for a lost relative." While I reached across to shake the DJ's hand, Andy pulled the pictures of Ken out of his jacket pocket.

Diggs Decker held the wide shot at arm's length to study it and then put his glasses on and held it close. Then he repeated the same action with the closeup. "Sure, I remember this guy. Not the best picture of him. We used to call him the Count. I'm sure that's who this is."

"The Count?" I asked wondering if he had become roller skating royalty.

He leaned it to make sure his voice could be heard. "First the Accountant, then we shortened it to the Count."

"Was he an accountant?" I asked without hiding the disappointment in my voice.

"Nah, but when he first came around, he dressed like one. Not in this rink. Down in Atlantic County. I used to have four rinks around the state. Four. Business was booming. Back in the day, every night was like this. If you think it's crowded now, you ought to see the late session. But the seventies ended. Disco died. Or so they said. In my mind, it never died. But roller disco wasn't the craze anymore. I had to close the other rinks."

"Is that when the Count stopped skating?" Andy interrupted.

Diggs stared at the photos for a few seconds. "I think so because I kind of remember noticing that he had stopped coming. No idea when. Geneva might know. He used to skate with her."

"Geneva?" I asked.

"Yeah." He searched the floor of whirling skaters. "There she is. In the white overalls." The term white overalls did not do justice to the stretch pants with a bib that covered the front of a sparkling silver tube top that matched the finish on her platform skates. She was spinning at that moment, so I found it hard to judge her age, but I had to think that Ken Patterson had thirty years on her. At least.

"When she was a child?" I blurted out.

"No. When he came back. Up here."

"He came back?" Andy and I spoke in unison.

"Yeah. He must have been gone for ten, fifteen years. Maybe twenty. But then, one day, he shows up here."

"This man? The Count? Ken Patterson?" I confirmed.

"I think that might have been his name, but I don't know for sure. He was old when he came back. He was maybe around the same age as me. I'd say fifty or more, but he could still skate. You should ask Geneva about him. She might know."

Before we could answer, he picked up a microphone and made an announcement. "Geneva to the booth, please. Geneva to the booth."

I should have felt elated that we were about to hear that Ken Patterson had survived his disappearance. That should have made me happy. It did, but the joy was mixed with a bit of disappointment that Donna Patterson had not killed him. More than a bit.

Chapter 29

Geneva was willing to sit down with Andy and me in the dining area where glass walls made a moderately successful attempt at keeping out the rumble of the rubber wheels on the wood flooring. We still had to talk over the music, but we got lucky and the mood became romantic with the BeeGee's "How Deep Is Your Love."

"Thanks for talking with us," I said.

"No problem. I don't much like skating to a romantic number without a partner, and I'm on my own tonight."

Other skaters with no interest in skating to a slow rhythm filled the tables around us. The mood was raucous, but at least we didn't have to yell over the rink noises to make ourselves heard.

"Can I get you something?" Andy asked Geneva. "A drink?"

"I wouldn't mind a Coke. Thanks."

I said I'd take the same, and Andy left the two photos on the table and went to get drinks. Geneva stared at me with a blank expression, which I attributed to the effort required to keep her eyelids in an open position given the heavy patina of eye shadow that resembled actual sequins. I couldn't ask her age, so I pegged her at around forty-five which meant Ken Patterson had around thirty years on her. I was so distracted by her appearance that I allowed an awkward silence before I spoke. Her puzzled expression prompted me. "Diggs thought you might be able to help us. I am friendly with a family that is trying to locate a missing relative whose daughter is ill. Diggs said you used to skate with the Count."

She pulled the photos towards her. "This the guy you're looking for?" She studied them carefully. "Well, the Count I knew was older than this."

If I'd shown the picture to anyone outside of the roller rink, they probably would have caught on right away that I was presenting them with an old picture simply because of Ken's clothes. They didn't appear so outdated inside the rink. "The close-up is cropped from the group shot taken in 1977."

She leaned over the close-up again. "So he'd be like old, now." Exaggerated facial expressions revealed the progress of her mental process. Puzzlement. Consideration. Doubt. Reconsideration. Recognition. "Of course, that is the Count. I'm sorry. I got fooled by the hair. He had a lot of gray hair when I met him, and it was shorter. No mustache. But that's the same guy. I always thought he had sad eyes. Why are you looking for him? Did something happen to him? Why doesn't his family know where he is?"

"There was a disagreement, but now, as I said, his daughter is ill and wants to see her father. Can you tell us where we can find him?"

Geneva let out a deep sigh and shook her head with broad motions. "I can tell where he was ten years ago. Something like that. Maybe more. Maybe twenty."

****Geneva****
Dolly's Roller Rink
1997

Geneva could feel the old guy staring at her, but he didn't give her the creeps. She thought he was admiring her skating, not her body. At least that was part of her fantasy. The rest? He was at Dolly's Roller Rink recruiting for a traveling roller-skating extravaganza. Never mind that she knew of no traveling roller skating shows. That would be why he was creating one, right? That's what the world needed, right? Starlight Express *had been a big hit. She wouldn't mind joining that cast but you had to be able to sing to get into a Broadway show. Even a revival. And she couldn't carry a tune to save her life.*

She'd seen him here before. That time he hadn't dressed for skating. He'd come to watch and talk to Diggs. Diggs seemed to know him, so she figured he wasn't an ax murderer or anything. Dressed in slacks and a sports jacket, he leaned on the railing and watched the skaters. That had been less than a week ago. And now, he was back for the disco session, and he was dressed for it. She wondered if his overalls dated back to the 1970s, but they didn't look bad.

Plain white over a plain white t-shirt. His skates were expensive—she could tell—but they weren't flashy seventies skates. They were plain black. Serious skates. She took that to mean he was a serious skater.

She'd shown off a bit the first night he came, and she did the same now. A few spins, a spread eagle, and a jump. Some basic stuff, but then she pulled out her specialty. Five jumps in a row. Right foot. Left foot. Right foot. Left foot. Right foot. To show her versatility she slowed the action to a long spiral traveling half of the rink on her left foot with her right leg raised behind her so her foot was even with her head. She knew she looked good doing it, although the move didn't exactly match the music. She stopped showing off her tricks and went back to dancing along with the Bee Gees. Showing him that she had rhythm. Just circling the rink, showing her basic moves. She forgot about the stranger and got lost in the music. Diggs's voice pulled her out of her daze.

"Geneva to the booth. Geneva to the booth, please."

Next time around the rink she embellished her backward toe stop with some arm motions to announce her arrival at the console where the stranger was waiting, chatting with Diggs.

"Geneva, meet the Count." Count? Was this guy a prince or something?

Diggs knocked that fantasy out of her head fast. "Not royalty. Just his nickname."

Diggs didn't explain why, but Geneva's mind raced ahead. It had to have something to do with money and the fact that this guy had a lot of it to count.

"Count used to be one of my best customers down in Atlantic County. He hasn't been skating in a few years and he wants to get back on the rink. He doesn't need a teacher. He needs more of a coach, a partner. Someone to get him back doing the tricks he used to pull off… What? Twenty years ago?"

She was wondering if the guy would ever speak for himself when he smiled and extended his hand.

"Nice to meet you, Geneva. My name is Ken but, as you heard, everyone calls me Count. I'll be happy to pay for your time. All I need is someone to skate with me. Critique me. Until I get my sea legs back. I've done some Rollerblading, but I haven't been on the wood in quite a while."

Geneva smiled, but she knew her face gave her away. She was disappointed. She thought he had more to offer, but she could use the $20 an hour he suggested.

"I don't want to interfere with your schedule, but if you could fit me in for three sessions a week, I'd be grateful."

The guy was so polite. She couldn't help but like him. "You look ready. I can start tonight."

His face lit up. His sad eyes changed to happy.

His basic skating was fine, so she got him to mimic her moves. By the end of the night, she knew he didn't need a coach, but she didn't tell him. She wanted the money. At the end of the third session, she admitted, "Count, I don't think you need me. Your skating is fine. Maybe we should get together once a week and add a new trick to your repertoire."

His big brown eyes again looked sad. "But it's more fun with a partner. I'd like you to continue."

She was happy to. Session by session Geneva grew to feel that they were friends. They would take long breaks and talk. She thought he needed the downtime to regroup. She'd never had an old friend before. She figured the Count was heading for sixty, but he didn't seem like the other folks she met who were his age. For one thing, he was in great shape.

At the end of the month, he suggested he would see if Diggs would rent him the rink for an hour each week. "We could have the entire space to ourselves. Can you imagine how that would feel? Roller skating made me feel freer than anything I've ever done in life." His eyes took on a dreamy look.

"Anything?" she teased to bring him back to the present.

He laughed but had a serious expression on his face when he answered, "yes, anything. Skating saved my life. I had done everything right when I was a kid. High School Honor Roll. Football team. Student Council. College. Marriage. Kids. Law School at night. Big practice. Big money. I did it all because I was supposed to. Because somebody wanted me to. My parents. My wife. My clients. I only felt alive when I was out sailing. Sometimes I felt as if I were flying. And in a way I was."

She barely breathed for fear of interrupting him.

"I thought I'd live on my boat, but until I could do that I needed something that made me feel I wasn't trapped, something that was always there for me. And that," he slapped his hands on his thighs, "was how I discovered roller skating and how I met Diggs." He took a drink of his root beer and slipped back into a dreamy mood. "When the air moves by you so fast, it's almost like sailing. I don't know why I stopped doing something that made me so happy."

"So did you stop when you started living on your boat?"

"That never happened. Things didn't work out exactly as I planned. I shouldn't have waited." He looked at her intently. "Promise me something. Promise me two somethings. One, don't ever walk away from anything you love. Two, promise you will never do anything because it is the accepted thing to do or because people expect you to do it. I did that and it almost killed me."

*****

"If that was how he felt, why did he stop coming?" I asked.

"He had a fall which was weird because he never fell. I mean before that. Amazing considering the moves he could do. He didn't break anything, but it scared him. I could tell. Knocked the breath out of him that's for sure. Took him a while to get back on his feet, his wheels. He needed help. He was an old guy by then. I'm not being mean. He was a senior citizen. He didn't skate like one. He would tell me how much better he had been before, but he was pretty good or I wouldn't have skated with him. We used to make up little routines to some of the songs. He loved it."

"But he stopped cold turkey when he fell?"

"No. Not right away, but he was never the same. He was always kind of tentative after that. Slowed down. Cut his sessions short. One night he came to thank me for being his partner but said he was quitting. He took a lap around the rink, took off his skates and left. Never saw him again."

"Do you know where he lived?"

"No. I never went to his house."

"Did he ever bring anyone along?"

"Not that I ever met. He always came alone. He was a nice guy. He seemed very, like, peaceful, you know what I mean. Like kind of Zen."

"Ken Patterson?"

"Yeah. I am pretty sure that was his name. He never told me the facts of his story. I think he was trying to tell me that he had some big life crisis and became a brand-new person."

"But he never talked about what that change was?"

She let out another theatrical sigh. "Let me think." She drummed her long silver nails on the table. "I don't remember him telling any stories at all. Like I said, he used to give me advice all the time. He would say that bitterness was a horrible trait, that it had ruled him for many years. *Don't let that happen to you.*" She waved a finger to mimic his actions. "He also liked to say not to be a fool, that not everything was forgivable. He told me that when I almost married a guy who abused me. If it weren't for him, I would have married the wrong guy."

"Did he think marriage was a good thing?"

"He didn't try to talk me out of marriage in general, just that marriage."

"Was he married?"

"He used to talk about a woman." Another big sigh. "I don't remember her name."

Andy slipped a cup in front of Geneva and me. I sipped mine, but she drained hers in under a minute. Seemed fair since she'd been the one doing the heavy exercise. While she finished up, I filled Andy in.

"Geneva used to skate with Ken, but he stopped after he had a nasty fall. He wasn't injured, but I guess he figured at his age he dodged a bullet. He always came alone. She never knew where he lived."

"Brigantine." Her straw made a crackling noise as she pulled air through it.

"What? I thought you didn't know." I turned to Geneva.

"I just remembered. He said he liked the ocean." She put her cup down.

"Did he say where in Brigantine?"

"Sorry, no. But he could have moved. That was a lot of years ago."

The Bee Gees came through the loudspeakers. "You Should Be Dancing"

"Oh God, I love this song." She popped to her feet. A bright smile crossed her face. "The Count did too. Find me out there if you have any more questions, I'll be skating." With that, she rolled out the door and onto the rink.

Andy and I looked at each other.

"How could he live so close and never run into anyone he knew?" I pulled out my phone and checked. "Brigantine to Avalon is only forty miles. From what she said, he came back fifteen, twenty years ago. Maybe more. How could he live there under his real name without being found?"

"He didn't turn up on any of your online searches?" Andy asked and then answered his question himself. "Of course, he didn't or we would be there. Did he have another name he used?"

"She knew him as Count but knew his name was Ken."

"Brigantine isn't a town you cut through," Andy noted. "You'd have a smaller chance of running into people there than most towns along the shore."

"I am still shocked he chose to come back so close to home, but it certainly sounds as if he is the Count."

"There's got to be other people up and down this coast hiding from each other. Cheating husbands and that sort. He can't be the only one." Andy made a good point.

"Do you think he's still there?"

"I think there is a chance."

I thought about the possibilities as I drained my Coke. "This was a fantastic surprise, Andy."

"I know you must be a little disappointed."

"I'll admit I feel a little let down that Donna isn't a killer."

"Don't write your theory off just yet. Cheer up. Maybe she did kill him. Just not when you thought."

As we left the rink, I wondered what had turned a man who appeared to be a button-down attorney into a disco king? The external changes would have been hard to miss, but there had to be some internal turmoil to turn the Ken Patterson Donna married into a man who felt comfortable skating under a mirror ball in fashions indisputably ranked as the worst ever.

Chapter 30

"What was that groan? Are you in pain?" Andy called from downstairs.

"Only the mental kind." Okay, that was a bit of a lie. My knees hurt. My calves hurt. My arches hurt. I was paying for those few spins around the rink. But what hurt the most? The likelihood that Donna Patterson had not killed her husband. I had been so sure. I'd envisioned a role for myself righting all the wrongs Donna had done. Now my fantasy had been crushed.

"I'm sorry," Andy appeared at the top of the stairs to the loft.

"Don't worry. You didn't wake me."

"Not for that. For destroying your dream of exposing Donna Patterson as a killer." He handed me a glass with Coke over crackling ice. Music to my ears.

"Where did you get the ice?"

"I ventured into the kitchen. I wanted to make a special effort for you, given your disappointment."

"The kitchen is thirty steps from the wet bar," I pointed out.

"It's a symbolic gesture."

"And much appreciated." The fizz tickled my nose as I got the caffeine into my body.

Andy slipped onto the bed beside me. "Don't forget she might have killed him another day."

"That's an optimistic thought." I sipped my coke and stared at the ocean. "I should be elated that Ken made it out alive, but there is something about Donna that made me want her to be guilty. I honestly believed she was capable of murder."

"Well, she may be, but I don't think she killed Ken. At least, not back then. I do believe that Ken Patterson is the Roller-skating Count."

"Me too. Just because I am a little disappointed, make no mistake, I am extremely grateful for your help tracking him down."

"You might want to keep it between the two of us that you are disappointed that he is alive."

"I accept that I need to focus on finding a seventy-something-year-old man. The only way I see that happening is if he stayed in Brigantine." I took a long drink of my morning caffeine.

"I want to get in a run before I head off to the library. Want to come?"

"We've met, right?" I asked Andy.

"I want you to understand you are always welcome." He kissed the air beside my cheek and disappeared down the stairs.

I enjoyed my morning Coke before I called Abby. I needed caffeine before I could think of facing her.

"Any word on my seeing your mother?"

"Explain again why you want to meet her?"

I didn't tell her the new, updated truth: because your grandfather may be alive in Brigantine and I can't just drive around town all day hoping to run into him in random spots. "I'd like another chance to get a better feel for her father. His likes. His dislikes."

What I needed was a clue about his interests, his activities that might have persisted, that might have been a lifetime habit. Something he might still be doing in Brigantine, if he was still in Brigantine. I didn't share that with her or the news that her grandfather had been alive and in New Jersey within the past twenty years. "The tiniest piece of information could help."

"Well, not today. How about tomorrow morning? No. Wait that's not good for me."

Abby and I agreed on Tuesday morning. "But we have to talk about how to communicate with her. If you ask her questions, she will freak out. I'm going to text you a link. It will help you understand how to speak to her."

I put a note on my calendar wondering what had happened to my plans for my Avalon stay before Abby and Elisabeth showed up in our yard. I have even specified a block of days on the calendar: *Do nothing. Enjoy Positano's couch.* I had already added the name DeMarco on Sunday.

It was ridiculous to think that I could engineer an accidental meeting with Bob DeMarco. Shortly after noon, I headed to his house. I was kind of interested in getting a look at his wife. No good reason. Just curious.

I pulled down our driveway and was waiting for the bike traffic to pass when one of the bikes stopped. One of the expensive ones. I couldn't identify the make, but I recognized it as an upscale model. I also recognized DeMarco. I slid down the window and called him.

"What a coincidence," he said moving the bike into position beside my car window.

Not really since I was pulling out of my own driveway, Ken's old driveway. DeMarco knew where that was.

"It's very handy actually." I didn't mention that I was on my way to his house. "I was hoping I'd run into you."

"Me too. I've been thinking about your project. I always believed Meitner completely. Maybe it would be better to let sleeping dogs lie. I don't expect you to find anything bad out about Ken, but what if you do? His daughter shouldn't hear that."

I didn't know what to say. I didn't want to argue. So, I lied. "I haven't found anything. Given her illness, Elisabeth may forget that she had a father at all, let alone one who gave no indication he loved her or even remembered her."

He opened his mouth, but no words came out. Some garbled sounds, but no clear thought.

I filled the gap. "It's a shame if he did love her. It would be great for him to return. But, as I said, I was hoping to run into you. I was wondering why you didn't tell me that you bought Ken's boat."

"What makes you think that I bought Ken's boat?"

"It's a classic. My fiancé knows a bit about boats, and he kept going on about how Ken's was a beauty. Not common. There's a painting of it in the main room." I pointed over my shoulder at the Positano house. "Andy was pretty sure he was looking at the same boat. He was surprised that Ken left it behind. The way I see it is he never intended to leave it behind. He told Donna he sold it, but he didn't. He changed the name to ME SAID LORDY. It's an anagram."

He cracked like an egg dropped from a height on a ceramic tile floor. "Yes, it is Ken's boat."

Here was a man who would not stand up to torture.

"Was Ken's boat. He changed the name as part of his escape plan. I don't know why he decided not to take it with him, but I got a call from Meitner asking if I wanted to buy it."

"Was this before or after Ken left?"

"After. When else?"

"Didn't you find that odd?"

"Meitner said that Ken had changed his mind. Meitner said the boat no longer fit his needs. I assumed his original plan was to sail away. I bought the boat. Meitner gave me a bargain-basement price, but it was all legal. I have the paperwork. I kept it quiet because I didn't want Donna to hear about it. We were still friends of a sort back then, and I wanted to stay out of her marital problems. Ken kept it in that slip down in Cape May. Part of hiding assets or rather separating assets. I left it down there."

"So Donna wouldn't see it?

"Partially. But it's a big boat for the yacht club in Avalon."

"What about his old car?"

"I think Meitner junked it. That was always the plan. It had no value, except that it annoyed Donna when Ken drove it. He liked that. Meitner told me Ken was going to drive it to the boat and leave it there."

"If Ken took the car there and left the boat there, how did he get away?"

"Not in that car. That's all I know. I drove when Meitner and I went down to the boat. He took the old car away. It's a long time ago. Details are sketchy but that is what I recall."

"And that didn't strike you as odd?" I pulled back. I was sounding like a TV cop. The bad cop.

DeMarco seemed annoyed with me. "I don't know. I didn't know, or care to know, the details of Ken's plans. All I knew is that Ken changed his plans. Meitner seemed thrilled that I didn't push for information. Maybe I pumped Meitner a little, but he didn't let anything slip. Nothing that stuck. Ken was gone. His boat and old car were there. I got the boat because he decided not to take it."

"Why didn't you tell me that?"

"Maybe it didn't seem relevant?" He asked a question.

"How could it not seem relevant?"

"I guess I got so used to hiding the connection to Ken, but not for any nefarious reason. Meitner said it would be best not to say anything and I went along. I didn't want to get involved. You know, end up in a tangle with Donna."

I leaned my head out the car window, so I could stare up into his eyes. "Bob if you know where Ken is, you owe it to Elisabeth to tell her. If you don't want to tell me, tell Ken that Elisabeth wants to see him."

"Don't you think that if I knew, I would tell you? I understand what she is going through, and I regret deeply the small part I played in creating her sadness."

"If you had known what Ken was planning, would you have driven him home that last night?"

He stared down Dune Drive as if the answer was down the road. "Yeah. I would have. I might have argued a case for Elisabeth, but knowing Donna…I would have dropped him off without any protest."

"Do you think he's alive?"

"I hope so, but I have no way of knowing." He didn't hide his rising frustration. "Why would I know that?"

"Do you think he left of his own accord?"

"Absolutely. I do. Meitner told me that and I trusted him."

"So why do you want me to back off?" I circled back to the beginning of our conversation. "I don't understand."

He stammered. "I told you. I've been thinking that I am contributing to this investigation, and I believe it could be causing little Lisa pain."

Of course. He had only altruistic motives.

"There is something else," he said.

I kind of thought there would be.

"No one did an investigation back then, but if they did? I was the last one to see him alive. I would have been a prime suspect. That isn't going to change because they waited forty years to investigate."

"What was your motive?" I didn't prompt him.

"I had none. You think I don't watch those mystery shows. It's always the victim's last known contact."

"That guy is always the prime suspect, but he doesn't always do it."

"I don't want to be the prime suspect."

"Then you're in luck. There's a good chance that he is still alive."

Bob appeared puzzled. Almost as if he didn't know how to react. If I were he, I would have been relieved for myself. Happy for Ken. I saw none of that on his face.

"I'm not going to push you, Bob, but you don't have to worry about being a suspect if he shows up. If you do know where Ken is, maybe you could tell Ken that Elisabeth needs to see him."

I swore DeMarco had a guilty expression on his face as he pedaled away.

I was already in the car and at the bottom of the driveway, so I figured I might as well take a spin around Brigantine. I was less than a hundred yards from the house and forty miles from Brigantine. I knew the idea was stupid. Futile. But I had to offer fate a chance to hand me a simple, quick solution. It could happen. I'd checked the population. Not long ago the population had been just under 10,000. I wasn't heading off to cruise Manhattan.

Brigantine was a lot bigger than I recalled. I'd been there years ago to visit a witness in a case, and my memory said I came over the bridge and turned right to find the house. I couldn't even find a street that looked familiar. I had visited last summer but with an address that I drove to directly. Before that my knowledge of Brigantine was visiting many years before with my parents and pictures of my grandfather there as a kid in the 1940s. I probably should have done some research before simply driving into town.

In many shore towns, I could have conducted a grid search. A few north-south through streets and lots of cross streets stretching from bay to ocean, most crossing at ninety-degree angles. A driver could get the feeling they had conducted a thorough search. Not my experience in Brigantine. I suspected I had searched several blocks four to five times, and others not at all. I couldn't even figure out if I had been to every part of town. Plus, there were a lot of condominium complexes, and I didn't even bother checking the parking lots.

I thought (fantasized) that I'd stumble upon a sailboat owned by Ken Patterson. I hadn't figured out how I recognize it as his. Maybe the name he gave it would offer a clue. *MISSING ELISABETH. HATING DONNA. NOT DEAD.* I did not spot a single sailboat in the water. Or a single powerboat either. I located and cruised by all the boatyards. I saw lots of powerboats sitting in the yard, but I had no idea where the sailboats would be in drydock. I ignored the powerboats. I was pretty sure that a diehard sailor like Ken would not be the owner of a powerboat.

Nothing I saw—house, boat, or car—remotely suggested that it might have some relationship to Ken Patterson. Pretty much the negative result I expected. Fate did not want to offer me a simple, quick solution.

I supposed if I sat on the seawall from sunrise to sunset for months, Ken Patterson might walk by. He probably would. If he was still alive. If he still lived in Brigantine. If he was still in good enough condition to walk.

I told myself I'd had a nice ride and headed out of town.

I was just heading into the tunnel when I realized I was being followed by a black Jaguar. Then I remembered. There weren't a lot of options when it came to leaving Brigantine Island. The car turned off for the Atlantic City Marina. I relaxed. I wasn't being followed. Who would want to follow me?

Chapter 31

Andy returned from school to find me sprawled on the couch.

"I've been working." I projected an Excel worksheet from my laptop to the movie screen that descended from the ceiling for those occasions when an eighty-five-inch screen was not adequate.

"I feel as if I am back at school, but with more comfortable seating." He dropped onto the couch beside me. "I assume I am looking at something to do with Ken Patterson."

I pulled out my pointer. I highlighted a heading. *Who might know what happened to Ken?*

"You bought a laser pointer. This is getting serious."

"If nothing else, it might impress Abby that I am serious. Want to see what I've come up with?"

"Will I need a beer?"

"It wouldn't hurt." When he returned, I was ready to make my presentation. "Let me run down the list. His brother Gerald." I hit Gerald Patterson's name with the laser dot. "The reasons are obvious."

Andy agreed.

"His friend Bob DeMarco." I highlighted Bob DeMarco's name. I told Andy about my encounter that morning. "I don't for a moment believe his line about worrying about being a suspect. Just a guess, but I suspect word has gotten out that someone is looking for Ken."

"And you're thinking that word got to Ken."

"Exactly, and Ken got to Bob DeMarco. Ken or Ken's rep."

"His did seem like a weak reason for asking you to abandon the investigation. Maybe he felt he had said too much." Andy suggested. "Or did he grow to regret the role he played and now feels ashamed to admit how much he knew back in '77."

"I did ask him that if he does know where Ken is he could let Ken know that Elisabeth is dying. It would work in my favor if he felt guilty." I hit DeMarco's name with the laser dot. "He might want to protect someone from something. Who and what? I have no idea. If Meitner were still alive...."

"If he were alive, he'd be the logical choice, but you're sure he isn't, right?" Andy asked. "Maybe you should replace his name with his wife's. She might know something even if she doesn't realize it."

I added her name and moved on. "Robin Carson seems so gullible. He doesn't know anything."

"And last on your list is Joey Facenda, a friend of Gerald Patterson."

"That's it."

"Not much of a list so far." Andy was not impressed. "My money is on Gerald Patterson. Maybe he didn't get advance warning that his brother was going away, but after all these years, I imagine Ken would want to get in touch. And Gerald is family." Andy said.

"And we are 100% sure that the Count is Ken Patterson?" I asked.

"99%. I realize you would love to keep your hope alive that Donna is a killer, but Diggs and Geneva seemed pretty convinced. Everyone, including his wife, believed Harris Meitner when he said that Ken got away. You're not looking for a murderer, remember?"

"Oh, right." I was as disappointed as I sounded.

"It wasn't as if he'd left notes for everyone. After he left, people read into what he said." Andy offered.

"What does it matter? Unless someone snaps and tells me, I will never find him." I threw down the pointer in frustration. It bounced towards Andy.

He scooped it up and pointed it at the projected image. "My gut says we can take Mrs. Meitner off the list. The question? Who can we add?"

Chapter 32

When I came downstairs on Monday morning, I didn't see Sally DeMarco sitting on the deck. If she hadn't moved while I was facing the ocean, I never would have spotted her. Apparently, people thought that after one visit they got lifetime visiting rights to this house. She was stretched out on a lounge.

I grabbed a jacket and my handbag and walked along the deck to the front of the house. "Mrs. DeMarco? Sally?"

"Ah, there you are. I rang the bell, but you didn't answer so I figured I would wait. You were probably in the shower."

"Yes, I'm on my way out," I lied. "Is there something I can do for you?"

With difficulty, she pulled herself off the lounger. I reached out to help her but she waved off my assistance. "I needed to stop by. I had a guilty conscience."

Had she stolen cash from my wallet during my visit? Probably not. She appeared more forlorn than guilty.

She sighed theatrically and glanced at the house, the sea, the floor, everywhere but at me. "I wasn't completely honest the other day. You can tell I really hate Donna Patterson. I should have gotten over my feelings by now. I don't sit around hating her all day every day, but when you brought her name up, all sorts of unpleasant memories came flooding in."

I didn't say a word. I didn't want to interrupt her confession whatever it involved.

"I know that more than anything Donna Patterson wants Ken to come back to her."

"I can assure you…."

"No. No," she interrupted. "I accept that is not your goal. I understand that you are searching for him on Elisabeth's behalf." She stared at the deck. "Which is why I felt so terrible that I lied to you. Well, I didn't actually lie. I simply failed to mention something."

I waited for her to tell me.

"Maybe four years ago, I was in Atlantic City with the girls. My girlfriends. We stayed in a hotel and all for the weekend. Just some gambling. Saw a show. Ate good food."

I smiled and nodded but didn't prompt her.

"And I wasn't sure at first."

I waited.

"I mean, it had been so many years. What, forty years?"

She finally let her eyes meet mine.

"But I knew. It was Ken. I was sure. He was one of those men who drew attention to themselves. Legitimately tall, dark, and handsome. He wasn't so dark anymore, but he was still attractive in an older, dignified, gray-haired way. His hair was mostly silver and cut short. He didn't have that ridiculous mustache he had the last time I saw him but there was something about the way he dressed. He still looked kind of flashy. I couldn't help staring. At the resemblance. He would never be my type."

I was feeling a mixture of elation and sorrow. More proof Ken was still alive even more recently. More proof that Donna didn't kill him. "Did he see you?"

She gazed into space as if watching the scene play out in space before her. "We made eye contact. He got this funny look. Puzzled. Like I was familiar, but he didn't know from where. And then he seemed to recognize me and then just as fast pretend he didn't. He didn't seem worried or scared. He grabbed the arm of this kind of floozy-looking woman he was with and strolled off. Not running. Not fleeing. Kind of calm but definitely heading out."

"Where were you? Which hotel?"

"The Artistical in Atlantic City. Do you know it?"

Know it? I had spent most of the previous summer there.

"When was this?"

"I've been trying to remember. Maybe three years ago. In the winter. I was up in Atlantic City for a girls' weekend with friends."

"Did any of them see him?"

"None of them would have known him. Never would have met him.

I didn't even tell them the story. I only saw him for a minute or two."

"Did you tell anyone?"

"I didn't want to. I figured if he were Ken, wherever the guy was, he was better off. If Elisabeth had been a child, I might have thought differently. But he's an old guy. He probably had a better life. A life he wanted. He'd gotten away from Donna. More power to him. I wouldn't rat him out to her. I'm not proud that I kept quiet, but I hated Donna. I loved the idea that her beloved Ken was so close and he didn't want to see her." She brushed back the hair the wind had blown across her face. "I feel guilty for Elisabeth, but I don't know her. She's a grown woman. I wouldn't recognize her if I walked right into her."

"And you didn't have any doubt?"

"No. And especially given the way he looked at me....It was Ken Patterson."

"And you didn't tell anyone?"

"Like I said, I didn't want to give Donna any clues about where he was or even that he was alive. I went home and didn't say a word." I could tell by her expression that she had cracked at some point. "It might have come out after a year or so. I was having lunch with the girls at the Princeton, and Donna was eating across the room. Turns out one of the girls knew her story—found it tragic. She bought Donna's version. Anyway, she talked about how he had been gone for so long and that he was probably dead. And, I said I wasn't so sure about that and they pumped me. I didn't say for sure I'd seen Ken, but I did tell them the story. But I never told anyone else."

"The woman who knew the story. Would she tell Donna?"

"I asked her not to. I said I wasn't 100% sure. But that wasn't the reason I asked her not to tell Donna. I wanted to protect Ken."

"But you didn't know if he lived near Atlantic City or if he was there on a vacation," I suggested.

"That's true."

I could tell. She didn't believe that.

"I watched their table. He seemed to be a regular. Maybe he lived around there."

My thought? She let the story slip hoping it would get back to Donna and hurt her. Just around the time Donna relocated to Cape May.

But why would Donna move after hearing that her beloved Kenneth was not so far away?

Chapter 33

After Sally DeMarco left, I kept my appointment at the Douglas home. My plan to interview Elisabeth was different now that I knew Ken had survived his disappearance.

Just before 10AM, I pulled up to one of the oldest and definitely the least impressive house on the block. As I climbed out of my car, I was greeted with the sentimental soundtrack of spring at the Shore, hammers and power tools echoing in the crisp air. Each year more houses of the Douglas's vintage would disappear to be replaced by taller houses that took advantage of every inch of a property. Set in the middle of a wide lawn, the Douglas house did not appear overwhelmed by behemoths.

Abby met me at the door before I could knock.

"She knows you're coming. I think she will recognize you, but follow my lead. Don't push the way you can." Abby, who thought I did not push enough, accused me of being too aggressive.

She led me down a short hallway. The walls were covered with black and white photos that appeared to tell the story of Elisabeth's life. At least, the part of it that happened after her father left.

"These are gorgeous." I slowed to admire the pictures.

"All from Donna. She fancies herself a photographer. She likes to create her personal version of reality."

To judge by the photos on the wall, Elisabeth had lived a happy, carefree life. I hoped that her smiles had not been forced.

I worked to hide the shock on my face when I looked into the living room. Elisabeth Douglas was barely recognizable from the night I'd met her. What I had taken as a feral look was probably a combination of fear and confusion, but sitting in her living room in a wing chair pulled into a spot of sunlight with a view of both the television and the dock outside the window, she appeared comfortable if not happy. I expected her to tell me that later in the day she would be off to meet the girls for lunch.

How had she come to look that way? Was she still able to dress herself? Fix her hair? Was that something she could accomplish on her own or did all of that fall on Abby? What a lot for a girl her age to handle. Maybe I shouldn't be so tough on her.

"Mommy," Abby smoothed a strand of her mother's hair that did not need smoothing as she knelt beside her chair. She plastered a wide smile on her face. She nodded at me. "Mommy, the lady who lives in your old house on the beach has come to visit. Her name is Meg." Her tone was soft and sweet—so different from what I was used to. "You met her the other night."

In the daylight, I could pin Elisabeth's age around fifty, but something in her expression, in her limited motions, made her seem much older. When she spoke, her tone was sweet. "You have that nice husband."

I didn't clarify that he was my fiancé. No need to complicate any of our exchanges.

"He was so nice. Abby told me. Where did I meet him?" She turned to Abby for the answer.

Abby knelt beside her mother gently gripping her hand. "You went to see your old house. He carried you to the car and I drove you home."

"Oh yes. I drove us there, didn't I?"

"Right," Abby said. Then she turned her head to mumble in my direction, "Never argue."

"Do you live in my mother's house?" Her intonation was tentative, childlike.

"Yes."

She didn't request any additional information.

"We had such good times there." Her smile broadened and her voice grew stronger. She seemed to be watching a show play out on a screen before her. "My father loved that house. He built it. I don't mean with his own hands, but he designed it. He couldn't stay. I wish he had. I wish he would come and visit." She tore her eyes away from whatever vision she was seeing. Her eyes and the tone in her voice beseeched me. "If he comes to visit, he won't know where we went. Will you tell him where to find me?"

"I will. Definitely. I will."

"Let me show you what he looks like." Elisabeth picked up a leather-bound album from a table beside her chair and flipped through the pages. They were full of enlarged shots of Abby and the man I assumed was Elisabeth's husband. In anticipation of a time when her disease would steal those memories, they were labeled in bold type—YOUR HUSBAND AL, YOUR DAUGHTER ABBY. Elisabeth passed by these pages until she found one labeled YOUR DADDY. The photo was a blow-up of one Abby had brought to my house. Pre-disco Ken Patterson holding his toddler daughter.

"What a nice picture! If I see him, I will be sure to tell him you want to see him."

"That's nice of you to promise, Meg," Abby squeezed her mother's hand.

"Hello. I see you have company, Elisabeth." A man about the same age as Elisabeth walked into the room.

Abby sprung to her feet. "Dad, this is Meg Daniels that I told you about."

"Nice to meet you. Al Douglas. Thank you so much for taking care of our Elisabeth the other night."

"Of course. We were happy to help."

Al Douglas smiled. An attractive man. Tall. Fit. Traces of gray at the temples. His looks were marred only by the worried expression that persisted even when he tried to cover it with a smile. Before she got sick, he and Elisabeth must have made a handsome couple. Donna might have had her faults, and all indications were that she had many, but she did provide her daughter with fine features. Aside from the thick, dark hair and eyes she must have inherited from her father, Elisabeth bore a decided resemblance to her mother.

"Meg can sit here right beside you. I just wanted to say hello. I'm going to get back to work." He placed a chair beside hers.

As I sat down beside her, Elisabeth reached for her husband's hand. She was smiling. "This lady is going to bring my daddy to see us." Elisabeth seemed so happy at the thought, I didn't protest.

"That's wonderful, Sweetie." He pulled his hand away to squeeze her shoulder, and she reached up a hand to pat his hand. With a *nice to meet you*, Al disappeared back to work.

Elisabeth turned to me with a warm smile on her face.

"What I love most about living in your old house is watching the moon rise over the water. I cannot wait for the full moon," I said.

"That is the best. My daddy and I would sit on the deck and watch it come up. He couldn't always be home at night, but he would be sure to be home on Big Moon Night. We called it Big Moon Night." She spoke slowly. I imagined more slowly than she had before the disease took hold of her.

Elisabeth spewed memories, one leading to another, that seemed to be playing out before her eyes. Abby sat on the couch, out of Elisabeth's sight but listening. When I glanced over, I saw her eyes glistening with tears.

After memories of Christmases, birthdays, and pool parties at the beach house, Elisabeth's tone changed. "My father was a handsome man. I suspect he still is, but he would be old now. Even I am old now." Her voice grew stronger with each word. "We had so much fun. Daddy and me. We would spend hours in the ocean. Right outside the house. We weren't supposed to go on the dunes, but we made a secret path just for us to get from the house to the beach. It was lovely except for the burrs. You really had to watch out for the burrs."

She changed the subject abruptly.

"My mother was never sad when my father left. She never let me be sad, but I was."

She glanced at the TV and switched to talking about the characters on the show. I wondered if she recognized the difference between their world and the one she shared with me. She turned to me and said, "Do you watch this show, Abby?"

Such a surprising glitch after such a good conversation. It drew Abby back to her side.

"That's Meg, Mommy."

"Of course. I am so sorry." Elisabeth seemed mad at herself.

"I was just thinking about my father. He smoked." I lied.

"Oh, boy," she giggled, "my father tried to smoke. Mother would have none of that in the house."

"Did he smoke outside?"

"He wouldn't dare. She would have found him. That's okay. Smoking isn't good for you."

"My daddy had hobbies," I said to keep the conversation going.

She did not react.

"People today run. My daddy did not like to run," I continued.

"Daddy had sneakers."

That was useful information although I hadn't encountered him running around Brigantine.

"My daddy liked to bowl," I said

No reaction.

"And play golf."

Again, she did not respond. I could see that she was lost. She had no idea what I was getting at.

"He did so much." I spaced out my comments, more accurately labeled lies, searching her face for a reaction. "Softball." "Rowing." "Skiing." I mentioned it even though I didn't know what good discovering Ken was a skier would do me as summer approached. Not one activity brought a glimmer of recognition.

"Pool," Elisabeth said.

"Your daddy liked to swim in your pool."

"No." She seemed angry. "Pool."

"Oh, he played pool. With sticks and balls."

"Yes, pool." She smiled and made a pretend shot. "But my mother would not allow a pool table in our house."

I foresaw my future hanging out in pool halls. Why didn't he love gourmet dining? Or did he? "What kind of food did he like?" A mistake. A question. I covered quickly. "My daddy liked Chinese food."

"Spaghetti. He was always eating spaghetti."

"That's very interesting. Anything else?"

Such a simple question, but a question. Elisabeth's warm expression disappeared. I could feel Abby's disapproval across the room. She jumped in quickly. "Meg, my Daddy is a surfer. I loved watching him surf when I was a little girl." But the momentum was lost. Elisabeth didn't seem to hear her. She was lost in her show.

When Abby walked me to the door, I spoke in hushed tones. "Maybe you should have hired a professional. I am not sure how successful I can be."

"Donna would never accept that." Abby didn't worry about keeping her voice down. "My mother would never defy Donna. She does everything Donna wants her to. Always has. For her entire life."

"I don't want to disappoint her."

"It's unlikely that she is clear enough to remember what you are doing. She won't ask. And, if we find something disappointing, we just won't tell her."

Chapter 34

Over the years, whenever I mooched off of—I mean visited—friends in Avalon, our days were spent pretty much the same way. Beach. Happy hour. Restaurant dinner. Bar. Usually, Fred's in Stone Harbor. Repeat. Never did anyone ever mention taking a walk on the Boardwalk.

I didn't realize the boards extended in either direction from the pizza place I'd seen from Dune Drive until I stumbled upon the information online. One-half mile of boards from 21st Street to 32nd Street. Not an exhausting trek. I decided to check it out. I needed a place to think. I had a feeling my search for Ken would be futile. I needed to find someone willing to tell me that Ken Patterson lives at 123 Main Street in Anytown, Some State. The only other option I saw was driving around Brigantine all day.

I parked and took the ramp to the Boardwalk on 21st Street and headed south. Abby cut me off at 23rd.

"I saw your car. What are you doing here?" She asked as if she were a cop, and I was holding a smoking gun.

"Taking a walk. I need to get to know the town. I've never been up here."

"Same view as from your first floor."

She eyed the thicket that blocked my view of the ocean.

"But listen to the sound of the waves! And, if I want to see it, I can walk down a path to the beach."

"You have an oceanfront home," Abby said.

"Are you telling me I should stay at home and out of the way of people who do not live in oceanfront property? Like the theory that rich people should fly First Class to free up space in coach." I waved an arm in either direction. There was no one in sight. "Oh, wait. It's getting to be a mob scene around here." A lone man came onto the Boardwalk at 21st Street.

Abby ignored me. "I thought I'd run a few errands while my parents were eating. When I spotted your car, I saw an opportunity to see if you thought over the conversation with my mother, to see if what she said was useful to you."

I only left your house twenty minutes ago. I didn't say the words out loud, but in my mind, my tone was quite impatient.

I resumed my walk. She tagged along.

"Anything can be a help. At the moment, I don't see how I can find him. All I can do is talk to people. Hope they let something slip. Or say something they don't even realize is important. You just never know, Abby. I will keep plugging along."

"Can I do anything to help you?" Her tone was different, solicitous, without a poorly-hidden agenda.

"Believe me. I will let you know."

She plopped onto a bench that had been donated by children of sorely missed parents who loved Avalon. So much for my walk. I dropped onto the bench beside her.

Abby stared across the dunes. "I am prepared for anything. Not my mother. She expects a blissful reunion with a wonderful man with some excuse to justify his actions that the rest of us can't even imagine. But I'm prepared for anything. You don't have to hold back. He may be dead. He may be a drunk. He may be mentally ill. He may be a criminal. He may be in Witness Protection. That's my favorite."

"If he were a criminal, I think the police would have contacted his family searching for him." I was trying to be helpful, but the familiar Abby was back. She looked at me with her *are you an idiot?* expression.

"What I am saying is I am prepared for the worst. If you find out something horrible, you can tell me. Then my father and I can figure out what to do about it. I'm not fragile."

One thing I'd never worried about.

"I realize I'm still a kid in your eyes, but I've had to grow up fast. I don't resent it. I am happy that I was able to take this gap year to see my mother through this. I've got lots of years to make up for lost time. Who knows what time she has left?"

In that moment, I remembered why I was helping Abby.

Then she leaned back and took a good look at me. "You know, your hair is pretty badly sun-bleached. I have a great hairdresser down here who could fix it for you."

The moment passed. I reminded myself. *You are doing this for Elisabeth. For Elisabeth. For Elisabeth.*

Chapter 35

I wasn't in the house long before I heard Beethoven's Fifth. The doorbell. I went down the indoor stairs and, through the glass, I saw a man staring off towards the ocean. I could have hidden. He hadn't seen me, but I was supposed to be investigating. I'd shown up at a lot of doors. Maybe it was only fair that someone showed up at mine. And, that I talked to them.

"Ms. Daniels?"

I was tempted to say who wants to know, but I treated him the way I wanted to be treated. "Yes, how may I help you?"

"I understand that you are looking for Kenneth Patterson."

My heart skipped a beat. "Why would you think that?"

"Word gets around. I heard from a friend of Al Douglas who's married to Elisabeth Patterson, Ken's daughter, that Elisabeth wanted to see her father and that someone was trying to find him for her."

I didn't press him on how he found out that someone was me. "Do you have any information?"

"Don't do it."

"Don't do what?"

"Don't look. Give up the search." His intonation was flat. Not threatening. He was offering advice, not delivering a threat. His words weren't delivered with that movie-mobster undertone that would have turned my blood cold.

"What can you tell me about Ken?"

"I don't have anything to say. I would simply advise you to stop the search."

"Are you a friend of Ken's?" He looked as if he might be old enough to have known Ken.

He snickered. "Hardly. When you were rooting around in Ken's history, didn't anyone mention that they suspected one of his shady clients knocked him off?" He seemed almost amused by the idea. His bright blue eyes twinkled. Did he imagine he might frighten me? He didn't.

"I heard there were rumors about some unsavory characters," I confirmed.

"That was me. At least one of them."

An unusual admission to say the least. He still didn't frighten me.

"Are you sure you wouldn't like to sit down for a few minutes? I'll get you a beer." I offered as if beer was an incredible treat that he could not get anywhere else in town. "But before I invite you inside, would you mind telling me your name? You know so I can scratch it out in my own blood when it turns out you are a nefarious character."

"Unsavory." He smiled. "Not quite as bad. Dodgy would work." He didn't add his name.

"And that would be Dodgy Dave? Dodgy Dan? Dodgy Dexter?"

"Just Dave. Dave Wendover."

I invited Dave Wendover to come inside because nothing makes more sense than inviting a self-described dodgy character into your isolated beach house. But Dave didn't appear unsavory or give off a nefarious vibe. He dressed well, professionally, carried a briefcase. What profession? Attorney? Investment banker? But unlike a lawyer or a banker, he seemed extremely polite and gentle. Almost shy. Just an impression. I had no proof. Even as I led him up the stairs, I decided that if this did not turn into a police matter, I probably would not mention to Andy that I invited a stranger into the house.

I grabbed a Corona from the wine refrigerator. "Would you like a glass?"

He said yes. A good sign. Would a killer accept a glass on which to deposit his DNA?

"How did you find me?" I asked.

"Tad, that's the mutual friend with the Douglas family, he said it had something to do with the fact that you were staying at the house." He took a chair at the kitchen island and looked around the great room. "It's been a long time since I've been here."

"I understand Ken liked to host parties."

"I wasn't invited to them."

"Oh."

"I was here when no one else was here. Sometimes Ken and I would meet here for privacy."

"Because you were nefarious." *You had to make a joke?* Sometimes I annoyed myself. Often.

I might have been angry with my attempt at humor, but the man seemed amused. "Dodgy, remember?" He shifted in his chair. "Let me clear the air right off. I spent five years in federal prison back in the eighties. People think those places are country clubs, but trust me, it's no fun, which is why I do not want to go back. There or to a real prison."

Why was he expecting to go back? What had he done?

"As you know there is no statute of limitations for murder."

My face froze. I guess my reaction was noticeable because he held out his hands. "No. No. I never murdered anyone. Certainly, not Ken. I mean no one. I never even thought of it. Killing anyone. But…." He took a long drink of beer. "Let me explain. Back when I found out that Ken had split, vanished without a trace, it occurred to me that he might have been murdered. Or, even if he hadn't been, people would think he might have been murdered. I was waiting for an investigation. I was terrified that I would be a suspect. He and I had worked together on deals that might not have been totally clean. Profitable, but on the edge. I had no reason to kill Ken. I kept Ken in the dark about some of my activities. He couldn't have done me much harm."

"Attorney/client privilege?" I asked.

"Not if they could prove that Ken and I were in a conspiracy together. Which we weren't. Although he did make an obscene amount of money off my deals. Before he left, I knew that time was running out for me. I saw signs that the feds were taking an interest in me." He took another drink of beer, and I sat in silence waiting for him to go on. "I was so scared. I thought the feds would think I murdered him to keep him quiet."

"But the feds never investigated?"

"Not then. Never as far as I knew about Ken. Later. I was young, fancied myself a hotshot. I never changed my ways. It took ten years for my tendency to bend the rules to catch up with me." He shook his head as if annoyed by his younger self.

"And you think if it turns out that Ken was murdered, the cops will do the investigation you feared now."

"Yes. No statute of limitation."

"Mr. Wendover, I have no proof that Kenneth Patterson is dead."

"You've found out he is alive."

"No. To tell you the truth...." I interrupted myself realizing that I was not going to tell him the truth, that I had reason to believe Ken was alive. "I've found nothing."

"Oh," Wendover said with a smile but the kind of smile that made my blood run cold. For the first time, I worried that Dave Wendover might not be the regular guy I imagined.

"Look, do you understand why I'm worried?" He leaned forward to ask.

I recoiled but just a little, but enough that he must have noticed. "Because if I find out that Ken did not disappear but was murdered, you will be a suspect?" In my opinion, not the prime suspect, but I could understand his concern.

"I am willing to make it worth your while to stop investigating."

I deeply regretted asking him in.

"I will pay you whatever the Douglas family is paying you, plus $10,000 to let sleeping dogs lie."

"I'm not doing this for money."

"So, let me give you $10,000 to stop."

"You would give me $10,000 to end my search for Ken Patterson?"

"I'd give you more if I had it. I have a nice life now. I run a small business completely separate from the financial markets. I have a wife I love. Two great kids in college. I started my family late after I got out of prison. I don't want to miss seeing them get married, have kids of their own. I believe Ken got away, but if he didn't, they will come to me. I know it. I worried about it for years. I can't worry about it now. Please, I beg you, stop looking for Ken."

I waited for an *or else*, but none came. At least that was good. No murder threat. Yet. He didn't sound that desperate. Yet.

"But what if I find out that Ken Patterson is not dead. That could only be good news for you." I forced a smile.

Wendover appeared confused. Hadn't he thought of that angle?

"Or what if I find out he died of a heart attack in 1999 in Cleveland? That would certainly help you."

He didn't have an answer.

"You're not going to tell me that's impossible, are you? Because if you do, I will have to assume the worst." I stared at him.

He was thinking hard.

"I can't take your money, Mr. Wendover. I am doing a favor for Ken's daughter. I am trying to find a living Ken Patterson. I have no interest in instigating a murder investigation." As of Saturday, no longer a flat-out lie. "Even if I did, how on earth could a murder this old ever be solved unless the police find a body along with the killer's wallet. You have nothing to fear." At least not before you made this stupid visit to me.

When I looked at Wendover's face, I saw disappointment. Not fear. Not anger. He just appeared to be feeling let down like a car salesman who hadn't closed the deal.

"Really, Mr. Wendover. You have nothing to fear."

He put his briefcase on the counter and snapped open the locks. He seemed so defeated, so sad, that I didn't even fear he would pull out a gun. He turned the case so I could see its contents.

"It's $10,000. Count it. Mostly twenties. Not marked in any way. It's yours. Please stop your search."

I'd never seen that much cash before. I had to admit all that money looked extremely appealing. The idea of taking it had its charms. Put the bills in a drawer and pull out what you need until the funds run out. But, then again, I wasn't about to go down for tax evasion. I'd learned a lesson from Al Capone.

"I can't take your money. I won't. I don't want to. Please, Mr. Wendover. Don't ask me to. Now, if you'll excuse me, my boyfriend is going to be home any second now." I fought saying my big, brute of a boyfriend who could break you in half. Too obvious a lie. I stuck with a more believable line. "I need to get ready." I closed the lid on the briefcase.

He stared at the case and wrung his hands. "Listen to me, Ms. Daniels. I might have liked money a little too much for my own good, but I am basically a stand-up guy. I am not sure that everyone who worked with Ken was. They might want the same thing, for you to stop your investigation, but they might not offer such a civil solution."

He stared at me. Hard. Long. But I sensed no desperation. Shouldn't he be sweating if he were fighting to hold onto the life he knew? Call it intuition, but I wasn't convinced he was scared or even particularly worried.

Looking sad, he didn't resist as I rushed him to the closest door and watched to make sure he went down the outdoor stairs. I didn't see his car, but I heard a car door slam, an engine start, and a vehicle head down the gravel driveway. The car didn't peel out as if in the hands of an angry driver but slowly, cautiously, politely. Nothing like I would have expected from a bad guy in a movie but more like the respectable role he had dressed for.

Chapter 36

Over dinner at the Princeton Inn, Andy and I had an interesting discussion of *The Feminine Mystique*. I was enjoying Andy's return to school.

"Okay, go ahead," he said when dessert arrived.

"Go ahead, what?"

"Go ahead and fill me in on today's news about Ken Patterson. You've shown great restraint. I know you want to talk about it. You had a big day."

"I had a sad day."

"You saw Elisabeth."

"True, but in addition, I finally accepted that I have to give up my dream of having Donna arrested for Ken's murder. Today, Sally DeMarco appeared on the deck to confess that she saw that Ken Patterson was alive five years ago maybe fewer. Maybe three."

"But you knew Ken had survived."

"I guess I held out a glimmer of hope that Count was not Ken."

"Meg, you are generally a kind person. It isn't like you to hope someone is dead."

"Don't worry. Wishing won't do it." I released a loud theatrical sigh to confirm my disappointment. "Sally was sure. She saw him at the Artistical."

"The Artistical? Our Artistical? Where we spent most of last summer?"

"Just think, Andy. We may have been there at the same time. We may have talked to him. Okay, that's unlikely, but from what she saw, she suspected he was a regular."

"Until he saw her there?" Andy made a good point. Why risk going back to a place you'd been seen?

"That may be the one place he doesn't go in Atlantic City."

"What did Elisabeth have to say?"

"Seeing her inspired me to keep going which is good because someone is putting on a full-court press to stop this investigation. Bob DeMarco yesterday. Today a guy who called himself Dave Wendover tried to buy me off."

"Buy you off?"

"He carried ten thousand dollars in cash. I mean I assume it was ten thousand. He said it was. I didn't count it."

I looked across the table and saw that Andy was scowling. Not really at me. More at the thought that someone would offer me ten thousand dollars.

I told Andy the story Wendover gave me. He didn't buy it either.

"I couldn't find anything about him online. I suspect it's not his real name."

"I'm not shocked. Except that you let him in the house, but that's a different topic. I can see only two people that would want you to back off. One, Ken's killer. But, if we accept what Geneva and Diggs told us and what Sally DeMarco saw, there is no killer."

I knew where he was headed. "That leaves one person who would make such an effort."

We spoke in unison. "Ken Patterson."

"He really doesn't want to be found. Why?" I asked.

"Maybe he never looked back after he left. He worked long and hard to get away."

"But people say he loved his daughter."

"People lie, Maggie." His pet name for me. He reached across the table and took my hand. "Maybe you have your answer. Maybe the answer is he does not want to be found."

I couldn't accept that. Not before I got to plead my case. Elisabeth's case.

Chapter 37

"Andy, it appears that the ocean disappeared overnight." I climbed over Andy and opened the balcony door.

"Couldn't have gone far. I still hear it." He mumbled. He wasn't ready to get up.

"The other possibility is that an intruder wrapped the house in cotton."

"Another good theory." He buried his face in his pillow.

I let a few seconds pass before I added, "Not clean cotton." The glass walls were solid sheets of light gray

He rolled onto his back and threw an arm over his eyes. He made no move to rise. "We, of all people, know that weather is not always perfect in paradise. Maybe it will burn off."

But it didn't. The fog transformed into a thin mist that made the thicket seem even more threatening, I was happy when a heavy rain cleared the air. I called Abby and invited her on a road trip.

"Why did you invite me to come with you?" Abby asked a good question as we pulled into the parking lot at the Artistical Hotel and Casino in Atlantic City.

"I heard a rumor that your grandfather was seen at the Artistical."

"When? Now? Is he still there?"

"No. Years ago. I want to talk to people there and see if anyone knows him."

"And you can't do that alone?' said the girl who complained that I didn't include her.

"I could but then our visit would take hours. I'd end up chatting with everyone." Even longer if I asked Andy, who knew just about every employee on-site, to come along. Besides, he had already been generous enough in sacrificing his school time for my project. "I can use you as an excuse."

"Thanks."

"An excuse to keep moving. You are an integral part of my strategy." I did not say that having her along was a move to rev up the emotional level of my visit, a Hail-Mary play I would pull out if needed.

"Can we eat while we are here?" She asked as I pulled into a parking space.

"Actually, I'm hungry. Let's grab something first." I didn't tell her why I picked the Bellini Bistro, but she asked why, after she suggested every other restaurant in the hotel, that I remained so insistent on going to the Bellini. "Because your grandfather may have been seen there."

Our research began before we hit the restaurant. I ran into three people in the hallways from the garage. I showed a maintenance worker, a custodian, and a front office worker the old picture of Ken Patterson. All had the same response. "Sorry, but that doesn't mean he isn't a regular. He might come when I am not on duty."

I thanked them.

"Is that the picture you're using?" Abby sounded astounded.

"It's the picture you gave me."

"Don't you know how to age it?" Her tone went from astounded to disgusted.

I stared at her and shook my head.

"I can't believe you call yourself an investigator. Give me that." She snatched the photo from my hand.

I watched her scan the photo into her phone. "By the way, I never called myself an investigator. I am doing you a favor."

She gave no indication she was listening to me. She was focused on her phone. I have no idea what she did next, but when she was done, I heard a ding on my phone and opened a text with a photo of an older Ken Patterson.

"That's pretty neat."

"Yeah, it's nifty."

I didn't react. I didn't care if she mocked my vocabulary. Just one more annoying trait to add to the list.

"Doesn't your PI boyfriend tell you how to do that?"

Sometimes I don't know how I tolerate you. I didn't say that out loud. "He hasn't worked as a PI in several years. If he wanted to do a similar photo manipulation in his last job, he could have done it on his computer at work." I had no idea if he ever had to do it or would have known how. Nonetheless, I defended him.

At the Bellini Bistro, Mario, the host on duty, was happy to see me. He asked about Andy and if we had made any wedding plans yet. "We've been busy, but we are going to start planning soon."

"I'm sure it will be lovely whenever you plan it. And wherever. Remember, we do lovely events here." He led Abby and me to our table.

"Do you really want to marry Andy?" Abby asked as soon as we were seated.

"Of course. I wouldn't get engaged to him if I didn't."

"Then, why aren't you planning your wedding?" She wasn't simply curious. She was confrontational.

"Who says I'm not?"

"You did. Just now. To the maître d'. You said you were going to get started."

"And I will. Abby, you don't know me or what's been going on in my life. Do you know that last year the cottage that I lived in for six years was destroyed by Hurricane Freida? Do you realize I lost almost everything I own? Do you understand I worked for six years at a job in the Bahamas in a career that I do not want to pursue? Do you grasp that I have no idea what I want to do next? I have a lot on my mind other than picking out frilly dresses and cakes."

"Don't you think you're too old to wear anything frilly?"

I paused and stared before I answered. "Do people tell you that you are a lot like your grandmother?"

"I resemble my father's family." She missed my point.

I changed the subject. "Order something nice. I'm treating. I appreciate your coming along."

She opened the menu but didn't focus on it. "Why didn't you show the host the picture?"

"Abby, there is such a thing as choosing your moment. We were chatting. I don't want it to appear that I only came here to pump him."

"But you did."

Did I really want to find Ken Patterson and subject him to this mini-Donna? *Think of Elisabeth. Think of Elisabeth.* I pasted a smile on my face. "I welcomed the opportunity to come. Andy and I had been meaning to visit, but did I mention time is an issue right now? I was thrilled for the opportunity to combine business and pleasure."

Her response was a sneer and one raised eyebrow. She snapped the menu once and studied it.

I will always believe that Abby ordered from the right side of the menu. The Bellini luncheon selection included sandwiches, salads, pasta dishes, cold platters, and a seafood combination platter featuring a lobster tail. I should have accepted wagers on what she would order. For an appetizer, she ordered a shrimp cocktail. "Are you having soup?" she looked at me.

"Maybe I'll have lobster bisque while you eat your appetizer." I hoped that put the kibosh on soup for her. I was wrong. She ordered the starter, the soup, and the daily seafood entrée before surrendering her menu to the waiter. I had the bisque and a chicken salad sandwich.

When the waiter left, Mario replaced him at the end of the table.

"Mario, I am so glad you are here today. I thought you might know a gentleman we are looking for. This is Abby, his twenty-year-old granddaughter."

Mario said he was pleased to meet her. Maybe he understood why I wanted to clarify that she was under twenty-one. Abby didn't figure out that I was afraid she would order a bottle of their best champagne next.

I felt pressure from Abby building as I chatted with Mario. She wanted me to ask about her grandfather. No buildup. No social niceties. Finally, it got too much for her.

"Are you going to ask him about my grandfather?"

I thought I knew how to shoot daggers from my eyes. Either I had lost the knack or Abby had some sort of protective shell. She was oblivious to my non-verbal messages. Why was I surprised? She was oblivious to most verbal messages. I pulled out my phone and showed him the computer-aged picture of Ken Patterson. "I think he may have shaved the mustache."

Mario studied it carefully. "This goes back a few years. We used to have a regular who came in here who looked a bit like that. What was the name?"

"Kenneth Patterson."

He shook his head. "The name might have been Patterson. I'm not sure. And I can't be sure it was the same guy."

I pulled out the picture from 1977 and passed it to Mario. "That is a picture from when he was in his thirties."

He studied the photo in his hand and then the one on my phone. "Yeah, I might recognize him. The man I am thinking of was tall, slender, in good shape for a man his age. He dressed kind of flashy. Used to come in with a woman who dressed real flashy. Older folks, right? If it's him. I haven't seen him in a while. I bet three. Four. Even five years. I wouldn't remember him at all, but he used to try to tell me jokes. The guy could not tell a decent joke. Funny. Takes a while to notice when regulars drop off. Looking at these photos, if it is the guy I think it is, he just stopped coming in. Sorry I can't help."

Oh, but he had.

Chapter 38

Even if I hadn't just done a stint as a VIP concierge, I could have pegged the guy as *somebody*, or at least a person who thought he was *somebody*. Of course, the baseball cap and sunglass combo was a dead giveaway, but the man loitering in the entrance hall to the Bellini Bistro hadn't stopped building his image there. I did a quick tally of his attire. The man was dressed in easily $5,000 worth of casual clothes, unless the trim on his sunglasses was solid gold in which case, I'd have to add another zero to my estimate.

"Did you enjoy your meal, Ms. Daniels?" The man lifted his sunglasses to reveal his identity.

"Mr. Maturi, why are you here?" I asked as if he did not have a perfect right to be.

"Ssh. I like to keep an eye on the competition. I was surprised to see you here. I assume it must be for your missing person project. It couldn't be for the food. I assume we'll see you back at A Taste of Maturi soon."

I sputtered. He was right. On both counts. The food at the Bellini Bistro was fine, but it didn't measure up to the meals that Maturi was serving. "As you know, I used to work at an Artistical property."

"So you suffer through the meals out of loyalty. Have you had any luck finding Mr. Patterson?"

"No. No."

"After your visit, I wracked my brain trying to think of anything that might help you, but it was so long ago. Most of what I remember, I can't remember."

I tried to be polite, but that made no sense. I told him so.

"The last time I saw Ken, he was cleaning out his office, and I helped him finish a bottle of scotch. I remember drinking, but I don't remember much of what was said. He was pretty far gone. Unlikely he remembers either."

"Ah. So it does make sense. Are you going to taste the food while you are here?"

"No. I am going to ask people who dined in the Bellini Bistro what they think of the food."

"Well, here is the person you should ask." She's the one who ate the most. "Why don't you tell this gentleman what you thought of your lunch."

"It was great." Abby described every dish in such detail that even Maturi appeared bored.

"So, all good then," he wanted the conversation to end.

"Not all good. Kind of expensive."

I guess she did look at the right side of the menu so she could be sure to order the highest cost items. *You're doing this for Elisabeth. You're doing this for Elisabeth.* I chanted silently.

"Time for me to get to work," Maturi said. He turned to me. "I notice you're wearing a ring. Why don't you bring your fiancé to our pre-opening tasting in the main room? Call my assistant. She'll have the tickets sent over."

I called while Abby made a stop at the ladies' room. I tried to give the hostess an e-mail address along with a long explanation of how our mail was being held and forwarded.

"Oh, but Chef Maturi wants everyone to get the lovely invitation. When you get it you'll see why. Give me your address. I'll have it delivered. Fedex. No biggie."

Chapter 39

I dropped Abby at home and lied. I told her I was done for the day, but I wasn't. I backtracked to Sea Isle City and Gerald Patterson.

I knocked three times before he opened the door a crack, I spoke quickly. "I don't know if you remember me."

"I remember you. Why haven't you given up yet?" His tone was oddly civil. Not an angry question. A simple inquiry.

"Because Elisabeth is still cognizant enough to ask about her father."

"You could just wait it out."

"That's…."

He interrupted me. "I know. That's cruel. I wish Elisabeth the best. I do. I just don't get this whole investigation bit, but I guess it's nice that you want to help Elisabeth."

He didn't ask me in, and I didn't ask for an invitation.

"I wondered if you had the names of any of the people that Ken dealt with that you might have considered shady."

"Me? No. Didn't I tell you about Maturi?"

"Him, I met."

Gerald seemed to have no reaction to that news. "Well, that's all I've got. I don't remember if I knew any other names in the first place."

"Do you know where they were located?"

"Most in Philly and then when gambling came to Atlantic City, some down here at the shore. Kenny passed the bar in both Pennsylvania and New Jersey."

I sensed that Gerald was being completely honest. So far.

"Do you know any company names or locations?"

"No. And I don't want to give you the wrong impression. They weren't mobsters or anything. They were just people who had interesting legal needs. More than drawing up a will if you get my drift. I don't actually know. I'm sorry. I realize your heart is in the right place."

I couldn't believe the warm conversation we were having, although he still issued no invitation to go inside. He stepped onto the porch and pulled the door behind him. Whatever was in that house he didn't want me to see.

"Have you been having any luck?"

"Not really. I guess I found out a lot about your brother's departure…escape…whatever people called it, but nothing other than what you told me."

"There never seemed to be any different explanation."

"I still find it hard to believe that after all these years, you've never tried to find him?

Gerald Patterson shook his head. "I explained that."

"Not even when the Internet came up?"

Again, he shook his head. "I'm not much for technology. Did you find anything online?"

"No."

"So it looks like I saved myself some time." He chuckled.

"Well, I should get going anyway. I thought I'd take a shot that you might have more info. Thanks for your help." I turned to leave. "Nice car." I nodded at the Porsche sitting behind the Lexus in the driveway. "You drive it much?"

"It's my son-in-law's. He and my other daughter's husband met here this morning to go fishing."

"Well, here they are now." He waved to someone behind me. I turned to see two in the thirty to forty-year-old range climbing out of a Mercedes at the curb.

"My sons-in-law. They know nothing about all this," he said though I hadn't asked. "No need to talk to them. They never met Elisabeth or Donna for that matter."

I nodded. "Thanks again for your help."

The two men stepped aside, and we said a polite hello to each other as we passed. Handsome guys in casual clothes chatting about car repair. "In any event, he said it would be ready by 5 PM if you don't mind taking me back."

I felt Gerald Patterson's eyes on me as I pulled away. I drove up 76th and circled the block. I was lucky it was off-season. I found a space on Landis from which I could watch the Patterson home and the Porsche parked in front of it.

Why had Gerald lied to me? He said his two sons-in-law had gone fishing in one car. Yet, neither of them was dressed for fishing. One had on expensive loafers and they both had on clothes more appropriate for a business-casual meeting than a fishing trip. According to Gerald, one of them should have been the owner of the Porsche yet the one man had asked for a ride to his car. Had he actually said car? He said it would be ready and he needed a ride. Was I jumping the gun thinking they were talking about car repair? I didn't think so. So who owned the Porsche? I had a guess. Kenneth Patterson loved his Porsche. Wouldn't he love to have another one?

I queued up an audiobook and sat for an hour observing no action until the two men Gerald described as his sons-in-law drove off in the same car they arrived in. For another half-hour, I waited for someone to drive the Porsche away, but no one came out of the house. Logic told me I'd put too much time into this project and that there was nothing to see there. Hunger and the need for a restroom made me start the car for the trip back to Avalon. I pulled away reluctantly. I had no reason to believe that Porsche belonged to Ken Patterson. No reason at all. But I did.

Chapter 40

Before I could check if Andy was home, I heard the ding dong of the doorbell at the deck door.

"What is that noise?" Donna Patterson snapped when I opened the door to the deck.

Guess the doorbell chimes had been a Positano addition. I almost said that the doorbells were added after she sold the house but caught myself. I was not supposed to recognize who she was.

"May I help you?"

"Don't play dumb. You know exactly who I am. I know what you are up to."

I didn't know how to play it. I went with her suggestion, dumb. "Excuse me?"

"I know who you are. I know why you are here in this house and, let me repeat, I know what you are up to." She swept past me in a move that seemed familiar. Oh right. Abby had swept in on her first visit as if reclaiming her territory.

At the edge of the great room, she stopped with her hands on her hips not allowing enough space for me to pass by. "I can't say the décor is very creative. Much different than when we lived here. I had a flair for decorating and could make even this hollow shell look comfortable." She strode to the window and stared toward the ocean. "Sometimes I wonder if I should have sold this place."

"Why did you sell it?"

She turned and glared at me. "It was my decision. I made it. I guess I must live with it." She moved to the side window to check out the pool deck.

"I never felt this house required a pool, but Kenneth, you know, my husband, has always been short on taste. He can be pretentious."

Conspicuously present tense.

"We are different in many ways." She spun on her heel and glowered at me.

I had nothing to say.

She moved to a spot in the center of the room. Her fragrance, unfamiliar to me, filled the large space. "I want you to stop this investigation. It will only bring sadness to my daughter. Her father has not been a part of her life for many decades. She did fine without him. He has now and has always had the option to return." She gazed into the distance, and I sensed that she wanted to make me see the pain that statement caused her. "So far, he has chosen not to do it. I still believe he will wise up, but it will serve him right if he shows his face after she is unable to recognize him."

What about Elisabeth's desires? What kind of mother was Donna? Everything was about her. "But Elisabeth wants…."

She interrupted. "I am thinking of Elisabeth. If he wants to come back, he will. I don't want him showing up here like a hero and hogging her deathbed. She deserves better."

"But Elisabeth…." Again, she cut me off.

"As much as it pains me to say this, Elisabeth is losing her mind. She doesn't know what she wants. Never has, really."

Never was allowed to figure out what she wanted was the thought that crossed my mind.

"She didn't pursue a lucrative career or marry a man who could take adequate care of her. I mean, Al did all right but nothing like her father."

The father that abandoned his family.

"I expected more, but Elisabeth wouldn't listen to me. It's not my fault her life turned out the way it did."

Which I expected Elisabeth saw as just fine. At least until her illness hit. Donna Patterson was a true genius at inspiring disgust.

"I didn't come here to discuss my life with you. I came here to tell you to drop your ridiculous investigation into my husband's departure from his family. He did not disappear. On July 4, 1977, after months of preparation, he left a party at the house of now-deceased friends here in Avalon saying that he had to take care of a business item. He did not tell me. He told a friend who drove him here to our home leaving me at the party. What happened after that I cannot tell you."

I hoped if I used a sympathetic tone—assuming I could get a word in—that she might soften her approach. I wasn't fast enough before she continued.

"Kenneth had been driving an old, beat-up station wagon around the shore. I assume he drove that to another destination where he transferred to another vehicle. I assume that because I was informed by his attorney, a man I had thought until that day was our friend, that Kenneth had made elaborate plans for his departure. Part of that plan was to leave the car to be picked up and junked. I can see why. That old heap was a disgrace. At any rate, he had taken care of every last detail. With the help of his attorney, he simply disappeared off the face of the earth. No one heard from him. Ever. Not me. Not my daughter. Not one of our friends."

"Do you have any idea why he left?" I tried my sympathetic tone but it didn't matter.

Donna didn't like the question, but she had an answer ready. She had probably delivered it many times. "In the years before my husband's departure, he was under quite a bit of stress at work. He didn't deal with it well and began to display odd behavior, dressing and speaking inappropriately. I think the stress escalated and he was unable to deal with the underlying issues. I tried to discuss the changes with him and be supportive, but he went temporarily insane. Our marriage was strong, and I believed he loved his daughter. I sometimes wonder if he left to protect us."

Was she leading me to the unsavory business partners scenario? I would ask a follow-up question whenever she took a breath, but I did not see such an opportunity in the near future.

"When he didn't return, of course, I barely had time to worry that something horrible had happened to him. I tried not to speculate, and then his lawyer visited and assured me that he was fine. Then and until this day I have simply waited for his return. He is welcome at any time."

I was dumbfounded by her admission that after forty years she expected him to turn up. My hesitation gave her a chance to turn towards the door.

"Wouldn't you like to have a seat?" I asked.

"No. I have no need to stay." Her sneer said hardly anything could be worse.

"But I have a few questions. For example, you mentioned the possibility your husband left to protect you and your daughter."

She stared at me.

"I wondered if you feared that your husband was involved with unsavory types in business."

"In the law, Ms. Daniels. In the law," she sniffed, "lawyers cannot deal exclusively with the type of people that they would choose to. Nor can they know what people are like before they become involved. I was not aware of such involvements, but I had heard rumors about some of his clients. If my husband inadvertently found himself in a bad position, he would never have wanted to worry me. He might have found himself a victim of an unsavory association. Perhaps that is why he could not return."

"Did you know the names of any of those people?"

"Were you listening to me? He would have protected me, I am sure. Kenneth could be extremely protective."

"Do you know what happened to his boat?" I asked.

For some reason, this question took her aback. "His boat. He owned a boat called the DonnaLisa," I added.

She stuttered briefly but recovered her imperious tone. "I am well aware that he owned a boat. When he developed new interests, he lost interest in it. I do not remember when he told me he'd sold it." She hesitated. "I have no idea where the proceeds went. He did keep a large portion of his fortune for himself."

She had more to say but she was having trouble saying it. Literally. She opened her mouth and tried to say a word but pursed her lips and shook her head in frustration. She paused and stared at the floor. When she spoke again, she seemed fine. She smiled. Until that moment I did not realize she could.

I leaped on her sign of weakness. "That must have been such a difficult time for you. I can't imagine what that night was like for you. Coming home. Realizing he was gone."

She seemed surprised by my sympathy and didn't figure out I'd asked a question. Not a particularly useful one. What could she say about her pain that would help me find her husband? I heard my grandmother's voice. *Nothing ventured, nothing gained.*

"I didn't realize anything was wrong. My husband had left a party for business reasons. That horrible old car he drove was gone. I assumed he had headed to Philadelphia for the night so he could get an early start the next day. That day was the last of a long weekend."

"How did his business associates get in touch with him in the middle of a party?" There were no cell phones in those days. Not even any voice mail.

"It is so long ago now, I can't actually recall. I assume he called them from the party to check in on their plans for the next day. He was like that. Always working. Work always came first with him."

Until the moment he walked away from his business and his profession. "Did you try to call him that night?"

"I…I don't recall that I did. I probably would not have. He had gone home to work. Or so I had been told. I wouldn't have disturbed him. He could get quite irate if I interrupted him. I don't recall if I tried, but I know I didn't speak with him."

If I was still viewing her as a murderer, I would have found this suspicious. Of course, I would have found it suspicious if she did call. "When did you realize that he was gone?"

Donna had an answer prepared for this question. I assume she had answered it many times. Anger crept back into her voice. "His attorney notified me. He drove from Philadelphia on July 5 and presented me with all the paperwork. He handled everything efficiently. Extremely so."

"That must have been horrible for you. Finding yourself all alone." Oops. I let it slip that I knew her daughter was away. What was the harm in that? She knew I was working for Elisabeth.

"To tell you the truth, I don't recall much about that day. I believe I went into some sort of trance. I just listened. I couldn't take it in. It was such a shock."

To her, but not many others.

Her arrogant mood had softened. "I appreciate that you are trying to help Elisabeth, but please for her good, don't pursue this. Who knows what she would discover if he were found? Now if he reappears? That is a completely different story. I go to church every morning and pray that he chooses to return." And then she said words that sounded awkward coming from her mouth. "God bless you for what you are trying to do." She grabbed my hand and squeezed it. Her largest diamond cut into my finger. It hurt. "I understand you mean well, but please you can only do harm."

She turned and, as she did, caught sight of the painting by the door. Seeing the watercolor of her husband's boat caused her to pause briefly. She adjusted the handbag on her arm. A nervous gesture, but she said nothing. She strode out the door without a goodbye, leaving her scent behind. Well, her scent and a small scratch on my index finger.

My mind was in a jumble trying to figure the woman out. I watched her walk to her car, strides confident, back ramrod straight. I noticed that she had locked the car even ten feet from the house in our driveway. As I watched her pull away, I realized I hadn't been asking the right questions, even of myself.

Chapter 41

Andy settled around the corner on the sectional, propped his feet up and listened. He had his copy of *The Feminine Mystique* with him, but if he had hopes of discussing anything but Kenneth Patterson, his dreams were quickly quashed.

"There is a full-court press on me to stop this investigation."

"Anyone new join the other team?"

"Oh, yes. Donna Patterson dropped by today."

"How did that go?"

"Pretty much as you would expect. She swept in and recited the story she's been telling for forty years." I filled Andy in. "Her visit did get me thinking. I've added a third theory as to why someone wanted the investigation stopped." I paused for dramatic effect.

"Go ahead." He bit into his cookie.

"We've already theorized that someone wants the investigation stopped because they murdered Kenneth Patterson."

"But now we know that isn't true."

"We are 99% sure that he was not murdered that night." Dreams die hard. "But I accept that Ken survived at least until twenty years ago. After that? Who knows?"

"Our second theory was that Kenneth Patterson is alive and does not want to be found."

"And your new theory? Theory number 3."

"Maybe someone wants the investigation to stop because it will reveal some malfeasance."

Andy nodded with a broad gesture. "Possible, but what? The statute of limitation would have run out for any crime other than murder and, despite your desire to reveal Donna as a murderer, we know that isn't the case."

"Let's begin with Donna. The question on the table is why wouldn't she not want me to find her husband."

"I thought she wanted Ken to come back."

"But of his own accord. What would be more humiliating for her than if I find him and he refuses to come back? She'd have to abandon her fantasies of his mental breakdown. Part of her might be afraid to find him. Everyone made it clear that she never launched any type of investigation. She doesn't want to face the truth."

Andy nodded. "Okay. Who else?"

"Leslie Meitner. Because her husband did something illegal in his dealings with Ken."

"Over forty years ago? The law wouldn't want him, and if Ken did, he knew exactly where to find him. I don't see it. Who else?"

"Bob DeMarco. Because he secretly wanted Donna?" I proposed.

"I think he secretly wanted the DonnaLisa." Andy was more cynical.

"You're projecting. Maybe Donna manipulated him."

Andy couldn't dismiss that suspicion out of hand. "Possible. Next."

I moved on. "I don't buy Wendover's story for a minute. He's a pawn. Someone is using him. Probably the same person who is manipulating Bob DeMarco."

"Possibly. Speaking of pawns. How did Donna find out what you were doing?" Andy asked.

"I guess Elisabeth could have said something, but I doubt it. And Abby knows to keep it a secret."

"Abby's father?"

"He wouldn't slip up. He wants whatever is best for Elisabeth. I believe that."

"So?" Andy stared at me waiting for an answer.

"Someone who wants the investigation stopped and knew she would help the effort."

"Who would know that?" Andy asked.

"Who do you think?" I knew who I thought.

"Someone who knows that Donna would not want him to found. A person who knows a secret we do not." Andy offered.

"Let's say it together."

"Ken Patterson." Andy and I said in unison.

I smiled. "A man who does not want to be found."

Chapter 42

The next morning, Andy and I drove to Sea Isle in separate cars so that he could continue on to school. I wanted to go into Gerald Patterson's alone, but Andy insisted on waiting outside. I kept my phone in my hand so I could signal if I needed help.

This time only the Lexus was in the driveway. I assumed Gerald was alone. I hoped Gerald was alone. When he opened his door, I opened with "May I come in?"

He seemed taken aback and stepped back to open the door wide. I stepped into a comfortable living room furnished, according to my guess, in the popular shore house decor from at least several decades before. It might not have been stylish, but the room was warm and inviting.

"Mind if I have a seat?" I didn't wait for an answer. I settled into an armchair, the one closest to the door in case he grew angry. "How have you been?" I asked expecting no reply.

Surprisingly, he answered, "I've been fine. What it's been what? Eighteen hours since you've been by? I didn't think I would see you again. Of course, I think that every time."

"Well, you probably wouldn't have, but Donna came to see me last night."

"Ken's Donna? My sympathies. What does that have to do with me?" He perched on the edge of a Windsor chair across from me. He wasn't going to settle in.

"She wanted me to stop the investigation."

"I told you that as far as I knew she never tried to find him."

"But how did she find out I was doing an investigation?"

"I.... You know that's a good question, but I am sure I wouldn't have the answer. You said you talk to her granddaughter. Maybe she told her."

"No. She knew Donna wouldn't approve."

"You said little Elisabeth isn't in her right mind, God bless her. She might have let it slip."

"Possible, I suppose. But I find it hard that she would get the details right."

"Well, I don't have any other ideas."

"I was thinking you might have gotten word to Donna."

"Why would I do that? How would I do that? I have no idea where she lives and would have no idea where to tell her to go. I know your name. That is it. I don't even know where you live."

"I mentioned I was housesitting. And, you have my phone number."

"Did she call you?"

He had me there. "She appeared on my doorstep."

"Why would I stir things up with Donna? Suppose Ken was alive. Would I want her searching for him?" Gerald shook his head as if disgusted.

"You know she wouldn't. She never looked for him. At all. She wouldn't have wanted to help the investigation. I don't understand why she would be so adamant about blocking it, but she would have wanted to stop it. I don't buy the whole 'he has to come crawling back' scenario. You would have known about that."

"I know no such thing. It's not me who told her. It makes no sense."

I watched for some nervous gesture, a tell, but saw none.

"It does if Ken is still alive," I said.

That got a reaction. Gerald sputtered and fought for words. "I don't understand."

"You realized that I was going to figure out that Ken was still alive. And, Ken does not want to be found. You knew that Donna had resisted any efforts to find Ken. I can't say I understand her, but she wanted him back only if he crawled to her. I'm not going to try to track him down and confront him. I would ask you to plead my case for me, for Elisabeth. I simply want an opportunity to talk to him so I can tell him about Elisabeth and Abby. My search has nothing to do with Donna. Nothing. I suspect family wasn't important to him." I glanced at the photos displayed on the table next to me, "I can see it is to you."

Gerald's back stiffened with pride as he gazed at the pictures. "I am a lucky man."

I studied the pictures of his family. Two daughters each with two children. One was with one of the men I had seen the day before. The other was with an African American man who looked nothing like the other man I'd seen before. Gerald had lied. The question was how often.

Chapter 43

I guess I shouldn't have been surprised when Gerald Patterson showed up at my door. But I was surprised he arrived only a few hours after he'd rushed me out of his house.

"Mr. Patterson? Gerald?" I didn't know what else to say.

"I need to talk to you." He nodded towards the ocean. "Do you mind if we sit on the deck? It has been so long."

Sure. House comes with rights to previous visitors.

"I've been lying to you."

No shocker there.

"Ken is dead."

I didn't believe him for a minute.

"When did that happen?" A trick question. Surely, he anticipated that he would have to provide details.

"Years ago."

"How did you find out?"

"Meitner told me."

"So Ken died before Meitner."

"Right."

"And you didn't mention this to me the first time I visited because…?"

"You caught me off guard. No one had come looking for Ken, ever. I didn't know what to say."

"You could have said, 'no need to search. He is dead.' If you wanted me to back off, why didn't you tell me this the first day I came to you."

Whoever prepped Gerald for this visit had not done a good job. Even though my tone was calm, he looked distraught as if I were browbeating him.

"I know why you didn't," I said. "You needed to check with Ken and find out what he wanted you to do. What I don't understand is why he didn't tell you to shut me down in the first place. All you had to do was say he was dead. I wasn't going to ask for proof. But instead, you let me get started, so you had to launch a ridiculous campaign to get me to stop."

"No. It wasn't like that. Ken simply wanted to know what was going on."

"He could have asked me."

"And you'd run back to Donna."

"I don't have any ties to Donna."

He didn't have an answer.

"There's no fraud involved here," I continued. "She never tried to have him declared dead. He anticipated everything. I can't imagine he left any insurance that she could claim. No crime. Meitner had all that under control." I hoped my stare would make Gerald uncomfortable.

Still no answer.

"I can imagine the pow-wow you had. What to do about this? At some point, one of you figured out that if you had told me he was dead in the first place, I would have gone away."

He looked sheepish.

"It's too late, Gerald. I know he's alive. I haven't told his family. I wouldn't without talking to him. I told you he could simply say, 'I don't want to see my daughter.' I couldn't force him. He's not wanted by the cops. Is he?"

Gerald shook his head.

"Then, I cannot fathom why it is so important to hide the truth. All I can figure is that he has some secret he needs to keep hidden. All I want to do is talk to him, to plead Elisabeth's case, but if he is willing to go to this extreme to hide that he is alive, I will tell the family I could not locate him. If I say he's dead they are going to want a death certificate or an obituary or something." Gerald kept his eyes cast down. "You go home and tell your brother he has nothing to fear from me. I will tell his granddaughter that I was told he was dead. That I have no proof to offer." Not a lie. "They will, of course, ask why you didn't tell me this before. I'll say I have no idea because the truth is I do not understand what you are up to."

"Elisabeth should feel loved. He'd like her to know that."

"I don't see any reason she would believe me if I told her."

"We had some wonderful times here. Can I sit here for a while? It's such a beautiful spot."

An audacious request, but I said yes. "Let me get you a beer." I wanted to give him time to think, to change his story, to open up, but by the time he finished his drink and drove away, he had not.

Chapter 44

I got the call the next morning.

"Miss Daniels. My name is Kenneth Patterson. I understand that you'd like to talk to me." I was taken aback by the voice. No one had told me to expect a deep, sonorous voice worthy of a television anchorman. "I have also been told that you will not give up until you do."

That was no longer true, but I thought of Elisabeth. "I would like an opportunity to plead my case."

He did not respond, but I kept to my rule to say as little as possible. I waited.

"This would be a confidential meeting."

"Of course. I'm not a professional investigator. I have no legal obligation to provide any information to your family." A moral obligation? That was different. I could deal with that issue later. I didn't want anything to interfere with my chance to present Elisabeth's dream. "I can come to your home."

"No. Are you familiar with the seawall at the north end in Brigantine?"

"I am."

"10 AM tomorrow. Park near the middle. Wait on the walkway. I'll find you."

I arrived early the next morning and got a morning Coke at the Wawa. I needed caffeine to face Ken Patterson. I found a parking spot that was, according to my calculations, as close as I could get to the center of the seawall. There were plenty of cars around, but their owners must have been eating breakfast across the street at Pirates Den. I didn't find a lot of people when I climbed the stairs to the walkway. It didn't take long to figure out that the wind might have had something to do with empty walkway. I assumed the same gusts that made the foam fly off the waves kept the seawall free of casual strollers. The only person who joined me was a single walker carrying what looked like leftovers. She climbed the stairs, spent thirty seconds admiring the sea view and left. I was alone with a view that made me wish I could paint. I didn't even try to photograph it, fearing the sight of my phone might scare Ken away.

At one minute to ten, I spotted an older man walking down the street. His was not a leisurely pace. He was on a mission. When he got closer, I recognized him. Not because of all the photos I had looked at. Not because of the aging app I had used to see what he would look like as an older man. No, behind his sunglasses I was sure I recognized our gardener.

I watched him walk towards me. His stride was not the one I had imagined for the young Ken, but also not the gait of an old man. His shoulders were slightly bent, but he was still tall. His hair, not totally gray, framed his face with a deep tan although it was early April. He appeared vigorous. Not the vigor of the young man who disappeared, but vigor.

I felt nervous as if I were meeting a celebrity, someone who had loomed large in my imagination and was now going to become real as if George Clooney had stepped off the screen. Well, maybe not George Clooney. Ken didn't look *that* good. Maybe a tall Anthony Hopkins.

He held the railing as he climbed the steps, but he had no trouble reaching the walkway. I could feel his discomfort as he headed towards me, but it wasn't physical.

"Ms. Daniels?" He did not extend a hand.

"Meg," I answered.

"At last we meet."

"We met once before if I'm not mistaken." I sounded so sophisticated as if Noel Coward had written the words for me.

"I didn't think you realized who I was." I heard the tiniest hint of amusement in his tone.

"I didn't until about two minutes ago."

"How did you find me?"

"Finding Gerald wasn't difficult." I explained my first step.

"But he was sworn to secrecy."

"And he did protect you," I said. "He never admitted you were alive until you gave him permission."

He seemed pleased by that information. He gestured towards a bench and we both settled in. The seat faced the water, but I kept my eyes riveted on Ken Patterson. I had waited so long to see him.

"I have to say, I didn't expect to find you so close to home. If the truth be told, I didn't expect to find you at all. I thought most likely you were dead." I didn't mention at the hands of his then-wife. "How did you manage to avoid being recognized while you lived so close to your old summer home?"

"I picked Brigantine because I knew no one here, but it was close enough to where I grew up that I felt as if I had come home. I'd lived in a dozen places, but I reached an age when I wanted to come home. I've made a life here."

"And you never felt the need to go back to your old life?" Even as I asked the question, it sounded dumb on my lips.

"How old are you?"

I told him.

"I left my old life before you were born. It seems like all that happened in a different incarnation on another planet."

"Your daughter doesn't feel that way." I figured I might as well move on to the reason I'd come.

"Lisa," he said the name with reverence. "I believed she would do fine without me. I cared about her. I did, but I would have been a rotten father for her even though I loved her."

"You named your boat after her."

He smiled. "Aren't you the brainiac? An anagram. What a dumb name, but I got all the letters in. For her and for Roddy. She had a little brother. He didn't survive." He paused as if observing a moment of silence. "When I left, I expected to come back into Lisa's life, but then things got complicated. It got too late. But don't go thinking I was a long-suffering saint doing what was best for my daughter. I was a self-centered jerk for a very long time."

I found that easy to believe but didn't tell him.

"Gerald said you were talking to people about me." He was seeking confirmation.

"Mostly friends, but I think you may know that. I got the impression I was being followed."

"I didn't ask anyone to do that. Gerald just wanted to help. He asked an old friend to help."

"Joey Facenda?"

Ken appeared shocked that I knew the name.

"I never spoke to him," I said.

He appeared startled by that news. "Then who did you talk to?"

"As I said, old friends of yours."

He didn't press for names, and I didn't offer any. "What did you find out about me?"

"That you carefully planned your escape. That you had been unhappy with the life you were living. That you wanted to keep up with the times. That Donna and you had different desires and expectations.

"You talked to her?"

"Your family did not want me to because she would not approve. But someone must have tipped her off that I was looking for you, and she came to see me, to dissuade me."

He smirked. "Yeah, I didn't think she'd want anyone digging into what happened to me."

"Everyone told the same story. She wanted you to come crawling back of your own free will."

"Did she now?" That thought seemed to amuse him.

"I talked to Bob DeMarco and his wife, ex-wife, Sally. Then Robin Carson. Several of your friends are dead. I talked to Malcolm Maturi. You remember him? He said you helped him get his business off the ground."

"He was a client I was happy to get rid of. I saw his name in a headline the other day. He's negotiating a deal for his property and his brand. I didn't realize he had a brand." Talking about something other than his own predicament seemed to relax Ken.

"You didn't know he was opening a restaurant in Atlantic City?"

"Does that mean he's around here?"

"That's where I talked to him."

"He remembered me?"

"All he said was that you were his first lawyer."

"That was a long time ago. He was just a kid. A snotty kid. Cocky. Fancied himself a big-time business tycoon. A big fish in the local pond, but he had bigger plans."

"In my opinion, he hasn't changed."

"That's too bad." He chuckled.

****Kenneth Patterson****
Patterson Law Offices
Philadelphia, Pennsylvania
July 1, 1977

One of the problems Ken was escaping was his relationship with guys like Malcolm Maturi. Guys who walked a fine line and fell off on the wrong side more often than not. Maturi was worse than most. He was still a kid. Thought he was invincible. A world-class manipulator. He wouldn't accept that Ken was not going to handle his business. He had shown up at his Philadelphia office unannounced and unwilling to accept he was no longer a client.

"Look Malcolm, I can't. I told you that. I gave you a referral. I am not your lawyer anymore."

"But I want you to handle this."

"I'm going away. Look, I haven't told everyone exactly what I'm doing. I need your promise to keep this quiet. I'm shutting down. Clearing out. I haven't taken any new clients in over a year, and I've handed existing clients over to other firms. I would have been happy to provide you with services, but I am leaving."

"Whatta ya mean, leaving?"

"Leaving, going, splitting, getting out of town, getting out of the business."

"Why would you do that? You got a pretty nice gig here."

"Yeah, well things are not always what they seem. You want to join me?" Ken pulled a bottle of scotch and two glasses out of a box. The kid was already half-loaded. That made him seem like a good drinking partner.

"Nice." The kid accepted the drink eagerly.

"I can't believe you're leaving a gig like this. I saw your house in Avalon. Pretty nice setup. You selling it? Maybe I'll buy it."

In your dreams.

"Must be a real chick magnet."

The kid was right. Too bad Ken would never get to use it for that purpose, but he'd never considered staying in the house an option. He wanted to go, to be somewhere else, to be anywhere else.

"You live there alone?"

"No. I have a wife and a daughter."

"They want to leave that place?"

"They aren't coming."

"What are you telling me, man?"

"I am telling you that come next week, I am going to be a ghost. This life… my life…it looks fine, but I'm not happy. I'm not that old." Ken knew why he was confiding in the kid. He'd approve. Everyone else he thought of telling would have disapproved, tried to stop him. But this kid? This kid would see him as a hero. He looked shocked but impressed. "Really, I am young enough to start over and I can."

"Where are you going?"

"That my young friend is a state secret. All I can tell you is it's somewhere where no one can find me."

"You're crazy. Giving up that place? You shouldn't go. You should make your wife go."

"You don't know my wife." He took a swig of the liquor and raised his glass in a toast. "Lucky guy."

"All the more reason to make her go. There are ways."

"Yeah, don't think I didn't fantasize about them." Ken was lying, trying to look like a tough guy, trying to impress a twenty-four-year-old kid. Why? Because the life he'd been living embarrassed him.

"Make your fantasies real. Live your fantasies. You want to know the way to do it? I'll share my plan." The kid leaned forward, his eyes sparkling. He could hardly contain his excitement. "Number one, you get your wife to withdraw a lot of money from the bank. My plan is I organize a charitable event with cash prizes. I will have called ahead to make sure it's ready. I'll ask for all different denominations. You know for the different prizes. At the last minute, I can't pick it up because I'm all the way across town where hundreds of people can see me. I phone her and ask her to pick it up. All she has to do is go get the cash. I'll make sure they only release it to her so she can't send anyone else."

"Yeah?" Ken wasn't sure where this was going.

"Then, I hire a guy. You must know that my dad's in construction. He and I, we run into some guys in the course of business, who know some guys. You know what I mean?"

Ken couldn't believe what a blowhard the kid was. Making himself sound not just tough but connected.

"These guys are real pros. You made a contract with them, they honor it forever. They never say a word. Until death."

Or until they need to make a deal to squirm out of some other crime. *Ken didn't say that. Let the kid role-play. He was enjoying the kid's act.*

"So, you get one of these guys and you find out how much they charge. Then know what you do?"

"Pay them?" Ken sounded tentative because he knew there had to be more to it.

"But how do you pay them? This is where it gets good. The guy shoots your old lady in a robbery. Pockets the money and leaves. If, despite your iron-clad alibi, the cops decide to check you out, they can look and look and never find where any money changed hands."

"Sounds like a good plan, but I don't need to kill my wife."

"Why?"

"I want out. I don't want to have to stay here and take care of my daughter. Fatherhood is not where I'm at right now. In the future? I can get in touch."

"You're going to leave your kid? That stinks, man."

"She'll have a great life. I have left her more than well-off. She'll want for nothing."

"I'm not giving up my daughter. I'm staying put. I'm keeping the kid. I'm keeping the house." Malcolm pulled out his wallet.

It fell open to a snapshot of a dark-haired girl with wide eyes. Younger than Elisabeth. Maybe five or six years old.

"Isn't she a beauty? This is my Marcella. I would never let her go."

"You think you can get custody of her in your divorce?"

"What makes you think there is going to be a divorce. Aren't you listening? What I told you. That's what I'm going to do. You watch the papers. I got it all planned."

Ken still didn't believe him. The kid was just trying to impress him. "Yeah, well, I'll say good luck now. I won't know a thing about it because I'll be gone."

*****

"What a blowhard. I thought I was a blowhard, but this guy really came up with some whoppers." He stared at me. "What's wrong?"

"Ken, Malcolm Maturi's wife was murdered. He was the prime suspect. The cops could never nail him."

"How did she die?"

"You just told me."

Chapter 45

The blood drained from Ken Patterson's face. "And you talked to him. You talked to Maturi."

"Yes." I felt as frightened as Ken looked.

"And you told him I was alive."

"I told him it was a possibility." I stuttered as I tried to recall what exactly I had said to Malcolm Maturi.

"And he knows you found me."

"No. No way." That I was sure of.

"And you think you were being followed."

"Only by people I suspected you sent."

"Today?"

"I didn't worry today. You'd agreed to see me. I figured you no longer needed to have me followed....Oh God." I hadn't checked for a tail. Why would I? No way Ken's people were still following me.

"He could have followed you." He surveyed the entire area.

There were no lone male walkers, but who could know who was hidden in the cars parked in the area. "But he told you that story so many years ago. His wife died so many years ago."

"There's no statute of limitation on murder. But it isn't the legal aspect that worries me. He has a big deal in the works. A scandal could kill it. He doesn't want a scandal."

"But all these years you never said a thing."

"I never knew." Ken shook his head.

"He doesn't know that. He doesn't even know you're alive. For sure."

"Doesn't he? Let me think. Let me think." He got to his feet with stronger movements than I'd seen before. He took two steps to the right, then two to the left, then two to the right. "I've got to get out of here. Go home. Wait for me to contact you. Do not contact me. Do not contact Gerald. Oh, God. I never knew. Oh, God."

"I'll drive you home."

"No. If he's here that's what he's waiting for. I'm better on foot. You stay here. Don't watch me go. Better if you have no idea what direction I went."

I was shaking. "I am so sorry. I never thought."

Ken said, "Hug me."

"What?"

"He doesn't know what I look like now. He only met with me a few times many years ago. For all he knows, you came to Brigantine to see your father. Give me a big warm hug. Maybe a kiss on the cheek."

I did.

He whispered in my ear. "This isn't your fault. You were trying to help Elisabeth. You couldn't have known. No one knew. For God's sake, I didn't know." He kissed me on the forehead. "Now, watch the water."

I slipped out of his arms and let go of his hand reluctantly as if saying goodbye to a beloved parent. I turned toward the ocean and fought the urge to look back. My legs were shaking. I didn't know if they would continue to hold me. I sank onto the bench that ran along the railing and sat facing north with my head turned to keep my gaze glued on the waves crashing against the rocks. After three or four minutes, I told myself Ken had to be safely away. I turned and saw no sign of him, but I did see a black Jaguar turning the corner a block away. The shape of the head was familiar. The pony tail. I told myself it couldn't be, but, in my gut, I knew. It was.

I ran to my car and made a turn into 11th Street. I could no longer see the Jaguar. At the corner, I spotted him. He'd slowed down while Ken climbed into a classic Porsche.

Malcolm wasn't checking to see if he was being tailed. He was busy tailing Ken. Ken was apparently oblivious. He didn't seem to notice the short motorcade following him through a series of turns that led to a modest house on the water. Ken pulled the Porsche into the driveway behind a gray compact car. Rushing across the lawn to his front door left him exposed. I held my breath waiting for a shot to ring out, but he disappeared into the house unharmed.

I would have let out a sigh of relief, but Malcolm didn't keep driving. He pulled past the house and stopped. I backed into a parking space before he could spot me and dialed Ken's cell phone. He didn't answer. Of course, he would have called me on a burner. He was still a man in hiding. He's told me not to contact him. He wasn't going to answer.

In front of me, Malcolm made no effort to get out of his car. Now that he knew where Ken lived, Ken would never be safe again. Because of me. I'd worry about that later. Right now I had to warn Ken.

There aren't that many trees in Brigantine, but luckily there was a row of trees along the Patterson property line. Dense enough for me to get to the house without letting Malcolm see me? I wasn't convinced, but I had no choice. I needed to warn Ken. And maybe someone else. The woman Geneva had talked about might live there and be at home. There were two cars in the driveway.

At least, I was all in black. I might not have matched the trees but, with any luck, I looked like a shadow moving through the brush. Or a bear.

When I cleared the front of the Patterson house, Malcolm could no longer see me. And I could no longer see Malcolm. I needed to rush.

I ran across a patch of lawn and pressed myself against the side of the house. I edged towards the back towards a high window. I jumped to see inside. The kitchen. The room appeared to be empty.

I knocked on the window gently. I couldn't assume Malcolm was still in his car. I jumped again with my arms waving. How did they not notice a jumping person outside their window?

I slid along the wall and around a corner onto the back wall of the house. No one was using the lovingly maintained back patio, lawn, and dock. I wasn't surprised no boat sat at the dock. I hadn't seen any boats in the water yet.

I felt my way along the back wall quickly expecting Malcolm to turn the far corner at any moment. I was relieved when I reached a sliding glass door. I saw Ken sitting in a recliner with a laptop in his lap. I knocked on the glass gently and waved frantically. He stared at me. I saw confusion. I saw anger. I saw frustration. What I didn't see was any motion indicating he was going to let me in.

I put my hands together in a universal gesture of prayer. Beseeching him to let me in. I didn't wait for a response. I tried the door. It slid open.

Ken reached the door just as I got it open. I pushed him back inside and pulled the door closed. "Do you have one of the bars to hold the door shut?"

He didn't question. He passed me what looked like a cut-off broom handle.

"I didn't follow you. I followed Malcolm. He followed you. He's out front. He's driving a black Jaguar."

Ken rushed to the front window and peeked through the sheer curtains. "I see the car. I don't see him." He handed me a cord. "Close the drapes."

I pulled the heavy drapes until they met and blocked any view of the room. Ken had pulled curtains across the sliding glass doors to the patio and disappeared into an adjoining room. I went to the door and found him in a bedroom peeking through closed curtains.

"I don't see him." Ken turned towards me.

"That can't be good." I waved my arms aimlessly. "He's got to be on his way in. You've got to call the police."

"And tell them what?"

"I don't know. I'm not a professional." I felt sick to my stomach. I had put this man in harm's way.

He handed me his cell phone. An out-going call was ringing. "I'll check the house. Tell my wife, tell Janice not to come home."

I watched out the bedroom window while I listened to the ringing but saw no sight of Malcolm. Janice's voice mail picked up. "Janice. This is Meg Daniels. Ken was meeting me today. He asked me to call. Don't come back to the house right now. It's a long story but trust me." Why would she? "Trust Ken. Don't come home. Wait for Ken to call. Please. Promise. He's fine. There's just…it's complicated. Trust him. Listen to him." I tried to think of something else to say. I left a long silence before I ended the call with the word "please" stretched out for three seconds.

Ken had left the room. I heard the voice a second before I would have stepped into the living room to find him. I jumped back, out of sight. The voice was Malcolm's.

"Long time no see, eh Kenny-boy."

"I'm sorry?" Ken sounded confused. He was doing a good job of faking.

"You don't recognize your old buddy, Malcolm. Malcolm Maturi."

"Malcolm? My God. I haven't seen you since you were a kid. I didn't recognize you. Now I can see it's you, but the ponytail kind of threw me, that and the gun in your hand. What's with the gun?" For a man facing a gun, Ken seemed bizarrely calm.

"Don't play dumb with me, Kenny."

I sank to my knees and crawled to the landline on the bedside table, grabbed the handset and crawled into the closet. I hit 911.

"This is 911. What's your emergency?"

My head was surrounded by cotton skirts. I pulled them around them to mute the sound. I whispered. "A man is holding a gun on a man in this house. He is threatening to kill him." I wasn't sure that was true, but it was a good bet Maturi was. Plus saying that was a good ploy to get help quickly.

"What is your location?"

"I'm in Brigantine."

"Your address?"

"I don't know." Thank God for landlines. I had no idea where I was. "Can't you see that on your screen? This is a landline."

"Are you in danger?"

"Not unless he figures out I'm here, but Ken is,"

She didn't ask who Ken was. "Okay, stay on the line with me."

"I will. I have to do one thing. I'll be right back."

I pulled a skirt off the hanger and covered the receiver to mute her protests.

With Ken's cell phone in hand, I crawled out of the closet and across a braided rug to the bedroom door. I saw both men at an angle which meant neither faced my way. I silenced Ken's phone, set it to record, and slid it into a spot so that the doorjamb held it in place.

I crawled backwards as quickly as I knew how to the closet. I stayed on my knees when I pulled the door in, leaving it open a crack. I positioned my ear beside it. As long as the two men kept talking in excited tones, I could hear them.

"I'm back. They are still talking."

"Stay with me now." The 911 operator sounded very supportive considering I'd just defied her orders. I whispered that I would.

Out in the living room, Malcolm asked Ken. "Who else is here?"

"My wife is out with friends. Only the two of us live here. She's never heard of you, Malcolm. Whatever gripe you have with me, she's got nothing to do with it." Ken switched to attempted bonding. "You look good. I had no idea you had done so well. I just heard about your success. That's wonderful. So I don't understand why you would screw up your success by holding a gun on me."

"You are right. I am doing great. I am about to sign a deal that means I never have to step into a kitchen or suck up to some vapid housewife again. I am selling my brand, Ken. You understand what that means?"

"I understand the concept."

"And you are the only one who can throw mud at that image."

"Me? How could I? Why would I?"

"Why? You forget, I knew you, Ken. I knew how much you wanted to be rid of your wife. You'd dumped me as a client. Did I get mad? No, I offered you a perfect plan. As a friend. And you wouldn't even consider it. Too moral. Too upright. Of course, that worked out for me. If you'd used it, my plan wouldn't have worked out so well a few years later. But all that good behavior proved one thing. You can't be trusted. Not with a secret like mine. You will want to do the right thing."

I hoped that Ken's voice memo app was working. What if I hadn't set it up correctly? I pulled my phone from my pocket and opened mine. "Be right back," I whispered into the landline receiver and stuck it back under the crumpled skirt.

Out in the living room, Ken forced a chuckle. "You can hardly say I would do the right thing. I left my wife and child. Disappeared. Never looked back."

I slid my phone into place behind Ken's and backed away. I could only see the side of Malcolm's head, but I could see Ken's face. He never took his eyes off Malcolm as he listened. I don't know if Ken realized what I was up to. Malcolm didn't catch the motion behind him as I crawled away backward.

Back in the closet, I picked up the landline phone. "I'm back."

The operator didn't bother with recriminations. "What did you see?"

"Nothing changed. They are still talking."

"Did you see the gun?"

"No. But Ken, the homeowner, is standing there as if Malcolm has a gun on him."

"You know the perpetrator's name?"

"Malcolm Maturi."

"The celebrity chef?" She sounded incredulous.

"The same." Had everyone heard of this guy but me?

"Hmh. Does he look upset?"

"I could only see the side of his face."

"Hmh."

I'd missed part of the conversation in the living room, but the topic seemed the same. "Hey, you played the good guy, took care of them. Your wife would have been simple to get rid of. Permanently. I gave you all the advice you needed, but you wouldn't listen."

"That's why you are here?" Ken sounded relieved, almost amused. Still acting. "Because of that idiotic conversation we had forty years ago?"

"You know, Ken, over the years you would pop into my mind. I heard you were gone, that you had no intention of coming back. But I always had this tiny little twinge in the pit of my stomach, when things were going great, this terrible feeling that you might reappear. *Especially* when things were going great. Like now."

"Because of that one drunken discussion? I could tell you I forgot it, but you wouldn't believe that. I do remember, but I never believed you. I lived all the way across the country. I had no idea you'd gone through with it. What could I have done about it if I had heard about it? That conversation is not evidence. Nothing I tell the police about your wife is gonna put you in jail."

"It's not jail that I am worried about. It's a different world, Ken. Social media. That will ruin me. You can ruin me. Twitter. Facebook. God, even Instagram. Innuendo can ruin my brand."

"I've been in hiding for forty years. You believe I have a presence on social media?"

"You can have someone do it for you."

"Why would I do that? I've got nothing against you. I have nothing to gain. You are not thinking this through. Anything you do now can only hurt you."

"But as long as you're out there, you're a threat to me. Your conscience is a threat to me."

"I've been out there for forty years since…when did you kill your wife?"

"She was killed in a tragic robbery in 1980."

"Ah right." Ken let a bid of amusement into his tone. How could he be so calm? "I'm a little hazy on the details, but it sounds as if your plot worked."

"Like a dream. The only mistake I made was sharing it with you, but I've always been a generous type. I thought you would take my advice. If you had, you would still be living in that palace in Avalon, not this dump."

"This house may be modest, Malcolm, but it is no dump. It is full of love."

"Which is why people will be so surprised at the murder/suicide."

Ken was no longer calm. "Do what you want with me, but do not touch Janice. She knows nothing. As far as I know, she's never even heard of you."

"Ken, you realize I am a planner. I believe that anything is possible with patience and planning. Did you think I would try to find you if I didn't have a plan to eliminate you? Me. Who committed, or rather commissioned, the perfect murder. I thought you were a smart guy."

"I am smart enough to see that you are making a big mistake. They will catch you."

"No one will connect me to you."

"That woman will. Meg Daniels. She knows you knew me."

An uncomfortable silence followed, At least it felt uncomfortable to me. The 911 operator chose that moment to ask if I was still there.

"Ssh. They're talking about me." I stuck my ear out the door.

"You didn't tell her why, did you, Ken?"

"Of course not. Besides, there is no statute of limitations for attorney/client privilege."

I hoped Ken was a good liar. His voice was convincing, but his face? Wait, this was the guy who lived a lie for a year while he planned his get-a-way. He'd do okay.

"She knows nothing more than I was your client?" Maturi asked.

"Nothing."

Malcolm couldn't know that he'd stated for the tape that he was no longer Ken's client before he spilled his guts about his murder plot. But then Malcolm was not aware that he was stating anything *for the tape*.

"And neither does Janice. I can see where maybe I would commit suicide. I'd been found after forty-five years in hiding. I was about to be exposed. Sure. I'll even write a note to that effect, but only if you promise that you will not harm a hair on Janice's head."

He didn't mention *my* hair.

"Waiting for her to return home is getting tedious." Malcolm appeared to be reconsidering the murder half of the murder/suicide plan.

"You'd better hurry. Maturi is revising his plan."

"We're coming. Just remain calm. Are you still in the closet?"

"I haven't moved."

"Don't. Is the door closed?"

"Well," I was reluctant to confess, "I left it open a crack. I wanted to listen."

"Don't worry about that. Close the door. We'll handle it."

I pulled the door shut. I heard nothing except the encouragement of the 911 operator for what felt like an hour. In fact? Three to four minutes passed.

At that point, the quiet was broken by a loud bang. I jumped but felt relief that it was not a gunshot. I assumed the hubbub that followed was the police arriving.

"What's happening?" I asked the 911 operator.

"Stay put," she advised.

"But what's happening." I couldn't control the need to ask repeatedly.

The last time I asked the question it was to a uniformed police officer who opened the closet door. He reached down and took the phone from my hand. "We've got her."

"I didn't get to say thank you." I reached for the phone but realized there were more important issues. "Is Ken okay? What happened?"

The young cop took my hand and helped me to my feet. I stepped out of the closet just in time to see Malcolm being led out the front door. His arms were behind his back. I assumed they were secured by handcuffs. I thought about taking the high road. Thought about it.

"Sorry I won't be able to make your grand opening," I called. "Not too sorry. Your escargot has too much garlic."

He turned his head to sneer at me. I hoped he got a long jail sentence. Otherwise, I had a feeling I'd pay for that comment about his snails.

"Ken?" I stepped into the living room. He was sitting on the couch talking to a uniformed policewoman.

"He's doing fine. We'll need to get a statement from you as well." The cop put his hand on his gun as I bent down for the phones.

I returned to an upright position without the phones. "May I pick up my phone?"

With the cop's permission, I retrieved the phones. He didn't question why I had two and didn't object when I checked both to see if the voice memos had been recorded. Ken and Malcolm's voices came through remarkably strong on both phones. "I think you might find these useful. I believe Mr. Maturi confessed to killing his wife."

Chapter 46

Unlike the first time Malcolm Maturi was accused of killing his wife, he was now a national figure. The national press made sure that his story was widely broadcast within hours. Social media went wild, but that was the least of Malcolm's problems.

The sun had not yet set when I heard tires on gravel. I stepped onto the deck expecting to see Andy returning from school, but the car was not his. I watched as Ken climbed out of the modest silver compact and walked around the front of the car to help an attractive woman from the passenger seat.

The woman seemed to be about the same age as Ken and Donna, but she was the anti-Donna. I didn't mean to sound pejorative describing her as flashy, but that was the best description I could come up with. No tailored pantsuit for her. She wore black leather pants that clung to the kind of skinny legs I'd always envied. Her top was loose and plunged at the neckline to reveal a dark tan and a half-dozen gold chains with diamonds hanging haphazardly from them. Donna would never have approved of her teased hair or her heavy makeup, but I thought the woman looked pretty, overdone but eye-catching. Based on what I heard about Ken Patterson, she would be the perfect woman for him.

"I tried calling you from my burner phone, but a cop answered your phone," Ken called to me.

"I should get it back tomorrow."

"May we come up?"

"Of course."

The woman arrived on the deck first. "You look so much prettier than in your pictures." She gushed.

"What? Have I been in the news?" I asked. I believed I had managed to keep my name out of the whole mess.

Ken moved into place beside her and stabbed an elbow into her side.

"That's a compliment." She didn't seem to grasp that the issue was not whether or not she liked the pictures, but rather why she saw any pictures.

Ken ignored her protest. "This is my wife, Janice. Since you understand my circumstances, I can tell you that we are not legally married, but no piece of paper could bind us more closely. Don't worry that I'm a bigamist, although we've been together for twenty-five years now." He reached for her hand and squeezed it.

When he removed his hand, I saw her left hand. No ceremony could bind them more closely than the collection of diamond bands on her third finger. There had to be four diamond bands lined up around a plain platinum band topped with a stone twice the size of mine, and mine was two full carats. Ken Patterson liked diamonds and, apparently, still had the money to provide them.

Ken followed my gaze and again placed his hand on the diamonds. "Janice taught me what marriage should be. I thank the Lord every day that I found her."

I thought of Donna sitting at home thinking about him for every one of those years. Every Christmas. Every New Year's. Every Anniversary. The image was a sad one, but I didn't feel any sympathy. She'd been clinging to a ridiculous illusion for decades. She hadn't tried to improve her life.

"I hope you don't mind that I brought Janice along. I wasn't going to leave her alone in our house. Besides, I wanted her to see this place. It's bigger than when I lived here." He pointed at the larger addition. "Traditional. Donna's doing. She never did like this house." He indicated the sections that were part of the original structure. "I loved how open this space was, how it called the outdoors inside. Donna filled it with furniture more suited to a stone colonial in hunt country." He pulled Janice close. "I can talk about Donna in front of Janice. She knows everything, and I do mean everything."

All the years later, I saw anger in his eyes, but more in Janice's.

"I realize it's chilly, but would you mind if we sat on the deck?" Ken asked.

"No. No." Whatever he wanted. I offered them refreshments, but they declined a full day's menu of choices from breakfast pastries to cocktails. All snack food.

I led them to the outdoor dining table.

"I kept our table here, too, out of the shadows in the evening. So we would get the last of the sun and its warmth."

"Given the time of year, we haven't been using it. Let me get a wipe."

"Please don't go to any trouble. I just want to let Janice see this place, feel this place, experience this place."

Is that why he had come? I had a related question. How frequently had he been experiencing this place? Only since I'd begun my investigation, or had he been having lunch on this deck for years? I wanted to ask but didn't. I needed to get the conversation on track and keep it there.

Ken pulled out two chairs, and Ken and Janice settled close together facing the ocean. I sat on the opposite side of the table facing Ken.

"We never got to finish our conversation about Elisabeth." He said.

I nodded and let him talk.

"I am going to assume that you are aware that I carefully plotted to disappear from the life I was living in 1977. I worked on my plan for over a year. My only confidant—at least until that drunken night with Malcolm—was a friend and lawyer, Harris Meitner. He helped me with the arrangements. After I left, he was the only one I was in touch with for ten years or so. I didn't even let my brother know I was alive for ten years. Did anyone tell you how Donna behaved after I left her?"

I nodded but said nothing. Let him tell me.

"You may know more than I do. Years later I learned she played the wronged woman to the hilt. She was angry that no one could find more of my money and, believe me, I left her plenty. She could live high on the hog for the rest of her life. She talked about my 'descent into madness.'" He ended the sentence with air quotes.

"I understand you didn't see it that way."

"No, I saw my escape as a way to save my life. Donna was killing me. Slowly, but surely, smothering me." Janice laid a long-manicured finger on Ken's arm. The nail color was a bright red that I am sure Donna would have found unacceptable. Cheap. Tawdry. I liked it.

"I understand leaving Donna. What I don't understand is abandoning your daughter."

"I was a horrible husband. But I suspect most men would have been a bad mate for Donna. She had no concept of what real life, of what real men were like. I lived in her world with her rules for many years even after the world started changing. And, believe me, there were social seismic changes during the years we were married. I wanted to evolve with a changing world. I might have stayed with Donna if she had been willing to change or even consider all that was going on, but she wouldn't."

He grew pensive and stared out to sea. Janice saw nothing but Ken. Her hand rested on his arm.

"I should have worked out a divorce with her. I did try, but she wouldn't hear me. She was so rigid. No compromise. I had to change. She knew every rule and every rule had to be adhered to. What to wear. Where to live. What restaurants to go to. What clubs to belong to. What stiffs we should have as friends. And, most significantly, no divorce. She told me ending the marriage was out of the question. I couldn't go on. She was killing me. She left me no choice but to disappear out of her life."

"Out of your daughter's life," I repeated what he could easily read as a condemnation.

"That wasn't my intention." He took a deep breath as if gathering his strength. "If I am honest, I didn't care at first. I didn't want the baggage of a kid. Life just seemed to move so fast and then Roddy was born and died. I felt that loss deeply. His death was inexplicable. An adorable, lovely little boy goes to sleep and never wakes up. If that doesn't make you question the meaning of your existence, nothing will."

His voice came close to cracking, but he took another deep breath and continued.

"Roddy's death should have brought Donna and me closer, but it didn't. She grew colder and colder. I came to feel I was trapped in this horrible domestic situation while the world was having fun. Donna only cared about her image. Dressing Elisabeth like a doll and having a husband as a prop at boring parties. And, of course, as a provider." He looked to Janice for support.

"I told Meitner, and I guess myself, that I would stay away and then come back after a few years when Donna accepted that our marriage was over. I hoped she would find someone else. I thought then she would agree to divorce terms."

"So why didn't you?"

I could see that Ken was struggling to answer.

Janice squeezed his hand. "Tell her, Sweetie. If you don't I will. You can't walk away letting her think you are the bad guy."

"I believed I had everything under control, but things didn't work out the way I planned. The night I left I slipped away from a party. I had Bob DeMarco drive me home. He was blocked in by other cars. I'd made sure I wasn't. He drove me home in our family car and took the keys back to Donna. I thought that she would assume that without a car, I wouldn't be going anywhere. I mean I had an old beater, but I never used it unless I was hauling stuff. I didn't think she would question that I was just working at home. In my mind, leaving the car for her would make her less suspicious. I was wrong. She was suspicious and she had wheels."

****Cape May****
Smitty's Marina, Cape May New Jersey
July 4, 1977

Ken felt happier than he had in years. Everything was falling into place. A few hours of sleep and he would be headed out to sea and north to Maine to a slip that would be his new summer home. His Porsche was waiting there for him, ready for a cross-country ride he had dreamt about since he was a kid. He'd enjoy the early change in foliage and then head west to California. A cliché? Maybe. But one he was happy to play along with.

The dock was close to deserted. He heard happy voices in the distance, but most partiers were out searching for the best view of the fireworks onshore or off. The night was overcast but the clouds had not stopped the festivities. He heard the fireworks starting in the distance.

He hoped Elisabeth was enjoying fireworks with Donna's parents that night. It pained him to leave her behind, but Meitner assured him getting custody was impossible. And to be honest, he didn't know if he could be a full-time parent. He loved her enough that he didn't want to drag her through an ugly custody battle. He understood what Donna was capable of. She would not hesitate to turn his own child against him, to use her to get to him. He'd left a letter for Elisabeth under her pillow saying that he had to go away for a while but he would miss her very much and would be in touch soon.

He would continue to write to her and explain that the time would come when they could be together again. He would remember her on her birthdays and Christmas. He'd keep sending the message so that someday, when they were older, they could be together. He would make sure she knew he loved her very much. He would hope for an opportunity to visit but he couldn't promise that. Donna might not permit it. He didn't even know how to get his gifts and messages past her. He might have to get Meitner involved. In the meantime, he would build a new life. A life he could bring his daughter into down the road. He chuckled. When they were both more mature.

He was looking forward to the next few days on the water. He couldn't wait for the dawn, but he was already feeling relieved, relaxing in the cockpit, taking the time to untangle extra lines. He was working on a difficult knot when he heard it.

"So this is where you were going."

The sound jolted Ken. He leaped to his feet and spun around. The rope and the knife dropped from his hand and landed on the bench. What he saw sickened him. Donna. Looking calm, cool and collected as usual. Still impeccably groomed and dressed in the clothes she'd worn to the party.

"You said you were going up to Philadelphia overnight, but you came here. Why did you bring our boat here? This is our boat, isn't it? Why did you tell me you sold it?" The voice was measured and emotionless. "What are you planning?"

"Donna. Why are you here?"

"Me? Why am I here? Did you really believe I would stay at a party making small talk while wondering what in the name of God you were doing? If I'd arrived a few minutes later, I would have missed you, but I saw you pull out of the driveway. I followed you. I assumed you were on your way to meet a girlfriend. Isn't she here yet?" She smoothed a hair.

Somehow her attention to her appearance enraged him. Following her husband when he went to see his girlfriend, why wouldn't she make sure every hair was in place? She wouldn't let emotions interfere with her image.

"Why did you tell me you sold the DonnaLisa?"

"It isn't the DonnaLisa anymore." He bit his tongue. Why had he told her? He didn't need her putting out a BOLO for the Me Said Lordy, the new name he'd chosen.

"Donna, you'll get a letter tomorrow. I've taken care of everything. You'll be quite comfortable."

"I don't understand."

"I'm leaving you."

"Leaving me?"

He was surprised at how calm she sounded.

"You can't do that, Ken. You made a promise, you took vows. That is not how it works. We are married for life." Her tone said the matter was not open for discussion.

"Donna, you will have everything you need."

"I need a husband. I need a family. Now get off this boat and come home."

He detected no trace of doubt in her voice. She'd spoken. She assumed he would obey. Maybe there was a time, but that time was in the past. "Donna, why do you want a husband who doesn't want to be married to you?"

"It doesn't matter what you want now. You made a vow. You've been in an extremely unpleasant and, may I say Kenneth, unattractive phase. It's time you get over whatever craziness this is, cut your hair, shave your face and get back to your real life."

"This is my real life. I want a new life."

"You're having a midlife crisis. A little early, I'll admit." Her intonation changed slightly, adding dismissive to factual. "People have been talking about your ridiculous behavior, but I've been faithful to you. I knew you would come to your senses."

"I have come to my senses. Those are the people with ridiculous behavior. People living lives they hate."

"Kenneth. If you insist on discussing this, we can talk at home." She gestured that he should follow her. "Let's get home before all the drunks get out on the road. You know I don't like to drive on holidays. You can ride with me."

Ken shuddered. This was going to be ugly, but he wasn't backing down.

"Donna, you must have known something was up. If not, why did you follow me?

"You left the party early for a business emergency? I don't think most lawyers have emergency business on weekends the way you do. Especially holiday weekends. Do you think I'm a fool? Was I supposed to think one of your clients had a sore throat and needed an emergency will? Really, Kenneth. You underestimate me. Now, come home. I forgive you."

"Donna, I don't want you to forgive me. I want you to let me go. You have to let me go. I am leaving. Tonight."

"You're not yourself. If need be, we can talk to Father Marx. He will straighten you out. Now get off that boat."

"No more talking. I've made up my mind. Do what you want but I am not coming." He'd talked to her long enough. For years. He had to get ready. He had to prep the boat. He was leaving at the first light of dawn. "I have things to do." He turned to start doing them. Behind him, he heard her board. "Donna...."

She didn't answer.

He spun around and saw her lunge. She had something in her hand. As it passed through a shard of light, it glistened and then it was in him. His sailor's knife. "You stabbed me." He felt her pull the knife out of his body, but the pain didn't lessen. His hand went to his side. Had she killed him? What organs were in there? What had she damaged? He was surprised at the warmth of the blood pouring out of him. He looked up and saw her coming towards him again. This time she had found the marlin spike. Thinner. Sharper. Easier to drive into him.

She seemed so calm. No tears. No anger. Just determination.

He grabbed her arm, but he couldn't stop the force of her forward thrust. The blade cut him but not so deep this time. She was going to try again and he wouldn't be able to resist. His strength was slipping away.

Help. He needed to call for help. He opened his mouth, but he couldn't find the strength to produce any sound. He was growing weaker and weaker, and the pain crippled him. His hand slipped off her arm. He sensed the knife moving towards him again. His knees buckled and his legs slipped out from under him. He reached for her and grabbed the leg of her pants. As he slipped into unconsciousness, he felt a small surge of satisfaction that he had ruined her white slacks.

He didn't know how much time he'd been out or how Donna had gotten him from the boat onto the dinghy, but when he awoke he recognized that was where he was, lying on top of a pontoon. He tried to remember all that had happened. He recalled Donna, crisp as ever, coming at him. Stabbing him. Hurting him. He was badly injured, too tired to move, barely able to think. Behind him, he heard the engine start and felt the dinghy pull away from the boat. He couldn't move and turn over and wondered if he should. In his condition, he could never fight Donna off. Who thought the day would come when he would say that? But he knew he couldn't win. He had to make her believe he was dead.

At the doctor's they always asked him to describe pain in numerical terms, one to ten. This pain was eleven. At a minimum. He opened his eyes and watched where they were headed. Even if his pain level hadn't made focusing difficult, the clouds blocking the moonlight made it hard to determine exactly where they were. Somewhere in the inlet. He'd always liked having a slip near the mouth of the channel. Easy in. Easy out. No need to maneuver between rows of docks. Now, he wished there were boats and revelers to see them pass by. But what would they see on the dark night? If they even noticed him, they would figure a woman was taking her drunken husband home from a party. Would it occur to them that she was transporting him out to sea to bury him? Unlikely.

He was aware enough to understand what she was planning. She was taking him out to sea for burial. He had to get off the dinghy before they reached the open water. If he stayed on the dinghy, he would not be able to fight her off. She had his knife. His strength was gone. He could see only one choice. Roll off the dinghy into the water before she got beyond the channel.

What could she do then? Catch him in the engine propellers? She wasn't good enough with the boat to do that. She wasn't strong enough to pull him back into the dinghy. Adrenaline might get him to the side of the channel. Yes, if he clung to a piling, she could get to him, but what other chance did he have?

He identified familiar sites go by and understood that his time was running out. He plotted. He had to make his move soon.

His thoughts were interrupted by the sound of Donna's voice. Still calm. Still devoid of feeling. "I'm sorry that you wouldn't listen. You know, Kenneth, it didn't have to end this way for you."

For you. No doubt he was right. She wanted to finish him off.

"The way you've been behaving. People don't do that."

He said nothing. He played dead.

"And walking away from our marriage. That just isn't done, Kenneth. Not by people like us. Not to a woman like me."

He had to fight the urge to groan. He could not give her a clue he was alive.

"I wish now I had made you listen before…well, before. Maybe it wouldn't have come to this."

He detected no emotion in her voice. No sadness. No regret. No doubt. She wasn't apologizing. She didn't see what she had done as wrong. No, she was correcting a wrong. Making everything right according to her rules.

He took a deep breath, let his leg drop over the side and shifted his weight so the leg pulled his body into the water. He rolled into the dark water with his eyes closed, trying to play dead. Sinking into the brackish water did something he thought impossible. It made the stinging sensation worse. The shock knocked the breath out of him. He needed air. He broke the surface and, through water-soaked eyes, saw Donna's form standing in the dinghy. She was probably considering her next move, but he knew his.

He could no longer play dead, but he could die. He flung his arms around as if struggling and took a deep breath, as deep as his wounds would allow, and slipped below the surface. He pictured her watching for his reappearance. She would focus on the place where he disappeared, but she wouldn't find him. She would watch for a moment and then, confident she had put things right in the universe, she would turn away to navigate the way back to the Me Said Lordy. *He wondered if she would find the rechristened boat. Let her figure that out.*

His thoughts were clear and practical as, staying beneath the surface, he clutched his wounds with one hand and propelled himself toward shore with the other. He had a plan. He felt calm, satisfied, the pain was fading. He didn't think that could be good. He sensed himself slipping away. Not now. Oh please. Not now. He had a plan. He didn't want to surface, but his breath wouldn't last. He kicked his way to the surface and let the current carry him to the nearest piling.

With painful and slow motions, he pulled his shirt off and used it to lash himself to the pole. He was cold but safe from sliding underwater if he slipped into unconsciousness. But anger kept him awake. Over a year of planning. Donna thought she thwarted his plan, but she hadn't. Sure, she forced a couple of modifications, but he would survive, and he would be free. He slipped his wedding ring off his finger and raised his hand as far as he could above the water. He managed to raise it five inches, far enough that he could watch it splash and then sink into the murky water.

*****

"It might have been only a few minutes, but it felt like hours before a powerboat overcrowded with partiers came by and picked me off that piling. I could barely speak and when I did, I was incoherent. I told them I made my girlfriend mad, and she pushed me overboard. Six guys on that boat. Not one of them questioned that story. I told them I didn't know how I cut myself. Something in the water. No need to call the cops. It wasn't her fault. I didn't want to get her in trouble. They all went along. They all claimed to have crazy girlfriends."

"But you'd been stabbed." If I sounded surprised, I wasn't. I had, in a way, been right all along. Donna had killed him or at least made her best effort.

"I found out later I had one very deep wound and several superficial ones. I was more scared of what I got in the wound while floating around in that water than I was about the wound itself. I admitted I didn't feel okay to drive, which had to be a colossal understatement. I didn't go back to the boat. Those guys drove me to Shore Memorial. In the car, I rehearsed what I would tell the staff at the hospital. I hit something in the water. The medical personnel were skeptical but more concerned with patching me up. On the fourth of July, the place was a mob scene. They didn't call the cops. I was lucky. About that and that Donna—although they had no idea I'd been attacked by an assailant—didn't hit a major organ. The doctors kept telling me that. I was meant to live. I was meant to have a second act."

From the little I knew of Donna, it never occurred to me to doubt his story. "And no one knew what happened to you. You just disappeared."

"And, since my exit was so carefully planned, no one came looking for me. Even better. I'd been afraid Donna might try to find me, to make a big show of missing me. But, given what happened, she didn't want an investigation. Why would she? She thought she killed me."

He stared at me hard as if waiting for a reaction. I stared back. I knew my eyes were open wide, but I had no idea what my expression was saying except maybe, *go on.*

"I wanted her to believe that."

My expression told him I was thinking over his position. I didn't find it outrageous. What floored me was letting the illusion go on for forty-plus years. But I said nothing. Ken was on a roll.

"I changed my plans. I never went back for the boat. Didn't have to. I had my wallet zipped into my shorts' pocket. Always did on the boat just in case I fell overboard. Turned out being neurotic paid off. I'd already mailed all my important documents to myself in Maine. Eventually, I had them forwarded. Meitner took care of everything else. He knew my plans changed, but he didn't know why. He didn't ask. He made the adjustments and told no one as I requested. No one ever came looking for me. Until you."

I found that hard to believe, although easy to see why Donna would have discouraged any investigation.

"So you can see, even now, I didn't want to be found. Gerald asked a few people to stop you. Or try. Bob DeMarco. He had no idea I was alive until Gerald approached him. He was willing to help me."

"Wendover?"

"He was the only one I could think of. Gerald scared him into helping."

"And Donna?"

"I knew Donna would not want an investigation. Back then or now. I knew she would try to stop you. So, I asked Gerald to get word to her. His friend Joey arranged an "accidental" meeting with her and asked if she knew the tenant in her old house was looking for me. I knew she wouldn't like that. The last thing she needs is someone finding the truth about what happened to me."

"All these years, she's believed she killed you. You let her believe she killed you."

"I despised Donna. Pure hatred. How would you feel about your murderer?" He leaned forward with his elbows on the table so he could get close. "You think I didn't love my daughter, but why do you think I hid the horrible truth about her mother? No matter how much I hated Donna, and I still hate her, I would never want to hurt Elisabeth. I didn't want her to grow up the child of a murderess. Attempted murderess. A criminal."

Janice reached over to caress Ken's hand. "Kenny loved the idea of leaving Donna squirming." Her voice revealed the pleasure that Ken's tone had tried to hide. She heard the intonation too and changed it to sympathy. "He thought that was enough suffering for her."

"I try not to think about how different all our lives would have been if I'd simply gotten in the car and driven away from that party. I told myself that I did the smart thing, that she would assume she'd find me at home, but there was another reason. I'd grown to hate Donna even before she tried to kill me, but I also pitied her. I had no problem deserting her. I even relished picturing the moment when she realized I was gone. But I couldn't have that moment happen in public. How would it benefit my plan to have her confess her dilemma and beg for a ride home? It wouldn't. It would be, as they say in football, unnecessary roughness."

Janice patted his hand. "Ken is a kind man."

His reluctance to humiliate Donna in that situation made me see 1977 Ken in a different light. But now? "I understand why you don't want to go back to Donna, but to abandon Elisabeth?"

"How can I face her? It's better if she thinks I'm dead. If I go back after all this time, I will want to explain. I would want her to understand." He shook his head. "If I come back, I will not lie. I will have to tell her what her mother did. The truth. If she believes it. That will destroy her life even more. I need to explain myself fully or not at all." He studied his hands.

I understood what Ken was saying, but I wasn't sure I agreed.

"Yeah, I enjoy knowing Donna worries she is never going to pass through those pearly gates into heaven. I wonder if she told a priest in confession."

"I understand why your hatred is still powerful, but she's lived her entire life with this. She's been punished," I argued.

"I realize we seem very old to you, Ms. Daniels, but she has plenty of years left to live. I prefer that for the rest of her life, she see herself as condemned to hell."

"More than you want to bring happiness to Elisabeth?"

"My return will not bring her happiness. Just confusion and more disconcerting emotions."

"You don't have to tell her the whole story."

"I am not coming back to lie. What lie could I make up that would explain my disappearance?"

When he put it so simply, his position made some sense.

"The cat is out of the bag. Abby, your granddaughter, is going to see you on the news. If she doesn't, someone will tell the family. We should get ahead of this. Are you ready to talk to your granddaughter?"

He didn't answer.

"Ken, you came here tonight. You must be willing. Why else did you come?"

"To thank you for saving my life."

"After I put it in danger? No. I think you want to see your family. What if I get us some hot chocolate to take the chill off? You can give me your answer when I get back."

The sun was gone by the time I returned to the deck. Ken and Janice were standing at the railing with their arms wrapped around each other. At the whir of the sliding door, they turned to face me.

"I have my answer. I'm ready."

Chapter 47

I slipped inside and was pleased to find the Positano's landline worked. My phone was at the police station along with Ken's.

"Why are you calling on this line? I almost didn't pick up." Abby was in her combative mode.

"Long story. I'd like you to drop by."

"Now?"

"As soon as possible."

"Are you going to say why?"

"I will tell you when you get here."

"Okay. Anything you need to tell me?"

"When you get here."

"Ten minutes." I told Ken when I returned to the deck. "I do not believe she has seen the news. She suspects you are here but doesn't know for sure."

I noted that Ken was clutching his mug as tightly as possible to control his shaking hands.

"Are you cold? Do you want to go in?"

"No, no."

"We should be seeing a moon soon," I offered.

"I haven't had this opportunity in a long time."

"May I ask? Where have you been?"

Ken leaned back. Relaxed. His manner turned to that of an old buddy telling fishing tales. "I had nothing but my wallet, but that was enough to get me started. I had a fair amount of cash on me. And some travelers' checks. Big denominations. There were ATMs, but we didn't rely on them the way people do now."

He sounded proud as if he had thought of everything. And so far it appeared he had.

"I talked my way out of the hospital the next day, settled my bill with cash, and got on a bus. Sent a telex from Ohio to Meitner, and he took care of the details related to my unforeseeable change in plans. I traveled all the way across the US. What a great trip that turned out to be! What an eye-opener! Of course, I would have enjoyed it more if I hadn't had to stop for medical care in Lincoln, Nebraska. Stayed there for a bit. Given my condition, I still wasn't certain Donna hadn't killed me."

Now he chuckled at the thought. He pulled up his shirt and pointed to jagged scars almost completely faded but still frightening. I don't know much about the human body, but I knew enough to recognize that the knife had struck near a nest of human organs.

The sight still horrified Janice. She reached out a single finger and traced the mark with a long crimson nail. "That infection could have killed him. She could have killed him."

Ken squeezed her hand and guided it back to her lap. "It took me seven days, but I pulled through. I got Meitner to settle the bill. Cash again, just in case. Never claimed any health insurance. I didn't want any bills, clues that I'd survived, going to the house by mistake."

He might have been injured but—I had to hand it to him—he'd been thinking.

"I wasn't feeling great, but I got back on the bus. Tell you the truth, I considered staying in Lincoln. Nice town. Nice people. But I stuck to my plan. My revised plan." He smiled at Janice. "Thank God."

"My Porsche—God, I loved that car—was waiting for me in Maine where I intended to go. Meitner got someone to drive it to California. I got it in LA, just in case anyone was watching, and drove it back to Nevada. I used my real name the entire time. Accessing money was tricky back then. No ATMs all over the place, but through banks I had access to the money I stashed away. Got an apartment. I didn't have to work, so I tried my hand at becoming a professional gambler. Did pretty well. I kept waiting to pop up as a missing person, but no one was looking for me. There was a stand there where I could get all the local newspapers. After a few weeks, I stopped checking. I stayed totally incommunicado.

Seems I'd done such a good job before I left, no one was looking. No one suspected foul play."

"Why didn't you go to the police? Donna tried to kill you." I made no attempt to hide my annoyance. Even I would love to see her in prison.

But not Ken. "And send Donna to jail? Sounds great, but I didn't want that for Elisabeth's sake. Besides, it would have been my word against hers."

"You had a big hole in your side. You had medical records."

"I'd lied to the guys who rescued me, the emergency room staff and to the folks at the hospital in Nebraska. As soon as I got to Vegas, I sent a statement to my lawyer that included every detail I could think of along with copies of my hospital receipts." He giggled. "And all these years Donna thought her murder attempt had succeeded. Can you imagine nightmares Donna must have had? I did. A lot at first. Waking up to find me covered in blood in our bedroom. Or emerging from the ocean water? I thought of staging something like that, but I'd gotten away. I wanted to stay away." He studied his hands. "It was a different time. I wasn't fit to be a father. I was never going to be a good father until I got stuff out of my system. Elisabeth was better off with Donna."

"But what if she hurt Elisabeth?"

"Physically? She would never do that. That would not look good. Child abuse was not in her rule book."

"But she was raising her. What kind of values was she teaching her?"

"She might not have been the warmest woman on earth, but she wasn't evil."

"Ken, she stabbed you and pushed you into the water. She thought she killed you."

"Can you blame her?"

"Yes. Yes, I can. I might get annoyed with my fiancé but I don't stab him."

"But you don't understand Donna. I got my revenge. I destroyed her world, her value system. I hurt her. I figured living with her secret had to be torture. Donna thought she was a killer. No statute of limitation on murder. I figure she must have waited every day for my bones to show up. Every new advancement in technology must have terrified her."

"All that time, your daughter, her daughter, was longing for her father. She thought you rejected her. Donna never said a word to console her."

"I believed she had the letter I left."

"No one said anything about a letter. I'm fairly certain Elisabeth never saw that letter."

"I wondered. Maybe Donna didn't want to give her false hope. She knew I wouldn't be back, that I couldn't be back, that I was dead."

"But you weren't dead."

"May I repeat, she didn't know that." He got up and walked to the railing. "I loved this place when I built it and being here now, I can see why. But I never missed it. Too many memories. Bad ones. Rage."

"Where were you living all this time?"

"Where wasn't I? I made a ton of money gambling. Then came the eighties. I got into the stock market. Made a lot more. When the magic stopped, so did I. I couldn't practice law without taking the bar in another state, so I took random jobs just to see people and stay even financially. I never lived extravagantly. I loved being a bartender, but when I moved to Brigantine I had to give that up. Too public. I got a job in security. Kept a low profile."

"You had a good life?"

"I did. I do. Listen," he leaned forward. "Janice says I owe you an apology."

I waited and didn't ask for what?

"She said I invaded your privacy. But I figured you were spying on me. Turnabout was fair play."

I didn't argue, although I wouldn't classify what I was doing as spying. I'd been out in the open about my goals. Mostly.

"When Gerald told me someone was looking for me, I was shocked. I knew Donna would never try to find me. I asked him to figure out why you were looking, what you were up to. Gerald repeated what you'd said, but I didn't know if you were telling the truth about Elisabeth. I didn't know who you were."

Had he never heard of Google?

"I just wanted to know what was going on."

"I told Gerald."

"Do you think a guy with my past takes everything at face value?" Ken waved a hand to dismiss my premise.

"Good point. What did you do?"

"The only thing I did was visit the house, that time you found me in the driveway. I wanted to check you out, but when you came back, I chickened out. I couldn't figure out how to get you talking."

"Were you sending people here at night to spy on us?" I asked.

Ken shifted his eyes to catch Janice's reaction. She nodded.

"Gerald sent a friend of his. The first night, but that was it. He took some pictures."

He didn't finish the sentence and I didn't force it. I heard the tires of Abby's car on the gravel. "Your granddaughter is here."

I ran down the outdoor stairs to greet Abby. "Come this way," I instructed her to follow me through the downstairs door.

"Why?" she asked in a familiar belligerent tone.

"Because I asked you to."

"What is it? What couldn't you tell me on the phone?" She complained as she climbed the indoor steps behind me.

"Sit down." I directed her to a seat at the kitchen island so her back would be to the deck. I didn't want her asking who the two people sitting outside were. Not yet.

"I want you to remain calm."

"I'm always calm. Why wouldn't I be?"

You're never calm. I kept that thought to myself. Aloud, I said, "Your grandfather is alive."

"He is? I knew it. Where is he? When can I meet him? What's his explanation? Where has he been?"

"He can tell you all that. I want you to meet him and decide if you think he should meet your mother."

"Meet him? Where is he?"

"I'm here."

I hadn't heard the door open or Ken step inside. Janice remained on the deck, but Ken was standing just inside the sliding door.

Abby slipped off her chair and turned to face him. Neither made a move in the other's direction.

"You are Kenneth Patterson?"

"I am. And you're Abby Douglas."

"I am."

"You must look like your father's side of the family," Ken said.

"Yes, my father's family is very nice. Intact. All members present." She paused waiting for Ken to respond, but he remained silent. "I expected you'd be better looking."

He didn't flinch at the insult. "I was once. I thought it mattered back then." Ken's manner was calm.

"And now we're supposed to think you're a changed man?"

"You never met me. Your mother never knew me. Not really."

"What do you have to say for yourself?" Abby didn't sound angry. Simply curious.

"I would like to talk to you. It's not a simple situation." I detected a quiver in Ken's voice.

"You two should talk. I'll be outside with Janice."

"Janice?" Abby's head shot around to face me.

"Your grandfather will explain." Then realizing what her greatest fear would be, I added, "He does not have another family. You two need to talk."

I crossed the room past Ken and went outside to take a seat beside Janice.

"How did that go?" She asked.

"It hasn't yet. Their first encounter wasn't promising, but Abby is the one who wanted to find him. She must have had a million imagined conversations with him. She is no shrinking violet. She'll get her footing."

"He's not a bad man. I've been with him for a long time. I should know."

"I can't say I understand."

"Yeah. Kenny is a complicated man." She returned to staring out to sea.

Forty-five minutes passed before Ken appeared on the deck. "Abby is going to talk to her father and let us know if I can see her mother. We'll get going now. We're not staying in that house tonight. We'll be at the Flanders in Ocean City."

I'd barely watched the taillights of Ken Patterson's car disappear down the driveway and settled on the couch when Andy returned home.

"I was getting worried. You didn't answer any of my calls or texts." He dropped a FedEx envelope in my lap. "Were you expecting this?"

I smirked. I don't often smirk, but the arrival of Maturi's invitation called for the reaction.

He leaned over for a hello kiss but stopped a foot short when he noted my expression. "Something happen today?"

Chapter 48

I finally achieved my goal of doing nothing on Saturday. At least my body did. My brain was wondering about what discussions were going on at the Douglas house.

The answer came on Sunday morning. "I got a message on my phone from Ken Patterson on my voicemail saying he will be here at ten this morning." Andy woke me before leaving for a morning run.

"Did he say why?" I groaned.

"Something about your driving him to Abby's. Abby told him you wouldn't mind."

Maybe I wouldn't. But what if I did? "Did he give you a number where I can reach him?"

"I can send you the number he called from." Andy pulled out his phone. "Oh no. I can't. Give me a piece of paper, and I'll write it down."

I stared at Andy. "I don't sleep with a notepad. My notebook is on the kitchen island, put it in there."

"Are you going to turn down his request?"

Of course I wasn't. I wanted to see this project to the end.

Ken Patterson arrived dressed in his Sunday best, an outfit Donna would find tawdry. Luckily, she would never see him. Or Janice who appeared to have dressed for New Year's Eve.

I was surprised that Ken brought Janice to this first meeting but thought again. He needed support. When he spoke he seemed nervous. "Do you think Janice could wait here while we go to see Lisa, Elisabeth?"

"Sure."

Ken thanked me, but it was Janice who appeared grateful. "You won't even know I was here." Her tone was apologetic.

"No problem. Help yourself to whatever is in our refrigerator." My turn to sound apologetic. I pointed out the little under-counter fridge. "You won't find much. I hope you ate before you came. On the bright side, we do have a great television." I provided instructions.

She said *thank you* with as much appreciation as if I had given her the house. "I might just enjoy the view."

"It's all yours." I turned to Ken. "Are you ready?"

He nodded. "I am. Yes, I am," he tried to convince himself. Again, he seemed nervous. I could certainly understand why. He pulled Janice into a long embrace.

"I am so happy for you, Kenny." She laid a light kiss on his cheek. "I am certain it will go well."

Ken's face made it clear he was not so sure, but he inhaled and exhaled dramatically, straightened his back and said, "Let's go."

Ken tapped his foot from the moment he climbed into my car until the moment he got out at Elisabeth's house. I would have told him to stop, but I suspected the movement was beyond his control. As was his chattering. On the ride, he filled the dead air with questions.

"Will she recognize me?"

"Abby said Elisabeth had a nice life. Do you think that is true?"

"Is Elisabeth's husband a good man?"

"Is her mother, is Donna, good to her?"

"Do you think what I did was wrong?"

That last question was hard to answer. "Ken, if I didn't know what happened between Donna and you…."

"You mean if you did not know that Donna tried to kill me?"

"Yes. Before I learned that, I must admit I did think the worst of you. Everyone I talked to confirmed Donna's shortcomings. I didn't hear a single positive word about her. Which means you left your daughter with a woman with no redeeming qualities. I didn't realize you thought you'd be back. Even then, you left Elisabeth to suffer a lot during her formative years."

"I hear you. I won't try to defend myself."

"I find it hard, but I will accept that you acted with what you thought was your daughter's best interest in mind. That doesn't mean I agree. I can't argue with your explanation that you didn't want to take her mother away from her. I don't quite understand. You thought so little of Donna."

Ken turned his face away from me and stared out the window. "Avalon has changed. So many big houses now."

I understood that wasn't the conversation he wanted to have. "Look, Ken, I have no way of knowing what I would have done in your position, but I suspect I would have turned Donna in so I could stay with my daughter." Not that I thought he was ready to be much of a father in 1977. I didn't mention that. "Maybe you did believe she would be the better parent."

We rode in silence for a few moments.

"What should I say to my daughter?"

"Haven't you ever fantasized about that?"

"I guess I did. Many years ago. But I gave up. I never thought this day would come."

"Well, it has. Try to remember."

"I am trying, but it is as if all my thoughts are caught in a tornado roaring around in my brain."

I didn't know what to tell him. I'd experienced those mental tornados myself on occasion. "You'll know when you see her."

As I pulled my car up in front of the house, I saw Abby standing at the kitchen window. She moved to the open door as we came up the path. Her father was standing behind her. I felt Ken might be going to reach out to hug her, but her demeanor stopped him.

"Grandfather," she said with a formal tone.

Al Douglas stepped forward and offered his hand. "I'm Al Douglas. Elisabeth's husband. She has been wanting to see you for as long as I've known her." No warmth, but no recrimination either. Al was willing to see how things went.

"Are you ready?" Abby asked her grandfather without any indication of warmth or encouragement. "We didn't tell her you were coming. You know, in case you didn't show up."

Ken absorbed the blow without emotion. "I understand."

"I'll be in the car," I said and turned to go.

"No, please." Abby grabbed my arm. "Come in. Mommy realizes you are the one who found her father for her."

Abby led us into the main room. Ken followed and Al brought up the rear of the family group. I trailed the others where Elisabeth sat staring out the window.

"Mommy, you have a visitor."

Elisabeth turned with a smile and surveyed the group. Ken stepped forward. Elisabeth stared at the stranger in her living room with a deep frown but within a moment her face broke into a big smile. Her eyes glistened. "Daddy?" I had no idea if she knew who he was or not. After all, she had called Andy Daddy, too.

"Yes, Elisabeth, sweetheart. It's Daddy. I've been away for a long time."

"Daddy?"

"Yes, sweetie, I am here." He leaned in to kiss her forehead.

"Daddy?"

"Yes." He knelt beside her but didn't reach out to touch her.

"I'm happy you're here, Daddy. Al this is my Daddy." Al sat on the arm of the chair and wrapped an arm around Elisabeth.

"I just met him, Elisabeth. He came to see you."

"Oh, Daddy, I am so happy you came."

From behind, I could see Ken's body begin to shake. Then, I heard his sobs. "Oh, baby girl. My baby girl. I am so sorry. So, sorry." He had no more words. The sounds he made were roars of emotion. Sorrow. Repentance. Regret. My eyes misted over but not for Ken, for Elisabeth. I didn't feel sympathy for him. He had a lot to make up for.

Elisabeth was smiling, a beatific expression. "Don't cry, Daddy. I knew you would come home."

Abby backed away and came to stand beside me. "That is the clearest she's been in weeks." She pulled a tissue from a box on the counter. I signaled her to pass me the box. We both wiped tears from our cheeks. Abby blew her nose with a vengeance that marred the sweet mood in the room. She didn't seem to notice. To be honest, no one did but me.

The sweet mood was shattered by the tones of a sea shanty. The doorbell.

"What day is it?" Abby turned to me with fear in her eyes.

"Sunday."

"Oh my God." Her entire body shook. "Oh my God."

"What's wrong?"

"It's her. It's her." She grabbed my arm.

"Who?"

"Donna."

"How do you know?" I asked.

"She stops by after church some Sundays. Not always on Sunday. Why today?"

Abby looked frantic. I pulled her towards the hallway whispering through gritted teeth. "You know that your grandmother stops by after church on Sunday and you invite your grandfather here at the same time?"

"I don't know....We wanted to move quickly but take a day to prepare my mother. I wasn't thinking. She was here last Saturday. She never comes two weeks in a row. It's not my fault."

With that sentence, Abby convinced me that she was more like her grandmother than she would ever have admitted.

"Do you think she saw the news?" I asked.

"She never pays any attention. Do you think someone called her?" Abby was worried.

A little late for that I thought. "Whatever, get rid of her."

"Can you go?" Abby begged me.

"She'll never catch on that something odd is going on if I answer the door, will she?" I was sarcastic but not nasty. "Go. Make something up, but get rid of her. Don't let her ruin this moment for your mother." I gave her a shove that I viewed as affectionate. "I'll be hiding in the kitchen. For moral support. Maybe it isn't even her."

The bell rang again. Twice. The visitor was getting impatient. I became more convinced that the caller was Donna. When Abby answered the door, she confirmed it.

"Grandmother. What a surprise?"

"Surprise? It's Sunday. I always stop by on Sunday." The imperious tone signaled Donna's arrival.

"Well," Abby stuttered, "not every Sunday. I guess I got distracted."

Oh, Abby. I wasn't shocked. I didn't know what motivated Abby, but I was convinced, whether on a conscious or subconscious level, she had engineered this confrontation. But she had to stop it. For Elisabeth's sake. The meeting would be awkward in any case, but I had no idea how Donna would behave. One thing was for sure. She could not be counted on to think of Elisabeth and her happiness first.

"Please, Grandmother, could you come back later?"

"Why would I come back later? I'm here now. Is your mother all right? Something's wrong. I can tell. I am her mother, and I should be told."

"No. No. Nothing is wrong."

I couldn't see the action at the door, but I envisioned Abby trying to restrain her grandmother, blocking her way.

Abby was trying to keep her voice light. Unconcerned. "There is no problem. She is fine. It's just not a good time." Abby tried to distract her. "You look nice. Is that a new pantsuit?"

Donna was not to be deterred. "You didn't answer me. Why?"

"Why what?" Abby tried to convince her grandmother she had forgotten the question.

"Why is this a bad time?"

"Oh, yeah." Abby was doing her best to play dumb. "She has company."

"What difference does that make? She is my daughter, and I will see her when I want." She tried to step around her granddaughter.

Abby backed to block the way to the main room. "Grandmother, believe me. It's not a good time."

"I can see you believe that, but you're being ridiculous."

I grew agitated anticipating what Donna was about to see. She pushed Abby hard to move her aside. At that moment, she caught a glimpse of me watching from the kitchen.

"What is going on in here?" She brushed by Abby. Only her first step down the hall was powerful. The next few slowed as the group must have come into view. What could she see? I slipped out of the kitchen and through the dining area to watch the scene unfold. She had not even seen his face yet, but the way she hesitated at the entrance to the living room told me she was afraid.

"Who is this?" She demanded. "Why is some stranger with my daughter?"

From her position at the door, all she could see was the back of a gray-haired man kneeling by her daughter's side, holding her hand. She might have been worried, but she clung to her imperious attitude even though the visitor could have been a kindly neighbor. "I have a right to know."

Ken straightened his back without so much as a glance over his shoulder. He got to his feet and then turned to face Donna full-on. She stared at him, and I stared at her. I wanted to see the parade of emotions across her face. Anger was quickly replaced by confusion, then puzzlement, then fear.

Donna knew that face better than anyone. She must have at least suspected that she was seeing Ken's face. She must have envisioned what he would have looked like as an older man. Hadn't she ever wondered if he had gotten away that night? Had she ignored the story that Sally DeMarco told? If she hadn't seen the news, one of her friends must have. If they called her, had she refused to accept the possibility that Ken was alive? I imagined her mind trying to put the pieces together. Would she try to dismiss seeing Ken in the living room as a hallucination? It could not be the man she killed.

"It's true...."

I guess she had heard the news.

"I thought...." She stopped. I watched her try to formulate a sentence. If talking to me at my house had caused a reaction, I couldn't imagine what seeing Ken would do. She tried again but did not say a word. She shook her head but didn't give up. She stood for a few seconds trying to compose herself. "No" was the only word she managed to get out. I wasn't sure if it was the intended word or not. Part of me enjoyed watching the show.

"Yes, Donna, it's me."

Her handbag fell from her shoulder to the floor. She made no attempt to retrieve it. She stood with her mouth open wide, saying nothing. I should have been concerned, but I didn't feel any compassion. She'd left this man for dead. She didn't deserve my sympathy.

Behind Ken, the smile on Elisabeth's face was tinged with confusion.

Donna started to mutter but stopped. She attempted a deep breath and tried again. She failed.

Ken took over. "It's been so long. I wasn't sure if you would recall the last time we met." His smile was mean, but why wouldn't it be. The last time she'd seen him, she'd shoved a knife in his torso. "I've been telling Miss Daniels, here, about that night."

Donna turned to me, and I smiled, at least my mouth did. My eyes told another story. I think she could read my expression. She knew what my face was saying. *I know Donna. I know it all.* I couldn't understand her response because when she tried to speak, she again failed. I heard a tiny squeak, but it seemed to have more to do with inhaling than with speech. She looked back to Ken. She stared at him for maybe five seconds before her eyes seemed to roll to the back of her head, her legs gave out and she collapsed to the floor.

The group watched as if a play was being staged for their benefit. She lay on the floor unattended.

"You'd better call 911. I'll take care of Elisabeth." Al issued directions to Abby. He helped Elisabeth to her feet taking care to block her view of her mother lying on the floor.

With no display of concern or emotion for Donna, Ken took his daughter's other arm. "Why don't we go outside. Can you show me the boats? When you were little, I used to take you on a boat."

Elisabeth smiled. "I remember."

Al's voice was calm and soothing. "You can tell your father about the boats we see back here."

Together Al and Ken guided Elisabeth out to the patio.

Abby was on her phone dialing 911. I went to Donna's side and knelt beside her. Her eyes were open, staring past me. I took her hand and told her she was going to be okay, but I was pretty sure she wouldn't be.

Chapter 49

Donna Patterson never regained consciousness. She never recovered from the massive stroke she suffered. She lingered in a coma for over a week before her lawyer, who had the legal authority, asked her son-in-law if he would agree to remove her from life support. Al Douglas consented. He and Abby were in the room when Donna took her last breath.

At Abby's request, Andy and I attended the funeral in the church where I had surveilled Donna.

"Nice size crowd," I whispered to Andy.

"Probably to make sure she's really dead," Andy whispered.

I frowned, but I wasn't convinced he was wrong. The turn-out was surprisingly robust in honor of such a miserable person. I assumed the mourners came for the living, not the deceased.

Abby's father stood beside her as she delivered her short eulogy that praised her mother more than her grandmother. I didn't spot a damp eye in the house including Abby's.

Andy and I weren't planning on going on to the cemetery, but after the mass Abby asked us to join the small group that did. The setting was bucolic, and a gentle breeze made the new leaves on the trees dance against the bright blue sky. I spotted Ken Patterson off to the side, hidden behind the trunk of an old oak in casual clothes with a baseball cap and sunglasses. He could have passed for one of the groundskeepers. Certainly for our gardener. I saw no sign of Janice. He had come alone. But I was certain, not for Donna.

Abby stood with her eyes on the casket as, one by one, mourners dropped a single white rose into Donna's grave.

"What could Abby be thinking?" I whispered to Andy as we trailed behind Al Douglas making his way back to the limo.

"I can't imagine the conflicting emotions. She didn't love the woman, but I think she did come to pity her."

Neither of us said aloud that Abby must feel some guilt. Maybe that guilt held Abby at her grandmother's grave until all the mourners had drifted away. Only after the last of the crowd had gotten into their cars, did Ken take a position beside her and wrap his arm around his granddaughter's shoulder. She didn't hug him back, but she didn't shrug off his embrace.

"I wonder if anyone knows that I was instrumental in killing Donna Patterson," I said.

"That isn't true. Abby told us her doctor said she was living on borrowed time."

"Yeah, but seeing Ken called in the loan."

He frowned. "Does that work as a metaphor?"

"Don't try to humor me."

"I'm not saying this to make you feel better. The doctor said her event was strictly a coincidence."

"What about almost getting Ken killed?" I found it hard to accept that as a coincidence.

"Okay, that one is on you, but you did solve a murder. And don't forget how happy you made Elisabeth."

"After I almost got her father killed."

"Stop saying that. You actually saved his life."

"That's the conventional wisdom, but that isn't the whole story."

"So, we never tell the whole story." Andy gave me a reassuring hug.

"I don't care how much people beg, but I am never doing a search for anyone again. I'm just lucky I never led any other potential assassin to their target. From now on, if someone disappears on purpose, that's good enough for me."

"Really?" Andy appeared skeptical.

"Really. I am through with this whole business."

"Making people happy?"

"Putting people in danger."

He looked at me. He didn't believe me.

"I'm out."

He stared.

"Really."

He stared.

"Why? Did somebody ask about me?"

"You won't want to hear the story." He headed back towards the car.

"What story?" With my high heels digging in the dirt, I had trouble keeping up. I touched his arm to make him stop. "Wait. What story?"

What harm could it do to listen?

Also Available From Plexus Publishing, Inc.

Florilla: A Pinelands Romance

A novel by Perdita Buchan

Granddaughter of "The Pinelands Witch," daughter of the self-styled Wizard of the Pines, and with powers of her own, eleven-year-old Florilla Munion finds herself abandoned deep in the New Jersey Pinelands. Rescued by the itinerant Dr. Peace, she is taken to Benderville, a model mill town in the heart of the Pines owned by the doctor's old friend, the eccentric, progressive Benjamin Bender. Benjamin Bender takes Florilla in, and she becomes his pupil when he discovers her talent for his beloved Latin and Greek.

But Benderville is only the beginning of Florilla's journey.

240 pp/hardcover | ISBN 978-1-940091-09-9 | Price $16.95
240 pp/trade paperback | ISBN 978-1-940091-08-2 | Price $13.95

The Carousel Carver

A novel by Perdita Buchan

This evocative historical novel tells the story of Giacinto, who emigrates from Italy in 1912 and becomes a carousel carver during the golden age of the craft in America, and Rosa, the eight-year-old orphan girl thrust into his care.

In 1939, with war looming and few new carousels being built, Giacinto leaves Philadelphia for the New Jersey shore, where his wildly popular creations require skilled attention after every summer season. The arrival of Rosa from Italy turns a solitary and predictable middle-aged existence on its head. Discovery, adventure, and danger are all met; youthful imagination brings carved stallions to life; and love blossoms in unexpected places.

The Carousel Carver vividly recreates the world of the immigrant carvers—from the inspiration found in fiery horses, big cats, and children's laughter to the clatter, sawdust, and politics of Philadelphia's bustling multicultural workshops. This is an engaging and insightful tale of tolerance, second chances, and what it means for those once adrift to call America home.

143 pp/hardcover | ISBN 978-1-940091-04-4 | Price $16.95
143 pp/trade paperback | ISBN 978-1-940091-03-7 | Price $13.95

The Last Newspaperman

A novel by Mark Di Ionno

Jersey in the '30s was Fred Haines's beat, though it was hardly worthy of the reporter who'd scooped the Ruth Snyder story back in '27. "The most famous *Daily News* cover ever," Haines bragged. His photo showed Snyder strapped to the electric chair. "Respectable" papers denounced it as vulgar, but it sold millions of copies and cemented Haines's reputation as the go-to "tabloid guy" just as celebrity worship was becoming an American obsession. But that was before Haines had the bad sense to publicly insult an even faster-rising media star named Walter Winchell. Haines wound up on the graveyard shift at the *Daily Mirror*, covering the most trivial stories his editor could dredge up. And Jersey.

"Strictly Sticksville," he said, remembering a cold March night in 1932. That was the night he drove down to rural Hopewell, near Trenton, oblivious that the story of the century was about to break under his byline. The infant son of Charles Lindbergh had been kidnapped, and Haines was about to become part of a media frenzy unlike anything anyone had ever seen.

224 pp/hardcover | ISBN 978-0-937548-74-5 | Price $22.95

Trenton

A novel by John P. Calu and David A. Hart

1774. The revolution brewing in the American colonies is set to erupt in violent conflict. In Hopewell, near Trenton, New Jersey, the nearly lifeless body of an orphan girl is pulled from the Delaware River by a son of John Hart, a man whose passion for independence has brought down the wrath of the British Crown and its many local sympathizers.

Thus begins an epic two-part saga in which the Harts become pivotal players in the cause of freedom, pitted against a powerful enemy alongside George Washington, Ben Franklin, and other patriots from throughout the colonies.

In the explosive second part, modern day Trenton comes into vivid focus as Luis Alma—son of Cuban immigrants, hero, and reluctant candidate for mayor—struggles to hold his family together. Against a backdrop of crime, corruption, and murder, a mystery unfolds linking the Alma family to the Harts of Hopewell, and a young man from the wrong side of the tracks discovers that the key to Trenton's future may lie in a secret from its past.

320 pp/hardcover | ISBN 978-0-937548-66-0 | Price $24.95